SUFFER IN SILENCE

SUFFER
IN SILENCE

A NOVEL OF NAVY SEAL TRAINING

David Reid

ST. MARTIN'S GRIFFIN

NEW YORK

SUFFER IN SILENCE. Copyright © 2011 by David Reid. All rights reserved. Printed in the United States of America. For information, address St. Martin's Press, 175 Fifth Avenue, New York, N.Y. 10010.

www.stmartins.com

The Library of Congress has cataloged the hardcover edition as follows:

Reid, David, 1976–
    Suffer in silence : a novel of navy SEAL training / David Reid.—1st ed.
        p.   cm.
    ISBN 978-0-312-69943-7
    1. United States. Navy. SEALs—Fiction.   2. Extortion—Fiction.   I. Title.
    PS3618.E5343S84   2011
    813'.6—dc22

                                                            2011019508

ISBN 978-1-250-00698-1 (trade paperback)

First St. Martin's Griffin Edition: June 2012

10 9 8 7 6 5 4 3 2 1

Dedicated to Lieutenant John Anthony Skop
Lost during Hell Week, BUD/S Class 235

ACKNOWLEDGMENTS

I would like to send my thanks to the instructors and trainees at Basic Underwater Demolition School/SEAL (BUD/S) Training for inspiring *Suffer in Silence*. The months I spent in Coronado were an unforgettable experience, and the memories of my own Hell Week are something I will always carry with me.

A writer rarely creates a novel in a vacuum, and I am no exception. At every step of the process, from entering BUD/S as a young officer to creating my first draft of this novel, I enjoyed the unwavering support of my incredible mother. In addition to providing invaluable editorial input, she has gracefully supported her sons' tendencies to put themselves in situations that would inspire heart failure in most mothers.

I would also like to thank Marc Resnick and Sarah Lumnah at St. Martin's Press for their hard work in preparing *Suffer in Silence* for republication. In particular, I would like to thank Marc for discovering my novel and taking a chance on a little-known author. Working with Marc and Sarah has been an incredible experience, and I couldn't have asked for the support of a better editorial team.

SUFFER IN SILENCE

ONE

THE TENDRILS OF FOG that snaked through the Basic Underwater Demolition/Seal (BUD/S) training compound only added to Grey's misery. The last rays of sunlight scattered into a luminescent haze, providing little warmth to his drenched, sand-encrusted body. The asphalt slowly wore away the skin on his ass as he completed sit-up 450. A stocky instructor with calves the size of bowling balls squatted next to Grey, scrutinizing his every movement through narrow eyes.

"You know why you're here, don't you?" The instructor's voice was an artificial growl that Grey would have found comical, had he not been in such pain.

"Why is that, Instructor Logan?"

"Because you're weak." Logan slowly stood up. "And stupid." He turned his back to Grey, took two steps, then spun around. Grey suppressed a groan.

"It's not over, fuck stick. Hit the surf. Wet and sandy. Two minutes. Go!"

Grey scrambled to his feet and sprinted out of the compound. He flew across the instructor parking lot, labored up and over the ten-foot sand berm, struggled across the beach, and charged into the surf. With the 58-degree water lapping at his knees, Grey did a belly flop and let the darkness of the Pacific close around him. He floated for a moment below the surface. He wasn't taking any chances. The instructors loved to line up the students after they had journeyed to the surf zone; an on-the-spot inspection often revealed telltale signs of cheating—a dry cover, a dry shoulder, a nervous facial expression. The punishment for cheating was always swift and severe. Satisfied that he was thoroughly drenched, Grey loped back to the beach and rolled in the sand. He powered up the berm, head tilted downward, eyes fixed on the sand. He looked up just in time to avoid knocking over Instructor Logan, who had been quietly watching Grey's progress from atop the berm.

"Thought you might just run me over, didn't you?"

Grey stood at attention, breathing heavily. He knew what was coming, and nothing he could say except "I quit" would change it.

"Running into instructors is bad policy, sir." Logan scratched at a sore on his neck as his eyes lazily scanned the beach. "Time to pay." The statement rolled off his tongue casually, as if he were commenting on the dreary weather.

Grey spent another half an hour somersaulting up and down the berm and into the ocean. By the time he was through, every muscle in his body screamed in agony. Life had not always been like this.

Mark Grey wasn't accustomed to failure. He was a masochist and a perfectionist, and these two qualities were generally enough to keep him out of trouble. In high school he had regularly logged eighteen-hour days in hopes of getting into a top university. At Stanford he had relaxed enough to find time for a string of girlfriends, but he never stopped working. After reading an article about the Navy Sea, Air and Land (SEAL) teams, he channeled all his energy into gaining admission to BUD/S. It was supposed to be the hardest military training in the world, and Grey couldn't read the word *hardest* without getting chills up and down his spine. He liked that SEAL officers and enlisted personnel went through exactly the same training. Months of mutually endured misery fostered a fierce loyalty between the two groups. Grey longed to lead men who had bled and suffered by his side.

With over one hundred applicants for ten officer spots, the competition for entrance into BUD/S had been stiff. To strengthen his physical fitness scores, Grey started competing in triathlons, eventually qualifying for a spot in the Hawaii Ironman challenge. Six feet one, with a lean, muscular body, Grey was a natural athlete. By the time his fitness test came around, he could run a mile and a half in combat boots and fatigues in less than eight minutes, do 130 sit-ups in two minutes, and perform thirty-five dead-hang pull-ups. Those scores alone virtually ensured him a place at BUD/S, so his 3.8 GPA was simply icing on the cake.

Immediately upon graduation, Grey reported to Officer Candidate School for twelve weeks of training. He easily rose through the ranks, attained the position of company commander, and graduated at the top of his class. In short, Grey had been the ideal candidate for SEAL training, which is why he found all the unwanted personal attention he had been receiving from the instructors baffling. Of the eight officers in BUD/S Class 283, Grey spent a disproportionate amount of time engaged in after-hours training.

Grey pulled off his soaked greens and stepped into the shower back at the barracks.

"Damn hombre, you look like you've just been raped!" Petty Officer Ramirez exclaimed. To emphasize his point, he grabbed the seaman showering next to him and directed a few pelvic thrusts toward the startled eighteen-year-old.

"Yeah, baby, you know I love it!" Seaman Jones drawled, playing along. He smiled, exposing a mangled set of teeth that betrayed his backwoods Tennessee upbringing.

"Rough day?" Ramirez asked, pushing Jones away with a feigned look of disgust.

"You could say that. Logan didn't like my sit-ups at PT this morning—claimed I showed a lack of motivation." Grey scrubbed his cuts with soap. "You know how it is—a little remediation session after chow, a little beat-down, a little surf torture." He winced as he touched his butt. The crack of his ass was as raw as hamburger meat, a phenomenon the students called "grinder reminder," in reference to the courtyard where they performed their daily physical training, PT. The grinder was hollowed ground; Grey swore he could smell the gallons of sweat and vomit that the asphalt had absorbed over the years.

"Who's leading PT tomorrow?" Grey asked.

"Redman," Ramirez answered. "You better sleep well tonight, my man, 'cause you're gonna need it come tomorrow morning."

Grey leaned his head against the grimy wall and let the hot water wash over him. The instructors hadn't broken his body yet, but they were sure trying. It was only the second week of training. Hell Week was over a month away, and graduation was too distant a goal to even contemplate. BUD/S was a six-month program, but by the time students graduated, most would insist all the abuse had taken at least five years off their lives.

Grey wrapped himself in a towel and stumbled into the room he shared with two other officers. Lieutenant Bell shouted into his cell phone in the corner of the room, and Ensign "Silver Spoons" Rogers spit-polished his boots. Bell was a former Surface Warfare Officer who had served two years aboard a frigate on the East Coast before transferring to BUD/S. He was an energetic man, prone to fits of profanity, and a shameless buttkisser who wasn't popular with his subordinates. As the Officer in Charge (OIC) of BUD/S Class 283, Bell was supposed to be accountable to the instructors for all the actions of the students. In reality, he rarely took responsibility for anything, instead managing to shift the blame for the class's many blunders to Rogers or Grey. At a diminutive five feet two, Bell was often addressed by the instructors as "Papa Smurf." With his receding hairline and slight paunch, he cut a comical profile. Bell wasn't overly athletic, but he somehow managed to pass all the physical evolutions. Nevertheless, he harbored a grudge against the exceptional athletes in the class, and this immediately put Grey out of favor. Grey felt certain that the fact that Papa Smurf had graduated from a poorly regarded state school didn't help matters, either. Smurf wasn't an "ivory-tower officer," a term he often used to describe his two roommates.

Rogers had earned the name Ensign Silver Spoons from the instructors, and the students frequently referred to him jokingly by this dubious title. In truth, he was a hardworking officer who had graduated from Princeton with honors. He meant well, but he was often misunderstood by both his subordinates and the instructors. They assumed he had a superiority complex, but he simply wasn't used to working with a bunch of rowdy sailors. A true gentleman, Rogers had been schooled in the classics and could recite parts of *The Iliad* from memory. The instructors often entertained themselves by making him recite poetry or translate insulting phrases into Latin. His baby face and close-set blue eyes only added to the comic effect as he played the part of the bookish intellectual.

"Inspection tomorrow?" Grey asked, eyeing Rogers's perfectly shined boots.

"Unfortunately. Didn't you get the word?"

"Nope. I missed our meeting today."

"What happened?"

"Just a little beat-down. Nothing big."

"Logan really dislikes you, doesn't he?"

"Seems that way, although I have no idea why."

"Maybe his wife was that doll you chatted up last weekend," Rogers suggested. "Remember? Over at Moondoggie's?"

Grey laughed. A rumor was floating around that a student had been medically dropped from the previous class after trying to impress an instructor's wife by claiming to be a SEAL. The woman had called her hubby and filled him in on the student's charming efforts. Three days later the student was dropped from training, his body utterly broken. Since hearing the story, the boys were careful about whom they flirted with, and even more careful never to claim to be SEALs. Becoming a SEAL was a process that took more than a year, and BUD/S students who thought their status as trainees afforded them bragging rights risked a painful lesson in humility.

Grey sat down heavily on the edge of his steel-framed bed. The thought of staying up all night polishing his boots and waxing the floor made him nauseous. If he was lucky he'd get two hours of sleep, maybe three. He pulled his combat boots out of his locker and started rubbing small circles of polish into the dry leather.

"What's on the schedule besides PT and the inspection?" Grey asked.

"The usual fun. Log PT and IBS. Maybe a little surf torture if we behave ourselves."

The instructors always made a point of beating the students a little extra on Friday afternoon, just so they wouldn't forget over the weekend that they were at BUD/S. Log PT consisted of a number of sadistic, back-breaking exercises performed with telephone poles. IBS, short for Inflatable Boat Small, involved a series of races, either carrying or paddling a hard rubber boat. The losing crew paid dearly. The winning crew occasionally got to sit out of the next race. Grey's boat crew was already notorious. Despite their best efforts, they often found themselves in last place.

Papa Smurf turned off his cell phone and surveyed his domain. "Boys, I'm hitting the rack. Don't work too hard tonight."

"It's only eight o'clock," Grey noted. "What about your inspection boots?"

"Done," Smurf answered. "Paid Owens ten bucks to polish them."

"And your knife?"

"Already sharpened." Smurf belched loudly. "Owens did it free."

Grey and Rogers exchanged glances. The concept of using money to pave the way to graduation disgusted them. They worked all night, finally crawling into their racks at two in the morning. Smurf's alarm went off at four o'clock, and the three roommates instinctively stumbled into the bathroom to shave, half blind from fatigue.

"Muster!" Petty Officer Burns strode angrily up and down the ranks of trainees, pushing people into their boat crews. "Muster, goddamn it!"

Grey glanced at his boat crew: Ramirez, Jones, Wallace, Stevens, and Tate. Someone was missing.

"Down one!" Grey called out.

"Who?" Burns asked loudly.

"Murray."

Burns shook his head in disgust and stormed into the barracks. He emerged a minute later pushing a barefoot, wild-eyed young man in front of him. The student's uniform wasn't buttoned, his belt buckle was turned backward, and his sand-encrusted boots dangled from his hands.

"What's the deal?" Grey asked, not sure if he wanted an answer.

Murray smiled sheepishly. "Sorry, boss. I was having a kick-ass dream. I must not have heard my alarm." He buttoned up his uniform and straightened his belt. "Won't happen again."

"I'd love to believe you," Grey said. "We'll talk later. We've got five minutes to be on the grinder for PT."

As Murray struggled with his boots, Papa Smurf motioned Grey over.

"You've got to control your boat crew," Smurf scolded. "We got ninety-five people out here on time, and we're waiting on one idiot. You better get him in line."

"Will do," Grey answered.

The class formed into sloppy rows and jogged in step toward the grinder. They called cadence as they went, hoping to impress the instructors with their volume. As soon as they rounded the corner of one of the beige buildings that surrounded the grinder, they sprinted to their designated spots. Over a hundred pairs of white footprints were painted on the asphalt. The students scrambled to fill up the rows.

"Drop!" The command echoed throughout the compound. Instantly, the entire class dropped into the push-up position and started counting out repetitions. When they reached twenty, Papa Smurf scanned the compound with panic-filled eyes.

"Who dropped us?" he whispered urgently. The students were required to call out the name of the instructor who dropped them in order to recover.

"I have no idea," Grey responded. "Try Redman, he's supposed to lead PT."

Papa Smurf inhaled noisily, then belted, "Instructor Redman!"

"Hoo-yah, Instructor Redman!" the class answered.

"Wrong!" the mystery voice bellowed. "Push 'em out!"

After twenty more push-ups, Papa Smurf looked back at Grey. "Well?"

Grey shook his head. "Beats me. Logan, maybe?"

"Instructor Logan!" Smurf shouted.

"Hoo-yah, Instructor Logan!" the class answered.

A brief period of silence followed, during which the trainees shifted their weight from arm to arm uncomfortably.

"Wrong! Push 'em out!"

"Who the fuck is it?" Smurf demanded. His face was turning beat red, contrasting sharply with his white T-shirt and green pants. With the blue vein running across his forehead and his thinning yellow hair, he was a veritable rainbow of color. Grey suppressed a laugh.

"C'mon. Give me a name."

"How about Chief Madsen?" Grey suggested.

"Chief Madsen!" Smurf called out.

"Hoo-yah, Ch—"

"Shut up!" the voice interrupted. "Push 'em out!"

The class pushed out twenty more repetitions.

"Push 'em out!"

Arms shaking with effort, the class did twenty more push-ups. By now everyone had assumed the leaning rest position. The trainees brought their feet in toward their hands until their butts were raised high in the air. This took some of the pressure off the triceps and chest. Unfortunately, this was not an exercise position sanctioned by BUD/S instructors.

"Get your weak little butts out of the air and I might recover you," the voice boomed. "I only want to see straight backs."

Suddenly the air was pierced by an explosive release of gas. This display of flatulence temporarily broke the tension. A few students even managed a quiet chuckle.

"Who did that?" the voice demanded.

Murray shifted his weight to one arm and raised the other.

"Go hit the surf, you dirty bird! Give that ass a nice scrubbing. I don't want any of your foul-smelling shit on my grinder."

Murray got up to start running.

"No! Bear crawl! And don't let me catch you cheating."

Murray's self-satisfied smile faded as he dropped into the push-up position and scampered the hundred yards to the surf on his hands and feet.

"Now, if the rest of you can keep your backs straight for exactly one minute, I'll recover you." The voice betrayed a high level of irritation.

The class snapped into proper push-up position. Grey knew they would never last a minute, but they had to try: giving up would only result in more punishment. Sure enough, thirty seconds into their endurance test a student let his back sag until his knees touched the ground.

"You are pathetic!" the voice screamed. "You are possibly the weakest class I've ever seen! Get your sorry asses down to the surf zone, get wet and sandy, and get back here! You have two minutes!"

Grey was growing used to this drill. The instructors would watch the students carefully. When it seemed they simply couldn't complete another push-up, they were sent to the surf. This way they were cold, wet, and physically exhausted all day—the perfect recipe for misery.

"This sucks!" a student yelled as they sprinted toward the surf. Grey looked over and made a note of his face. Students who complained excessively tended to disappear. If a trainee didn't truly want to be at BUD/S, he would go away. No doubt about it.

Grey leaped into the dark ocean, cringing reflexively as the water closed over his head. Although he hated the cold, he found his current situation perversely romantic. All his life he had dreaded the prospect of a desk job. He longed for adventure, and here it was, aching in every bone, coursing through every strained muscle. The bite of the ocean, the briny smell of rotting kelp, the sand abrading his legs—it all pointed to one glorious conclusion: he was living his dream. A smile broke out on his face as he sprinted back to the grinder.

"Are you fucking crazy?" Ramirez asked, eyeing Grey's ecstatic expression. "Sir, with all due respect, I think you've lost it."

The horrifying scene that greeted them back at the grinder quickly shattered Grey's private revelry. A dozen instructors were stationed at various points on the pavement. Two held hoses, one brandished a bullhorn.

"Morning, gents! Ready to PT?"

"Hoo-yaaaah," the class answered. They sustained the traditional battle cry, holding it for minutes on end. The brick walls of the compound magnified the eerie sound until it reached a fevered pitch. Grey could easily imagine that they were Viking warriors preparing for a raid, emptying their lungs in a display of raw masculinity. He felt alive: every nerve in his body was on edge. This was the instructors' motivation check. They were always eager to find out who really wanted to be at BUD/S and who was just along for the ride. Grey yelled until his voice cracked, and then yelled some more. The result was a hoarse cry that modulated in pitch like the voice of a pubescent schoolboy.

Instructor Redman raised a clenched fist, signifying that he'd heard enough. He was an imposing figure: six feet four, arms bulging with muscle, a chest that seemed impossibly big. His skin was leathery, and his beady black eyes peered from beneath a prominent brow. A thick patch of spiked black hair crowned his head, and his nose looked like it had been broken at least a dozen times. The students were terrified of Redman. Especially Grey . . .

I'm invisible. Grey knew what was coming. *You don't see me. I'm not here.*
"Grey!" Redman bellowed.

"Hoo-yah," Grey responded. He winced as his voice rose an octave.
The class laughed. Redman's eyes narrowed even farther.

"Is that what they teach you at Stanford? How to scream like a woman?"

Grey felt like melting into the asphalt. At Officer Candidate School the instructors had stressed the importance of maintaining an aura of professionalism in front of the enlisted men. Over three-quarters of Class 283 was comprised of enlisted personnel, and they were currently having a nice laugh at his expense. So much for image.

"Think you can do proper sit-ups today?" Redman asked.

Grey nodded.

"What?"

"Hoo-yah," Grey croaked, straining to keep his voice low.

"We'll see about that." Redman laid a foam pad on the platform and assumed the sit-up position. "Sit-ups . . . ready?"

The students dropped onto their butts. "Ready!"

The instructors strolled between the ranks of trainees, hosing them down and assaulting them with a torrent of verbal abuse. Grey felt the scab on his ass scrape off as he completed sit-up after sit-up. The salt that clung to his uniform ground its way into his open wound, making his eyes water uncontrollably. The sit-ups progressed into push-ups, then lunges, pull-ups, dips, leg lifts. An agonizing hour later the madness stopped.

"I'm not impressed," Redman said, shaking his head in disgust. His blue T-shirt rippled as he tensed and relaxed his muscles. "Look at me." He jumped off the platform. "I'm not even sweating, and you guys look like a bunch of underfed refugees. You've got ten seconds to get off my grinder. Move!"

The students tripped over one another as they scrambled out of the compound, eager to put as much distance as possible between themselves and the instructors. The sun peeked over the coastal mountains, casting a pale glow over the base's cream-colored buildings. Grey gathered his boat crew up in the open space next to the barracks that was simply referred to as "the pit." It was a patch of concrete hidden from instructor view yet large enough to accommodate ninety-six trainees—an ideal place to spend a few precious seconds getting reorganized.

"It's zero six hundred," Smurf announced to the class. "We have to be back here by zero seven. If you guys want a decent breakfast, we better get moving."

Murray jumped onto Grey's back and clung to him like a koala bear. "I'm tired, sir. How about a piggyback ride? You've got enough endurance for both of us."

"Murray, lock it up," Grey commanded. "We're late."

"Get in line, *puta!*" Ramirez yelled. "If I miss breakfast 'cause of you, you'll be wishin' you were dead."

Murray reluctantly dropped to the ground as Petty Officer Burns formed the class into ranks and led them onto the beach. The chow hall was a little over a mile away, a distance that at first seemed trivial. However, Grey quickly learned that six extra miles of running a day took its toll on the body. Many students in the class were already coming down with shin splints and stress fractures. The energy the class had displayed on their first chow run last week was gone. Grey noted with amusement that his fellow students naturally settled into the crippled gait known as the BUD/S shuffle. By shuffling their boots along the pavement rather than picking up their feet, they saved precious energy and minimized chafing. As they made slow progress toward the chow hall, Petty Officer Liska, a mild-mannered student with a golden voice, began calling out a jody. He sang a refrain, and the class echoed his declarations.

> *I don't want to be no Army Ranger,*
> *I want to live a life of danger.*
> *I don't want to be no Green Beret,*
> *They only PT once a day.*
> *I don't want to be no fag Recon,*
> *I'm gonna stay 'til the fightin's done.*

The jody and the high morale of his class lifted Grey's spirits. The thought of eating a nice hot breakfast made his stomach churn in anticipation. At BUD/S Grey learned to live moment by moment. Some days were too painful to contemplate as a whole entity. Instead of focusing on getting secured for the day, Grey focused on surviving until the next meal.

Class 283 stopped in front of the chow hall and formed into ranks. Papa Smurf ushered the first group of enlisted students into the building. The officers always ate last. It generally left Grey with little more than five minutes to scarf down his favorite morning meal: bacon and eggs, hash browns, five pieces of toast with peanut butter and jelly, hot cereal, orange juice, milk, and a huge piece of coffee cake. All told, Grey estimated that he took in about three thousand calories a meal—and he was still having trouble maintaining his weight. The constant shivering combined with up to six hours of physical conditioning a day turned his body into an insatiable furnace. Rogers often joked that he saw Grey's food catching on fire before he even swallowed it.

"Hello, Mr. Grey." Felicia flashed a pearly white smile from behind her cash register. She was Grey's favorite food-service worker, and like everyone else who worked there, she had the lilting accent of a recent Filipino immigrant. Several of the members of Class 283 had a crush on the five-foot beauty.

"How's it going, Felicia?"

"Not bad, Mr. Grey." Her smile faded. "I worry some, though."

"About what?" Grey leaned in closer and motioned the other officers to pass him in line. Felicia waited until they were out of hearing range to answer.

"Someone say bad things about you." She looked down at her feet. "I think he want you to go away."

"What do you mean?" Grey felt his heart constrict. If an instructor didn't want you to make it through BUD/S, you almost certainly wouldn't.

"He say you think you so smart—you know, too good for the rest."

"Who?" Grey's hoarse voice faltered. "Who said that?"

"Big guy, dark skin, sticky hair. Mean-looking."

Redman. Grey felt the excitement that had coursed through his veins on the way to chow slip away. *Motherfucker.* He pressed Felicia's hand gently as a show of thanks and made his way down the chow line. After collecting his usual assortment of nourishing navy foods, he found Rogers sitting alone at a table.

"You look like you just saw a ghost."

"It's worse than that," Grey confessed. "I just learned that Redman thinks I'm a self-righteous, cocky son of a bitch, and he's going to try to get rid of me."

"Does that surprise you? Redman hates all officers."

"I know, but I think it's different this time." Grey forked a load of scrambled eggs into his mouth. "The only thing that comforts me is the fact that we're graduating from Indoc tonight. I probably won't see him until Hell Week."

Rogers played with the last bits of hash browns on his plate. After mashing them into an inedible greasy sludge, he looked up at Grey apologetically. "Redman's going into First Phase with us."

"Shit." Normally the instructors in charge of Indoctrination were replaced by an entirely new crew for First Phase. The room suddenly grew quiet. Grey lowered his voice. "You've got to be kidding me. Can he do that?"

"That's the rumor."

"Two-eight-three, on your feet!" Smurf stood up and walked toward the door, signaling that chow was over. Grey had only managed to fork in one mouthful of food. He turned his back to the class, then greedily used his hands to scoop a massive handful of bacon and eggs into his mouth.

"Barbarian," Rogers muttered. "Cretin."

TWO

GREY FLUNG OPEN THE door to his locker and pulled out his pressed camouflage uniform. Inspection was in five minutes, hardly enough time to change. Rogers rooted around frantically in the locker next to him.

"Where's my knife?"

"I have no idea."

"Where's my knife?" Rogers repeated, this time more urgently. Staying calm under pressure was not his forte. Grey sometimes wondered if being a SEAL was a wise career path for his scholarly friend.

"Check behind your seabag," Grey offered.

Rogers dropped to his knees and pulled his seabag out of the locker. "Eureka!" He stood up holding his knife appreciatively, as if he had never seen anything so beautiful. "Thanks for the tip, chum."

"You better get your ensign asses moving," Smurf said. "Don't make me look bad." He dropped to his knees, pulled a stack of dog-eared magazines from the bottom of his locker, and carefully arranged them on his neatly made rack.

"Why the magazines?" Grey asked.

"Bribery," Smurf said. "It's the only sure way to pass a room inspection."

Grey stepped closer and glanced at the titles. *Backdoor Babes, Barely Legal, Uncensored XXX, Buttman*—an astonishing array of hard-core pornography.

"Nice," Grey muttered sarcastically.

"Hey, I don't make the rules," Smurf said defensively. "I just want to pass." After admiring the glossy finish on his boot tips, he adjusted his belt buckle and strode out the door.

Grey and Rogers threw on their uniforms as they raced the clock. Grey finished first by a long shot; he tied Rogers's boots while his room-mate frantically buttoned up his top.

"Let's go, Socrates," Grey urged. "Time waits for no one, and Redman certainly won't wait for me."

A minute later Grey stood in formation outside the barracks. A quick glance around suggested everyone had done their homework. Boots were shined, uniforms were starched and pressed, covers were blocked, hair-cuts were fresh.

"Stand by!" Petty Officer Burns yelled. "Feet!"

The class snapped to attention. A string of instructors clad in blue shorts and sweatshirts strolled to the front of the formation. They all sported nearly identical, ultratrendy sunglasses and wore the same disgusted scowl on their faces.

"Silver Spoons, front and center!" Instructor Logan yelled.

Rogers clumsily broke ranks and jogged to the front of the class. He towered over the stocky instructor, and for a lack of anything better to say, shouted, "Hoo-yah, Instructor Logan!"

"Hoo-yah yourself, you stupid, overpaid cake eater." Logan looked Rogers up and down and then hocked a mixture of sunflower seeds and spit onto his boot. "Boots look like shit," he observed. "What's your ex-cuse?"

Rogers remained silent.

"Excuses are like assholes: everyone's got one." He spit again. "What's yours?"

"No excuse, Instructor Logan."

"Fine. You'll pay later. For now, recite."

"Recite?"

"Yeah, stand up on that table and let the class hear some Greek shit."

Rogers jumped onto the picnic table behind the instructors and cleared his throat.

The man for wisdom's various arts renown'd,
Long exercised in woes, O Muse! resound;
Who, when his arms had wrought the destined fall
Of sacred Troy, and razed her heaven-built wall,
Wandering from clime to clime, observant stay'd,
Their manners noted, and their states survey'd.

The instructors began their inspection as Rogers continued. The soothing sound of the recitation combined with the instructors' furious yelling sent Grey's head reeling. He tuned out the verbal abuse and tried to focus on the beauty of *The Odyssey*. The epic poem had a timeless quality that seemed to rise above the chaos surrounding him.

"Drop down, fuck stick!"

Grey snapped out of his reverie. Everyone in the class had dropped into the push-up position. Instructor Redman's angry face was inches from his own. Grey dropped down and started cranking out push-ups.

"Recover!" Redman yelled.

Grey jumped to his feet.

"Drop!"

Grey dropped. This sequence continued until his breath came in heaving gasps—drop, recover, drop, recover.

"Think you can pull your head out of your ass now?" Redman screamed.

"Hoo-yah!" Grey answered.

"We'll see about that. Let's check out that uniform of yours." Redman looked Grey over quickly and smiled deviously. "What did we say before? Each inspection hit is worth a hundred push-ups?"

"Hoo-yah," Grey answered quietly.

"Well, let's have a look." Redman grabbed a tiny thread between his fingernails and started pulling. Once the thread had unraveled several inches, he turned to show off his prized find.

"Instructor Logan, check this out!" Redman shouted. "Have you ever seen an Irish pennant this long? I could rappel off it!"

"I think that's worth at least three hits," Logan suggested. "Maybe four."

Grey felt like disappearing again. Special attention was becoming a way of life.

"And look at those boots," Redman clucked. "Scuffed."

"And all that sand on his chest," Logan added. "Dirty bird!"

Grey felt his face flush with anger. The six-inch Irish pennant was one thing, but nailing him for messing up his uniform while doing push-ups was absurd.

"Jesus Christ!" Redman bellowed. "You are pathetic! Hit the surf! You have two minutes."

Grey dutifully immersed himself in the ocean and returned to find Redman standing in front of a ring knocker. Although the term *ring knocker* had lost its prestige years ago, Grey still used it to describe the U.S. Naval Academy officers in his class. They rarely messed up, always managed to land the choicest collateral duty assignments, and were fiercely protective of one another. They were secretive and defensive, yet they always managed to put on a cool, friendly face. Rogers had once likened the phenomenon of the insular Academy brotherhood to the Freemasons. To be fair, Grey had met a number of Academy officers he thought were outstanding leaders and fine human beings, it just happened that none of them were in Class 283.

"Nice boots, Mr. Wright," Redman stated. "Good uniform, clean haircut—over all, not bad."

"Thank you, Instructor Redman." Ensign Wright smiled broadly.

"Don't thank me, dumb-ass," Redman muttered. "You want to hit the surf, too?"

"Negative, Instructor Redman." Wright's gap-toothed grin disappeared.

As Redman moved down the line, Grey noticed that he would glance in his direction frequently. The devilish look on the instructor's face suggested that he delighted in the knowledge that Grey was keenly aware of the unfairness of the situation. He only sent one other student to the surf, and that was because his buckle was on backward. The last student Redman inspected was Seaman Jones, the "Tennessee Wonder."

"What are you smiling about, you inbred, backwoods, banjo-strumming fool?" Redman asked.

"I was just thinkin' about what a nice day it is and all," Jones drawled. "This here is real outdoors weather."

"Real outdoors weather," Redman repeated, poorly imitating Jones's accent. "Well, ain't that nice." He brushed some imaginary dirt off Jones's shoulder. "You a fag, Jones?"

"Negative." Grey could hear the nervousness creeping into Jones's voice.

"You sure about that? Cause I sure could imagine you and Murray getting hot and heavy back there in the shower."

Jones tottered perceptibly. Grey hoped he didn't pass out.

"C'mon, Instructor Redman!" Murray cried, breaking the silence. "You know I could do better than that old hillbilly piece of ass. I'm a sexy bastard." He cupped his pecs and rubbed them provocatively. The class laughed.

"You are one sick fuck." Redman covered the distance to Murray in a few gigantic strides. "And you are not allowed to be funny. Only instructors should attempt humor. And just to drive the point home, I'm going to beat the shit out of you. Time for some reindeer games out on the beach. Jones, you can join us."

Grey tried to magically narrow his body so that it disappeared behind the student next to him.

"Grey, you too." Redman started to walk away when his eyes fell on Rogers. "And you too, Persephone, or whatever your name is."

The four unfortunate students ran to the beach together. They lined up and stood at parade rest in front of the sand berm. Several minutes later Redman strolled out.

"Two officers and two enlisted. Perfect." The instructor's enormous pecs twitched beneath his T-shirt as he spoke. "I'm sure you gentlemen are familiar with wheelbarrow races. One trainee gets in the push-up position, the other picks up his legs, and away you go. I bet you guys did this shit all the time when you were Webelos, or Cub Scouts, or whatever the fuck that organization is called." Redman drew a line in the sand. "You'll start here, and you'll finish when I tell you the race is over. Assume the position."

Grey dropped onto his stomach. He knew upper-body strength wasn't Rogers's strong point, so he took the dreaded bottom position. His triceps burned in anticipation of the beating that was in store. Grey looked over at Murray and smiled when the seaman winked at him.

"Instructor Redman, can you give us a direction or something?"

Murray asked. "For all I know, Rogers might take a turn and race right over the sand berm."

"Go straight ahead, dumb-ass. If I want you to turn I'll tell you." Redman held his arm up and waited a few seconds. Murray false-started, and when he realized what he had done, he locked his elbows to stop his forward progress. Unfortunately, Jones kept pushing on his legs and unwittingly plowed his partner's face into the sand. As Murray and Jones scrambled to reorient themselves, Redman dropped his arm to start the race. Rogers and Grey took off.

"Pays to be a winner!" Redman yelled as he jogged backward in front of the struggling pairs.

Grey started to falter after a hundred yards. Each time he planted an arm he felt his elbows strain under his weight. Each step was a jarring reminder of how ludicrous SEAL training could be. His bowed back screamed for relief as Jones and Murray caught up.

"Let's go, girls! Almost there!" Redman yelled. "Just make it to me!" He stopped ten yards ahead of the racing human wheelbarrows. Grey knew something was amiss: Redman's tone was far too encouraging. He conserved his effort and let Murray and Jones pass him up.

"Sorry. Changed my mind," Redman stated cheerfully as Murray collapsed into a heap, bringing Jones down with him. Grey and Rogers blew by their fallen comrades. With deliberate slowness, Redman cut a path toward the sand berm. He angled up the sandy slope, smiling with delight as Grey repeatedly fell onto his chest as his arms gave out.

"Just think, gentle ensigns, you could be sitting behind a six-foot stack of paper aboard USS *Neverdock* right now. Or you could be at flight school, eating donuts and piloting a cutting-edge aircraft. There must be a better life. You don't need to be here."

"Fuck that," Grey gasped between fiery breaths.

"What?" Redman asked.

"I said fuck that!" Grey yelled.

"All right then, sir. Don't get your satin panties all in a tangle. Just follow me, if you please." With a frilly arm movement, Redman bowed in mock deference. He continued up the berm and down the other side toward the ocean. Grey placed one hand in front of the other, willing his drained body to keep up. Shortly after he reached Instructor Redman,

Jones and Murray appeared at his side. The defiant smile was gone from Murray's elfish face. Strings of spittle streamed from his open mouth, and his normally sparkling blue eyes had clouded over.

"Hydration break!" Redman pointed at the churning surf zone. "Take your wheelbarrows out into the surf, gents. Lubricate those rusty parts with some salt water."

Grey and Rogers continued their forward progress. The icy ocean water progressed up Grey's arms, eventually reaching his chin. He inhaled deeply and held his breath as a large breaker rumbled toward them.

"And halt!" Redman yelled.

The three-foot wall of whitewash slammed into the pair, knocking them backward with surprising force. They tumbled a short distance before regaining their footing.

"Enough practice being a garden tool," Redman stated. "Let's practice being icicles. After all, Christmas is only two months away." He hocked a yellow plug of phlegm onto the sand, then wiped his hand across his mouth. "Take your seats."

The four trainees linked arms and sat down. Jones sat to Grey's left, Rogers to his right. In the last two weeks Grey had learned that you were valued by your fellow students not only for how much you "put out" during team evolutions, but also for the amount of heat your body produced. Strangely enough, some students were virtual heaters while others were cursed with a chilly touch. Grey counted himself among the blessed. Two days ago several members of his boat crew had gotten into a dispute over who got to sit next to him during surf torture. Unfortunately for Grey, the two trainees greedily clinging to his arms at the moment were frigid specimens. They pressed their arms into his torso and exhaled in soft staccato breaths.

"We're gonna be here all day, gents. You'll have plenty of time to consider your options," Redman called from the beach.

Jones stared straight ahead as his jaw involuntarily jackhammered. The ghostly sheen of his pale skin gave Grey the creeps.

"Hang in there, Jones. We all know he can't keep us out here more than twenty minutes or so."

"Yeah, there are specific medical regulations on this sort of thing,"

Rogers added. "He knows that surf torture without an ambulance standing by is against the CO's orders. Besides, he can't kill—"

A wall of whitewash rushed overhead, interrupting Rogers's speech.

"Oh, yes he can," Murray contradicted. He coughed loudly before continuing. "He most definitely could freeze our sorry asses, but it would end his career in a hurry. Let's hope he loves his job."

Oh, he loves his job all right. Sick fuck lives for this stuff. Grey closed his eyes and used the sound of incoming surf to time his breath holds. His body grew used to the rhythm of the ocean. The wave lifted his torso as it passed overhead, then pushed him flat against the bottom as the water receded before the next set. Up, down, breathe, hold. If it wasn't so cold, Grey might have found it relaxing.

"Feet!" Redman yelled.

Thank God. Grey slowly stood and tried his balance. He wasn't nearly as stiff as he expected. Jones was another matter. The Tennessee Wonder stood up, then promptly fell back on his ass. Rogers and Grey each grabbed an arm and helped him to the beach.

"Well, well, it's looks like we've got a cold one," Redman said. He stared intently into Jones's eyes. "You want the silver bullet?"

"Hell no," Jones stammered. "I ain't never takin' that thing." The silver bullet was rumored to be an anal thermometer six inches in length and about an inch in diameter—a special treat for hypothermia victims. Rogers claimed it was just another manifestation of the SEAL obsession with homosexuality. References to gay sex were ingrained in BUD/S culture. It was as much a part of life as breathing, and both Grey and Rogers found it a sad display of insecurity. Of course, they could never say that.

"Hillbilly Bob, start doing jumping jacks! The rest of you get back out there!" Redman yelled.

As Grey trudged back into the gray Pacific, he could think of only one thing—his gorgeous girlfriend. He let his body go numb as his mind drifted back to his days at Stanford.

The first time Grey set eyes on Vanessa, he knew he had met his match. She was the sassy daughter of brilliant Indian immigrants—a true New York City girl—and she seemed completely unimpressed by the fact that Grey aspired to be a SEAL. In truth, she really had no idea what a SEAL did. With perfect mocha skin, ebony hair, and almond-shaped eyes, Vanessa was breathtakingly beautiful. Her curvaceous body turned heads, yet she remained oblivious of the stares of her admirers. Grey was instantly charmed. When they first started dating, Grey had explained what his career aspirations entailed and hinted that maintaining a relationship past graduation would be difficult at best. But it turned out that beneath all her sass, Vanessa was a romantic, and she proved willing to take a chance on him. All Grey could think about now was curling up next to her warm body.

Feet. Grey felt a tugging sensation on his arms.

"Let's go. He said 'feet,'" Rogers stammered.

Grey snapped out of his reverie and into the world of the living. Rogers and Murray helped him to his feet.

"Goddamn!" Murray yelled. "Isn't this shit just tons of fun? And just think, we've still got a month until Hell Week."

Apparently a little surf torture had revived Murray's spirit. Grey was grateful. A student with his personality was invaluable for two reasons. Not only would he improve morale by keeping things light, but he would also serve as a lightning rod for some of the instructors' wrath. Although Grey protected Murray from the anger of Papa Smurf as much as possible, like everyone else he occasionally succumbed to the "better him than me" philosophy when it came to the instructors' attention. Something about being frozen and beaten continuously all week shifted students into their primal survival mode, and Grey was no exception. Earlier in the week Jones had become a class favorite by passing out during log PT, ending the evolution prematurely. The class had been exuberant at this turn of events: martyrdom was fully endorsed by Class 283.

"No time to waste, ladies," Redman scolded. "Log PT starts now. Don't be late."

The four chilled trainees broke into a sprint back toward the compound. Rogers fell twice as he struggled to squeeze some coordination into his frozen limbs. Grey yanked him to his feet, and they scampered up the berm together. As they stumbled down the other side, Grey noted with horror that the class had already started log PT. Each boat crew held a telephone pole at extended-arm carry. Grey cursed under his breath as he realized his boat crew was currently making do with four students rather than the usual seven. While Murray and Jones had suffered alongside Grey, the four other members of his crew had been left to hold the log above their heads by themselves. Although he had no idea how long they had been struggling with their log, the pleading looks on their faces suggested they could use a little assistance.

"And here they are!" Instructor Logan boomed. "Just in time to help out their pathetic boat crews!" A prerecorded cackle burst forth from his megaphone, followed by a high-pitched scream. He spat a glob of sunflower seeds into the sand.

Grey took his position at the rear of the log and pressed his hands into the splintery wood. He immediately felt the trainee in front of him ease up. He could tell his boat crew was fading fast. The log bobbed unevenly as individuals caved in and released pressure on their arms.

"Who's going to be the big loser?" Logan asked. "Who's going to drop their precious log?" The megaphone emitted another hideous cackle.

The front end of the log started to drop.

"Fire it up, Ramirez!" Tate yelled.

"Fire it up your ass," Ramirez groaned. "You try being up here. This shit ain't easy."

Teamwork. It was such a beautiful concept, yet so difficult to orchestrate when inordinate amounts of pain entered the equation. Grey watched helplessly as Ramirez lowered the front end of the log onto his right shoulder.

"We have a winner!" Logan yelled, imitating a circus barker. "If you gentlemen would kindly step over to Old Misery, I believe Instructor Redman is waiting to fulfill your every physical need."

"Waist carry," Grey commanded. His crew lowered the log to waist level. "Right hand starting position." They dropped the log on the sand. Grey's stomach dropped as he got an eyeful of Redman standing over the fabled torture device. Old Misery was at least twice as heavy as a standard PT log, yet it was considerably shorter in length. The result was an unwieldy piece of wood that was too thick to get a good grip on and too short to fit everyone underneath comfortably. The cryptic inscription "Old Misery Never Dies" had been gouged into its rough surface, a reference to a favorite BUD/S story. Legend had it a group of vengeful trainees had once floated Old Misery far out into the ocean, hoping they would never see the cursed log again. The next morning, however, Old Misery had washed up on the beach directly in front of the BUD/S compound, soggier and heavier than ever. Since then, Old Misery had commanded a fearful reverence among the superstitious students.

Instructor Redman sat cowboy style on top of Old Misery and gave it an affectionate pat. "I think it's time for a ride, Old Mis," Redman cooed as if he were subduing a horse. "Let's see what these girls can do." He waited expectantly. "Well? Take me for a ride, damn it!"

For several seconds Boat Crew Nine froze in confusion. Grey was sure Redman was joking. They couldn't be expected to lift Old Misery with an extra 250 pounds tacked on.

"Don't test my patience," Redman warned.

Grey looked around helplessly. Suddenly a blur of camouflage flashed toward the overbuilt instructor. Murray threw his small frame directly against Redman's chest, catching him completely off guard. The pair fell backward into the sand. Grey seized the moment.

"Right shoulder carry." As the rest of the class looked on in hushed amazement, Grey's crew hoisted Old Mis onto their shoulders. Meanwhile, Murray and Redman engaged themselves in an all-out wrestling match. Murray was only able to hold off his huge opponent for a few seconds. The instructors laughed hysterically as Redman put Murray in a choke hold. The laughter subsided as Murray's complexion shifted from an overcooked red to a shade of blue. His mouth worked silently, as if to beg for mercy.

"Enough!" Instructor Logan barked as he pulled Redman away. Murray gasped noisily for breath while Logan whispered into Redman's ear. After kicking a cloud of sand into Murray's face, Redman angrily stormed off the beach.

"What are you looking at, shit birds?" Logan yelled. "Keep those logs up."

A shaken Murray joined Boat Crew Nine as they hoisted Old Mis. Although Grey knew Murray had expected a violent reaction to his playful attack, his manner had changed dramatically. *He's scared.*

"If you're lucky enough to make it to the end of the day, you sure as hell won't make it through First Phase," Logan growled. "You're one dumb motherfucker, Murray, and I don't envy you. Redman's gonna tear you a new one." He spat seeds and walked away.

Grey felt certain his back would snap in half at any moment, and his arms weren't faring much better. Old Mis grew heavier by the moment. Just when he was sure a womanly scream would slip past his lips, the instructors found a new game to play—log push-ups. Boat Crew Nine held Old Mis at a waist carry, crossed their legs, and plopped backward onto the sand. Grey felt his rib cage flex under the weight of the log as they assumed the starting position. The push-ups themselves weren't overly difficult; it was keeping Old Mis balanced that Grey found terrifying. The log rocked dangerously as they pushed it up and down. Several times the behemoth came close to rolling off of their palms and onto their faces. Grey could handle breaking a rib or two, but contemplating a crushed skull wasn't pleasant.

"*Coma me mierda, mayate.*" Ramirez told Instructor Logon to eat shit through clenched teeth.

"*Chingate.*" Jones added a strained "fuck you," exhausting his knowledge of gutter Spanish.

Up down, up down, up down. Old Mis worked her magic. Grey felt as if his eyes would pop out from the strain of keeping the log off his chest.

"Treat your logs kindly," Logan growled. "Give them the love they deserve. Take them down to the ocean and give them a nice bath." He spat a gob of sunflower seeds into the wind. "Hell, let's make it a race. Last boat crew back here gets Old Mis."

Thank God, Grey thought. If only they could make it to the surf and back. He winced as his boat crew rolled Old Mis off their chests and down their legs. With a coordinated surge of energy they hoisted the log onto their shoulders and started up the sand berm. Each step resulted in enormous amounts of wasted effort as their feet slipped backward. White flashes erupted like tiny volcanoes in Grey's field of vision, and the muted morning light shimmered off the churning ocean. *Not a good sign.* Suddenly Old Mis grew considerably heavier. Grey turned to yell in frustration and found Murray sprawled out on the sand. In an instant Logan was by his side.

"Everyone put your logs down and go sit in the surf," Logan ordered.

He led Murray to the back of the white ambulance and pushed him inside. The door slammed shut, and the diesel truck roared off.

"Get out there and link arms!" His growl had morphed into a full blown yell. "Just because your teammate passes out doesn't mean training is over!"

"Oh, yes it does," Ramirez whispered. "This shit is paradise."

Grey waded into the ocean, which suddenly did not seem quite as cold, and happily took his place in the line of students sitting in the surf. He pulled Ramirez and Jones close to either side, basking in the temporary relief from the overflowing lactic acid in his muscles.

"Thank you, Murray," Jones murmured reverently.

Grey leaned forward in the line and picked out Rogers's face several places down. "How about a poem to commemorate our friend's noble sacrifice? We need to pay our respects."

"Right," Rogers answered. "Give me a moment."

The line of students lurched forward and back as the breakers pushed them into a U-shaped formation.

"Get back on line, you turds!" Logan kicked sand into the air. "You have ten seconds, or I'll have you doing buddy carries up and down the beach."

The students on either end of the lineup suddenly sprang into life and scooted backward through the water. Miraculously, the line straightened out. Rogers cleared his throat loudly.

"A poem, gentlemen," he offered. "Your attention, please."

> With ceaseless courage and unbridled fire
> Old Murray saved us from the mire
> Of logs and pain and cruel Mr. Redman,
> If he were here, we'd all be dead men.
> And now we sit in frosty bliss,
> Bathing in each other's piss.
> A true, good friend became a martyr,
> And saved our class from working harder.

Rogers smiled triumphantly as the students groaned. Although his fellow trainees teased him mercilessly on account of his archaic mannerisms, they always enjoyed his antics.

"Well, I didn't have time for anything better," he explained as the jeering continued. "If you give me more time, I might be able to come up with something in iambic tetrameter, or maybe a nice Italian sonnet."

Grey closed his eyes and tried to capture the moment for posterity—the numbness creeping into his limbs, the scratch of sand against his butt, the pull and surge of the tide, the playful laughter, the gentle sun on his face, the wheeling cry of restless seagulls, the taste of salt on his lips. He braced himself for the ominous sight of the white ambulance as it returned from the medical clinic. When it finally rumbled onto the beach, he was mentally prepared to go back to battle with the logs. Apparently his classmates weren't. A collective groan rippled up and down the line as they stood up in the surf and marched toward shore.

Murray climbed out of the ambulance and met his class in the shallows. As they reached the beach, Logan moved his hand in a circle above his head.

"School circle," Smurf yelled, suddenly taking charge. Frothy spit flew from his mouth. "Let's go, let's go!" The class responded sluggishly to spite him. Much to Grey's delight, it was becoming common knowledge that Papa Smurf was out for only one person—himself. Gradually everyone dropped to their knees and fixed their eyes on the stocky instructor in front of them.

"Before we continue, I want to make a point," Logan began. "We have a weak link in this class. A dangerous one. He's like a plague, a pestilence, a virus." Logan lowered his voice to a conspiratorial tone. "A pussy. He'll destroy your class. He'll bring you down. He'll make you weak. Hell, he'll even try to make you crave cock."

The class laughed to humor Logan, but Grey could tell they were shaken. Murray's eyes narrowed as he stared at an invisible point somewhere up the coast. A student next to him placed a protective hand on his back.

"Murray, front and center," Logan commanded. "The rest of you back away."

Murray pushed through the crowd and stood before his class.

"This is your weak link." Logan jabbed a finger into Murray's back. "This piece of shit is only holding you back. If I were you, I'd take him behind the sand berm tonight and do it the old-fashioned way. Give him a choice: either he can leave, or you beat the crap out of him." Logan scanned the crowd. "Is there anyone here who will come forward and honestly tell me that Murray is worth a rat's ass? Do any of you really want to work with this shitbag?"

The class fell silent. They all feared being singled out as a turd. Everyone knew that once you appeared on an instructor's shitlist, life was bound to get very colorful in a hurry. Murray's stone face suddenly melted. His lower lip trembled as he looked at the blank faces before him.

"I'd work with Murray any day," Grey said, stepping forward. He grabbed Murray possessively by the arm and yanked him back into the crowd. "He's got a bigger heart than half the people out here."

Logan glowered. "Well, well. A shitty officer stands up for his shitty enlisted buddy. You two make a great pair."

"I'd take Murray as well," Rogers said quietly. "I think he adds a lot to our class."

"See what's happening, gents? The bottom of the BUD/S barrel is foaming to the top. All the people you should be concerned about are coming forward." Logan threw up his hands. "Anyone else want to join the goon squad?"

"Count me in," Ramirez said. "I stand by my boat-crew leader."

"Me too." Jones raised his hand. "I'm not lettin' you suckers have all the fun."

"All right," Logan growled. "Enough bullshit. Everyone back on their logs."

The log push-ups, sit-ups, side-straddle hops, and extended-arm drills lasted well into the morning. Grey puked twice, and the taste of bile stayed in his mouth until chow. As the day wore on, the class became less and less enthusiastic. The journey to and from chow seemed impossibly long, and Grey silently cursed the sand that stripped away the flesh between his legs. Thankfully, Instructor Redman didn't show his angry face for the remainder of the day. After hours of boat drills, a thoroughly chilled Class 283 filed into the First Phase classroom for their pseudograduation from Indoctrination. Indoc was simply a warm-up for the rest of BUD/S. Its termination marked the beginning of six more months of torture.

"Drop." Logan peeked his head through the doorway. The class immediately assumed push-up position. He disappeared again, and the class adopted the leaning rest. Five minutes later Grey's arms were trembling violently. Following the lead of his classmates, Grey started alternating body positions. First he would rest his stomach on the tile floor so that his back ramped downward, then he would lift his ass high into the air and rest his arms. Unfortunately, even this tactic couldn't salvage enough strength from his sorely depleted triceps and chest. Grey's arms gave out and he crashed to the floor.

"Get up," Rogers pleaded. "Don't let—"

The door crashed open, and a string of instructors filed into the room. Grey tapped into the adrenaline coursing through his veins and managed to push his chest off the ground. He was too late.

"Who the fuck are you?" A black-haired instructor with small dark eyes pointed a long finger in his direction.

"Ensign Grey, instructor."

"Why the hell was your stomach on the ground?" Something metallic flashed in the instructor's mouth as he talked. Grey was caught off guard, and it took him a moment to respond.

"No excuse, instructor."

"Damn right, no excuse." His mouth gleamed again. Grey realized the flash came from a metal tongue stud.

That can't be regulation. Grey glanced around and found that his classmates were equally mesmerized. Something about a BUD/S instructor with a tongue stud was perversely intriguing. *How am I supposed to take this guy seriously?*

The new staff arranged themselves in a single-file line and glared at Class 283. A tall, rangy instructor with a handlebar mustache stepped forward. He spoke slowly, as if addressing a classroom full of children.

"Welcome to First Phase," he droned. "I'm Chief Baldwin." He casually paced back and forth in front of the class as he spoke. "You can call me Chief Baldwin. You will not call me simply 'Chief' or 'Baldwin' or 'Dude' or 'Man' or any of that other crap you dope smokers picked up in high school. Is that clear?"

The class responded with as much volume as they could muster: "Hoo-yah, Chief Baldwin."

"What the fuck does that mean?" Chief Baldwin asked, his brow furrowing in anger. "Someone tell me what you meant by that pathetic 'hoo-yah.'"

"It meant, 'Yes, we understand,'" a voice blurted out.

"You will never use 'hoo-yah' to answer a question. Is that clear?"

"Yes, Chief Baldwin," the class answered.

"Good, because I refuse to speak hoo-yah-nese. That lame-ass expression can mean 'yes,' it can mean 'fuck yeah,' it can mean 'I heard you,' it can mean 'I'm only saying this because I have to,' or better yet, 'If it were up to me I'd stick my foot up your ass.' I only speak English. So if I ask you a question in English, I expect a reasonable answer." Chief sat on the edge of a table. He arched a dark eyebrow as he watched Class 283 drip sweat onto the floor. "I'll be your proctor, which means it's my job to take care of you sorry little dimwits. First off, recover yourselves."

The class thankfully scrambled to attention. Chief Baldwin motioned for them to take their seats.

"Here's what I'm not going to do: I won't hold your hand when you pee, or find you a tampon when that time of the month rolls around, or pop the zits on your adolescent faces. I will listen to your serious grievances, and I'll try to keep First Phase running smoothly. That doesn't mean you can come up to me and say, 'Chief Baldwin, Instructor Osgood keeps making me hurt. Tell him to stop.' I'll either laugh in your face or beat you, depending on my mood. However, if you say, 'The chow hall stopped serving food; we're starving,' I'll see what I can do. Now, on to the fun. I'm going to introduce you to the First Phase instructors. They're going to say their names once and only once. I expect you to remember them. Understood?"

"Yes, Chief Baldwin."

One by one, the instructors blurted out their names: Instructor Dullard, Instructor MacLean, Chief Lundin, Instructor Osgood, Instructor Barefoot, Instructor Furtado, Instructor Smith, Instructor McNeil, Senior Chief Ortiz, Instructor Petrillo, Instructor Heisler, Instructor Johnson, Instructor Heffner, and Chief Nebrinski. Grey frantically tried to attach faces to names, but the only one that stuck in his mind was Instructor Furtado, the tongue-studded warrior.

"Let's jog your memory." The suggestion came from a bald instructor built like a fireplug. He smiled mischievously. "Drop."

The tiny desks squealed as the students pushed them aside. Due to a lack of space, they did their push-ups crowded together like toppled dominos. All the eyes were on Papa Smurf, who by virtue of his position as class leader was responsible for calling out the instructor. He squirmed uneasily.

"Instructor Heisler," he yelled in a faltering voice.

"Hoo-yah, Instructor Heisler," the class answered.

An uneasy silence followed. The instructors stood by, coiled and ready to spring. Grey held his breath reflexively as he prayed for mercy. *Please be Heisler.*

"Wrong!" the stocky instructor yelled, and the room erupted into chaos. Instructors danced about, punishing students with push-ups when they couldn't recite the correct name.

"What did you call me?" incredulous instructors asked as they leaped from desk to desk. "What's my name?"

When Grey was sure he would pass out from the strain, his tormentors stepped off their desks and stood by passively. Seconds later a lieutenant clad in dress blues walked in the room.

"Sir, what can we do for you?" Chief Baldwin asked pleasantly.

"Don't mind me," the officer said. "Please, carry on." He was a friendly looking fellow, and Grey sincerely hoped that he would end their misery.

"Class, meet Lieutenant Fuchs," Chief Baldwin said. "He's the director of First Phase."

The class watched his face expectantly. The lieutenant merely smiled and strode out of the room. The interruption diminished the instructors' zeal for punishment considerably. They filed out the door, leaving only Chief Baldwin behind.

"I expect you're having a class-up party tonight. You invite women?"

"Hoo-yah!" the class screamed in reply.

"What'd I say about answering my questions with that lame-ass phrase? You'll pay later. Now, I'll give you some advice. . . ." He paused and stroked his mustache thoughtfully. "The command does not condone using class funds to hire strippers. The last couple of parties involved strippers, and I was happy to attend. Catch my drift?"

"Yeah, you just want to see some ass. Fuck the command policy, right?"

The class looked around in horror. Sassing the class proctor was as close to suicide as anything a BUD/S student could imagine. Grey immediately recognized the voice. *Damn it, Murray.* Much to the surprise of the class, Chief Baldwin grinned broadly, showcasing his tobacco-stained teeth.

"I like an honest man," he said. "I also like a student who isn't afraid. Just watch your attitude, 'cause most of my cohorts aren't quite as genial as I am. Catch my drift?" He squatted in front of Murray. "What's your name, son?"

"Murray." He lifted his head and eyed the instructor warily.

"Well, Murray, you just finish those push-ups you were working on. I'll keep my eye on you." Chief Baldwin stood and walked out of the room. "Recover yourselves," he yelled over his shoulder. "I'll see you ladies tonight."

The students of Class 283 hobbled to their feet and headed for the door. They formed two columns and limped across the grinder, dripping salt water, sweat, and sand across the pavement as they went. Once they reached the pit, Papa Smurf gathered everyone around him. "Passing word," or reviewing the day's events and planning for tomorrow, always took far too long. Grey liked to keep things moving so the guys could get a shower and get on with their nights.

"Listen up," Smurf ordered. He assumed his defensive body position—legs spread wide and arms crossed tightly over his chest. "Today went better than it could have, so good job on not screwing things up even more. Murray, thanks for passing out." The class cheered loudly, and Murray got his butt pinched and his head slapped several times. "One thing we need to work on is respecting the chain of command. We are in training, but that doesn't mean that you can blow off your boat-crew leader, even if he is a lowly ensign."

"Fuckin' A, sir," a sandy-haired seaman named Larsen cut in. "I know you're talking about me. I didn't mean any disrespect when I told Ensign Rogers to go fuck himself. I was simply suggesting that we might actually win a race if we cheated like the rest of you bastards. Sir, with all due respect, most of our boat-crew leaders don't know what the hell is going on."

A silence followed, in which the gaggle of ring knockers stared incredulously at the enlisted puke who dared to defile their leadership. A red-faced ensign named Pollock stepped forward.

"Look, I don't know where you guys went to boot camp, but at the Academy I was taught to show a certain amount of respect to my superiors. I know BUD/S is a vacuum. You can say whatever you want and get away with it, because we're all classmates here. Just remember that when and if you graduate, everything will change. We'll be giving you orders, and you'll either be following them or getting the hell out of the teams."

"That's bullshit, sir!" Larsen yelled. "If you want your every command executed without question, you should have joined the surface community. Nearly half of us have college degrees. The only reason we're not officers is that we couldn't get billets, so we enlisted. If I have a good idea or a suggestion, I expect you to listen, bars or no bars."

"You want EMI?" Pollock yelled back. The class groaned. Threatening Larsen with Extra Military Instruction, aka punishment, was a cheap shot.

"You can have me stand all your watches! I'll stay up every goddamn night. But just know this: you won't have one ounce of my respect." He gestured at the crowd behind him. "Or any of the other lowly enlisted folk in the class."

Grey stepped into the center of the circle. He had to restrain the urge to take both Larsen's and Pollock's heads and knock them together.

"Listen up, everyone!" Grey called out. The noise level quickly died down. Grey rarely spoke out, and the class immediately gave him their attention. "I want you all to step back and take a look at the situation we're in. We're setting ourselves up for disaster. Come next week, you know what the instructors will be looking for?" He wiped a hand across his sweaty forehead. "They'll be looking to see if we work as a team. If we can't handle petty disputes like this, they're gonna tear us apart. If they sense a lack of teamwork, we may as well kiss our chances of graduating good-bye."

"So what do you suggest, sir?" Larsen asked.

"Well, first of all, the officers in the class, myself included, need to listen more carefully to the suggestions of the enlisted. Second of all—"

"Excuse me, brother," Petty Officer Jackson said. "I know what you're trying to say. With all due respect, I'll take it from here." Petty Officer Jackson was the only black student in Class 283. He was well liked by everyone, and he had a notoriously sharp wit. He launched into his fabled preacher routine. "My brothers in Christ-uh. What we have here-uh is a failure. A failure of brotherly love."

"Amen," the class responded. Smiles broke out all around.

"The Lord—the Lord above-uh—he's a watchin'. He's a wishin' that e-dogs and o-dogs could struggle hand in hand. Yes-uh. That's right. Struggle together."

"Sing it, brother!" Murray yelled.

Jackson picked up the intensity. "And we need respect, brothers. We need it now like no other time. Yes-uh. We should be like Moses. Like Moses in the face of the Lord's awesome power! Yes-uh! Respect, brothers."

"Hallelujah!"

"But we need just rulers! Yes-uh! Like the people of Israel, who were delivered from the oppression of the pharaoh, we need fair leadership! What we need-uh, is the shepherds and the sheep united together. Yes-uh. Show me the love." Jackson grabbed Pollock and Murray by the wrist and jammed their hands together. "That's right, brothers. Show me that brotherly love!"

Students embraced and wept theatrically.

"That's right-uh. I feel it now! I feel it in my achin' bones. We must strive to understand. Yes-uh! We will listen and understand each other! We will not fight! No-uh! We will unite together, and we will escape from this place! We will be delivered from the tyranny of BUD/S."

"Amen!"

"We will struggle and toil, but we will leave it all behind one day. Yes-uh. We will pin on that trident, and we will know we earned it together, brothers! Yes-uh. Together!" Jackson raised his arms to the sky. "Let me hear a 'together'!"

"Together!" the class yelled.

"Let me hear you say, 'united in brotherly love'!"

"United in brotherly love!"

"Let me hear an 'amen'!"

"Amen!"

A profusely sweating Jackson stepped back into the crowd. Class 283 erupted into applause. Papa Smurf stepped forward.

"That's a hard act to follow, but I think Petty Officer Jackson's point is well taken. We need to get beyond all this petty shit and start working together. Now, on to business. Don't forget we're moving into our new rooms this weekend. That means all of your trash should be packed up and ready to go by seventeen hundred Sunday afternoon. Ensign Rogers has the list of new roommates, so contact him if you don't know who you're living with." Smurf cracked a rare smile. "Big party tonight. Murray and Ramirez set it up, so if it sucks, blame it on them. Be there, nineteen hundred, Gator Beach. That's all I have."

Grey turned to walk toward the barracks but was intercepted by an apologetic Jackson.

"Sir, I didn't mean to steal your thunder back there. Just thought I could work the crowd a little and get people excited again. Hope you don't mind."

"Not at all, Jackson." Grey slapped him on the back. "It's people like you who keep this class together. Nice work. Your powers of persuasion are definitely more effective than mine."

"Thanks, sir. You've got the right message. You just have to learn to deliver it with a little flair—a little soul." He winked playfully. "You got to tell it from the mountain, brother!"

"I'll keep that in mind." Grey laughed. He turned and hobbled toward the barracks. "You've got the gift, Jackson," he called over his shoulder. "You should have been a preacher."

"Sir, I am."

THREE

GREY AND ROGERS WALKED together down Trident Way toward Gator Beach. The sun slowly slipped below the horizon, casting an explosion of color into the evening sky. The clouds glowed with a purplish hue, and the oversize sun radiated spikes of orange and yellow across the churning blue sea. Grey stopped and studied the horizon. *Nothing.*

"You always do that," Rogers commented.

"What?"

"You always look for the green flash. Why the obsession?"

Grey put his hands in the pockets of his blue jeans and started walking. "Don't you ever make promises to yourself? Don't you ever swear that you'll do something before you die?"

"What, like sail the seven seas?"

"Sure. Or run a marathon, climb Mount Everest . . . or marry the woman of your dreams."

"Yeah, but I'm missing a crucial link here. Are you telling me you promised yourself you'd see the fabled green flash before you die?"

"Exactly. I had a physics teacher who explained the whole phenomenon to me. It's for real—has something to do with diffraction. I figure if I watch the sunset every time I get a chance, I'll get to see it eventually, right?"

Suddenly the stillness of the air was shattered by a crude rendering of Metallica's "The Unforgiven" on the electric guitar. *Larsen.* The excitable trainee had been a member of a failed heavy-metal band before enlisting in the navy. Grey and Rogers turned toward the party. Several picnic tables laden with chips and salsa were arranged in a horseshoe shape around a concrete slab that served as the stage. Three kegs lay buried in the sand nearby.

"Welcome, esteemed sirs." Murray gestured toward the kegs. "Have a drink. Make merry. The chicks will be here soon."

"You go ahead," Grey said to Rogers. "Murray and I need to have some words."

"Now?" Murray's face fell.

"It'll only take a second." Grey threw his arm around Murray's shoulder as Rogers walked off. "Look, Murray, I like you. You're an important part of our class. You help everyone step back and take themselves less seriously, and you absorb more than your fair share of instructor love. I just want to make sure you make it through this program. That stunt you pulled this morning was not cool. You just can't be late for musters, okay?"

Murray nodded. His eyes were glued to the ground.

"Look, I'll do anything I can to help you out. If you know you're going to screw something up, let me know and I'll smooth things over as long as I can. Just remember, I can only cover for you for so long. You're going to have to pull yourself together and really start making an effort."

"I know, sir," Murray said quietly. "You're the only person in this class who watches out for me. Without your help I would have been dropped like a bad habit days ago. I'll never forget that." He raised his eyes. "I'd follow you any day—anywhere."

Grey searched for words but came up empty. He was suddenly embarrassed. A large blue bus pulled up next to the beach, and the door popped open with a hydraulic hiss. A string of scantily clad girls filed out.

"You hit the sororities?" Grey asked.

"Of course, sir."

"Nice work." Grey walked toward the party and left Murray to greet the girls alone. The BUD/S students who were gathered around the stage turned toward the new arrivals and cheered loudly.

"What are you standing here for?" Grey asked the class. "Go mingle."

He sat down on a wooden bench as the trainees fanned out into the crowd of college girls. Larsen was still playing guitar, but he had switched to an acoustic model and wisely toned down the music. A slightly skewed version of "Margaritaville" filled the air. Grey ran a hand through his blond hair and cringed when he realized it would soon be gone—and cut off by a stripper, no less. The thought of some big-breasted naked woman shaving his head made him laugh.

"What's the matter, Mr. Grey? You gay?"

Grey turned his head. Chief Baldwin sat nursing a beer several feet away. Grey felt his pulse jump involuntarily.

"Negative, Chief Baldwin."

"Then why the hell aren't you out there trying to get laid? Even an ugly guy like yourself has a chance with that bunch of harebrained college skanks."

"Thanks." Grey relaxed. "I've actually got a pretty serious girlfriend."

"Where is she now? Can you point her out?"

"She's at UCLA law school," Grey answered. "She doesn't exactly have a lot of free time these days, but she promised she'd make it over here sometime soon."

Chief Baldwin wiped the beer foam off his mustache with the back of his hand. "She put out?"

"Like a champ." Grey hated himself for adopting the false bravado that was expected, but he didn't want to seem like a prude. A long silence followed.

Finally Chief Baldwin asked, "Does your woman really understand what you're getting into?"

"I think so," Grey stated. "At least as much as I do."

"I'll tell you now, being a SEAL and having any kind of serious relationship is the hardest thing you'll ever do."

"How so, chief?"

"Well, before I became an instructor, I spent an average of about twenty days a year at home. That's not enough time to keep a woman satisfied."

"What were you doing for the rest of the year?" Grey asked.

"I was either deployed or training somewhere." Chief Baldwin belched. "There's a reason we have over a ninety-percent divorce rate."

Grey shook his head in disbelief. "Ninety percent?"

"Yup. You better believe it." He moved to the keg and refilled his plastic cup with beer. "Well, have fun tonight, sir. Enjoy yourself while you can, because Monday is gonna be a serious kick in the ass." He stood up and raised his beer in salute. "I'm out of here."

"Have a good one," Grey said.

"Yeah, fuck you, too." Chief Baldwin flashed a smile and walked away.

Fuck you too? Grey poured himself a drink as he pondered this response. *At least I'm on his good side.* He sat back and relaxed as the party picked up in intensity. A brawl nearly broke out near the kegs as trainees elbowed one another out of the way, fighting to deliver drinks to their waiting sorority girls. Grey watched Rogers work on a beautiful auburn-haired girl. She was near tears with laughter, and Rogers casually put his hand on her arm. The girl played with her hair and fidgeted nervously. *He's got her,* Grey thought. *Not bad.* Now Rogers's mouth was inches from her ear, and he appeared to be whispering something. She smiled and nodded, and they walked off.

"You believe that shit?" Ramirez asked as he sat next to Grey. "The Shakespeare-spoutin' motherfucker is smooth. I didn't know chicks still went for that."

"Apparently so." Grey laughed. "What about you? Why aren't you busy seducing some sex-crazed senorita?"

"Married, bro." Ramirez winked. "Got three kids." He jumped to his feet and pointed toward a group of dancing girls. "Let's see those moves. I know you Stanford types can get funky."

"I don't know where you get the energy," Grey said. "This is the only move I can handle tonight." He raised his beer to his lips and lowered it again.

"If you say so, sir." Ramirez jumped into the middle of the dancing circle and whooped loudly. Two pretty young girls immediately sandwiched him, pressing their bodies against his as they moved to the music.

A black SUV pulled up onto the beach and honked several times. A beefy man with a belly that hung over his belt stepped onto the sand. With a flourish, he opened the backseat door, and two voluptuous women dressed in ridiculously tight tops stepped out. A platinum blonde with a store-bought tan sulkily strutted toward the party, her huge breasts bouncing in a leopard-print top. A raven-haired woman with a heavily made-up face followed close behind. The dancing slowed to a stop as the guys gawked at their new guests. The sorority girls turned away, clearly annoyed at the loss of attention. The blond woman talked briefly with Murray, and an exchange of cash took place. She handed him a CD and stepped onto the concrete stage. A pulsing beat soon echoed across the beach, and the women started to dance.

Grey felt a pair of hands close over his eyes.

"You weren't actually planning on watching that, were you?" a sultry voice asked.

"Of course not," Grey answered. "Would I do something like that?"

"Yes." Grey felt a pair of lips brush against his neck.

Grey peeled the hands from his eyes and kissed them gently. He turned and pulled a dark-skinned beauty into his lap. "I didn't expect to see you here."

"I know." Vanessa planted kisses on his face. "I just couldn't let some stripper shave your head. I think I deserve the honor." She reached into her purse and brandished an electric razor. "When do I get to expose your lumpy head to the world?"

"Soon enough." Grey gestured at the strippers, who were already topless. "They're going to start cutting hair as soon as their little show is over."

"And what a show it is," Vanessa said. "There's enough silicone out there to fill a bathtub." She wrapped her arms around his neck. "Lucky you, baby. I'm all real."

"Tell me about it." Grey closed his eyes and pulled her close. "I'm glad you came. This week has been horrible."

"Are the big bad instructors beating you up?"

"More or less," Grey said. "I'm pretty much a wreck right now."

"You tell them they better leave you alone or I'm gonna start kicking ass."

"I'm sure that's really intimidating, hon."

"What?" She pushed against his chest. "I can fight. Don't you start with me, boy. I'll take you downtown."

Grey laughed. "I love you." He rested his head on her shoulder.

"Oh, looky here, how cute. Two little lovebirds." Jones flashed his broken-toothed smile. He was wearing a ridiculous black cowboy hat, and a toothpick rested jauntily between his lips. "I reckon you owe me an introduction, sir."

"Of course. Vanessa, this is Jones, aka, the Tennessee Wonder."

"A pleasure to meet you," Jones drawled. "I just had to lay my eyes on the woman who stole my boat-crew leader's heart. I can see he's whipped for a good reason."

"Thanks." Vanessa smiled. "I try to keep him in line. If he gets too bossy, just let me know. I'll set him straight."

"Will do, ma'am," Jones said. He tipped his hat. "Be good, you two."

The music slowed and the strippers sauntered over to a picnic table. Murray provided them with electric razors, and they went to work. The last of the sun's rays had long since faded away, but the huge full moon provided enough light to make out the excited faces of the students. The crowd yelled encouragement as trainees had their heads shaved one by one. Grey watched with interest as Jones sat down in front of the busty blond stripper. She playfully grabbed his hat and perched it on her head. The luxurious bounty of her enormous chest pressed against his neck as she gently razed his hair away. A big goofy grin split his face from ear to ear as he reveled in the crowd's attention.

"Lookin' good, Tennessee!" Grey yelled. Jones gave him a thumbs up.

Vanessa ran her fingers through Grey's hair. "It's time, isn't it?"

"It sure is. Feel free to get naked at any time," Grey said playfully.

"Not on your life. This will be a strictly G-rated event, at least until I get you to myself." Vanessa stood up and positioned herself behind him. With a click, the electric razor whirred to life, and soon clumps of yellow hair were falling to the ground in waves.

"Baby, you have an ugly head," Vanessa said sweetly. "I've never seen a paler, lumpier skull in my entire life."

"Thanks. You're a real morale booster." Grey reached up and touched the scratchy surface of his head. It felt repulsive, like a growth of five-o'clock shadow. "You sure you still want me?"

"Yes, I'm sure. However, I'm not introducing you to any of my friends for a few weeks." She put away the razor and pulled Grey to his feet. "You look like you could use a break. How about we get a hotel room and I give you a nice back rub?"

"Do you have to ask?"

Grey woke up at three thirty with a terrible case of the cold sweats. Fever dreams had become a regular occurrence over the last few nights. He wasn't alone; most of Grey's boat crew had been having the same experience. He suspected that hovering at the edge of hypothermia was a contributing factor, and the constant nightmares couldn't help matters much. Grey had taken to calling the twisted dreams of surf torture and drowning "BUDmares."

Vanessa opened her eyes and gently touched his forehead. "Baby, what's wrong with you?"

"I don't know," Grey answered. "This happens every night. Just try to go back to sleep. I'll be fine."

Vanessa was clearly too tired to argue. She instantly closed her eyes and nodded off. Grey stepped into the shower and instinctively began shivering as the water splashed over him. His body naturally prepared itself for the shock of the fifty-seven-degree ocean; experiencing warmth and wetness simultaneously was becoming a foreign concept. The numerous cuts on his legs and the raw crack of his ass flared painfully as he scrubbed them out with soap. The last thing Grey needed was a serious infection. A member of his boat crew had already been dropped from his class because an infected boil had to be cut out of his ass. Anytime stitches were used, the afflicted individual was forced to cease training. If the doctors deemed staying dry necessary for recovery, the instructors deemed it grounds for a medical roll to the next class. Being wet and miserable was a fiercely protected aspect of BUD/S training. Nobody slipped through on a medical chit. Grey suddenly felt weak. He sat down on the hard shower floor and closed his eyes. The patter of warm water on his weary body quickly lulled him to sleep.

"Grey!"

He opened his eyes to the sight of his naked girlfriend standing above him.

"Wake up. You look like a drowned sewer rat." She pulled him to his feet and stared in his eyes. "Baby, you sure you're okay?"

"Yeah. Tired," Grey muttered. "No. Yeah. Tired." He groaned.

"You're making no sense." She turned off the water and stepped out of the shower. Seconds later she reappeared with a towel and started drying him off. His mind vaguely registered pleasure as she gently wiped the water from his body.

"You're the best."

"I know." She stopped drying and kissed him on the lips. "Too bad you're so tired."

"I'm not," Grey protested. In fact, he was. BUD/S students talked about women and sex constantly, but in reality most of them would gladly take a nice massage followed by cuddling over a night of steamy passion. *Just hold me.* Grey laughed. He couldn't bring himself to say it.

"What's so funny?"

"Nothing." His mind created a conversation. *Vanessa, all you think about is sex. Sometimes I think it's all you care about. Can't we just cuddle? I'm tired.* He laughed again. The words were so foreign to his gender, he knew they would never escape his lips.

"Someone better tell me what is so damn funny," Vanessa said as she pushed him out of the shower and onto the bed. Grey found her incredibly attractive when she was annoyed. Naked and annoyed was even better. Still, his body wouldn't respond.

"Sleep," Grey murmured peacefully. He curled up into a ball.

"Yes!" Vanessa yelled. "I win!"

"Win what, babe?" He opened one eye skeptically.

"The bet. Remember? You told me there would never be a time I wanted to have sex and you didn't. Well, guess what, buddy? You lose."

"I never lose," Grey grumbled. He felt energy slowly creeping into his muscles.

"You lose," she whispered. "*You* lose!"

"I don't think so." Heat rushed into his face. "Not tonight."

"Well, look at you. You're just lying there like a sack of potatoes."

"Okay, you're right," Grey said. He faked a yawn. "Let's just go to sleep."

Vanessa sighed and stretched out next to him. He counted to ten, then quickly rolled on top of her and kissed a trail down her body.

"Take it back," Grey demanded playfully.

Vanessa laughed. "You're so predictable. I love you."

Saturday was a sleepy blur of blissful indulgence. Grey had been pampered with back massages, his favorite Chinese takeout, and more loving attention than he could handle. His lack of energy only seemed to make Vanessa more amorous, a phenomenon he would mercilessly tease her about when training was over—if it ever ended. She kissed him good-bye Sunday morning, and Grey had to suppress the strong urge to jump in the car and disappear to L.A. with her. At the moment, law school seemed like an incredibly luxurious lifestyle. Although by attending BUD/S he was fulfilling a dream, Sunday mornings were an inevitably depressing experience. Floors had to be waxed and buffed, boots shined, uniforms squared away. And on top of everything else, Grey had to move into the new barracks. Rogers was packing up his belongings when Grey walked in to the dank room they shared with Papa Smurf.

"What's up, John?" Grey was the only student who occasionally addressed Rogers by his first name.

"*Rien,*" Rogers answered in a sneering French accent. "*Je deteste Dimanche.*"

"There he goes again," Smurf grumbled from his corner of the room. "Mr. Sophistication himself. I really wish you'd cut out that French crap."

"Imbecile," Rogers huffed, then cracked a smile. "You need to learn to appreciate France, sir. Many of the finer things in life are French in origin."

"Like?" Smurf folded his arms over his barrel chest.

"Cheese, wine, escargot, the Tour de France . . . French fries."

"Look, all I know is that we saved their sorry asses during World War Two. They don't have to play their self-righteous, holier-than-thou games with us. Without our help, they'd all be doing the goose step right now."

Rogers's smile widened. "Excellent point, sir. Well-taken."

"You two are ridiculous." Grey pulled his uniforms from his locker and laid them on his bed. He smashed everything into his seabag and slung it over his shoulder. "Sir Rogers, Papa Smurf, I'll see you at our new home. Don't kill each other while I'm gone."

"Are you suggesting I'm capable of violence?" Rogers looked offended.

"I sure as hell hope so." Grey made for the doorway. "You'd better be."

As he walked away he heard Rogers call after him, "I'm no sissy, mind you. I'll challenge you any day, my warmongering friend. Perhaps a duel . . ."

Crazy, Grey thought. *Absolutely crazy.* The more stressed out Rogers got, the more frequent his bizarre antics became. The stress of the impending beat-down on Monday was getting to everyone. When the weekend was the only aspect of life students had to look forward to, starting a new week was a somber event. Grey slowly walked down Trident Way toward their new barracks, kicking loose pebbles across the asphalt as he went. A few wispy clouds slid overhead in the strong sea breeze, interrupting the bright blue canvas of the sky. The smell of seaweed was strong in the air, and the gleaming white sand berms rose up against the barbed-wire fence that surrounded the SEAL Teams. *Trapped in paradise.* Grey's thoughts scattered as an out-of-breath Murray appeared at his side.

"What's up, sir?"

"Not much." Grey was struck by how horrible Murray looked. The man obviously hadn't slept. "Thanks for putting together a good party on Friday."

"Not a problem. Glad you enjoyed it." Murray waited a few breaths before continuing. "The rest of the night was interesting."

"What do you mean?"

"Redman came through my window at four in the morning."

"You're kidding."

"I wish I was. I should have known better than to leave it unlocked. The fucker was drunk as hell."

"So what did he do to you?" Grey asked, genuinely disturbed.

"First he peed all over the room. It just so happened that my uniforms were sitting conveniently in a pile. Go figure. Then he dragged me out to the beach and beat me until the sun came up. I spent some quality time in the surf, did a few thousand push-ups, played in the sand, whipped out my dick—"

"Whipped out your dick?"

"Yeah. He thought he'd get a good laugh at the size of my cock. Unfortunately for him, I'm hung like a horse—even when it's cold." Murray wrapped his arms tightly across his chest as he looked out toward the ocean. "That was some fierce surf torture. I don't think I've ever been so cold in my life. I could laugh the whole thing off, but Redman said something that really got to me."

"What's that?"

"He told me that he isn't the only one who wants me out of here. He said that every instructor in First Phase was going to make it their personal mission to force me out of training."

"Bullshit. He's just nursing his wounded ego. It's not every day he gets tackled by one of his students."

"I know. But I think he had a good point. I'm dead if I don't change my ways. Being the class turd might be entertaining for you guys, but I don't want my sense of humor to force me out the door."

No shit. Grey looked away. "I've told you a million times, Murray, you're a good guy. You just attract attention. You're a lightning rod among BUD/S students. If you want to fix the problem, you need to learn to shut the hell up."

"You're probably right." Murray cracked his knuckles. "I've got other ideas, though."

"Explain."

"Redman's bad news, sir. We both know that. He has to have a past, a few skeletons in the closet."

"What's your point?"

"I'm not going to let him force me out." Murray kicked at a pebble, launching it down the street in a graceful arc. "Sir, he won't get rid of me. I won't let him. If he wants me to ring out, he'll have to tear my arm off and beat the bell with it." Students who had reached their breaking point and wanted to be dropped from training were required to ring a polished brass bell near the grinder.

Grey chuckled at the macabre image of an instructor whaling away at the brass bell with a severed limb. His smile faded and he regarded Murray coolly. "I'm still not following you, Murray. Are you suggesting blackmail?"

"That's one way to say it."

"Bad idea," Grey stated firmly. "Real bad idea."

"Sir, what am I supposed to do—just stand by passively and let him destroy my life's ambition?" Murray spat on the ground. "No fucking way. If he wants to play that game, I'm not beyond defending myself."

"Okay, so let's pretend this is a reasonable idea, which it isn't. How are you going to dig anything up?"

"Jeff Thompson, one of my brother's buddies from high school, is an East Coast SEAL. He's the guy who got me interested in the Teams in the first place. Redman spent a tour over in Virginia. I'm sure Jeff could dig something up."

"What if there is no dirt?"

"I'm willing to bet that there is, sir."

"And what if you get caught snooping around? Redman's not someone to be trifled with."

"It's a chance I'm willing to take."

Grey shook his head. "Murray, I still think it's a bad idea, but I'm not going to stop you. Just be careful. I think you're taking a bigger risk than you realize." Grey started up the steps that led to the courtyard of Building 618. "One more thing, Murray."

"What's that, Mr. G.?"

"Why do you look like crap?" He gestured at Murray's sunken eyes. "I understand you had a bad time Friday night, but you should have been able to rest up yesterday. What's the deal?"

"Oh, sir, you wouldn't believe me if I told you."

"Try me."

Murray flashed a self-satisfied smile, then drew in a deep breath as if preparing for a long speech. "Well, I met these two sorority sisters last night. They're both hot—tight little asses and nice perky tits." He cupped his imaginary breasts to emphasize the point. "Anyway, these two hotties were drunk off their asses and horny as hell. Little did I know they were bisexual. We took a cab to their apartment, which cost me about thirty bucks, but it was well worth the money. Sir, these chicks were on to me so quick, we didn't even step through the door before one chick had her hands down my pants. Then they started kissing each other. I almost had a heart attack at that point. Have you ever seen two girls kiss? You've got to see it to believe it, sir. But it gets better. Then they—"

"Enough, Murray. If I want to hear any more, I'm sure I can just pick up a copy of *Penthouse* and read all about it." Grey looked Murray in the eye. "Just don't forget, if you start pissing flames because you catch some VD, it might affect your training."

"You serious, sir?"

"Yeah, I'm serious. How'd you like a nice case of herpes during Hell Week? Little sores are very prone to infection. I wouldn't be surprised if you got a little flesh-eating bacteria on Mr. Happy. And you know what happens then. There's no cure; they just have to cut out the affected area."

The color drained from Murray's face. Grey was amused to see he'd grossed out the raunchiest student of them all. Murray instinctively reached down his pants and felt his package. "No more messing around, sir, at least until Hell Week is over."

"Good. Now go square away your crap for the inspection tomorrow. I'll come by your room later tonight to make sure you're done." Grey walked off toward his new room. The horseshoe-shaped three-story building was officially the bachelor enlisted quarters, but all the officers in BUD/S called it their home. The central courtyard contained three metal drying cages where students stored their wet gear. A rusty pull-up bar leaned heavily to one side next to a battered tree. The concrete court-yard was surprisingly well swept, and the few patches of grass on the perimeter were actually green. The place wasn't bad looking. Most importantly, it was a quarter mile from BUD/S, which meant instructors wouldn't be dropping by quite as often. Grey walked around to the western side of the building. He climbed up the stairs to room 310 and admired the view. The Point Loma peninsula jutted out into the Pacific, and the old lighthouse sat at its tip, a majestic crown jewel wedged between the limitless sea and sky. Several ships steamed out of San Diego Bay, slowly making their way past the Mexico-owned Coronado Islands. *Once again, it should be paradise,* Grey thought. He looked down over the walkway wall and froze in disbelief.

"No!" Grey yelled. His stomach churned as he watched his classmates apply the last coat of green paint to their helmets. He had completely blown it. His helmet currently sat unpainted at the bottom of his seabag.

"What's the problem?"

Grey looked over at a smug Ensign Pollock, who was carefully applying the sticker numbers 283 to his helmet.

"I forgot about my helmet. I'm dead."

"That sucks," Pollock added helpfully. "You haven't even started sanding yet?"

"No. How long does it take?"

"A couple of hours." He admired the placement of his numbers before continuing. "Then you have to apply a few coats of primer. After that dries, you can start with the paint."

Grey turned and banged his head lightly against the door to his room. *I'm finished.* He shuddered when he imagined the poor impression a crappy-looking helmet would make with the First Phase instructors. The next eight weeks of his life would be unimaginably bad. Grey opened the door to his room. At least his living conditions would be greatly improved. Instead of four beds, there were two, and in addition to metal lockers, the furniture included wooden nightstands and cabinets. Grey sat on one of the saggy mattresses and closed his eyes. *Another sleepless night.* He sat motionless for several minutes before pulling himself together. After digging his rough-edged, chipped helmet from his seabag, he made his way downstairs. As he walked, he examined his helmet closely. The Kevlar dome was in worse shape than he remembered. Smoothing its surface out would take most of the night and might even require a power sander.

"Watch yourself, sir," Murray said as an oblivious Grey bumped into him.

"Sorry." Grey held up his helmet. "I've got a small problem."

Murray snatched the helmet from Grey's hands and felt its surface. A smile slowly spread across his face. He waved the helmet in front of Grey, then quickly flung it over his shoulder, launching it across the courtyard. It landed on the concrete with a crack, sending chips of old paint flying.

"What the hell did you do that for?"

"Sir, it's my turn to do *you* a favor." Murray placed a hand in the middle of Grey's back and pushed him toward his room. He opened the door and gestured toward his bed. Two identical green helmets sat side by side on his mattress.

"Take your pick."

"What?"

"I said take your pick. You can have either one."

Grey looked at Murray in disbelief. "How'd you get two?"

"I bought one at a surplus store. I heard the instructors like to smash helmets—throw them against the concrete. That way we have to stay up late repainting them. With two helmets I'm a step ahead of the game."

"Good thinking," Grey said, genuinely impressed.

"Thanks. Now hurry up and grab one before I change my mind."

"You sure?"

"Sir, I'm sure. I'm not going to let my one opportunity to save your sorry ass slip away."

Grey picked up a helmet and admired its shiny smooth surface. He was torn. Although he had covered for Murray more than once, by taking a helmet, the balance of debt would swing in Murray's favor. Grey felt nervous about the prospect of owing the troublesome sailor anything. After a moment of deliberation, he came to a compromise.

"I'll take it, Murray. But only for two days. That way I'll have time to get my own helmet ready while I wear one of yours." He reached out to shake Murray's hand. "Thanks. I owe you one."

Murray gripped his hand firmly. *"De nada, señor.* What goes around comes around."

"Right. See you tomorrow." Grey climbed back upstairs and rode on a wave of relief, enjoying the release of anxiety that comes after a close call. *Thank God for Murray.* The thought was an amusing one, if only because it seemed so improbable. Having something to thank him for was a refreshing change of events. Grey stepped through the door to his room and was surprised to find Rogers standing naked in front of his locker. He appeared to be checking himself out in a small mirror mounted on the locker door.

"Grey!" Rogers exclaimed. An awkward silence followed. "What's up?"

"Not much. Is there a reason you're naked, besides wanting to check out your sexy body in the mirror?"

"Yeah, I was about to try out our new shower." Rogers turned toward the bathroom. "You know, see if it works and everything."

"Right." Grey plopped down on his mattress. "John, do you ever think you would have been happier growing up in ancient Greece?"

"What? So I could have sex with older men?"

"No. I was thinking more along the lines of being able to train buttnaked."

"That would be excellent," Rogers mused. "I could have a harem of slave girls rub me down before I went to compete at the stadium." His voice took on a dreamy quality. "The fearless warrior, muscles rippling and glistening with oil, strides into the arena. The boisterous crowd suddenly falls silent at the sight of the champion. With the victory laurel in view, he fearlessly tackles his opponent and pins him to the dirt. The slave girls rejoice as they anticipate the night of lovemaking that lies ahead."

"I always imagined you as a warrior poet," Grey stated. "You know, the perfect fusion of mind and body—the Greek ideal."

"I'm flattered." Rogers disappeared into the bathroom. His voice became slightly muffled. "No really, I am. I take that to be the highest compliment anyone could receive."

"Well, one thing's for certain. You're probably the only BUD/S student who can recite Homer in ancient Greek." Grey curled up on his mattress and closed his eyes. He still had a lengthy list of chores to complete before tomorrow morning rolled around, but he found the pull of gravity on his eyelids irresistible. *Just a short nap.*

FOUR

MORNING PT, IBS, INTRODUCTION-TO-KNOT-TYING *brief, chow, knot tying, conditioning run, core values.* Grey ran over the schedule of the day's events. Briefs provided a nice break, although they often involved quite a few push-ups. IBS, however, was always a painful experience. The evolution involved crews racing one another through the surf in hard rubber boats. If the surf was big and boats were being overturned at a sufficient rate to keep the instructors entertained, the punishment on shore was light. If the ocean was flat, the instructors utilized a wide array of torturous land drills to keep things adequately difficult. Grey prayed for large surf.

Morning PT blurred into a haze of discomfort. *Drop. Get wet. Surf and back, two minutes. Push-ups—ready? Crunches, pull-ups, dips, leg levers, flutter kicks, atomic sit-ups—ready?* As he struggled through his push-ups, Grey looked to his left and listened as Instructor Furtado whispered into Rogers's ear. The instructor was bent at the waist, hovering over the prone trainee.

"You gay, sir?" The question came with a silver flash of tongue stud.

"Negative, Instructor Furtado."

"You don't sound so sure about that. I've heard you like to hang out at those gay bars over in Hillcrest. I bet you're some old guy's little bitch." Furtado spat on the ground, nearly missing Rogers's head. "In fact, I bet that's how you got through college. I bet you dished out blow jobs like candy. Anything for the grade, right, sir?"

Rogers didn't answer. Grey knew he had maintained friendships with a handful of gay students back at Princeton. The subject was a sensitive one.

"Come on, admit it, sir. You crave cock." The silver stud flickered. "Say it. Say, 'I crave cock.'"

"And what if I did?"

"Then you'd be gay," Furtado said stupidly.

"No shit." Rogers's words rang out across the grinder.

Grey smiled to himself as Instructor Furtado strolled away, at a total loss for words. *Chalk one up for Rogers.* After three trips to the surf and countless push-ups, the class finished PT and sprinted off the grinder. Grey walked over to Rogers and threw an arm around his shoulder.

"I see you've made a new friend," Grey observed.

"Unfortunately," Rogers said. "That guy definitely has a problem. I suspect he was abused as a child. If I was a better person, I'd almost feel sorry for him."

"But you don't," Grey said. "You want him to go to hell."

"Not hell. The man needs to be reformed. I think he should spend some time in San Francisco—you know, the Castro District. I'm sure he'd eventually come around."

Papa Smurf limped over to the smiling roommates. His faltering stride suggested he was already suffering from shin splints. "I expect you two to listen," he hissed. "I'm trying to keep this goddamn class together, and I could use your cooperation."

"Can we help you with something, boss?" Grey asked.

"We're already late for chow. How about getting your boat crew in line?"

"Right away." Grey turned and surveyed the gaggle of trainees loosely clustered in the pit. "Jones!"

The Tennessee Wonder immediately appeared at this side. "Yup?"

"Will you help me get everyone in line? We need to get out of here now if we want any breakfast."

"You got it." Jones disappeared into the crowd. Seconds later a handful of the milling trainees snapped into a line. Grey counted their heads. *Six.* Even Murray was present and ready to move out.

"Ready to go, sir," Grey said, turning to Papa Smurf.

Smurf merely grunted and strode away. Grey gave Jones a thumbs-up

and got a wink in reply. He felt his chest swell with pride. He was beginning to love his crew. They were a ragged bunch, but they got the job
done. The class started shuffling slowly, but the pace escalated, and they
ended up sprinting to make it to chow on time.

"Hi, Felicia," Grey said, still breathing heavily from the run.

"Good morning, sir." A loose strand of silky black hair had slipped
out of her ponytail and rested along her smooth brown skin. She looked
radiant as always.

"Any gossip for me?" Grey asked. "Is Redman still talking trash?"

"Oh, no," Felicia said. "Haven't seen him since last week. Mean man."
She tilted her head downward and glanced up at Grey with her big brown
eyes. "Something wrong with anybody who don't like you."

"Thanks, Felicia. That's nice of you to say."

"You're welcome, Mr. Grey." She squirmed nervously. "You better
eat. No time to talk today."

"Right. See you at lunch." Grey moved down the breakfast line and
grabbed a handful of wrapped cream-cheese cubes. After glancing around
to make sure the mess manager wasn't watching, he stuffed them into the
pockets of his camouflage pants. Because he would only have a matter of
seconds to sit down and eat, a few hidden slices of toast and some cream
cheese would serve as an essential snack on the run back. Sure enough, no
sooner had Grey sat down with his tray of scrambled eggs and bacon than
Papa Smurf ended chow.

As the class shuffled back to the BUD/S compound, Grey pulled
sandy, salty toast from his pockets and jammed it into his mouth. Next
he peeled open the tiny cream cheese cubes and wolfed them down. The
gritty combination wasn't exactly a bagel and cream cheese, but it did the
trick. As he chewed, Grey continually readjusted the position of the helmet on his head. It kept riding forward until the front rim rested on the
bridge of his nose. Although he was grateful that Murray had lent him
the helmet, it was a few sizes too big, and running with it was a chore.
Eventually he gave up and ran with one hand against his head.

"Headache, sir?" Ramirez asked.

"Nah. Big helmet. Had to borrow one of Murray's."

"Are you telling me my boat-crew leader isn't squared away?"

Grey detected a hint of sarcasm in Ramirez's voice. He glanced over his shoulder. Sure enough, an ear-to-ear grin dominated the sailor's face.

"I thought you officers were on top of things." Ramirez sighed dramatically. "I should have known better. No wonder us enlisted pukes make everything happen around here. *Ay caramba.*"

"You're right, Ramirez. I'm a dirtbag. I think you should be in charge." Grey took off his helmet with its distinctive white stripe and passed it back. Ramirez passed forward his own helmet. Grey tried it on and found that it fit much better.

"How do I look?" Ramirez asked Jones.

"Dang. I think you just lost a few brain cells. It's that whole officer thing."

"Shit, hombre. I think you're on to something." Ramirez grasped his head in his hands and crossed his eyes dramatically. He spit the words out slowly, as if uttering them took all his energy: "Losing common sense, losing brain power . . . must get helmet off before it's too late."

The trainees running next to Ramirez caught on to his ruse and started shouting encouragement.

"Fight it! Fight the power!"

"Don't sell your soul to the cake eaters!"

"Keep it real, Ramirez! Fight the man! Get that thing off!"

Ramirez played along, rolling his eyes and foaming at the mouth. The theatrics continued until he suddenly composed himself and adopted a warbling British accent. "Rogers, fetch me my pipe," he quipped. "That's right. Don't keep an officer waiting. And while you're at it, fetch me my bathrobe and my slippers. I didn't attend Stanford for nothing, you know. I'm a gentlemen, and it pains me to associate with you ruffians."

"Enough." Grey snatched the helmet from Ramirez's head. "You can make fun of me all you want, but don't knock my alma mater."

Ramirez punched Grey playfully in the shoulder. "It's all love, boss."

"I know."

Class 283 turned onto the beach, sending clouds of dust aloft on the gentle breeze. A series of explosions rumbled on the far side of the berm as waves crested and erupted into a frenzy of whitewash. The students fell into a hushed silence; they knew boat drills would be dangerous if the sets stayed large. They shuffled into the pit and fell into a rough formation.

"We have five minutes to be on the beach, standing by our boats," Smurf yelled. "Make it happen."

Grey gathered his boat crew around him in a football huddle. "Ramirez, take Tate, Wallace, and Stevens and get the boat out. Murray, grab seven life jackets. Jones, get the paddles. I'll find a pump." He stepped back and the group scattered. Grey snaked through the class and made his way to the drying cage where they stored their gear. The class only had a few pumps, and not every boat crew would have time to use one. Grey knew their boat had a small leak, but due to BUD/S politics, he wasn't allowed to patch it. He could handle automatic weapons and demolitions, but not quick-drying glue. *Far too dangerous.* Without some extra air, paddling his boat would be next to impossible. It would drag through the water, and his crew would never get past the breakers.

Two trainees cradling pumps in their arms squeezed past Grey as he entered the chain-link drying cage. Apparently other boat-crew leaders were also plagued by leaking boats. A lone pump rested against a pile of orange buoys in the corner. Grey quickly moved toward it, but a pair of arms snapped it up before he could get there.

"Shit!" Grey flung his arms up in despair.

"You need this?" It was Rogers.

"My boat's trashed. I'm dead unless I get some air," Grey explained. "But you got here first. Fair is fair."

"Take it," Rogers offered.

"Thanks." Grey gave Rogers an affectionate slap on the ass as he reached for the pump. He would have refused the favor out of principle, but he knew his boat crew was counting on him. "I owe you one."

"You can buy me dinner sometime."

"Will do," Grey said as they exited the cage together. "Anywhere you want."

"Shouldn't have said that," Rogers warned. "I like French food. Expensive French food."

Grey ran to his boat and went to work. Murray held the hose in place as he inflated the main tube.

"Two minutes!" Smurf yelled.

Several crews shuffled past, their boats positioned on their heads. Grey pumped frantically. His progress seemed impossibly slow. Up down, up down. The air wheezed through the rusted pump as he raced the clock.

"We better go, sir," Jones said. "Time's a wastin'."

Grey pulled the hose from the plastic valve and set the pump on the asphalt. He moved to his position at the stern of the boat and grabbed a plastic handle.

"Prepare to up boat."

The boat crew leaned over, anticipating his command.

"Up boat." In one fluid motion, they hoisted the boat onto their heads. Grey glanced around and discovered to his dismay that they were alone. He didn't need to say anything. His boat crew sensed the urgency of the situation and naturally started running. The unmistakable rumble of a diesel engine rose up behind them.

"Fuckers are ten minutes early!" Murray yelled.

The run escalated into a sprint, and a mélange of curses echoed through the air as the hard rubber boat bounced violently on their heads. Grey gritted his teeth as his already tender scalp took a beating. The gurgling grew in intensity as the truck pulled up behind them.

"Boat Crew Nine, bringing up the rear." Chief Baldwin's voice echoed through the truck's PA system. He chuckled devilishly. "Down boat!"

Grey's crew immediately lowered their boat. They stood at attention, eyes locked on the horizon.

"Go cool off your slow asses in the surf," Baldwin ordered. "Stay there a while. We can't have you turds getting heat stroke."

They left the rubber craft lying in the sand and sprinted toward the surf. Grey led the charge, sending a sheet of cold spray into the air as he tromped through the shallows. Once he reached waist-deep water he linked arms with his crew and sat down.

"Fuck us. We're fucking cursed." Murray clung tightly to Grey's arm.

"How many times can you say *fuck* in one sentence?" Jones asked.

"What? Am I offending your hillbilly sensibilities?"

"Nah. All I'm saying is you don't got to swear so much. You know, stay positive. Ain't that right, sir?"

"Exactly," Grey agreed. "Murray, lighten up."

"You can all go to hell."

Grey was about to respond in anger but caught himself. A glance at

Murray's face tempered his frustration. The wily sailor's eyes sparkled mischievously. His face darkened as the instructors' truck pulled up to the surf line.

"Hide the trainee!" Baldwin's voice boomed.

Grey counted to three before lowering his head underwater. A few seconds later he came to the surface, and the heads of his boat crew members appeared shortly thereafter.

"Not good enough! I want synchronized submarines. If you can all come to the surface at the same time, I might spare you."

"How generous," Murray muttered.

They tried Baldwin's game again and failed. Grey still came to the surface before the rest of his crew.

"You lose. Time to pay. Stand by your boat."

They rushed out of the ocean and scrambled to their boat. Grey took his position at the rear of the craft and waited for instructions. He didn't wait long. Instructor Furtado flung open the passenger door of the truck and casually strolled in their direction. He was clad in blue shorts, combat boots, a blue T-shirt and sported an expensive pair of sunglasses. His curly black hair glistened in the sunlight.

"Extended-arm carry," Furtado ordered nonchalantly.

Grey gave the command and they hoisted the boat above their heads. Furtado watched the crew for several minutes before grabbing a paddle and silently hurling sand at them. Grey looked on with dismay as the rest of the class carried their boats into the surf, marking the beginning of the first race. *We're screwed.* The sand continued to fly, and the weight of the boat quickly became unbearable. Furtado whistled a cheerful tune as he flailed away with his paddle.

"*Mierda,*" Ramirez cursed. He dropped both of his arms, and the rest of the boat crew yelled at him to carry his weight. The boat wobbled unsteadily. Grey's lower back flared up, and streams of sweat ran down his forehead. After violently shaking out his arms, Ramirez rejoined the effort.

"Ramirez, you Mexican pussy," Furtado yelled. "You better put out. There's no place for buddy fuckers here."

Jones gave out next. "Sorry," he groaned as his hands dropped.

"You too?" Furtado walked up to Jones and held up his middle finger.

"This is how long you have to get your weak little arms back in action."
His tongue stud clicked against his teeth. "One—"

Jones quickly put his hands under the boat, but Furtado was unimpressed.

"Too late. Your boat crew doesn't need you. Drop down."

Jones started doing push-ups as the remaining six members of his
crew struggled to keep the boat aloft. Furtado walked underneath the boat
and made his way back to Grey.

"Sir, you think you can keep this thing in the air for five minutes?"

"Hoo-yah."

"Is that a yes?"

"Yes." It was a lie. Grey's arms trembled violently.

"We'll see about that." Furtado stood with his wiry arms crossed
over his chest. As an afterthought, he pressed a button on his watch,
emitting a quiet beep. "You're on the clock."

The boat surged back and forth as they struggled to keep it off their
heads. Grey felt like screaming in frustration but refused to give Furtado
the satisfaction of seeing him upset. The front of the raft suddenly dipped
amid a string of Spanish curses. Grey quickly moved forward to compensate.

"Ramirez, drop down next to Jones. You two are equally worthless."
Furtado smiled at Grey. "Getting pretty hard, isn't it?" He ran his tongue
along his lips. "All you have to do is say, 'I quit.' Be honest with yourself,
sir. You don't need this crap." He checked his watch. "I don't think you're
gonna make it."

Fuck you. Grey repositioned his arms and let his eyes focus on the huge
breakers rolling toward shore. With an effort, he tuned out the curses and
groans of his fellow boat-crew members. Time stood still as the world
swirled in his head and the roar of the surf filled his ears. The greasy-haired
instructor with the tongue stud appeared to be shouting, but his glistening
lips made no sound. Grey felt his legs wobble. The waves continued to roll
toward shore, and the thunderous whitewash roared even louder in his
ears. *Down boat.* Grey felt a hand push against his chest. Suddenly the tumultuous ocean faded into the background.

"I said *down boat*, sir!" Furtado yelled.

"Down boat," Grey stammered, regaining his senses. No sooner were the words uttered than the boat crashed to the beach. Grey fell over backward and wound up sitting in the sand.

"Get up," Furtado ordered. His voice was scornful, but Grey detected an undertone of grudging respect. "Join your class."

Murray extended a hand and pulled Grey to his feet. Jones was already frantically shoveling the sand out of their boat with a paddle. The rest of the crew joined in with their hands. The flurry of sand settled back on the beach as they hoisted their boat onto their heads and ran to join the class. Instructor Redman stood on the berm with a megaphone in his huge hands. His scowling face suggested he was in his usual frame of mind—angry. The crew leaders lined up in front of him while the rest of the class stood at attention next to their boats. Grey found a place for his boat, grabbed his paddle, and ran to join the lineup.

"We have a latecomer." Redman stared at Grey through dark, narrow eyes. "You feel like reporting, sir?"

"Right." Grey stood at parade rest. "Uh, Ensign Grey reporting. Boat Crew Nine standing by, uh—manned, rigged, and ready for sea."

Moving with lightning speed, Redman snatched the paddle from Grey's hand and hurled it over his head. It somersaulted through the air and disappeared on the other side of the sand berm.

"Next time say it like you mean it," Redman snarled. He turned his attention to the rest of the boat-crew leaders. "Next race—out to the buoy and back. First boat crew to line up on the truck wins." His brow furrowed as he looked over their heads. Grey knew Redman was surveying the surf; he would time the sets so that the big waves rolled in just as the class paddled out. Several tension-filled seconds passed before Redman yelled, "Bust 'em."

Grey swore under his breath as he stormed down the wrong side of the sand berm. He couldn't start the race without his paddle. The instructors constantly reinforced the notion that a paddle should be treated like a weapon. In other words, leaving one behind would carry dire consequences. Grey leaned over and snapped up his paddle before charging back up the berm. His crew looked helpless as they stood by awaiting instructions.

"Go!" Grey yelled as he sprinted toward them. They reacted immediately, each grabbing a handle and running the boat into the shallows.

Seconds later Grey joined them, pushing against the bulbous rear of the craft.

"Ones, in!" Grey commanded. The first pair jumped into the boat and began paddling at the bow of the craft.

"Twos, in!" The next pair jumped in just as a huge breaker crashed toward them. Grey was between the boat and the beach—not a desirable situation. The boat would plow right over the top of him. At the last moment, he moved around the side and grabbed a handle with his free hand. The whitewash picked the boat up and flung it toward shore like an insignificant toy, dragging a sputtering Grey alongside. His fingers burned as he struggled to maintain his grip. Several seconds later the wave released them, and Grey quickly got a muster. Four students lay slumped in various positions inside the boat, their paddles firmly clenched in their hands. Murray clung to the handle next to Grey's, giggling like a schoolgirl, and the top of Jones's head was barely visible on the other side of the boat. *Seven accounted for.*

"Let's hit it!" Grey yelled as he eyed an approaching wave. "Everyone in."

They scrambled aboard and began paddling as a wall of whitewash rumbled in, carrying two overturned boats along with it. Grey leaned back and thrust his paddle into the water, straining to keep the boat perpendicular to the shore. As coxswain, it was his job to keep the boat lined up. Failure to perform would have disastrous results; his crew could easily end up like the poor bastards bobbing in the surf, watching helplessly as their overturned boats rushed away.

"Stroke through it," Grey yelled. "Don't stop paddling."

The whitewash hit them, and for a brief moment Grey felt the claws of the wave dig in, pulling them backward. But the crew kept paddling, and with a jolt they popped over the frothy breaker and continued their journey through the surf. Grey surveyed the wreckage that the last wave had left behind. At least a dozen students were swimming toward shore, riding high in the water in their bright orange life preservers. Grey picked Rogers out of the crowd.

"Having trouble, comrade?"

Rogers was clearly out of breath. He simply shook his head.

"Let's move," Grey shouted as another swell approached. The mound of water grew in size exponentially, and the crew paddled furiously to clear it before it broke. Grey estimated the size at about seven feet—big enough to hurt. The lip started to curl over as they surged up its massive face. Grey realized too late that in an attempt to keep the bow from drifting starboard he had overcompensated, digging his paddle in too hard. The bow swung to the port side. Instructor Baldwin's muffled laughter echoed from the truck loudspeaker. Grey looked down and yelled a warning to his crew: "We're going over." For a moment Grey experienced the exhilaration of being weightless. Bodies and paddles floated in the air next to him, spinning in slow motion. Grey rotated backward and found himself staring at the clear blue sky. *Shit.* With a crack, his back broke the surface. The huge black form of the boat bore down on him. Grey instinctively ducked below the surface, and the boat slapped the water above his head. In the next instant he was tossed like a rag doll, his body crashing against hard rubber, other bodies, an unforgiving paddle. Finally the force of the whitewash passing overhead plowed him into the bottom, mashing his face against the sand. Out of breath and disoriented, he popped to the surface. All hell had broken loose. The boat was nowhere to be seen, and several unattended paddles bobbed ominously next to him. Grey grabbed as many paddles as he could and kicked for shore.

A group of instructors madly dashed about the beach, apprehending any boats that drifted into shore unattended. Grey thrashed his way out of the ocean and joined his crew as they ran toward their boat. A scowling Instructor Redman kneeled over the rubber craft, releasing air from the main tube. Grey's heart sank as he watched the rigid hull slowly collapse.

"Want your boat back?" Redman's eyes gleamed like obsidian. "Come get it. It's all yours."

Grey threw his armload of paddles into the boat and took a muster. *Ramirez, Jones, Wallace, Stevens, and Tate.* He was down one.

"Missing someone, sir?" Redman asked. "You better have a full muster."

"I'm down one."

Redman's chest muscles twitched under his blue shirt. "That's fucking unacceptable. Never leave a man behind." He violently snatched the paddles from the bottom of the boat and hurled them one by one far out

into the surf. Jones and Ramirez dutifully sprinted after them like fowl-
ing dogs chasing fallen birds. Grey was fumbling with the valve caps in
an attempt to save any remaining air in their sadly sagging craft, when
Murray limped over. Redman finished flinging the last of the paddles
out to sea and stood with his hands on his hips, watching the wild antics
of Jones and Ramirez with undisguised satisfaction.

"Sorry for the delay, sir," Murray sputtered, his sides heaving violently. "I got my ass kicked coming through the surf."

Redman spun around at the sound of Murray's voice. His eyes narrowed to slits. "Drop down, fuck stick."

As Murray dropped into the push-up position, a putrid stream of salt
water poured from his mouth. It pooled in the sand below his pale face.

"You don't belong here." Redman kicked a flurry of sand toward Murray. "Your boat crew doesn't need you. Hell, Ensign Jackass over here has
enough trouble leading this worthless boat crew. And you—you're the icing on the cake."

Jones and Ramirez emerged from the ocean, their arms laden with
wooden paddles and amber strands of kelp. They rushed to the boat and
dumped their loads.

Redman pointed a finger at Ramirez. "You're in charge now. Ensign
Grey and Seaman Murray have some business to attend to. They'll join
you later."

Ramirez gave Grey a questioning look. Grey nodded, then subtly
jerked his head toward the surf.

"Get your ass in gear!" Redman boomed. "And don't lose your boat
this time!"

Ramirez dropped two paddles onto the sand as the crew portaged
their limp craft toward the ocean. Redman snatched up a paddle and
handed it to Grey. "Here's your task, sir. I want you to dig a nice little hole
with this paddle. Make it about the size of your worthless friend's body. I
want him buried. That means I only want to see his ugly face. When you
finish you can catch up with your boat crew."

Grey started clumsily digging away at the beach with his paddle.
Murray remained in the push-up position, salt water dribbling from his
nose, eyes fixed blankly on the sand. Redman watched stone-faced as
Grey's crew floundered in the surf. Grey occasionally slowed his pace to

look over his shoulder, hoping to catch a glimpse of his boat. Ramirez obviously had no experience as a coxswain, and the four paddling crew members barely wielded enough power to move the deflated boat. Wave after wave battered them and swamped their craft.

"That's good enough," Redman barked, surveying Grey's hole. It was about two feet deep and six feet long. The burly instructor nudged Murray in the ribs with his foot. "Get in."

Murray lay on his back in the hole. He gave Grey a wink.

"Bury him."

Grey started shoveling, quickly covering Murray in a loose mound of soft sand.

"Pack it in."

Grey gently pressed the sand flat over Murray's chest. Redman shook his head in disgust and snatched the paddle from his hands.

"I said, 'Pack it in!'" Redman yelled as he whaled at the sand. Murray winced slightly with each crack of the paddle. The instructor worked himself into a rage. His skin glistened with sweat as he hammered away, oblivious to the world around him. With a snap the wooden paddle broke in two pieces. Redman stared at the handle in his hands for a few moments, then hurled it over his shoulder.

"Get out of here," he yelled. "And hurry the fuck up."

Grey picked up the other paddle Ramirez had dropped and started digging Murray out. With a groan, Murray pried himself from his hole. Redman strode away, headed for a group of instructors gathered in a conspiratorial cluster down the beach.

"You all right?" Grey asked.

"No problems here, boss."

"See our boat anywhere?"

They both scanned the frothy ocean. The surf had died down, a result of a rare lull between sets. Murray pointed slightly to the south.

"There."

Sure enough, Ramirez sat alone in the virtually submerged raft, yelling at a cluster of students who sloppily swam toward him.

"Let's go." Grey handed Murray the functional paddle while he carried the bottom half of the broken one. He could at least try to steer with it by holding the blade below the surface. They took off at a run. Farther down the beach two other crews sat next to their boats. Apparently they were the only students who had successfully paddled through the breakers and around the buoy. The rest of the class still floundered in the surf. Grey and Murray waded out into the ocean and started stroking awkwardly out to sea. Suddenly the ocean sprung back to life: the swells picked up, and huge breakers started thundering toward the beach. Because of their buoyant life jackets, Grey and Murray had a hard time diving under the waves. The charging whitewash constantly carried them backward. To prevent themselves from separating, they linked arms each time a wave approached.

"We're screwed." Murray nodded toward an unusually large wave forming offshore. Ramirez was still alone in the boat, paddling furiously in an attempt to keep the boat perpendicular to the shore. The wave continued to grow. A frustrated Ramirez hurled his paddle into the sea and raised a defiant middle finger toward the approaching monster. The wave curled just as it swept the boat into its grip. Ramirez made no last-minute effort to dive overboard or get a better grip on a handle; he simply sat motionless, his gesture of defiance unbroken.

"Fuck me," Murray whispered reverently as he watched the scene unfold.

The boat surged up the face of the wave and then flipped over, launching Ramirez headfirst into the impact zone. He disappeared below an explosion of whitewash.

"On my count," Grey commanded. The wave rumbled toward them, flinging the empty raft ahead of it. "One, two, three. Dive!"

They both took a deep breath and struggled beneath the surface. The wave flung them flat against the seafloor. A split second later it peeled them away and sucked them into the whitewash. Grey lost Murray's hand as he tumbled toward shore. *Never lose your swim buddy.* The world rotated wildly as the surf pummeled the air from his chest. Finally the whitewash deposited a breathless Grey in waist-deep water.

"Murray!" he yelled.

"Right here." Murray swam over and pointed farther out to sea. Ramirez kicked feebly toward shore, and as he got closer, Grey immediately noted a large wound on his head. Blood trickled down his face in thick rivulets. He appeared dazed.

"Let's bring him in," Grey said.

Together they sloshed through the shallows until they reached him.

"You don't look so good, compadre," Grey noted. "What happened?"

"What?" Ramirez looked at him blankly.

"What happened?"

"Hit bottom." Ramirez touched his head. "Hard."

Grey and Murray each slung an arm over their shoulder and helped Ramirez toward shore. A siren sounded from the beach as the ambulance's red lights whirled. Two corpsman instructors were waiting on the beach with a backboard when they arrived.

"Get your boat crew together and give me a muster." A lean instructor with spiky blond hair named Heisler waved them off. "And get the hell out of our way."

"Hang in there," Murray said quietly.

"We'll see you soon," Grey added.

"Ay," Ramirez moaned. "My fucking back."

Grey and Murray reluctantly stepped away and directed their energy toward assembling their boat crew. Training would stop until the ambulance returned from the medical clinic. Gradually students stumbled into shore and formed into boat crews. A long ten minutes later, the ambulance returned without Ramirez. The rest of the morning slipped away in a blur of overturned rafts, lost paddles, and bruised bodies.

"He's here," Felicia whispered as she handed Grey his change.

"Who?"

"Him." She nodded toward a table teeming with instructors. "You know, the big one."

"Oh." He stuffed his change into a ziplock bag and slid it into his shirt pocket. "It's okay, Felicia. You don't have to worry so much. He's supposed to be mean."

"Maybe, but why is he staring at you now?"

Grey felt his skin prickle. "He's staring at me?"

"Saying bad things, I think."

"Do you do this to me just to make me paranoid?"

"No. I do it because I like you. You deserve to make it."

"Thanks." Grey grabbed a tray and some silverware. "I've got to go. I'll see you tomorrow."

"Bye, Mr. Grey."

Grey began his meal in silence, stuffing forkfuls of macaroni and cheese into his mouth. Rogers sat across from him, carefully removing a long black hair from his mashed potatoes.

"Do you think Redman has a thing against me?" Grey asked.

Rogers looked up. "Of course."

"What do you mean, 'of course?'"

"It's obvious. He looks over here all the time."

"Maybe he's looking at you," Grey said. He turned in his seat, and his eyes locked into Redman's for a brief second. "Or maybe not."

"He hates you. He hates Murray." Rogers shrugged his shoulders. "There's not a lot you can do about it. Besides, we all have our enemies. Instructor Furtado and I aren't exactly chums. I wouldn't care to run into him in a dark alley."

"Yeah. He might rape you."

Rogers raised his eyebrows. "You think it's funny. I think it's a legitimate concern."

"Give me a break." Grey threw part of his roll at him. "You're absurd."

Rogers threw his head back and poured a glass of water down his throat. He always drank the same thing for lunch—three glasses of water and a glass of milk. Any variance in this routine was sacrilege. He was halfway through his glass of milk when a thought struck him. He lowered his glass, leaving a thick milk mustache above his upper lip.

"Where's Ramirez?"

"At medical."

"He should be back by now. Something's wrong."

Suddenly Grey felt like a lousy boat-crew leader. He resisted the urge to run back to medical and check on his friend.

"You could always ask Instructor Heisler what happened."

Grey stood up. "Good idea." He pushed his chair back.

"Are you crazy?" Rogers asked. "Not now. At least wait until he separates himself from the group."

Grey didn't acknowledge Rogers's suggestion; he was already marching toward the instructors' table. They all turned and watched him approach.

"What the fuck do you want?" Redman demanded.

"I was hoping I could have a word with Instructor Heisler."

"Go ahead and talk. He's here, isn't he?"

Grey looked at Instructor Heisler and started to open his mouth but was cut off by Redman.

"Speak or get out of here, shit-for-brains."

The instructors stared. A brief, tension-filled silence followed. Grey couldn't seem to start a sentence. Heisler pushed back his chair and stood up. He motioned toward the door. Redman shot his fellow instructor an angry look.

Heisler stepped outside and turned toward Grey. "He won't be coming back."

"Who?"

"Ramirez. He's finished. That's who you came to ask me about, isn't it?"

"Yeah, but . . ." Grey felt his stomach drop. "What happened?"

"Probably a cracked vertebrae. He's lucky he wasn't immediately paralyzed. He's at the hospital right now getting X-rayed."

"Fuck!"

Heisler gripped Grey's arm with a strong hand. "Hey! It wasn't your fault. This is BUD/S. Shit happens."

"Yeah, well shit doesn't happen to my boat crew." Grey felt nauseous. A series of images swept through his head: Ramirez posturing as an officer in his borrowed helmet, defiantly giving the finger to a huge wave, and lastly, lying helpless on a spinal board, his face contorted in pain.

"It's a reality of life here, Mr. Grey. Most of your friends won't make it through this program. Most will quit. At least Ramirez can live on knowing he never gave up."

Some comfort. Grey turned to walk inside.

"Sir."

"What?"

"This accident doesn't reflect on you as a leader. You realize that, right?"

"Sure." *I could care less.* "Thanks."

On the run back to the compound, the class broke into song. Grey didn't appreciate the high spirits. He shuffled along in mental isolation as rough voices belted out a SEAL version of "Winter Wonderland."

Through the woods, we're a walking,
The VC, we're a stalkin'.
One-shot kill, oh, what a thrill,
Walking in a sniper's wonderland.

Grey watched the pavement slide by below his feet. The ocean breeze started to pick up, and the cool air caressed his damp uniform, sending chills down his back. A gray pall fell over the street as the sun slid behind the eastward-moving coastal clouds. The traffic light separating the amphibious base and the BUD/S compound glared a defiant red. They were running late.

"Moving out!" Smurf yelled. "Road guards, post!"

Two students wearing orange vests charged onto Silver Strand Boulevard and planted themselves in the way of oncoming traffic. The sharp squeal of brakes pierced the air as several cars skidded to a stop. The class sped up their shuffle as they crossed the street. A few students waved at a pair of high school girls waiting impatiently in their VW bug, hoping to solicit a smile or maybe even a flash of forbidden, creamy high school skin. Nothing but icy stares. Grey pulled his T-shirt up over his mouth as they jogged down the beach; the air was saturated with airborne sand particles that crept into every moist part of his body. Their eyes watering, the trainees of Class 283 finally turned into the compound and fell in step. After they sprinted across the grinder, a glut of terrified students clotted the doorway to the classroom, leaving them wide open for instructor harassment.

"Drop."

The students dropped in place, falling all over one another. Grey found his face inches from the butt of Aniston, a generally unpleasant kid from New Jersey.

"Push 'em out."

Grey started cranking out push-ups, timing them carefully so that his nose wouldn't break as the bony ass in front of him jerked up and down. At twenty they stopped. *Safe.* Smurf was wedged between two students several feet away. He looked over at Grey pleadingly and mouthed, *Who was it?*

"Furtado," Grey said quietly. As he shifted his weight from one arm to another, his body jerked forward, and his nose unwittingly plowed into a hard butt. Aniston slid forward and sprang to his feet.

"Instructor Furtado," Smurf yelled. Aniston dropped back into the push-up position as the class called out the instructor.

"Recover." Furtado strolled into the room, quickly scanning the pathetic array of students before him. "Except you." He pointed at Aniston. "You recovered too early."

"That's only because Mr. Grey was sniffing my ass," Aniston protested.

You will die, Grey thought. *I will finish you.* He briefly toyed with the idea of sweeping Aniston's legs out from beneath him. He could barely contain his rage. To be singled out was one thing, but to drag someone else down with you was unforgivable.

"Really?" Furtado pushed through the crowd of students until his face was inches from Grey's. "You like male asses?" he asked quietly, almost pleasantly. His breath was sickeningly minty, and his tongue stud flashed as he spoke. "I know Mr. Rogers does. He told me so this morning." He bobbed his head to maintain eye contact as Grey tried to look away. "Who's your roommate, sir?"

"Rogers."

Furtado was ecstatic. "Would you fucking believe it? It's perfect." He turned to the class. "You assholes going to tolerate this? Who lives next door to these fairies?"

Pollock raised his hand.

"You ever hear the bed banging against the wall late at night?"

Pollock smiled. "Negative, Instructor Furtado."

"Not at all?" Furtado sounded disappointed. "Maybe a few screams of pleasure? The occasional crack of a whip?"

"Nothing," Pollock answered.

"Well, then. You must be in on it, too. Pollock, Grey, Rogers, and Aniston—drop down for being gay."

Grey started his push-ups as Furtado launched into his lecture, "Introduction to Underwater Knot Tying." The rest of the class took their seats.

"You all had this class in Indoc, right?" Furtado asked. "This shouldn't be new material." He picked up a twenty-inch piece of rope and twirled it. "This shit isn't rocket science. Hold your breath, swim to the bottom, tie your piece of rope onto the line, wait for the instructor's approval, then swim to the surface. Easy, right?"

"Hoo-yah," the class answered.

"Good. That concludes my brief." He flashed a white smile. As an afterthought he added, "Everyone knows the five knots, right? Square knot, clove half hitch, right angle, bowline, and becket bend?"

The room was silent. Grey shifted weight from one hand to the other at the back of the class.

"Good. Now let's talk business. Who has a good story?"

Murray immediately jumped up.

"You're a turd," Furtado said. "Drop down."

Murray dejectedly assumed the push-up position.

"Who else?"

"I've got one." A squat kid built like a diesel truck stood up.

"What's your name? You bald losers all look the same."

"Swenson."

"Okay, Swenson, let's hear it."

"All right, so yeah, I was at this bar last weekend," Swenson began, his gravelly voice the epitome of forced masculinity. "And I met these two chicks—"

"You're lying. Drop down. You couldn't meet anything with that bald melon of yours." Furtado looked around. "Next?"

A student with a pronounced black eye raised his hand.

"Let me guess. You got in a fight?"

"Yup."

"And you won, right?"

"Yup."

"More lies. But I like hearing about fights. Who was it?"

"Two big ole Marines." The student stood up and held his hand high above his head. "About this tall, and beefy as all get-out. They started saying shit about the SEALs, so I punched this guy in the face. I had to jump like this to get him." He sprung into the air and threw a punch at the ceiling. "He was out right away, but the other guy landed me a good one. Lopez over there had my back, and he was about to get in on the action, but the bartender was already on the phone to the shore patrol, so we bolted."

"Sit down, Mike Tyson," Furtado said. "Weak story, but a good delivery. Take your seat." He addressed the class. "While I enjoy a good bar brawl as much as anyone, you guys need to realize that it can be a career ender. Try to stifle your urge to brag, especially around officers. You never know who might turn you in."

Grey felt beads of sweat pop up on his forehead. Maintaining the push-up position was getting old. He wanted to cry out in frustration, both because of Ramirez's accident and because he had been betrayed by a classmate.

"Now it's my turn for a story," Furtado said. "You better like it." He got comfortable and sat on the edge of the table. "This weekend I was downtown at Club Safari. By the way—stay away from that place. I work as a bouncer there, and I sure as hell won't let any of you turds in. Anyway, so I'm working there Saturday night, and these two fine girls stroll up. And I mean, they were built. Perfection itself. You know when girls have that nice, heart-shaped butt?" He sprang to his feet and stepped over to the whiteboard. He pulled the cap off a pen and proceeded to sketch a butt. "Like this." He stood back and admired his artwork before turning back to the class.

Unreal, Grey thought. *I'm sitting here in pain, and some jackass is drawing pictures of a girl's butt.*

"They're both hot as hell—big old titties and everything. So naturally I introduce myself. Unfortunately, I have to work, so I don't get to chat with them much, but on the way out one of the bitches grabs my ass. This naturally starts a conversation, and within an hour they're both back at my place, and I'm giving it to them hard." Furtado thrust his pelvis at some imaginary harlot for emphasis. "We do it all night, and in the morning right before they leave, they let me in on a secret. Yes, gentlemen, they were both porn stars. I boned two porn stars last weekend."

Grey felt his stomach turn. *And you're proud of this?*

Murray propped himself up on one hand and raised the other.

"What?"

"Instructor Furtado, I'm very impressed by your story. But shouldn't you also tell us about the consequences of your actions? I mean, the itching and burning must be horrible. . . ."

Furtado's cheerful demeanor melted. His mouth twitched as he struggled for words. Finally he hissed, "You'll pay, Murray." He turned and walked toward the door. "You have ten minutes to be at the pool, ready to go."

Oops. I guess we fail. Imagine that. Grey's mood wasn't improving. It took at least fifteen minutes to get to the pool, and two minutes to change. Ten minutes was an impossibility. *Fuck it.*

"Let's go!" Smurf yelled. "Form it up on the beach!"

A wave of students poured out the door and sprinted across the grinder. Grey moved through the crowd until he was lined up next to Murray.

"Are you out of your mind?"

Murray flashed his patented, insane smile. "Yes. Aren't you?"

"No, seriously. You're going to get yourself killed."

"Someone has to keep life interesting around here, don't they?"

"Sometimes interesting isn't good, Murray." Grey fell into the formation and took a quick muster of his boat crew. "Surviving is good."

"You worry too much, boss."

"We'll see."

The class moved out at a fast trot. Their breath came in ragged gasps by the time they reached the stoplight. Once again, the road guards blocked traffic as the class stormed across the street. No one had enough wind for a battle cry. They ran past the base McDonald's, the Exchange, and several low-slung storage buildings before reaching the pool.

"They're not here yet," Smurf said, encouraging them. "I don't see a truck."

They rushed through the gate and onto the cement pool deck. The class skittered to a stop as the front-runners noticed an instructor perched on the diving platform. Furtado casually checked his watch.

"Thirteen minutes." He shook his head. "Close, but no good. Get wet."

The class stampeded into the pool like a group of lemmings. Grey felt a foot connect with the back of his head as students jumped farther and farther out into the pool to clear their teammates. The water was surprisingly chilly. The instructors must have turned off the pool heater for their benefit. *How touching.* In waves of a dozen or so, the students pulled themselves from the pool and lined up next to the chain-link fence that surrounded the facility.

"Murray, get up here," Furtado ordered.

Grey watched Murray climb the steps that led to the three-meter diving platform. Furtado and Murray conversed for a few tension-filled seconds, and then Murray walked to the edge of the platform and stood looking down at the water. He stripped off his top, his boots, his pants, his undershirt, and his socks, leaving only a pair of butt-hugging khaki underwater-demolition-team (UDT) shorts. After mashing his clothes into a bundle, he tossed them toward the class. He walked to the rear of the platform, turned, broke into a run, and launched himself into the air. The class watched in silence as Murray extended his arms in the beginning of a perfect swan dive. At the apex of the dive, however, when Murray should have dropped his head and streamlined his body, he remained stretched out horizontally.

"Belly flop!" Jones yelled. The class cheered.

Murray accelerated downward, his head, legs, and arms thrown back theatrically. At the last second he chickened out and rolled into a ball. A geyser of water exploded into the air as Murray's body broke the surface. Seconds later he swam to the side.

"Do it again," Furtado yelled. "And do it right this time."

Murray climbed back onto the platform and faced the class. He took a bow as the class shouted encouragement. After rolling his shoulders and neck, he pointed toward the pool and accelerated down the concrete platform. He executed another perfect launch, arcing high into the air. And once again, as he fell, his body remained horizontal. His eyes were shut tightly and his jaw clenched as he made contact with the surface. A distinct crack echoed throughout the complex as Murray disappeared from sight. A long five seconds later, he floated to the surface and took feeble strokes toward the wall. His face was pale and his eyes were wide with pain.

Grey rushed to the side of the pool to help him out.

"Get the fuck away, sir!" Furtado yelled. "He can take care of himself!"

As Grey reluctantly turned away, several diesel trucks rumbled into the parking lot. Smurf quickly called the class to attention. Furtado ran down the diving-platform steps and disappeared out the gate.

"Call them out for me," Smurf ordered as he nervously fidgeted in his wet uniform.

"I don't know their names any better than you do." Grey shrugged. "I'm sorry."

"Just do it."

The class tensed up visibly at the sight of Smurf's insecurity. Seconds later a string of instructors filed through the gate, and Grey started spouting off names, hoping for the best.

"Senior Chief Ortiz, Chief Baldwin, Chief Lundin, Instructor Heffner, Instructor Furtado, Instructor Redman, Instructor Heisler."

Grey allowed himself a small smile of satisfaction. It appeared he had correctly guessed the order of seniority—a small miracle. Suddenly the decontamination showers hissed to life. The decon area consisted of ten shower nozzles that shot high-pressure water from three directions. While maintaining the hygiene of the pool was the ostensible purpose behind this torture apparatus, the instructors liked it for one reason: standing under it was extremely uncomfortable. The water was always freezing cold.

"You forgot me, dipshit." A short, well-built, mustachioed instructor with a shaved head addressed Grey. "I'm not someone you want to forget. In fact, I'm going to make sure it never happens again. Go stand in the decon, arms extended. I want you to repeat my name a thousand times. When you're done, you can get out. And don't even think about cheating."

Grey stepped into the path of the blasting water and started chanting, "Osgood, Osgood, Osgood—"

"Use my proper title. And shout it out," Osgood snarled.

"Instructor Osgood! Instructor Osgood!"

"Louder!"

Grey yelled at the top of his lungs. The cold water bit into his skin, and in less than a minute he was shaking hard. Five minutes later, when he reached repetition three hundred, Murray joined him. They both checked to make sure the instructors weren't watching, then hugged each other tightly, striving to conserve as much body heat as possible.

"Why you here?" Grey asked.

"Redman."

"What'd you do?"

"Nothing."

Grey continued shouting out Instructor Osgood's name. By the time Grey reached repetition nine hundred, he was becoming deliriously cold. His speech started to slur, and he clutched Murray like a lost child.

The rest of the class bear-crawled around the pool deck. Instructor Osgood walked behind them, urging the slower students to crawl faster. Red streaks marked the concrete where trainees had left behind skin from their tenderized hands.

A new instructor walked over to the decon showers and regarded Grey and Murray impassively. Grey was so cold that he refused to let go of his fellow student.

"Who sent you here?"

"Instructor Osgood."

"Have you been in here since we came?"

"Yes."

"Get out—both of you."

Grey gratefully stepped out of the shower. He had never met Chief Lundin, but he could already tell he was a godsend. The man was completely ordinary looking, with a slight paunch, unremarkable muscles, a thinning head of brown hair, and dull brown eyes.

"Why'd you join the navy?"

"Excuse me?" The question caught Grey off guard.

"I said, why'd you join?"

Grey thought for a while. His teeth were still chattering. "I thought being a SEAL sounded like an interesting profession. Sure beats investment banking, anyway."

"Does it?" Lundin asked. "You could be making truckloads of money."

"Fuck the money." Grey looked Lundin in the eye. "My brother went that route. One-hundred-and-twenty-hour weeks and certain heart failure by age fifty. I can think of better lifestyles."

"If you say so, sir."

In the background, students groaned as they completed their third lap around the Olympic-size pool.

"What'd you study?"

"History."

"Focus on anything?"

What the hell is this guy up to? "U.S. foreign policy."

"And you?" Lundin looked at Murray. "What's your story?"

Murray eyed the instructor skeptically. "I grew up in Stockton. High school drop out, vagrant—you know the story."

"You realize about half the enlisted men in this class have college degrees—"

"And?"

"You're a little behind the power curve. Not to say you couldn't catch up, but the only tour I can think of that gives you the time to attend classes is"—Chief Lundin laughed softly—"BUD/S instructor."

"I didn't sign up for the SEALs to get an academic education," Murray said. "I want to kick down doors. Shoot and loot!"

Chief Lundin smirked. "Right. You and everyone else. The reality is somewhat different."

"What do you mean?" Murray looked confused.

"Don't worry about it. Go join your class."

Grey and Murray jogged over to the school circle that had formed around Chief Baldwin. He held up a short piece of rope and deftly tied a series of knots, his nimble fingers working from memory.

"And there you have it," he said, holding up a bowline. "Instructor Furtado already went over all of this in detail, so I won't beat the subject to death. I want five lines of students at the deep end of the pool. Each line will be assigned one instructor. When he waves you out, you swim to his position. From there on out, it's his show. He'll tell you when to swim to the bottom and tie your knot on the line. Once you've got your knot tied, you'll give him the okay sign. He'll examine your knot. If he likes it, he'll give the okay sign back. Then you'll give him a thumbs up. You will not surface until he returns the signal. Understood?"

"Hoo-yah, Instructor Baldwin!"

"What did I tell you about answering my questions? Hoo-yah means nothing to me! Drop down, assholes!"

The class quickly cranked out twenty push-ups.

"Now form five lines, and make it quick."

Grey quickly glanced at the instructors in the water and herded his boat crew toward Instructor Heisler. He had a good reputation, and he generally treated the students with a modicum of respect.

"Hey, Jeff." Instructor Redman swam over to Heisler. "I want that group," he said, pointing at Grey's boat crew. "Mind if we switch?"

"Of course not."

Fuck. We're dead.

"Officers first, sir." Redman waved Grey into the pool. "Let's go."

Grey lowered himself into the cold water and sidestroked over to Redman. The burly instructor splashed water in his face.

"Nervous?"

"No."

"Bullshit." Redman splashed water in Grey's face again. "Here's the deal: you have micro lungs, I have manly lungs. I'm going to stay on the bottom the whole time. You get to come to the surface between each knot—"

"What—?"

"You doubt me?" Redman cut in. "Just do it, dumb-ass. The trick is this: the longer you keep me waiting below, the more upset I'll get. The more upset I become, the less likely it is that I will approve your sorry little knot. Catch my drift?"

"Sure."

"Here's the order: square knot, bowline, half hitch, and becket bend. Don't mess it up." The hint of a smile formed at the corner of his mouth. "Okay, sir. Whenever you're ready."

Grey exhaled several times, then drew in a huge breath. The surface closed over his head as he lowered himself toward the bottom. A white line ran across the pool several inches from the concrete floor. He swam over to it and started his first knot. *Left over right, right over left.* Seconds later he had a perfect square knot tied to the line. He gave Redman the okay sign. Seated cross-legged on the other side of the line, the instructor looked like he was meditating. He grabbed the knot and regarded it carefully for a few seconds. He pulled on both loose ends of the line, ensuring that it was snugged down sufficiently, then slowly formed the okay sign. Grey eagerly flashed the thumbs-up and waited for acknowledgment before bolting for the surface.

The eerie silence of the pool gave way to the heckling of instructors as he drew in several ragged breaths. *This is going to suck.* He allowed himself a few more seconds on the surface, then dove below and executed his second knot. Redman nixed his first bowline, forcing him to try again. As he carefully worked the soft knot line into the appropriate configuration, he began to chicken-neck, instinctively gulping and thrusting his head forward. By the time he reached the surface, he was on the edge of panic. Hypoxia was on the way.

The third knot went perfectly. It helped that a half hitch was an easy knot. However, by the time he reached the surface, he was once again dangerously short of breath. He still had to execute a becket bend, a bitch of a knot.

Redman looked like the picture of stoicism as Grey swam to the bottom. His arms were folded across his chest, and he sat nearly motionless. Grey started his becket bend. His fingers worked frantically, and his heart surged as he presented the completed knot for inspection. The cross-legged instructor examined it, then shook his head. *No good.* Grey felt a warm cloud of urine escape his UDT shorts as his bladder released its contents.

I'm finished, I'm finished. Dead. Dead. Dead. The knot refused to come together. The chicken-neck dance began in earnest as Grey fought to stay focused. He felt as if he would explode. Panic had set in, and there was little he could do to hide it. He finally managed to complete the knot, and he thrust it toward Redman urgently. The instructor took his time, tugging at the knot, examining it. Blackness started to creep in from the corners of Grey's eyes. His field of vision was shrinking rapidly. Redman looked at him expectantly.

The okay sign. Grey formed the signal with his right hand. Redman promptly returned it. Without wasting a second, Grey thrust out his thumb, requesting to surface. Redman held out a closed fist. *Is this some kind of sick joke? Fuck this!* Grey violently pushed off the bottom, his eyes fixed on the surface. Suddenly his upward acceleration stopped. Redman had him by the ankle and was dragging him back to the bottom. Once Grey's face was level with his own, he stared into his eyes and extended his thumb. Grey shot to the surface, kicking with all his might. Fresh air rushed into his empty lungs as he struggled to regain his composure. Redman surfaced a short while later.

The two eyed each other for several seconds. Air was still sawing in and out of Grey's lungs. Redman breathed quietly.

"Pass."

That was all Grey needed to hear. He swam to the side of the pool and slowly pulled himself out. His head spun crazily as he stood up, causing him to totter dangerously and nearly fall backward into the pool. Chief Lundin rushed over and took Grey by the arm.

"Steady there, sir."

"Thanks."

"Don't thank me," Lundin said quietly. "It makes me look bad."

"Right." Grey slowly regained his balance.

"Go join the winners."

Walking slowly, Grey joined the two students who sat facing the chain-link fence. As he gingerly sat down, he looked over and was pleasantly surprised to see Rogers's pensive face staring back at him.

"Not nearly as bad as I expected," Rogers said quietly. "Not bad at all, really."

"Sure thing, champ," Grey said. "Who'd you have? Heisler?"

"How'd you know?"

"Try it with Redman next time. I almost drowned."

"It was that bad?"

"Worse." Grey looked over his shoulder and saw a lone student climb out of the pool and assume the push-up position. "Who is that?"

"Jones."

"Jones?" Grey shook his head. He hated to see any of his men fail. *Damn it.*

"Do you realize this is as relaxing as BUD/S will ever get?" Rogers was smiling. "I mean, how often are we going to get to sit here and bask in our success? This is paradise."

"You worry me sometimes, Socrates."

"Oh, come on, Mark, lighten up."

They sat quietly for several minutes, enjoying the unusual silence. Grey had just closed his eyes when an instructor jumped into the pool and dragged Murray out.

"Breathe, you asshole, breathe."

Murray got on his hands and knees and puked a stream of water onto the concrete.

"Get up, you turd." It was Furtado. "Don't play sick with me. Get in the push-up position."

A shaky Murray assumed the position as the cluster of winners grew steadily bigger. By the end of the test, only twelve students had failed, a remarkable showing for a class that still had close to a hundred people.

"You have two minutes to get dressed and get out of here," Osgood told them. "Don't be late." With a snap of his fingers the instructors began moving between the rows of frantically dressing students, tossing any loose articles of clothing they could find into the pool. Students raced across the concrete and launched themselves headfirst into the water.

"Just put on anything!" Smurf yelled. "I don't care whose it is!"

Grey wound up wearing a camouflage top from one of the smaller members of the class. He couldn't button it, and it only came halfway down his stomach. Worse yet, the boots he pulled on were several sizes too small. Smurf was frantically rolling up his pants legs when the instructors called time.

"Not even close," Osgood observed angrily. "You'll pay later. We're running behind schedule. Take a chilly dip, then form it up on the beach for a conditioning run."

The class jumped into the pool then squeezed out the gate and fell into formation on the road. They ran until the diesel trucks crammed with instructors rumbled past, then stopped and quickly exchanged boots. After the flurry of activity, Grey found he had been jilted. The boots he held definitely weren't his. They felt a little better, but they were still at least a size too small. *Tough shit.* The class started running as Grey finished tying his boots. By the time they reached the beach, hot patches had popped up on his feet, a sure sign that blisters were on the way.

"We don't have any time to waste," Smurf said as they stopped on the sand. "If you're wearing someone else's boots, give 'em up."

Grey stepped forward and pulled off his boots, which were clearly stenciled ROSARIO on the back in big white letters.

"Rosario!" he yelled.

"Here, sir." A lean Hispanic petty officer meekly took the boots and passed over the ones he'd been wearing. His manner was polite, almost deferential. Grey almost forgot he was at BUD/S.

"Thanks." Grey pulled on his own boots and stripped off his camo top. Standard running gear consisted of pants and an undershirt. Just as Grey began to relax, two diesel trucks roared through the gate to the compound and parked themselves on the beach. Three instructors followed behind: Chief Baldwin, Instructor Heisler, and Osgood. Chief Baldwin was notorious for his runs. He didn't look exceptionally fit, but rumor had it he would run the pants off anyone. And Osgood—well, Osgood was said to run a brutal goon squad, an unfortunate collection of students who just couldn't keep up.

"Form it up!" Osgood yelled. After a short pause he added, "Too slow. Hit the surf, wet and sandy."

The class charged into the frigid ocean and then rolled in the sand.

"Too slow. Do it again."

After four trips to the ocean, Osgood tired of his game. Either that or Chief Baldwin got sick of waiting. Without warning, the lean chief took off down the beach at a full sprint.

"Better keep up," he yelled over his shoulder.

Grey smirked as he sprinted to the front of the pack. He was in a terrible mood, but at least running was something he could handle. Quiet arrogance was the attitude Grey preferred when his running skills were put to the test. His determined eyes bored holes in Baldwin's back as the instructor took off over a sand berm. *I'll take you any day. You're nothing.*

The diesel trucks gurgled at the back of the pack, and after a few minutes of berm running, a steady stream of encouragement spouted from the trucks' PA systems.

"Just give up. You'll never make it." It was Furtado. "If GI Jane can do it, so can I," he squealed sarcastically. "Never give up. Never surrender."

Chief Baldwin took a turn onto the hard-packed sand and proceeded south along the water's edge. Grey was surprised at the old man's speed.

"You realize you don't have to be here, don't you?" Furtado said. "Didn't you know you can get your SEAL diploma over the Internet? All you have to do is fill in your name on an online form, and the next day you get your official SEAL diploma in the mail."

The voice coming from the truck loudspeaker grew fainter and fainter as the pack spread out along the beach. Grey ran directly behind Chief Baldwin, his eyes glued to the instructor's back. He felt strangely alone. The pack was several strides behind him and falling back by the second. Chief Baldwin kept increasing the pace, pushing on, dragging Grey in his wake.

The chain-link fence that surrounded the demolition pit was visible a quarter mile ahead. Grey knew Baldwin would stop there and wait for the class to catch up.

"C'mon. Pick it up." The words slipped out of Grey's mouth before he could censor himself.

"Excuse me, sir?" Chief Baldwin looked over his shoulder.

"Nothing."

"Nothing my ass." Baldwin picked up the pace. "If you can stay on my shoulder for the next minute, I won't beat the shit out of you. How's that for a deal?"

Grey didn't answer. He focused every ounce of energy on the considerable task of matching the instructor's stride. The chain-link fence danced toward them as they accelerated into an all-out sprint. Baldwin opened a gap of several feet for a few seconds, but Grey threw in a surge at the last minute and closed the distance. After slowing to a jog, the chief turned and regarded Grey with one raised eyebrow.

"You run in college?"

"Marathons," Grey answered, "and triathlons."

"Not bad. You're safe—at least for now. But you sure as hell better keep up on the way back, because I'm not tired." Baldwin stripped off his shirt, revealing the lean chest of a runner. Ghostly white skin stretched over his ribcage. "You better take off your shirt, too, sir. It pays to be a winner."

Grey peeled off his shirt and watched as his class struggled toward the demolition pit. Jones was the second student in. He ran like a wild man, arms windmilling out of control, head titled back.

"You! Get over here."

Jones came to a sudden halt at Baldwin's feet.

"Where you from?"

"Tennessee," Jones drawled.

"You hunt?"

"Sure." Jones rested with his hands on his knees. "Got a couple of hounds."

"No kidding?" Baldwin smiled, and his brown eyes danced. "I have a soft place in my heart for backwoods freaks like you. I think every class needs a bona fide hillbilly, don't you, Mr. Grey?"

"Oh, undoubtedly," Grey said. "Jones is the real deal." He winked.

"Yup. Real deal, that's me. Hillbilly born and raised. Yes, sir."

"Jones, I almost don't want to hurt you," Baldwin said. "That's a compliment, in case you were wondering. You'll be the cutoff today. Take off your shirt."

Jones stripped off his shirt, revealing a build similar to Baldwin's.

"Stretch out on your own. This might take awhile." Baldwin jogged north as the bulk of the students approached. He cryptically held out an arm and pointed toward the ocean. The students dutifully charged into the surf. Fifteen minutes of lunges, squats, and assorted physical activity followed. Osgood took a particular liking to Smurf Jacks, which consisted of doing jumping jacks in a full squat position. Students fell over, students collapsed, students retched. It was a mess.

"It sure is good to be alive, ain't it, sir?"

Grey looked over at the Tennessee Wonder and laughed. "You're so goddamn positive, Jones. Can't you let me stew for a while?"

"And what good would that do? I know what's troublin' you. Dang, I like Ramirez as much as you do, but you got to realize there ain't a damn thing you can do. At least his heart's still tickin' and his brain's buzzin'."

"Still . . ." Grey's voice trailed off. He sifted a handful of sand through his fingers. "I'm gonna go see him tonight in the hospital, if he's still there. You want to come?"

" 'Course I do."

They sat and stretched in silence, gazing at the blue ocean, trying to ignore the grunts of pain that came from their classmates. Eventually Baldwin whistled and pointed north. By the time they started running, the fleet-footed chief already had a sizable lead. Grey relaxed and let his legs fall into their natural rhythm. Disassociation was a trick he had learned as an endurance athlete. Running was the only BUD/S activity solitary enough for it to have a real effect. He let his cheeks slacken, relaxed his hands, opened up his stride, and let his breathing flow naturally. His vision blurred slightly as he shifted his attention inward, retreating to the shelter of his mental fortress. Vanessa danced at the water's edge, laughing, spinning, her brown skin shining in the afternoon light. The water sprayed up around her knees as she twirled in the shallows. Grey reveled in the image, impervious to the lactic acid building up in his legs.

"Hey." Baldwin thrust an arm in front of Grey's chest. "I need some space, champ."

Vanessa disappeared in a snap. He backed off, allowing Baldwin to run a few paces ahead. Fire spread through his legs, and his breath became uneven. They were almost to the dive tower. Surely Baldwin would stop there.

"You up for another mile?" Baldwin asked, looking back over his shoulder.

Grey smiled weakly.

"Good." He picked up the pace even faster.

Fighting the urge to fall back proved nearly impossible, yet somehow Grey managed to stick with the instructor. Several hundred yards later, Baldwin stopped abruptly and started jogging in place.

Thought you could break me? Grey allowed himself a small dose of pride. *Think again, Chief Twizzelstick. I called your bluff.*

Baldwin eyed Grey warily, opened his mouth as if to say something, then thought better of it. He simply pointed at the section of beach where the class had left their uniform tops and their canteens. Grey walked away in silence. After unscrewing the top from his canteen, he greedily poured a thick stream of water into his mouth, spilling the cool liquid down his chest in the process. Jones joined him moments later.

"That Chief Baldwin sure is a fast one." Jones was breathing heavily. "I bet he's surprised as hell you kept up. I would be."

"Thanks." Grey plopped onto the sand and started stretching his hamstrings.

"I'd give him a run for his money back home, out in the mountains. This sand is new stuff to me. It just sucks the energy right out of my legs."

"You ever go to the beach as a kid?"

"No. It ain't exactly next door, sir."

"When was the first time you saw the ocean?"

Jones snorted. "About three weeks ago, give or take a few days."

"And here you are."

"And here I am."

Grey stood at rigid attention, dripping sand and salt water onto the grinder. Instructor Osgood had assembled the class for a special occasion. He paced back and forth in front of the students, stroking his mustache. Suddenly he stopped and leaned in close to Murray.

"Quit."

"No."

"No?" Osgood yelled. "Is that all?"

"No, I will not quit, Instructor Osgood."

The stocky instructor spit at Murray's feet. "You will." He moved down the line, picking out individual students, harassing them. Suddenly a trainee broke from the ranks.

"I want to quit," he said softly. It was a young kid, fresh out of high school.

Osgood threw an arm around the student's shoulder, acting like an old chum. He walked away with his new friend, talking quietly. The student disappeared into the First Phase office. Osgood came back smiling.

"See, it's not so hard. Just say 'I quit.' Just say 'D-O-R.'"

Chief Lundin walked past them, then stopped and retraced his steps, a mischievous smirk on his face. "As a class, spell *Dorito*," he commanded.

About half the class chanted, "D-O-R—"

"Ha!" Lundin yelled. "Got you! You just asked for a Drop On Request!"

The class groaned. Lundin walked away chuckling to himself.

"In all seriousness, if you're thinking about quitting, now is the time," Osgood said. "I'm about to beat the shit out of you, and I really mean it. Spare yourself the pain. Why suffer? So you can spend your entire career away from home, getting shot at, sleeping in the mud? It's only going to get harder from here on out. That's a promise."

Another student stepped forward, then another, and another.

"Good. Keep it coming, gents. There's no shame in what you're doing."

Yet another student stepped up, and another, and finally one more. Apparently the knot tying and the run had taken their toll. Osgood *had* run a particularly mean goon squad. A good quarter of the class had lost their lunch while performing muscle-melting calisthenics at one of his famous "rest stations."

"Just one more, and I won't beat the class." Osgood was beginning to sound like a used-car salesman. *Just one more, and I'll even throw in a free set of tires. . . .*

Another student stepped forward.

"Two more, and I'll give you all your BUD/S diplomas right now."

"Bullshit." Murray's voice was scornful. "Why don't you just beat us and get it over with?"

Grey felt a rush of pride. Murray was deflecting the attention away from Osgood's propaganda in an attempt to stem the steady flow of quitters.

"You'll get a beating, Murray. Don't you worry." Osgood turned his attention back to the class. He wasn't playing along. "Just two more . . ."

The general aura of desperation had passed. There were no more takers.

"On your backs!" The command came quickly, violently.

The class dropped onto their backs.

"Your bellies."

Students flipped onto their stomachs.

"Feet."

They jumped to their feet.

"Backs, bellies, feet. Backs, bellies, feet . . ." *Backs, bellies, feet, backs, bellies.*

Grey's eyes stung as the sweat streamed down his forehead in rivulets. The endless litany of commands continued. The unforgiving asphalt rubbed Grey's hands and bottom raw. He cursed under his labored breath as his ass scab tore free.

"Hit the surf. Wet and sandy."

Thankful for any change of routine, the class sprinted across the parking lot, climbed the berm, and charged into the ocean. Osgood was waiting when they returned.

Backs, bellies, feet. Backs, bellies, feet. The sand only made the abrasion worse. Grey knew he was bleeding. His ass was on fire, the pleasant result of salt water on an open cut. He fell into a battered trance, and the minutes blurred into an undistinguishable tangle of pain.

FIVE

GREY CAUGHT UP WITH Murray on the run back to the barracks. He grabbed him by the arm and pulled him away from the pack of limping students. The pair slowed to a walk.

"What's up, sir?"

"Whatever happened to your quest for dirt on Redman? Did your contact work out?"

Murray allowed himself a self-satisfied smile. "It sure did."

"And?"

"Jeff pulled through for me. I called him up, and he gave the number of someone out here who worked with Redman—a retired chief named Scott Armstrong. I gave Armstrong a call, and he agreed to meet me at a restaurant in Imperial Beach last night. Let me just say my hunch was right. Redman is one dirty fucker."

"What did Armstrong say?" Grey asked impatiently.

"He served with Redman on Team Four before Redman transferred to BUD/S. Apparently our favorite instructor wasn't the most popular guy around. He didn't get along with anyone, and more importantly, no one would operate with him."

"So he was worthless."

"Essentially. It gets better, though." Murray's blue eyes sparkled. "He got removed from Team Four well before his tour was up."

"Why?"

"Let's just say the team had inventory problems. Ammo and demolitions seemed to grow legs and walk off the compound. Armstrong says they were never able to pin the problem on Redman, but the platoon commander had little doubt it was him. Apparently it's not uncommon to keep wet suits, H-gear, and other personal equipment, but taking any kind of weapon home is bad news."

"You've got to be kidding me. They think Redman was stealing ammo and explosives?"

"That's it. Not many people know about it. Armstrong got involved because he was the platoon commander's right-hand man. The two of them discussed the situation, and rather than launch a formal investigation, they convinced the commanding officer to relocate Redman. That way they got rid of him without destroying his career and possibly even sending him to jail."

"Isn't it hard to pull off that kind of thing? I thought inventories were tight."

"Not that tight. Stealing an M-60 would be one thing, but bullets and explosives are another story. You use them, and they go away. Catch my drift?"

"So he went to the range and kept ammo instead of expending it?"

"You got it. And on top of that, Armstrong said that while it was rare to lose a weapon, they lost track of a huge number of older parts from cannibalized M-4s—"

"Meaning Redman could assemble his own firepower from spare parts," Grey mused. He shook his head in amazement. "It worries me that this criminal has the authority to beat the shit out of us."

"Kind of scary, isn't it?"

"Scary is an understatement. It just goes to show that you shouldn't press it further. If Redman catches on to your snooping, there's no telling what he might do to you. He probably has a basement full of torture equipment."

"Very funny." Murray shifted his gaze away from Grey's face. "I'm not satisfied yet. I've got some good leads, but I don't have any hard evidence. I want to see what I can dig up here in San Diego. Redman's been here awhile—long enough to get into some trouble."

"It's your life and your body, sailor. Just don't say I didn't warn you."

"I can handle it. You worry too much, sir."

They walked back to the barracks in silence. Grey punched Vanessa's number into his cell phone. He was still soaking wet and covered with small cuts and bruises from the day's events.

"Hello?" Vanessa's voice was sleepy.

"Geez. You sound worse than I do."

"Mark?"

"Is everything okay? How's school?"

"Who cares about school? How are *you* doing?"

"I'm alive. Bleeding out the ass, but alive."

"Okay, babe. Some things you don't need to tell me. You can spare me the details of your love life."

"You're nasty," Grey said. "It's from sit-ups, silly."

"Right." Vanessa laughed softly. "So what's new? They beat you up today?"

"Of course. Same old story," Grey said, "but I lost a guy in my crew—"

"Baby, that's horrible! He died?" Her voice rose an octave. "Do you have to do this? I mean, can't you be an accountant or something? I'm sure you could land a good job, maybe grad school, law school, medical school. . . . Please? Baby, don't do this. . . ." Her voice trailed off.

Grey was silent. Someone was clearly having a bad day.

"Okay, I'm sorry," she said finally. "I know I'm being ridiculous. But please tell me he didn't die."

"He's alive," Grey said. "I think he broke his back, though."

"Was he a friend of yours?"

"We're all friends."

"I mean, were you close?"

Grey sagged against the wall. Vanessa wasn't making this any easier. "Yes, we were pretty close. He was a good kid."

"I'm so sorry, baby. That's horrible. How did it happen?"

"The boat . . . We were in the boat . . . I mean, he was . . . I was in the water. . . ." He couldn't finish. He felt a crushing weight on his chest, and he felt his eyes tear up. He bit his lip, his embarrassment growing rapidly. *I need sleep. That's all. Just sleep.*

"I have to go." His voice was uneven. "I'm sorry. I'll call you tomorrow, okay?"

"Please don't go. Not like this."

"I'm sorry," he repeated.

"Just tell me you'll be okay."

"I'll be fine," he said. "I love you." Grey struggled to understand how he could swing from joking around to almost shedding tears in a one-minute conversation. *Nice warrior you'll make, Grey. Real stable.* After limping to his room, he jumped in the shower and scrubbed out his cuts. He dressed quickly, throwing on a pair of jeans, a T-shirt, and a sweatshirt. It wasn't cold outside, but being wet all day made wearing a dry sweatshirt a luxury. Jones was sitting on the hood of Grey's jeep when he walked into the parking lot.

"Ready?" Grey asked stupidly.

"Well, I sure as hell ain't sittin' on your hood for kicks."

Grey unlocked the doors and Jones climbed in. Soon they were racing across the Coronado Bay Bridge toward Naval Medical Center San Diego. The clouds had rolled in again, and the downtown lights glowed weakly through the gloom. To the south of the bridge, a series of gray ships sat heavily in the bay, tethered to their gray piers. To the west, the lights of Point Loma glimmered through the haze, marking the position of the unobtrusive submarine base. The lighted runway of the North Island Naval Air Station lay directly behind him, and the old Marine Corps Recruit Depot sat quietly at the north end of the bay. Grey loved San Diego, even if the military presence was a little overwhelming at times. The day he would actually have time to enjoy the many delights of "America's Finest City" seemed impossibly far off, and his mood only blackened as he weaved through traffic.

"You think the instructors are tellin' the truth?" Jones asked.

"About what?"

"About it never getting easier . . . even after we graduate."

"It depends. Yes, you will travel constantly, and you won't see much of home. But no, you won't have an instructor screaming in your face." Grey spoke loudly to be heard over the rumble of his jeep as he accelerated past a semi. "Before I came to BUD/S, I had temporary duty at the Special Warfare Command. Let me tell you, the SEALs I worked for are incredibly laid-back. It threw me off at first. They are about the furthest thing from a BUD/S instructor. Just a bunch of friendly guys who surf on their lunch breaks. It's a whole different world, Jones. You walk a quarter mile down Trident Way, and the nightmare of BUD/S seems far away."

"Traveling so much must be hard on the family, though." Jones mused. "I wonder how many guys are married."

"Why? You planning on tying the knot?"

"Well, there is this girl back home. . . . I love her to death, but I told her we'd at least have to wait until I got out of BUD/S. She still lives with her parents. Wants to be a schoolteacher." He smiled to himself. "I'd love to marry her; I just know staying hitched ain't easy in the Teams."

"It can be done," Grey said, "although Chief Baldwin said the divorce rate hovers a little over ninety percent."

"Damn. Ninety percent?"

"Something like that. It's not easy. Imagine being gone eleven months of the year. Your wife might not even know where you're going." Grey thought of Vanessa, and tried to imagine leaving at a moments notice, disappearing for months. "It takes a special kind of woman to put up with that crap."

Jones sat quietly, staring wistfully into the distance.

"Women," Grey said. "The great complication."

"No kiddin'. But they sure are nice. . . ."

Grey pulled his jeep into the hospital parking lot and cut the ignition. Several minutes later they were standing in a nicely appointed reception room. A handful of flower arrangements dotted the premises, and a small-scale model of the hospital sat in the center of the room under thick glass. Grey walked to the bathroom while Jones approached the front desk. When Grey strolled back into the reception area several minutes later, Jones was standing with his back to the desk, hands in his pockets, staring out the window.

"What's the news?" Grey asked.

"We can't see him," Jones said softly. "He had a stroke. Hemi-plooga, or something. Can't move his left side."

"What do you mean? I thought it was a spinal injury. A fractured disk—"

"You can ask the lady, sir."

Grey wheeled around and strode over to the reception desk.

"Can I help you, sir?" A young petty officer with silky black hair and full lips looked up from her magazine.

"What happened to Ramirez? I thought he was going to be fine."

"You're referring to Petty Officer Angel Ramirez, sir?"

"Yes," Grey replied impatiently. "I'm his division officer." It wasn't exactly true, but it was easier than explaining the function of a boat-crew leader.

"I called in several minutes ago on behalf of Seaman Jones," she said, "and I was told Petty Officer Ramirez has suffered a brain hemorrhage. Hemiplegia. He's lost motor control of his left side. Of course, he only got here this morning. I'm sure you could talk to his doctor tomorrow."

"I want to see him tonight." Grey folded his arms across his chest.

"Sir, I can't let you do that." The receptionist's green eyes burned into him. "He's had an incredibly traumatic injury, and he's in no condition to receive visitors."

"Fine." Grey knocked his knuckles against the desktop impatiently. "Can you at least give me his room number so I can send him something on behalf of his division?"

"If you drop something off here, we'll be happy to deliver it. Or I can give you the hospital's mailing address." She regarded him suspiciously.

"Okay, Petty Officer—"

"Grant."

"Right. Petty Officer Grant . . ." Grey shifted approaches. "You are doing your job very well. I understand you have orders, but I just want you to hear me out. I'll be perfectly honest with you: I feel like Ramirez's accident is my fault. He was my responsibility. He was alone in a boat that I was commanding. When he took the fall, I was there to witness the whole thing. He wanted nothing more out of life than to become a SEAL. Dreams die hard, but the knowledge that his classmates haven't forgotten about him would make all this a lot easier."

"You mentioned sending something," she said, her demeanor softening. "Maybe if you got the class to sign something and sent it over . . ." Grey noticed she was quite attractive now that she had dropped her guard slightly. Her eyes were truly startling, the deepest green he had even seen.

"That's a nice idea, but it's not the same." He leaned forward slightly.

"Please. Please tell me his room number. I'll do anything. He's like family." Unethical or not, Grey had to see Ramirez.

Grant propped her hands against her forehead and bit her lip. "Like family?"

"Like family," Grey repeated.

She smiled slightly, and Jones swayed unsteadily. She wasn't just good looking. She was gorgeous. "I'll see what I can do."

"Thank you."

"No promises, though."

"Of course not," Grey said. "A chance is better than nothing."

"Right." She picked up a phone and chewed on her nails nervously. After a short wait she said, "Yes, this is Grant at the front desk. I have two gentlemen here who want to see Seaman Ramirez. . . . Yes, they're family. Brothers through adoption . . . I know it's a bad time, but they're both scheduled to leave the country tomorrow. . . . Yes, that would be great. Thank you." She hung up and sighed heavily. "Don't ask me to do that again!"

"I wouldn't dream of it. You're a princess."

Grant smiled shyly. "Sir . . ."

"Sorry. We're not used to being in the presence of good-looking women."

"And that's the truth," Jones added.

She was blushing now. "Someone will be here any minute."

"Great." Grey stepped away from the counter and waited. A young corpsman strode into the room moments later.

"You're Angel's brother?" the corpsman asked, raising an eyebrow.

"Through adoption," Grey corrected quickly.

"Right. Follow me." He walked at a quick clip, navigating a series of empty corridors with ease. The corpsman stopped in front of a white door. He opened it and peeked in. "It looks like he's resting."

"We'll just wait by his bedside," Grey offered. "We'll let him sleep."

"Fine. Give a holler if you need anything. I'm just down the hallway."

Grey stepped into the room and immediately felt an intense pressure on his chest. Ramirez looked so out of place in the sterile hospital room. His cheeks were tear-stained, and his closed eyes were swollen and rimmed below with bluish skin. Grey walked closer and stood at the bedside. Jones stared at the floor. They stood motionless for several minutes before Grey turned and nodded toward the door. *There's nothing we can do. . . .*

"Sir."

Grey jumped. Ramirez's voice sounded weaker; the sarcastic edge was gone.

"Thanks for coming." His eyes were slits. He smiled weakly. "I thought you might show up. And Tennessee, well that's a nice surprise."

"What? You expect any less from me?" Jones acted hurt. "Where I come from it ain't no surprise when the whole town turns out for someone."

"Of all the people to bring along, sir," Ramirez said with a smirk, "you have to bring Mr. Sunshine Country Bumpkin. Next thing I know, that hillbilly hog's gonna be telling me it's for the better." He looked at Jones's face, and realized he was pushing it too far. "Jones, you know I'm just messin' with ya, bro. I'm glad you came."

"Anything for the sexiest man in BUD/S."

"Oh, you better stop before I climb out of this bed and give it to you good."

"Enough, guys. You're starting to worry me," Grey said.

"Tell me with a straight face that you don't think I'm sexy," Ramirez challenged.

Grey smiled and shook his head. *What a piece of work.* He missed Ramirez already.

"See? It can't be done. I'm sexy."

An awkward silence filled the room. Jones fidgeted nervously and kept his gaze firmly planted on the white floor.

"Hey, this ain't no damn morgue," Ramirez said. "I'm still alive."

"I'm sorry," Grey said. "I was just thinking about how much we're going to miss you."

"Yeah," Jones agreed. "What's a boat crew without a loudmouthed Mexican?"

"Well, at least you still got a dumb-ass hick to keep things exciting."

"Any idea what's going to happen to you?" Grey asked quietly. "How serious is it?"

"Pretty bad." His smile faded. "I can't feel my left side so good. The doctor said something about full disability. I don't know what I'm supposed to do. I've got three kids, bro."

"Things will work out," Grey said. "Sometimes these things happen for a reason."

"Yeah, like I was a dumb-ass and gave the middle finger to a ten-foot wave. That's the only reason I can think of."

"I meant maybe things will work out better in the long run. You'll regain mobility, invest your disability money, and eventually become a corporate raider on Wall Street. We'll come visit you in your Manhattan penthouse. You'll have a whole gaggle of sexy senoritas waiting to fulfill your every desire, and all the disgusting cow-tongue burritos you can eat."

Ramirez laughed. "Fuck Manhattan. If I'm going East Coast, it's the Bronx for me. You know any Mexicans that live in Manhattan?"

"Then the Bronx it is," Grey agreed.

"I don't know a damn thing about those places," Jones mused, "but I don't really care, so long as this half-breed stays away from me. He's nothing but trouble."

"Aw, honey, stop acting like you don't love me." Ramirez raised his right arm and beckoned. "Give me a hug."

"I'll pass on that one, compadre."

"Come on. You're hurting my feelings."

Jones darted in, pressed his chin against Ramirez's shoulder, and darted out.

"Much better." Ramirez smiled slightly and closed his eyes. "You boys need to get back to base, no? It's getting late for a bunch of tadpoles."

Grey gave an exaggerated bow. "We're at your service, Ramirez. You need anything, you give us a call."

"Thanks." His eyes were still closed. "I mean it. I don't know what I'd do without you guys. Now get out of here."

At the door, Grey turned and said, "Just in case anybody asks, we're all brothers by way of adoption, right?"

Ramirez laughed softly. "Later, bro."

SIX

GREY LINED UP ACROSS from Murray on the beach. He propped his fins by his left foot, held his sharpened knife in his left hand, and cupped his polished CO_2 cartridge in his right hand. He turned around.

"Murray, check me out."

If any strap on his gray inflatable life jacket was twisted, it meant an inspection failure, and an inspection failure meant pain. Grey had experienced enough pain over the last few days. Things had been going poorly ever since Ramirez took a nosedive into the bottom on Monday. It was Friday now, and Grey knew he should be excited for the weekend, but all he could think about was getting the swim over with.

"You're fine, sir. No twists."

A diesel engine roared to life somewhere off the beach. *Instructors on the way.* Grey came to attention as the truck bounced onto the beach, followed by a gaggle of instructors in wet suits.

"Drop." Osgood's voice echoed through the truck's PA system. "Corpsmen, give me a water temp."

Immediately two students dashed for the water. They trotted from the surf dripping wet moments later. One of the corpsmen produced a metal thermometer and handed it to Instructor Osgood.

"Fifty-five degrees," Osgood boomed. "Wet-suit tops stay on."

Several instructors started moving down the two lines of swimmers, inspecting knives, checking life vests, and dishing out harassment to their hearts' content. Instructor Heisler moved down Grey's line from the right side, Instructor Furtado from the left. *Please, please let it be Heisler.* The two moved closer, and suddenly Heisler stepped away and walked to the truck.

"Nervous, sir?" Furtado asked. "You look like shit." He snatched the knife from Grey's hand and ran the blade across his arm. Grey watched a series of hairs collect along the blade's edge; it was sharp. Furtado grunted and returned the knife. "You know how to use that thing, sir?"

"Hoo-yah, Instructor Furtado."

"You sure about that? You think you have the balls to gut a man, watch as his intestines spill out on the sand?"

Very nice. "I don't know, Instructor Furtado."

"You don't know?!" Furtado yelled. "Well, you better find out, sir, 'cause we're in the business of killing, and I sure as hell don't want some chickenshit officer trying to lead a bunch of warriors." He grabbed Grey's CO_2 cartridge and turned it over in his hands. "Looks like you scrubbed a toilet with this thing. You shine it?"

"Yes."

"Put your shit away and drop down, sir."

Grey obediently sheathed his knife and screwed in his CO_2 cartridge before assuming the push-up position. Furtado didn't let him stop at twenty; at repetition one hundred Grey started to sweat beneath his wetsuit top. This definitely wouldn't help his swim time. Minutes passed as Grey shifted uncomfortably, waiting for the command to recover.

"Hit the surf," Osgood boomed. Murray grabbed Grey's life jacket and pulled him to his feet. They ran toward the surf together as Grey struggled to pull on his Neoprene hood. The icy water stung as it moved up his legs, a crescendo of pain that peaked when the frigid ocean slapped into his balls. Grey turned around and sat down in the water to pull his fins on. Murray smiled next to him.

"You like this, don't you?" Grey asked as the white water foamed around them.

"It's the easiest thing we do," Murray replied, "except for maybe the obstacle course. There's no goon squad, and the instructors can't really give us a lot of shit."

Grey hated the swims—the cold, the boredom, the challenge of trying to stay on course, the stress of staying within arms length of Murray. He'd rather run.

"Let's hit it," Murray said as he pulled on his mask.

They sidestroked through the surf, diving for the bottom when a breaker rolled in. Grey tried to establish a comfortable rhythm. Swim pairs were required to stay close together, which demanded a mutual understanding of pacing and a healthy dose of courtesy. If the lead swimmer was pulling away, he would back off the pace a little, and if a swimmer wanted to change sides, he would tap his partner on the shoulder. They fell into a groove as they reached the orange buoy that marked the starting line.

As they bobbed in the current, Murray asked, "You coming tonight?"

"Where?"

"A bunch of us are going out—probably downtown. You up for it?"

"I don't know. I told Vanessa she could come visit tonight."

"Sir," Murray scolded, "there is a time for pussy, and there's a time to hang with the boys. Who's gonna have your back when you get caught in a firefight? Vanessa? I don't think so. You need some quality bonding time with the rest of us: drink a shit-ton, get in a fight or two, chase some tail."

"I'll pass on the fighting and chasing tail, but I'll give it some serious thought."

"Sir, you're being a nerd. Don't think too hard."

Grey laughed and splashed water in his swim buddy's face. Murray always looked absurd with a face mask on. It pulled up his upper lip and stretched out the skin around his eyes, lending him an uncanny fishlike appearance.

"Go!" Chief Lundin shouted, catching them off guard. They kicked hard with their fins, trying to get a lead on the pack. Grey hated having to swim over other students; it could lead to hard feelings. His world became a series of flashes—gray, green, gray, green. The sky and the murky ocean passed in series before his eyes as he propelled himself forward. The briny taste of salt water mixed with the faint aroma of gasoline created a nauseating concoction in his mouth. And Murray's big fish eyes, wide open and blank, were unavoidable. *Stroke, kick, kick, kick, glide.* Grey became a machine, thoughtless, unfeeling, uninterested. His mind drifted away as he headed north toward the turnaround buoy. The two miles went quickly, and Grey was pleased when they easily passed the required time.

"Bottom sample," Chief Lundin requested pleasantly. He watched them from the boat floating at the finish line. *Crap.* They were too far offshore.

"You ready?" Murray asked.

"No," Grey answered. "But let's get it over with."

They counted to three and slipped below the surface. Grey immediately started kicking, struggling against the buoyancy of his wet-suit top. Ten feet, twenty feet . . . The bottom failed to appear. Grey cleared his ears. Thirty feet. The bottom was still nowhere in sight. He kicked harder, and suddenly his outstretched hand touched sand. The visibility was horrible. Grey swam along the bottom, his lungs burning. Finally he found what he was looking for—a rock. Sand was acceptable as a bottom sample, but there was always the chance it would disappear by the time a diver reached the surface. Rocks were safe. Grey grabbed the smooth stone and kicked hard for the surface. Murray was already there, waiting with a sand dollar perched on his head. Grey held up the stone for Lundin's inspection.

"Get out of here," he said, dismissing them with a wave.

They kicked toward shore on their backs, taking their sweet time. Because they had been the second pair across the finish line, having enough time to change wouldn't be a problem.

"You *have* to come tonight," Murray said as they neared the surf zone. "That's an order, sir."

"An order, eh?" Grey snorted. "Well in that case, count me in, captain."

"Right." Murray eyed an approaching swell. "Now's it's time for a little bodysurfing."

"But we're supposed to keep a low profile in the water, just like a mission," Grey protested.

"Mission, shmission. The instructors won't see us. Stop worrying." Murray turned onto his stomach and started kicking hard. With a shrug, Grey did the same, timing his surge of power so that the wave would pick him up. Sure enough, he felt the wave grab hold and launch him forward, pushing him fiercely down the face of the wave. Just as the white water crashed behind him, he glanced to his left and saw Murray cut toward him with one arm extended Superman style. They collided lightly and managed to stay stable, riding the wave together toward shore.

"That wasn't so bad, was it?" Murray asked, standing up in the water. He pulled his fins off and dropped his mask so that it hung around his neck.

Grey spit out some salt water and wiped a hand across his mouth. A loud belch rumbled up from his gut. They sloshed through the inshore area and crossed the beach, stopping next to Osgood's truck.

"Swim Pair Nine, Grey and Murray," they chanted in unison.

"Drop down, you sorry sacks of shit. You don't think I saw you joy-riding out there? Time to pay the man."

Murray looked over apologetically as they started cranking out push-ups.

"I'll give you three minutes to wheelbarrow around that beach marker and back," Osgood said, "and if you make it, I'll let you go."

"Hoo-yah!" Murray yelled.

"You're on the clock."

Murray immediately jumped up and grabbed Grey's legs. *Well, I guess that settles it.* It seemed more appropriate for Murray to take the bottom position, considering he had masterminded the bodysurfing that got them into trouble in the first place. But there wasn't any time to argue now. Grey lurched forward and started running on his hands. Three minutes would be tough, but it was do-able. The old familiar burn started in his arms, and by the halfway point he was ready to pass out in the sand. *Pain is weakness leaving the body.* He repeated the mantra over and over in his head to no avail. Pain was pain; everything else was bullshit. He collapsed in a heap in front of the truck as Osgood casually consulted his watch. The bald instructor deliberated for a moment, then jerked his head toward the decon showers. Grey scrambled to his feet and bolted to safety with Murray at his heels.

They quickly rinsed the salt water from their gear, then hurried to the pit, where their pants, shirts, and helmets were arranged in a neat line. After yanking off their wet-suit tops and stowing their swim gear in their seabags, they fumbled with their pants, their limbs shaking violently from the cold. The class trickled in slowly, and Grey and Murray helped the stragglers change. They were running out of time.

Smurf waddled around the corner, waving his arms frantically. "Four minutes. We have four minutes to be on the obstacle course." Out of breath, eyes rimmed with red, pale skin, he looked like a madman. *Must be the pressure.*

"I give him a week," Murray mumbled quietly.

"Hell, why not make it a day," Grey countered. "He'll be gone this afternoon."

Smurf was panicked; he stumbled over everything and accomplished nothing. Suddenly Grey felt sorry for the midget class leader. He looked so hopeless.

"Let me help you," Grey offered, picking up a swim fin and throwing it in his bag.

Smurf was taken aback. The two of them generally did not enjoy a close relationship. Moments later the whole class was on the beach, sprinting toward the obstacle course. Once they reached the first obstacle, they lined up from fastest to slowest. Grey would start second. He always started second. His only competition came from a brute of a student named Warrior. The last name was real, and it fit. He had a grim-reaper tattoo on his left bicep, and his muscular arms seemed too long for his body. The width of his iron lats forced him to hold his arms away from his body, and the end result was a torso that looked like an upside-down triangle. Warrior muscled his way over obstacles while Grey finessed them. The last time they ran the course, Grey finished only five seconds behind his teammate.

"Hey, Stanford," Warrior said, punching Grey in the arm. "Think you're gonna beat me today?"

"Maybe," Grey said, "but you're the man, Warmonger. A mere mortal such as myself would naturally have trouble taking you down."

"Damn straight." Modesty was not one of his virtues.

The dreaded rumble of diesel trucks echoed from the beach. The class snapped to attention. Chief Baldwin pulled the lead truck to a stop in the sand and stepped out.

"OIC, what's your muster?"

Smurf waddled over and said something quietly.

"Eighty-six, eh? We'll see about that." Baldwin approached the line of students. "Give me a count."

A series of numbers rippled down the line, ending as Warrior grunted, "eighty-five."

"What?" The usually unflappable Baldwin kicked a spray of sand toward the students. "I try to help you out, and this is how you repay me? False muster?" He stormed up to Smurf, bent over, and yelled louder. "False muster, sir?"

Smurf just quivered in place.

"Fucking false muster? You are finished, sir. You are fucking finished!"

Grey felt his body tense up. Those were not good words from the class proctor.

"Hit the surf, sir, and think hard while you're gone. You better be able to tell me who's missing when you get back here."

Smurf grabbed his swim buddy, a petty officer, and bolted for the ocean.

"Who can give me a muster?" Baldwin bent over, scooped up handfuls of sand, and hurled them toward the class. "Someone better give me an accurate muster, because your class leader is a failure. A fucking failure!"

A hand shot up in the middle of the line.

"Let's hear it."

The student stepped forward. It was Rogers. "The correct muster is eighty-five, Chief Baldwin. Petty Officer King is presently at medical."

"At medical," Baldwin mused, stroking his mustache. "At medical . . ." A palpable wave of heat flowed into Baldwin's pale face. "Okay." He sounded calm. Too calm.

"I didn't get a chance to tell the OIC," Rogers said quietly.

Baldwin spun on his heels and stormed over to the truck. He came back with a shovel and an orange cone. "Murray, get out here." Murray obediently trotted forward. Baldwin whispered something, and Murray flailed away at the sand with the shovel. By the time Smurf and his swim buddy returned from their lengthy journey to the surf, Murray had created a shallow pit.

"Smurf. Mr. Rogers. Get comfortable," Baldwin ordered, pointing at the pit.

They dropped onto their backs.

"Bury them," he said, turning to Murray. Within a minute only their heads showed above the sand. Baldwin pulled the orange cone down over Rogers's head, hiding him from sight.

"School circle!" Baldwin yelled. Once the class had gathered around, he lowered his voice. "Leadership lesson number one: never, ever leave a man behind. I thought I already went over that, but apparently I wasn't clear enough. Next time this happens, someone will go away. I mean it. You don't have to quit, gentlemen; we can get rid of you." Baldwin nudged the orange cone with his foot. "Mr. Rogers is wearing the dunce cap because he is the source of the problem. He neglected to tell the class leader that King was at medical, thereby causing a false muster. Mr. Rogers is a safety hazard. And the OIC is always at fault, which is why Smurf is buried alongside Rogers." Baldwin regarded the buried students thoughtfully. "These two can keep me company. The rest of you line it up."

Several instructors clambered out of the diesel trucks and took their stations along the obstacle course. Warrior stood ready at the starting line, flexing and relaxing his enormous lats. Larsen, the argumentative sandy-haired seaman, stood next to the first obstacle with a stopwatch. As owner of the slowest obstacle-course time, he had the dubious honor of reading off times until someone from the front finished and took over.

"Sub-six today," Warrior grunted. "Watch me."

"You go, girl." Grey gave him a cheesy thumbs-up. Thirteen minutes was a passing time on the obstacle course. Under ten minutes was good. Sub-six was incredibly fast. Grey's personal record was 6:18.

"Go!" Warrior lifted himself off the ground and muscled his way down the parallel bars. Grey had thirty seconds before he started. He watched Warrior drag himself over the low wall before bringing his attention back to the start. "Three, two, one, go!"

Grey jumped onto the parallel bars and raced forward, carrying all his body weight on his arms. Next were the tires, which he ran through with ease. Then the low wall, the high wall, and then the dreaded barbed wire. Someone had obviously filled the pit. Occasionally students would venture out at night and deepen the crater beneath the barbed wire. Apparently the instructors had caught on and filled it in: the last wire was strung a matter of inches from the sand. Grey dropped onto his stomach and wormed forward, keeping his body pressed flat against the ground. The last wire dragged across his back as he squirmed beneath it, ripping a large hole in his shirt. He bolted to his feet and ran to the cargo net. At approximately fifty feet, the vertical net was no joke for students who were afraid of heights. Grey clambered up it with confidence, flinging himself over the top with ease. Instructor Furtado waited impatiently at the bottom.

"Give it up, sir. It's not your place to beat an enlisted man."

"We'll see," Grey said quietly as he stepped on the first balance log. It rolled freely from side to side, and he had to walk slowly to keep from slipping off. Furtado walked alongside him.

"Your balance doesn't look so good, sir. If I didn't know better, I'd say you've never done this before."

Grey continued on to the second log, then the last. Suddenly the log stiffened beneath his feet. It wasn't rolling. Grey looked over his shoulder. Furtado had a boot firmly planted on it.

"Whoops," the instructor exclaimed, pushing the log with his foot.

Grey flew backward through the air and landed on his back in the sand. *Whoops my ass.*

"Better do it again, sir." The tongue stud flashed in the sun.

Grey ran back to the start of the obstacle. *I'm not going to let this fucker slow me down.* He ignored Furtado, blocking out the instructor's crude taunts. He reached the end of the last log and moved on without hesitation. The rope transfer was a piece of cake—two ropes with a metal ring between them. Grey climbed up the first rope and used the ring to swing to the second. Then came the Dirty Name. The cursed obstacle had broken countless ribs over the years. Grey jumped up and caught the first log at stomach level. He carefully pulled himself to his feet, then he lunged for the second, higher log. With a thud his torso crashed into it, and Grey immediately threw his arms over the top to keep from slipping ten feet to the sand below. He jerked his legs rhythmically, pulled himself over the top, and dropped to the sand on the other side.

"Don't let an officer catch you," Heisler yelled to Warrior, who was losing his lead. "Don't disgrace us. You'll pay if you do."

Grey accelerated the pace as he whipped through the metal bars of the Weaver and across the unstable Burma Bridge. Warrior grunted above him, muscling his way up the three-story wooden tower. Grey slowly closed the gap, skillfully and effortlessly pulling himself upward. They reached the top platform at the same time. Now came the most famous obstacle of all—the Slide for Life. Two parallel ropes ran at a shallow angle to the ground thirty feet below. They each grabbed a line and hooked their feet over the top of the rope. Then, moving like inchworms, they hung below the line and scooted themselves downward.

"Let's go, Warrior."

"It's not over, sir."

"You had a thirty-second lead." He couldn't resist rubbing it in. "I'm way ahead."

Warrior suddenly increased his pace, hurling himself down the rope at the edge of control. He was moving too quickly.

"Careful," Grey warned, but it was too late. Warrior lost his grip and slipped through the air, landing with a thud on his back. The drop was less than twenty feet, but it was enough to do serious damage. Immediately the ambulance roared to life and raced over. Two instructors jumped out and leaned over Warrior.

Grey hurried to the end of the rope, then turned back to where Warrior lay.

"Get out of here. Finish the damn course," an instructor yelled.

Warrior wheezed loudly, his hands clutching at his chest. Burning with guilt, Grey reluctantly turned away and finished the course, his enthusiasm gone. Instructor Baldwin was waiting at the finish line.

"6:59." He looked down at his clipboard. "Major backslide. Hit the surf."

"But—"

"I said hit the surf!"

Grey did a 180 and jogged across the sandy plain toward the berm. It didn't matter how fast he navigated the obstacles. If he didn't improve his time, he got wet. *Goddamn ridiculous policy. Do professional athletes set a personal record every time they compete? No. But BUD/S students, hell, they just need to try harder.* Grey was not impressed with the logic behind punishing fast students for not improving constantly. It didn't matter if he gave it his all each time: some days would be better than others.

Grey watched with interest as Warrior rose to his feet, tenderly rubbing his chest. *Thank God.* He probably wouldn't be the only sand dart of the day. Years ago a BUD/S commanding officer had strung up a safety net below the Slide for Life. It had an unintended effect; students were no longer afraid to drop off the line, and the number of trainees who failed that particular obstacle increased. Fear was a great motivating factor.

The cool ocean was refreshing for a change. Grey sat in the shallows, resting his sore muscles. The day was far from over: drown-proofing would take up most of the afternoon. Although he was comfortable in the water, Grey didn't relish the thought of having his hands and feet tied and being thrown into a pool.

"Having fun?"

Grey looked up. Furtado stood on the berm, glaring down at him. *Fuck.*

"Since you seem to enjoy the ocean so much, why don't you stay awhile?" the instructor yelled. He walked down the berm and approached Grey. "What the hell do you think you're doing?"

"I was on my way back—"

"Bullshit. You were taking a break." Furtado ran his tongue along his moist lips. "Go ahead. Get comfortable. Lie down."

Grey lowered his torso until he was flat against the bottom and his mouth rested just above the surface of the water. Furtado's mouth moved, but Grey couldn't hear a word: the rush of the ocean flooded his ears. The tide surged and he held his breath. His initial relief faded as his body cooled. *Just another day in paradise.*

The chili macaroni sloshed in Grey's stomach as he shuffled away from the chow hall. For the first time in the history of Class 283, they actually had more than enough time to eat. In fact, they still had half an hour before they needed to get to the pool. As they were sitting in the chow hall, playing with their food, Petty Officer Young had uttered "Bat Cave" and received blank stares. The Bat Cave was a small empty plot of land sandwiched on all sides by low buildings—an ideal place to hide out. Young knew about it because this was his second time through BUD/S. He had been a member of Class 280, but three weeks from graduation he failed a run by ten seconds. Rather than drop him, the instructors had decided to send him back to day one. Grey admired the kid's tenacity.

The class jogged for several minutes before turning abruptly and filing down a narrow alley. The passage opened into a weed-infested lot paved with patchy asphalt and littered with trash. Grey knew that most people would find the place unappealing, even depressing, but to him it represented sanctuary. The class immediately flopped down and got comfortable. Grey used Rogers's stomach as a pillow.

"This is better than a warm slice of poontang." Murray sighed, closing his eyes.

"You ain't never had good poontang then," Jones drawled. "I could use a nice fat momma right about now."

"You're right about that," Rogers added. "Think of the warmth . . . her luscious bosom pressing against your back as she lovingly spoons your tired body. The release of tension, the complete relaxation . . ." He sighed dramatically.

"You're a strange cookie, sir," Murray said.

"Thanks."

"I'm sorry, but that's the truth. You should be proud of your weirdness. I've never met anyone quite like you, sir. Besides, normal is boring."

"Is that why you're such a scoundrel all the time, Murray? You're afraid of normalcy?"

"Scoundrel?"

"Scoundrel, ruffian, troublemaker—pick your word."

"I rest my case."

Grey turned his eyes to the heavens. It was gray as far as the eye could see, but a small patch of blue sky opened over his head. He watched it change shape, growing and shrinking, pulsing like a jellyfish as it slowly inched eastward. His eyes grew heavy. Suddenly he was back at school, dancing with Vanessa, holding her tight as they turned circles in her dorm room. He lifted a hand and touched her cheek. She smiled and gazed at him with bedroom eyes. He leaned in for a kiss.

"Feet!"

Grey snapped back into the world and wiped a string of drool from his chin.

"I thought we had twenty minutes to rest," Grey said to no one in particular.

"You've been asleep at least that long," Rogers said. "Now get off my stomach."

Weird. Grey reluctantly stood up. The class formed into ranks and shuffled out of the alley. Within a few minutes they were undressing on the pool deck. Grey felt his stomach churn. *Shouldn't have eaten so much.*

The rumble of diesel engines echoed from the street, throwing the class into a panic. Grey quickly bundled his clothes together and jumped to attention just as Osgood ran into the compound.

"Get wet!"

Some of the students were still undressing. They lurched to the pool with their pants around their ankles, much to the amusement of Osgood, who seemed unusually jovial. The class reassembled next to the chain-link fence.

Redman stepped through the gate. "Get wet."

The class disappeared into the pool. Heisler appeared as they climbed back out.

"Get wet."

The cycle continued until all twelve instructors were standing in the compound.

"Anyone know what all the excitement is for?" Baldwin asked. He didn't wait for an answer. "Chief Lundin got picked up for Senior Chief today." Baldwin stepped aside. "Senior Chief, they're all yours."

Senior Chief Lundin stood uncomfortably in front of the class and scratched his head. He looked at the drenched students and then at the pool. Finally he said quietly, "Get wet."

The class reappeared in front of him seconds later.

"Right." He clasped his hands in front of his stomach. "Drown-proofing. You've all practiced this before, right?"

The class mumbled an affirmation.

"Good. I'll run over the procedures real quick, just as a refresher. Your partner will tie your ankles together and your hands together behind your back. Then you get dumped in the pool. Then you bob from the bottom of the pool to the surface, back and forth, back and forth. That lasts"—he looked over at Osgood, who held up five fingers—"five minutes. Then you float on your stomach for five minutes. After that, you travel one hundred yards across the pool and back. You can start bobbing once you return to your spot. And finally, you sink to the bottom, complete a front flip, a back flip, and then retrieve your mask using your pearly whites. Any questions?"

"What if we break our restraints?" Rogers asked.

"You fail. Pick a good partner—someone who can tie a knot." Lundin scanned the group of students with red-rimmed eyes. "Anything else?"

"What if we can't float?" asked Jackson, the Mississippi Minister.

"Once again, you fail."

"But it's a racial thing, Senior Chief. Black men don't float."

"Cry me a river." Lundin chuckled. "I've seen black men pass this test." He poked Jackson's stomach with his finger. "You've got enough of a belly to keep you afloat."

"Senior." Osgood pointed at his watch.

"Right. Everyone partner up and line up at the nine-foot section. Let's get this thing started."

Rogers poked Grey in the arm. "Partner?"

"Sure. I'll go first." Grey sat at the edge of the pool and Rogers tied his hands behind his back. Once his wrists were secured, Grey strained against the line, testing the knot. "Tighter," he said.

Rogers retied the knot and moved on to Grey's ankles.

"Hurry the fuck up!" Osgood yelled. "Some of you shitheads are slower than my high school girlfriend!"

"That's pleasant," Rogers mumbled. "What a gentleman."

"Prepare to enter the water!"

Grey took a deep breath and let it out slowly. *Relax.*

"Enter the water!"

Rogers nudged Grey gently, and he slipped into the pool. He exhaled slowly, letting his body grow negatively buoyant. Soon he was standing on the bottom nine feet below. He pushed off gently . . . too gently. His momentum ran out three feet from the surface. He had a choice: let gravity slowly pull him to the bottom and try again, or thrash for the surface and look like a fool. Grey chose the former, preferring not to attract any extra attention. The pool bottom slowly rose to meet his feet, and he pushed off harder this time. *Not a good start.* His head broke the surface and he inhaled deeply. A glimpse of Rogers's face wasn't comforting; he was obviously worried. Grey smiled to reassure his friend as he exhaled through his nose. Soon he was bouncing off the bottom rhythmically, a strangely comforting motion. The silence of the pool was a nice change—no yelling, groaning, grunting, cursing.

"Float!" Rogers yelled, moving his hand horizontally back and forth.

Grey nodded and descended below the surface one more time. He collected himself as he rose off the bottom. Floating was the one aspect of drown-proofing Grey had trouble with. He was lean enough that staying on the surface required him to kick his legs steadily like a jellyfish pulsing its tentacles. As soon as his head broke the surface, Grey leaned forward and exposed as much of his back as possible to the air. *Kick. Kick. Kick.* He traveled slowly in a tight circle; the rules only allowed him a three-by-three-yard area to move around in. Every time he lifted his head for a breath, he slipped backward into the water and immediately had to lean forward again and wait patiently until his gentle kicks brought him to the surface. By the time his five minutes were up, he was on the verge of panic. He just couldn't get enough air.

"Travel!" Rogers yelled, pointing to the other side of the pool.

Thank God. Grey porpoised across the pool, moving toward the other side. Turning around presented the only challenge. He jerked his body violently and swung his legs around, all the while sinking below the surface. With a powerful kick he rose back up and began traveling in the other direction. For a little excitement, he poured on the speed, adopting the motion of a butterfly stroke without the benefit of his arms. He was the first one back, and he resumed bobbing immediately.

"Back flip!"

Grey sank to the bottom, kicked off, and immediately threw all his weight backward. He arced in a painfully slow circle as water rushed up his nose. He sank to the bottom again and pushed off, spraying water from his nostrils as he broke the surface. A hurried breath, and once again he was sinking for the bottom.

"Front flip!"

It started smoothly enough. Grey pushed off the bottom and leaned forward. His graceful circle came to a halt as his head struck the concrete. He found himself in a disheveled heap nine feet under. Grey thrashed his body, trying to get his feet beneath him. No luck. He looked up at the surface and suddenly felt an overwhelming sadness grip him. Strangely, all he could think of was his desire to someday have children and start a family. He stopped thrashing, and lay quietly on the bottom for several long seconds. *Get a grip.* With a furious lurch he managed to get up on his knees. From there he struggled to his feet and bolted for the surface.

"Front flip!" Rogers repeated, his eyes wide with concern.

Grey sawed in a ragged breath and started his descent. He learned from his previous mistake and executed a perfect flip. When he surfaced, Rogers was holding a diving mask in his hands. Grey watched the mask drop into the water several feet in front of him. He descended, touched the concrete, and pushed off at an angle, hoping that on his next descent he would be directly over the mask. Another breath, another descent. His positioning was perfect. Sinking to his knees, he leaned forward and gripped the rubber facemask strap with his teeth. After struggling back to his feet, he pushed for the surface. The mask dragged below his chin, and the force of his rapid ascent pulled the strap from his mouth. *Shit.* He bobbed several times before coming down on top of the mask again. Exhaling further, he sank down on his side and gripped the strap in his teeth. He wiggled to his feet and gently pushed for the surface. He felt the mask drag below him, spurring him to clench his teeth even harder. Rogers winked as he broke the surface. Grey bobbed two more times until he was at the side of the pool. On his last ascent, Rogers grabbed him under the arms and yanked him onto the pool deck.

"Nice job, Mark."

"Jesus," Grey groaned. "That was a bitch. I don't know why they call it drown-*proofing*. Just *drowning* would be more accurate."

"Thanks. You're really cheering me up."

"I'm just saying—"

"Silence." Rogers made a cutting gesture with his hand. "Just send me to my watery grave, Mr. Grey. I will go down like a gentleman."

"Oh, but you are a gentleman," Grey said. "I must say though, I don't think death suits you. Do me a favor and survive. But first untie my hands."

"Of course." Rogers untied Grey and they switched places. The dreaded hiss of the decontamination shower made Grey's stomach churn. He looked over his shoulder and saw a dozen students standing dejectedly under the spray of cold water.

"Failures," Rogers explained. "Smurf's in there."

"Listen up, motherfuckers!" Osgood yelled. "Two minutes and we're switching. Don't be late!"

Grey finished tying up Rogers and stood by, ready to push him into the pool. The Reverend Jackson sat a few feet away, staring blankly at the water.

"Hey, Reverend," Grey said, "I know you can handle this. Just stay calm."

"Right. Stay calm," Jackson repeated quietly.

"Enter the water!" Osgood yelled.

With a slight push, Grey sent Rogers to the bottom of the pool. He divided his time between watching Rogers and Jackson. He was definitely more worried about the preacher. Rogers appeared to Grey to be comfortable in the water, but even looking at Jackson in the pool made Grey feel panicked. They both made it through the bobbing phase without incident. Time for the floating.

"Float!" Grey yelled.

Rogers came to the surface and immediately began floating. The Reverend bobbed a few more times and finally spread himself flat, exposing nearly every inch of his body to the air, doing everything he could to stay on the surface. Grey shook his head in disbelief. Something wasn't right. He looked again. Yes, the Reverend was sinking. He wasn't thrashing, splashing, or showing any other signs of panic. His body was in the correct position, and he was sinking. Quickly. As he settled on the bottom, an instructor swam down and pulled him to the surface.

"Failure!" the instructor yelled, dragging Jackson to the side. "Petty Officer Jackson!"

"Roger that," Osgood said, scrawling the name in his notebook. "Jackson, join your friends in the decon." He jerked a thumb toward the group of students huddled together in the shower.

Grey shot the Reverend an apologetic look and received a weak smile in reply. *Racial,* the preacher mouthed silently.

Rogers made it through drown-proofing without incident, and he and Grey sat together in the winner's corner while a half dozen students, including Murray, retook their knot-tying test. Half an hour later Murray had passed the test, and the class assembled on the road and jogged back to the BUD/S compound. A brutal conditioning run followed, during which Grey puked a stream of chlorinated pool water onto the sand. Despite his intestinal trouble, he managed to avoid being gooned. After eight miles of agony, Chief Baldwin stopped in front of the compound and dismissed the class.

"Friday dance!" Murray shouted. He put a hand on his crotch and bounced forward across the sand. "It's Friday, it's Friday!" He slapped an imaginary ass. "Friday, baby, Friday!"

"Let's get out of here," Grey suggested. "The sooner the better."

Murray's dance came to a sudden halt. A serious look crossed his face. "Not yet, sir. We have some business to attend to."

"We?" Grey asked. "*You*, not we."

"I need a swim buddy. It will only take a second. I just want to talk to the Master at Arms."

"Murray, I told you I'm not getting involved in your crap."

"Please." Murray dropped to his knees. "Please. I'll owe you one."

"Get up," Grey ordered, pulling him to his feet. "You're embarrassing me."

"Then let's go before I really make you look like a jackass."

Grey reluctantly followed Murray to the edge of the grinder and waited while Murray knocked on the door to the armory. Several seconds of silence passed before a wiry man with Coke-bottle glasses pulled the door open. He wore a wrinkled camouflage uniform, and his oily brown hair lay in a tangled mess on his small head. He was one of the many non-SEALs who kept the base running smoothly.

"What?"

"Chief, I was wondering if I could have a word with you," Murray began. "I just had a few questions about—"

"Come on in," he said quickly. "I'm finishing up an inventory and I want to go home, so forgive me if I'm a little blunt."

"I just wanted to ask you about exactly that—your inventory. Apparently the guys in Third Phase are having a hard time keeping track of everything, and I heard the instructors will really beat the crap out of us if we slip up. I was wondering if you had any pointers or suggestions so we can stay out of trouble when we start practicing at the range."

"That's still a long ways off," the chief said, "but I like your attitude. Better to start preparing early than never." He adjusted his enormous black military-issue glasses. "The main thing is to keep accurate logs. Check everything in and out, keep a close tabs on the ammo you're actually expending, and for God's sake, don't try to keep any rounds as souvenirs."

Murray nodded attentively. "So it's true then?"

"What?"

"You've been having inventory problems?"

The wiry chief chuckled. "Let's just say it's a good thing I made chief six years ago, because I wouldn't have a prayer the way things are going now." He dropped his clipboard on a metal countertop. "It takes an act of Congress to take away the rank of chief, and they wouldn't bother, because I'm about to retire."

"It's that bad?"

"I'm exaggerating a bit," the chief conceded. "That's a privilege of old age." He flashed his tobacco-stained smile, and the skin around his eyes wrinkled. "I'm getting to be an old fart. Just looking at you young kids makes me a little envious." His smile faded. "To answer your question, though, ammo is the main problem. I just don't feel like I'm getting enough of it back. I'm suspicious that one of the students is fixing the logs. God only knows why you'd do something stupid like that. And I've been tracking our demolitions carefully for a year." He shrugged. "Something's just not right. On top of everything, my spares also seem to be walking off, but I suspect that's because those dang SEAL instructors keep taking parts to fix the M-4s without properly signing them out."

"Well, chief, rest assured that when we're in Third Phase, we'll do a better job for you," Murray said. "Ensign Grey and I will keep the class squared away."

"I hope you do, for the sake of the chief that relieves me. I don't want to leave a mess behind for the poor bastard."

"Thanks for the tips, chief, and let us know if we can do anything for you," Murray said as they moved toward the armory door.

"Good luck, sailor." The chief shifted his gaze toward Grey and acknowledged his presence with a stiff nod. "You too, ensign."

"Thanks." Grey followed Murray out into the fading sunlight.

"Interesting," Murray murmured as they limped toward Building 618. "Old chief confirmed my suspicion. Redman took his bad habits with him when he left Team Four."

"Maybe it's just sloppiness," Grey suggested. "Or maybe it's just really hard to maintain a good inventory. We don't know Redman's responsible."

"Sir, are you kidding me? It's got to be Redman."

"Could be," Grey said. "I wouldn't rule it out. I'm just playing devil's advocate."

"Big bad instructor's gonna go down!" Murray exclaimed. "Now I'm armed and dangerous!"

"You have no proof," Grey reminded him. "*And* I still think you're a fool if you mess with him. This isn't child's play."

"I know. I wish you'd stop saying shit like that," Murray said. He glanced at Grey uneasily. "No disrespect meant, sir. I know you're my superior, but it's not *your* BUD/S career on the line."

"That's not true, Murray," Grey said. "You and I both know it."

"They want me, not you." Murray punched Grey lightly on the arm. "But enough shoptalk. It's Friday night. Time to go out and kick a little ass."

"Sounds good to me," Grey said. "I could use a beer or two."

"Two?" Murray laughed. "Try ten."

They hobbled together toward the barracks as the sun arced toward the sea, their groggy heads filled with thoughts of hot showers and pints of beer.

SEVEN

VANESSA, PLEASE LISTEN. I really wanted to see you tonight." Grey swallowed nervously and gripped the phone so hard his knuckles shone white. "I mean, I still want to see you. I always want to see you. It's just that tonight is sort of a boys' night out." He waited for some kind of response. Nothing. "Please try to understand—"

"Oh, I understand, Mark. I'm just wondering why I'm driving down Interstate Five all dressed up for a nice dinner with my boyfriend."

"You're already in your car?" Grey felt his face flush hot. "I didn't know—"

"The beauty of cell phones, babe. I left when I said I would."

Grey felt his heart constrict in his chest. "I'm so sorry. I wish you would have told me that."

"It doesn't really matter, does it?"

"Yes, it does. Let's just forget everything. I'm sorry. Let's go to dinner."

"No," Vanessa sighed, "I think the mood's spoiled. Don't you?"

"No. Just keep driving. I'll make it up to you, I promise. We can even eat Japanese." Grey thought this was a big concession. He absolutely hated Japanese.

"Thoughtful, but no thanks. Listen, I'll get over it. I'm just a little fed up with this whole situation. I don't care if you want to go out with the boys, but a little prior warning would be nice next time."

"Just come. Please come."

"I'm exiting the freeway. I'm turning"—she paused—"and I'm heading north. I'll talk to you later." The line went dead.

Grey called back and waited anxiously for the line to be picked up. After ten rings he slammed the phone down and stormed back to his room. *You're a real Casanova, Mark.* He heard Rogers singing Johnny Lee's "Lookin for Love" in the shower before he even opened the door.

Suddenly he switched moods and launched into an aria, his pseudo-operatic voice warbling uncontrollably. Normally his friend's antics would have cheered Grey up. Tonight they just made him more frustrated. *My girlfriend hates me, and I'm rooming with a lunatic from Princeton.*

Suddenly the warbling stopped. "Stop being so melodramatic!"

"What?" Grey asked incredulously. "What?"

"I said stop the melodrama. Everything's going to be fine." Rogers voice echoed from the bathroom. "First you slam the door, then you hurl your boots into your locker. Just relax."

Grey sat down on the floor, thoroughly perplexed. "You're a freak, you know that?"

"I know. But then again, aren't we all?" He picked up his aria where he had left off.

Holding his head in his hands, Grey waited for his turn in the shower. He ran over his conversation with Vanessa a million times in his head and cringed with each rehashing of the dialogue. *Jackass.* What to do? He sat motionless for a while, then suddenly jerked his head up. *Flowers.* That was it. He grabbed his cell phone.

Ten minutes and 120 dollars later, flowers were on their way to L.A. The florist had been unhappy about making a delivery when she was closing shop in ten minutes, but an extra sixty dollars did the trick.

"Welcome to my world, sir," Murray said, gesturing at the dance floor full of grinding bodies. "More pussy than you can shake a stick at."

"Fabulous." Grey walked over to the bar and ordered a beer. It arrived in a plastic cup. *Classy.* They had all ridden the bus to downtown San Diego, and Murray had led them to his favorite club. Now they were in the basement of some building, buried amid a mess of sweaty bodies in a fine establishment called either the Hurricane, Tsunami, or Tidal

Wave. Grey couldn't remember. He sipped his beer and watched the crowd. The Reverend Jackson emerged from the cluster of dancing bodies and strolled over to the bar.

"How's it going, sir?"

"Not bad, Jackson. Buy you a beer?"

"Don't drink," he answered. "My daddy drank, and it was an ugly thing. Almost killed him."

"So I guess you came for the scenery?"

"That's right," Jackson said. "I'm bringing righteousness to the wicked. Consider me a missionary, bringing God's word to the lonely women of the world." He laughed easily. "Don't buy into my act, sir. I like a pretty woman just like the next man, but I *am* a strong Christian. I'm not going to stick it in just anything that moves, unlike some of the characters in our class."

"Speaking of . . ." Grey said, gesturing toward the other end of the bar. Ensign Pollock, the redhead Academy grad, was licking salt off an amply endowed woman's neck. He threw back a shot of tequila then used his teeth to pull a lime slice from her mouth. Murray approached the couple with a mischievous twinkle in his eyes. He tapped Pollock on the shoulder, and when the ensign turned, Murray ducked the other way and kissed the woman forcefully on the lips. Pollock swung back around, and his eyes went wide. Before he could react, Murray was gone, swallowed up by the crowd.

"Impressive." Grey downed the last of his cheap beer. "Let's see your moves, Jackson. Time to get your groove on."

"Look at you," the Reverend said, "trying to talk like a black man and all."

A marine standing next to Jackson overheard the conversation. He belched loudly and put his arm around Jackson's shoulder. "Take it to the bone, brother jive. Slap my fro. You dig, home slice?"

"Shut up before you embarrass me." Jackson looked around warily. "It's all good with me, but some brothas wouldn't appreciate your antics. Know what I mean?"

"What? You don't like jive?" The man's eyes were a glazed blue, his nose red. "C'mon man. I can hang." He burped again. "Or do I have to be a Negro to talk like that?"

"You better stop, brother, or I might get the impression you're insulting me." Jackson was no longer smiling.

"And what if I was?" The marine leaned in close. His breath stunk of alcohol.

"Then I'd say you were a dumb-ass jarhead who was about to get his ass beat."

"By who?" Another sickening wave of tequila breath.

"Me."

The marine put his hand against Jackson's chest and pushed hard.

"Do that again and you'll be sorry."

"Ooohhh, scary." Another push.

"I warned you." With a few deft movements, Jackson had the man on his stomach. He twisted an arm behind his back and asked, "Now are you going behave, or do I need to break your arm?"

The marine didn't answer. As the crowd gathered around, Jackson released him. He stood up slowly and brushed his clothes off. Jackson turned back to the bar and pretended nothing had happened.

"Watch out," Grey yelled, but he was too late.

A meaty fist connected with Jackson's head, and the Reverend jerked forward, temporarily stunned. Grey gave the marine a hard uppercut, resulting in a satisfying *thunk* as the jarhead's chin jerked up and he fell over backward. It had been at least fifteen years since he had hit anyone, and he was enthralled by the experience. Suddenly a fist connected with Grey's kidneys, and he doubled over in pain. He turned just as another punch slammed into his eye. Pain radiated through his skull as he staggered backward. The crowd erupted into a frenzy, and Murray jumped up and delivered a powerful kick to the attacking marine's back. The jarhead's body bowed backward unnaturally, and he groaned with pain as he fell to the ground. A dozen BUD/S students entered the fray as a group of marines materialized from the crowd.

"Shore patrol!" the bartender yelled. "Shore patrol!"

Just as quickly as it had begun, the fighting stopped, and there was a mad rush for the door. An overweight bouncer wearing gold chains tried to stop Grey by holding out a beefy arm.

"Step aside, shithead!" Warrior yelled, pushing the bouncer flat up against the wall. "After you, sir!"

"Thanks." Grey rushed up the stairs and stepped outside. He ran down the sidewalk and turned at the next corner. A group of BUD/S students stood huddled together football style, discussing their next move. One of them lifted his head and saw Grey approaching.

"Get in here, you animal!"

Grey joined the huddle.

"I think we should find those marines and beat the shit out of them," a skinny kid from Nebraska was saying.

"Nah. I think we oughta go over to McP's and tell war stories," Jones drawled. McP's was a bona fide SEAL hangout; BUD/S students were not welcome there.

"Bad idea," Murray said. "I know one thing for sure. We need to get Mr. Grey shit-faced. He deserves it after landing that beautiful uppercut."

"Amen," Jackson said, joining the group. "Whitey here avenged my ass."

Grey smiled. "Whatever you guys want. You buy the drinks, I'll drink 'em."

"It's settled then," Murray said. "Let's go."

They descended into another seedy club, and the drinks started rolling in. Grey lost count somewhere after twelve and decided he'd had enough. His fellow students disagreed. He sampled the finest concoctions the club had to offer—a Gorilla Fart, a Cement Mixer, a Mind Eraser. The room started to spin.

"Enough!" Grey held up an unsteady hand. "I'll puke in your face."

"I dare you," Murray taunted.

"Fine." A rumble started deep in Grey's stomach and moved its way up his throat. He thought back to his childhood and rehashed the gross-out contests his brother had enjoyed so much. *Mmmm, tasty. A greasy slab of pork served up in a dirty ashtray. French-fried eyeballs floating in a bowl of blood.* Grey felt his throat unclench, and a stream of vomit flew through the air. Murray stepped back just in time, and the puke splattered on his shoes.

"Impressive, sir," Murray said, unfazed.

"What the fuck, guys?" the bartender asked. He was a pasty-skinned young man with a series of chains connecting his numerous facial piercings.

"Shut up or I'll pull that shit off your face," Murray said.

The bartender stalked off toward the back of the club.

"Time to go." Murray grabbed Grey by the arm and dragged him up the stairs. They stumbled outside into the cool night air. Grey thought of something funny to say, but by the time he opened his mouth the thought had passed. He suddenly became embarrassingly aware of his drunkenness.

"Take me home."

"I am, boss."

"Please just take me home."

They finally reached the bus stop and plopped down on the curb. After sitting in silence for several minutes, Rogers ambled over.

"How now, brown cow?"

"Fuck, Rogers. You been drinking, too?" Murray asked.

"Aye. A pint of ale is a fine thing—all the sustenance a man needs."

"Right. What next? You gonna break out in song."

"Not a bad idea, shipmate." Rogers cleared his throat noisily. "This little ditty is a fine thing I picked up from our instructor friends. It goes something like this:

> Drink, drink, drink, drink,
> Drunk, drunk, drunk, drunk.
> Drunk last night, drunk the night before,
> Gonna get drunk like I never have before.
> 'Cause when I'm drunk I'm as happy as can be
> 'Cause I am a member of the Frog Family.

Grey and Murray stood up and joined in for the second verse. They wobbled back and forth together, their arms linked over each other's shoulders.

> Well, the Frog Family is the best family
> That ever sailed across the seven seas.
> There's a highland frog and a lowland frog,
> An underwater frog and a gosh-darn frog.
> Singin' glorious, glorious! One keg of beer for the four of us!

Thank God that there are no more of us
'Cause one of us is drinkin' all the beer, damn near!

Just as they were launching into the third verse the bus pulled up and the door opened with a hiss. They spent a few frantic seconds scrounging in their pockets for change, finally finding the right amount and clumsily depositing it in the receptacle. The bus driver looked them over with tired eyes.

"Know where you're going?" he asked.

"To the Isle of Coronado," Rogers answered, "where the finest warriors in the land keep their quarters."

"Whatever, guy." The door hissed shut and the bus took off. They collectively decided that the coolest kids always sat at the back of the bus, so they stumbled past a few passengers and took their seats. Just as they were nearing the Hotel del Coronado Rogers suddenly stood up and pulled the stop cable. The bus groaned to a halt at the next stop.

"But we're not back yet," Murray protested. "What's your deal, Rogers?"

"Just trust me." Rogers stepped down onto the street and beckoned for the others to follow. Grey followed Murray off the bus and checked his watch. It was only eleven thirty. A lot had happened in three hours. Rogers led them around the back of the hotel and they stumbled along the umbrella-lined sidewalk. The faint hum of conversing voices rose up nearby. Rogers suddenly stopped and opened a door, and they found themselves staring into a luxuriously appointed bar. With a pompous gesture he brushed imaginary lint from his cheap jacket and made a grand entrance. Grey and Murray shrugged and followed him in. All eyes in the room were on the newly arrived patrons.

"Can I help you?" the bartender asked.

"Yes. I'm here to play," Rogers said in a clipped British accent, pointing at the piano.

"I'm sorry. Maybe you should try back tomorrow. We're winding down."

"No. I must play," he stated with finality and strolled toward the grand piano at the front of the room.

The bartender started to pick up a phone, but Murray grabbed his arm. "I'm sorry. We'll get him out of here. Please."

Rogers began to play, and suddenly the room grew quiet. He launched into a difficult piece, his body swaying slightly, his eyes nearly closed. The bartender gaped. Murray stopped breathing for several seconds. Grey felt like he was going to puke. The crowd *ooh*ed as Rogers continued his flawless performance. When a scowling security guard stalked into the room and headed for the piano, a distinguished-looking gentleman wearing a tuxedo shooed him away. The music was amazing, uplifting, absolutely perfect. Grey bolted out the back door and puked in the flowers. He dropped to his knees on the concrete sidewalk and heaved in silence. The muffled sound of Rogers's playing floated through the air, and Grey wiped the vomit from his chin and smiled. The music continued for several minutes, surging, pulsing, silencing the crowd. Finally it eased to a stop, and the crowd erupted into applause. Rogers and Murray bolted out the door seconds later.

"The charm has worn off. Let's get out of here," Rogers suggested. They ran past the hotel's tennis courts and onto the beach.

"Hold on." Grey dropped to his knees again and retched. "Better." He took off his shoes, and they continued out to the water's edge. The surf roared into shore, surging on the high tide.

"Look at that." Rogers pointed at an extensive pile of rocks that extended out into the surf. "Rock portage. We get to land our boats on those beauties." Just then a wave slammed into the rocks, sending a curtain of spray into the air. "Get caught between your boat and a rock and kiss your legs good-bye."

Murray whistled. "That's some bad shit. Too bad Ramirez isn't here. He'd eat those rocks for breakfast."

"Shut up," Grey said quietly. He thought of Ramirez in a sterile hospital bed, immobile, alone.

"I didn't mean anything bad."

"I know. Just shut up." Grey picked up a stone and threw it into the surf. It made a tiny blip on the surface and then disappeared. "I'm sorry. Let's go."

They turned to the south and moved slowly toward their barracks, occasionally stopping to throw a rock into the ocean. *Blip.*

A loud knock on the door wrenched Grey from his alcohol-enhanced slumber. His head pulsed and throbbed as he stood up and groped his way toward the door. Clumsily he pressed his eye against the peephole and was shocked at the sight of Vanessa's grotesquely bloated face peering back at him. *Damn peephole.* It could even make beautiful people like Vanessa look like trolls.

"Hi, baby," Grey mumbled, swinging the door open. The sunlight blinded him momentarily, and he closed his eyes to block out the glare. "What are you doing here?"

"You look great, honey," Vanessa said, glancing at Grey's black eye. "And you smell like a rose. . . ."

Grey could only imagine the stench. He didn't remember brushing his teeth, just crawling into bed. "Sorry. I had a rough night."

"Apparently." She pushed past him and sat on his bed. "Enough of the chitchat. What the hell happened to your eye?"

"I fell."

"Into someone's fist? Mark, that isn't like you. You never fight."

"I know." He gestured toward the other bed, where a shapeless lump was shifting groggily beneath the covers. "Rogers isn't up. Let's talk outside. Just let me brush my teeth first."

He walked into the bathroom and did a double take. The man in the mirror was completely foreign. Grey liked to think of himself as reasonably good-looking. The character staring back at him looked like a neo-Nazi fresh from a barroom brawl. His face was tan, but his shaved head was ghostly white, and his left eye was a swollen purple mess. *Jesus.* He touched his eye and winced.

Vanessa was standing with her face to the ocean when Grey stepped outside of his room. Her long black hair was blowing in the gentle breeze, and her stance, arms crossed, legs planted firmly apart, suggested she was either pensive or upset.

"Hi," Grey said softly, placing a hand on her shoulder.

"Hey." She took a step back, forcing him to drop his hand. "Let's walk." She led the way, striding swiftly over the sand berm and onto the beach. The briny smell of the ocean was strong, and it made Grey recoil instinctively. The ocean made him think of one thing: *cold.*

"I'm sorry about last night," Grey said.

"I know. I got the flowers."

"And?"

"I was touched, and I came here to make passionate love to you to show my gratitude."

"But?"

"Well, besides the fact that you smell like puke and look like a battle-worn paramilitary freak, I'm a little concerned about how this place is changing you."

"What do you mean?"

Vanessa stopped walking and turned toward Grey. "What do you think? When was the last time you got in a fight?"

"Sometime about—"

"I know when. Third grade. I'm just making a point. It's not like you."

"Look," Grey said, "when we started going out I didn't hide anything from you. I told you I wanted to be a SEAL more than anything else, and nothing would stand in my way. Right?"

Vanessa nodded.

"And didn't I warn you that I might change during training?"

"Yes, but—"

"Let me finish," Grey said gently. "I feel like I have to say this. It's hard to describe what I'm feeling right now. I'm revolted by the face I see in the mirror, but I have to tell you, knocking that asshole marine on his back was one of the most satisfying things I've done in a long time."

"Mark!"

"I'm serious. I really enjoyed it. Fighting for a friend when you know he would do the same for you—it's an amazing feeling. It's why I want to be a SEAL. It's a brotherhood. You suffer together, eat together, fight together. . . ."

"C'mon, Mark. You sound like a damn navy recruiter." Vanessa searched his face. "Where is the boy I used to know?"

The throbbing in Grey's head grew more intense. "I'm still here."

"Is this going to be forever? This violence thing?"

"SEALs are trained to take lives, Vanessa. It's irresponsible to sign up for this line of work without considering the possibility of killing."

"But you don't have to enjoy it."

"And you know I wouldn't. Just because I threw a punch at some loudmouthed jarhead doesn't mean I'm on some downward moral spiral. It's just that I'd give the world for my boys, and if it means throwing a punch, so be it."

Vanessa pulled off her shoes and dug her toes into the sand. "This is going to be harder than I thought."

"What is?"

"Us. Surviving this thing. Being apart constantly."

"But is it worth it to you?"

Vanessa drew a circle in the sand with her toe. The silence was overwhelming.

"Is it?"

"If you can promise me you'll be the same man I met four years ago when you get out of this place."

"You know I can't do that." Grey reached out and gently grazed his hand against her cheek. "But I can promise I will always love you."

Vanessa stood on her toes and kissed him on the forehead. "I should go."

Grey watched her turn and walk back toward the barracks, shoes in hand. He thought about following her and convincing her to stay, but he couldn't do it. Instead he sat in the sand and watched the angry ocean throw whitecaps toward shore. The urge to cry competed with the urge to hurt something. He picked up a handful of white sand and let it run through his fingers. A seagull landed near his feet and pranced back and forth, strutting fearlessly across the beach. Grey picked up a pebble and threw it. To his surprise it hit the gull's neck. The bird squawked angrily and took to the air.

"What?" Grey yelled irritably. He had crawled back into bed an hour before, and he still felt horrible. The loud knocks on his door presented an unwelcome distraction.

"Sir, it's me." The voice belonged to Murray.

"I'm having a bad morning. Go away."

"I have something important you should hear about."

"Later."

"Sir, it will only take a minute."

"Make it quick." Grey strained to pry his eyes open. He squinted against the sunlight that flooded the room as Murray opened the door. "There was a murder yesterday," Murray stated, waving a newspaper in Grey's face.

"Who died?"

"A gun-shop owner in Imperial Beach. He was out on bail after being arraigned on charges of selling illegal weapons and explosives."

"So what?" Grey was more concerned with his splitting headache than a murder in Imperial Beach.

"Sir, make the connection. Work with me here," Murray pleaded. "He was found garroted in his own house. It was a clean job. The police don't have any suspects yet. The guy was selling illegal shit. He had been nailed earlier selling C-4, automatic weapons, ammo. Whoever knocked him off must have either been in competition with him or, more likely, didn't want him to squeal about something." He slapped the newspaper against the top of Grey's head. "This is some serious shit, sir. You think that the inventory problems at BUD/S might somehow be tied to a small-time arms broker? Can you think of a better source of C-4? That shit is expensive as fuck. You could make a tidy little profit selling it."

"It's possible," Grey admitted reluctantly. He tried to hide from the light, burying his head beneath a pillow. "I think you should worry about making it through training. The police will figure it out."

"Fuck the police. I could be done with BUD/S by the time they figure anything out."

Grey struggled into a sitting position. "Murray, this whole blackmail idea just reached a new level. The stakes are higher. Leave it be."

"I don't think so, boss. I think I'll wander down to IB and pay a visit to this gun shop. If it gets too crazy, I'll back down and forget the whole thing."

"You're a stubborn fool, you know that?" Grey said.

"Sir, I know my shortcomings," Murray said. He pulled open the door and stood profiled against the bright morning light. "Get some sleep."

"Good luck," Grey mumbled. "Be careful." He dropped his head back onto his pillow and fell into a restless sleep.

EIGHT

*M*ONDAY MORNING, SIX DAYS *to Hell Week*. Grey toed the line drawn in the sand and tensed his body in anticipation. He had twenty-four minutes to run slightly over four miles. Redman expected improvement every week, and Grey was feeling less energetic by the day. BUD/S was supposed to make students stronger, but he knew every day he spent in training he lost a little bit of his edge. It was almost as if he were being punished for showing up in exceptional shape. The other students started from ground zero and finished training as decent runners. Grey felt that he started as an unusually good runner but that he would most likely graduate from BUD/S as a mediocre athlete. The daily beat-downs took their toll on his body.

"I want no failures today," Chief Baldwin stated. He leaned out the window of the big diesel truck. "Failure means surf torture, and I'm not in the mood to hammer anyone today." He glanced at his watch. "Ready . . . go!"

The line of students erupted into a sprint. Grey never understood why the class always felt compelled to bolt from the starting line when the race was four miles long. He ran in the middle of the pack, pacing himself. The second half of the run was crucial. It wasn't even six in the morning, so the beach was deserted. Grey occupied his mind with thoughts of Vanessa. He had always worried about the toll BUD/S would take on their relationship. Now it seemed his fears were being played out. He was tired, he was angry, and he was letting the love of his life slip through his fingers.

"I'm running with you today, boss," Murray said as Grey moved up to his shoulder.

"Good. I could use some company."

They continued north past the rock pile and the Hotel del Coronado. Murray fell off the pace in a matter of minutes. The white truck that marked the halfway point was parked facing south, and Grey ran around it counterclockwise. Instructor Furtado read off his time: "12:30, slow-ass motherfucker." Undaunted, Grey picked up the pace. He almost always ran negative splits—the second of half of his run was faster than the first. The rest of the class streamed past in the opposite direction, yelling encouragement as Grey flew back to the starting line. He flashed a smile and a thumbs-up. Several hundred yards behind the pack, a figure appeared, hobbling down the beach alone. Grey recognized the massive shoulders and arms immediately. *Warrior.*

"Pick it up, Warrior!" Grey yelled. "You need this run!" He desperately wanted to stop and physically push his classmate down the beach, but he knew that stopping would only make the situation worse for both of them.

Warrior shook his head in disgust. He was limping badly. *Must be stress fractures.* They were the bane of everyone's existence at BUD/S. At least a fifth of the class suffered from them at some point during training. Grey refocused himself as he continued down the beach. The run started to hurt, and he started to feel alive. He tilted his head back, a bad habit he acquired in high school and that he had never been able to shake. The faster he ran, the sloppier his form became. He raced past the hotel and past the high-rise condominiums. A lone jogger clad in a bright blue sweat suit and headband eyed him curiously as he sprinted past. His breath grew ragged.

Grey felt anger flood his mind like a shot of adrenaline. He was mad at Vanessa, mad about Ramirez and his paralysis, mad at Furtado for being an ass, mad at himself for getting in a fight, mad at BUD/S for making him mad. The anger burned through him, and he punished himself by turning up the pace a notch. He was flying. Redman stood at the finish line, silent, waiting to pounce. *Fuck you. You're not going to get me. Not today.* His pace was impossibly fast. Grey looked toward the sky. *You better kill me, God, because I'm not slowing down.* Arms churning, legs swallowing whole lengths of the beach at a time, Grey flashed across the finish line. He stopped next to an instructor truck and leaned against it for support. *Don't lie to me. I passed that run.*

Redman glanced at his watch and then turned toward the ocean. *I passed the damn run.* Redman stood in silence, watching the surf. Grey knew this meant he had passed. It was Redman's ultimate compliment—no words of encouragement, just silence. Heavy, brooding silence. As suddenly as Grey's anger had come, it passed. The endorphins crashed in, leaving him elated and dizzy.

Jones crossed the line minutes later, then Murray, and then the bulk of the class. As soon as thirty-two minutes had passed, Redman sprang back into life. The students unfortunate enough to fail the run ran directly to the surf. Heads hung low in shame, they linked arms in the shallows and lay on their backs. The truck driven by Furtado trailed Warrior down the beach. Furtado had his head out the window and was undoubtedly yelling insults at the limping student. *Asshole.* Grey ran toward Warrior and stopped at his side.

"Get out of here!" Furtado yelled. "He doesn't need you!"

Grey ignored the comment. "C'mon, Warrior, let's pick it up. I'll run you in." He stayed on the muscle-bound student's shoulder and gradually increased the pace. They crossed the finish line together.

"Thirty-seven minutes," Redman noted. His perpetual scowl dominated his dark face. "You'll pay for that, you slacker. Hit the surf. Grey, you too. Since you obviously care about your buddy so much, you can keep his worthless ass warm."

They ran into the surf together and joined the lineup. The other students were already twitching and shaking, and Grey closed his eyes as the icy water closed over his shoulders.

"Thanks, bud," Warrior said quietly. "I owe you."

"You owe me nothing," Grey responded. "Nothing at all."

They locked arms and wormed close together, conserving as much warmth as possible. As the minutes slipped by, Grey lost track of time. His world was dominated by one thought: *cold.*

As the class ran to breakfast, the feeling slowly returned to his frozen limbs. Sixteen students had failed the run—sixteen too many. The tone was set for the day. Punishment would be the theme, and the battered students of Class 283 would be the unfortunate players. Grey could hardly wait to discover what twisted new torture regime the instructors would cook up.

The enlisted students filed through the chow line, followed by the officers. Grey stopped for his traditional chat with Felicia.

"How's it going, beautiful?"

Felicia giggled and turned her eyes downward. "Not bad, Mr. Grey. Same thing as always."

"You like working here?" Grey asked, leaning his elbows on the counter. "This hardly seems like the place for someone of your caliber."

"What does that mean—*caliber*?"

"You know, someone of your quality. Your good looks, your charm."

"It's not bad," she mused. "But I would like to be a movie star." Her eyes lit up. "Hollywood," she said slowly, drawing out each syllable. "What a place. Everyone rich there, right?"

"Not exactly," Grey said. "There are the lucky few who make it. But there are even more burned-out waitresses who never got their big break. Hollywood eats people alive. I was thinking more along the lines of having you go back to school, maybe get a degree."

"But I don't speak well, and I write even worse."

"So?"

"How would I go to college?"

"Well, you could start with community college. Then move on to one of the universities. It would be worth your time, I promise."

"I'll think about it," Felicia said. She opened her mouth to say more, but nothing came out. Her eyes went wide.

Grey started to turn to see what had caught her attention, when a steely hand clamped down on his shoulder.

"Can I have a word outside, Mr. Grey?" Redman asked. Before Grey could answer, he was being pushed out the door and onto the sidewalk.

"Is there a problem, Instructor Redman?" Grey asked, looking up into the familiar angry black eyes.

"Yes, sir. Just a minor one." Redman leaned in close. "You better stop that thing of yours right now."

"What thing?"

"You know what I mean," Redman growled. "It's hardly appropriate for an officer to be banging the food-service lady. That could get you in a lot of trouble." He sneered. "I bet she's a good fuck, though, isn't she?"

Grey felt his face flush red.

"I bet she's a nice piece of work. A real LBFM. She'll do everything, won't she?"

"First of all," Grey stated angrily, "I am nothing more than a friend. Second of all, it's really none of your business. She is a contract employee, not a member of the navy. Fraternization is not an issue. You're way out of line—"

"Don't lecture me, you superior piece of shit," Redman snarled.

"Fuck off." Grey could hardly believe the words coming from his mouth. "Mind your own damn business."

Redman's eyes went wide. "Sir, if you make it through this program it will be a miracle. I'm going to make it a matter of personal pride that you fail. You and that loser Murray. And don't you ever, ever lecture me again, or I'll throw away my career just for the opportunity to kick your ass."

Grey bit his tongue. There was nothing he could say to diffuse the situation. Redman spat at Grey's feet, then turned and disappeared back into the chow hall. *I'm dead.* Grey took a deep breath, collected himself, and walked back into the building. Felicia gave him an inquiring look, but he just shook his head and continued down the line. He heaped a huge load of scrambled eggs and bacon on his plate, followed by pancakes with syrup, sausage, yogurt, and coffee cake. The extra calories would be crucial during Hell Week, when students routinely burned ten thousand calories a day. Grey found Murray sitting alone at a table.

"What's going on, boss man?" Murray asked in between spoonfuls of hot cereal.

"You're not the only one Redman wants out of this program."

"What happened?" Murray asked, raising an eyebrow. "I need details."

"The asshole called Felicia an LBFM and told me I shouldn't be banging her."

"A little brown fucking machine?" Murray asked, smiling. "I haven't heard that term in a while. So what's the problem?"

"I told him to fuck himself and to mind his own business. His reply was that he is going to make it a matter of pride that you and I don't make it."

"That wasn't the smartest thing to say, sir."

"I know," Grey said. "My anger got the better of me." He poked at his pancakes. "So tell me about your little investigation of the gun shop. Any luck?"

A shadow passed across Murray's face. He spoke quietly. "I don't want to talk about it. You were right. I was a fool to even go down there. I'm done snooping around."

"No kidding?" Grey asked. "What happened?"

"Nothing," Murray stated with finality. His big eyes never left his plate.

"Well, if that's it, we need to focus on getting out of here in one piece. Redman hates you, and now he hates me, and we're going to have to work that much harder to make it out of this program." Grey intently looked Murray in the eyes. "We need to make a pact."

"Okay. What about?"

"That we'll both make it. That we won't quit no matter what. Hell Week is coming up, and if we can make it through that, I think we'll have a chance." Grey extended a hand.

Murray clasped it firmly in both of his. "What are we swearing on again?"

"That we won't quit no matter how thick the shit gets."

"Deal. But we should make the pact official."

"What do you mean?"

Murray grabbed a dull knife with serrated edges and brought both his arms under the table. He winced for a second, then passed the knife over to Grey. "You know what to do."

"Are you kidding me? Are we in fifth grade?"

"Sir, I'm bleeding all over myself here."

"Let's stick with something symbolic. We'll make up a secret handshake or something."

"Sir . . ." Murray shot him a dirty look.

"Unbelievable." Grey looked around to make sure no one was watching, then sawed into his arm until a trickle of blood started flowing.

Murray extended his bleeding arm across the table. Grey reached out and they pressed their arms together.

"You better not have any blood-borne diseases," Grey joked. "This feels like part of a bad Western film. Either that or some antiquated Boy Scout ritual." He smiled. "So I guess we're blood brothers now?"

"Exactly. This is fraternization at the highest level. You could get court-marshaled for this, sir."

"Fuck it. If they want to cart me away, let them try."

Murray pulled his arm away seconds later. "It's official now. Neither of us can quit. To give up would be to shame both of us, and the penalty for cowardice is eternal damnation."

"Right." Grey held a napkin to his arm to stop the blood flow. "Brothers."

"Brothers in pain, brothers in glory," Murray said quietly. "Let the fun begin."

The urge to collapse nearly overwhelmed Grey. He was in the push-up position on the concrete pool deck, shoulder to shoulder with half of his classmates. The other half either crawled over the prone students' backs or low-crawled beneath them. Grey's lower back screamed with pain. A constant series of knees jabbed into his spine, sending wave after wave of nausea into his stomach. He puked, and the acidic mess filled his mouth. Although he wanted to spit it out, he knew that would only get the class in more trouble. Puke anywhere near the pool was not tolerated. He swallowed it, and cringed as the half-digested food burned its way back down his throat.

"Faster," Osgood yelled. "You guys are slow as molasses. The slower you go, the longer we'll play this game." The bald instructor paced back and forth in front of the line of prone students, urging those who were crawling along on top to pick it up. Grey rarely prayed, but just this once he made a silent request that Osgood be struck down by lightning. He knew it wasn't good to ask for the suffering of others, but Osgood could be nothing less than devil spawn. He was sure God wouldn't mind.

"Enough," a gentle voice cut in. "We need to get back on schedule."

Senior Chief Lundin stepped in front of the line. Grey could almost see angel wings sprouting from his back.

"It's your show," Osgood acknowledged, stepping into the background.

"Today," Lundin began in his lazy voice, "you're going to take your lifesaving test. You've already practiced the various carries and breakaways with your classmates. Now you get to try them out with instructors. There will be five instructors in the pool, including myself, acting as victims. You will execute one of the rescue techniques on each of the victims. If you fail to bring them back to the edge of the pool safely, you will be allowed one more try with a different instructor acting as victim. Make sense?"

The class nodded.

"Good. We'll all start at the opposite end of the pool, which means you'll have to cross-chest-carry each victim about twenty yards. If your victim is active, this might be quite a challenge. Just remember, you swam across the pool and back underwater earlier this month. Towing someone twenty yards shouldn't be a big deal, even if your head is stuck underwater the whole time. Questions?"

The class stood in silence. Grey was not looking forward to this evolution. He already had a lifeguard certificate, but the test he took didn't involve victims that actively tried to drown their rescuers.

"Form five equal lines at the edge of the pool. When we give you the signal, you will execute the indicated rescue. Okay? Okay."

The class rushed to create five lines, but everyone refused to line up in front of Instructor Redman. Grey knew the class would get hammered if they didn't straighten it out soon, so he stepped in front of the burly instructor and met his scornful gaze. The rest of his boat crew reluctantly filled in behind him.

"Bold move, sir," Redman noted. "You realize I'm taking you straight to the bottom, right?"

"I would expect no less of you," Grey replied.

Redman dove into the pool and swam to the far end. "Reverse head hold!"

Great. That was the hardest rescue to execute. Grey dove in and swam toward the instructor, stopping a few yards away. He turned around so his back was to Redman. This particular rescue required that the victim wrap both arms around the rescuer's neck. It was the hardest hold to escape from, and you never knew when the victim would strike. Grey waited uneasily. Suddenly the water exploded behind him, and he instinctively tucked his chin in to his chest and let himself sink down in the water. It was a futile gesture. Redman managed to get both arms around his neck. Grey sank to the bottom of the pool with the muscular instructor clinging to him from behind. *Drowning once again,* Grey thought. He pried at the instructor's arms, trying to break them free from his neck. No luck. Redman was far too strong.

Grey's mind raced. He had no idea what to do, so he finally settled on going limp. He closed his eyes and tried to wait it out. *Burning, burning, burning.* Hypoxia rushed in, and the urge to bolt for the surface flooded his brain. Despite the discomfort, Grey remained motionless, waiting for the instructor to give in. The meaty arms relaxed around his neck, and Grey pounced on the opportunity. He pried them lose and bolted for the surface. A quick breath was all he could manage before a hand grabbed his ankle and pulled him back below. This time Redman faced him, and the sight of the hulking instructor's face was terrifying. Despite sitting on the bottom without a breath for close to a minute, a smile rested on his lips, and his coal-black eyes regarded Grey hungrily. Grey fought the panic that stormed into his mind. Surrendering to panic meant certain failure. *Maybe he really will drown me.* Redman had a firm grip on his shoulders. Once again, Grey played dead. He relaxed completely, conserving as much oxygen as he could. When he thought he could bear it no longer he sprung into action, kneeing Redman in the stomach. The instructor floated back in surprise, and Grey raced for the surface. As soon as he sucked in a lungful of air he swam toward the side and pulled himself out of the pool. He lay on the cold concrete, his sides heaving.

"Mr. Grey! Failure!" Redman yelled after coming to the surface. Osgood marked it down on his clipboard and pointed to the back of the next line. "Better luck next time, sir."

Grey staggered to his feet and fell into line. His mind whirled and spun out of control, his vision a blurred mess of muted blues and grays. Rogers grabbed him by the arm.

"You all right, chum?"

"Not really." Grey struggled to clear his head. "Chalk me up for another near-death experience."

"Redman?"

"Of course. Who else?" His vision slowly returned to normal. "What instructor do I have the pleasure of rescuing next?"

"Furtado."

"Beautiful." Grey focused on relaxing as the line shortened. His heart was still racing, and he didn't want to start the next rescue already winded. Minutes later Rogers jumped in the pool and swam toward Furtado. Grey watched the action with interest. His friend managed to get a good grip on the wiry instructor and began the cross-chest carry without incident. Halfway back, though, Furtado tried to roll Rogers beneath him. Rogers kept fighting, trying to keep his mouth above the surface. With a gasp he sucked in a mouthful of water and tapped Furtado on the shoulder, signaling defeat. *Shit.* Furtado released his grip, splashed water in Rogers's face, and pushed the flustered student toward the edge of the pool.

"Good luck," Rogers croaked.

"Thanks." Grey rolled his neck and psyched himself up. *You're mine, Furtado. Don't even try me. I'll tear your tongue stud right out of your face.* Furtado smiled at the other end of the pool.

"I need to repeat the reverse head hold," Grey called out.

"Roger that, sir. Come get me."

Grey jumped in the pool and stroked to the other side. He stopped and turned around several feet from Furtado. Now the wait, the horrible wait. *Tick, tick, tick.* Grey heard the splash and tucked his chin. Furtado tried to get a grip around Grey's neck, but Grey was ready for him. He broke the instructor's hold, spun him around, and threw an arm over his chest. Furtado immediately started to fight, thrashing violently. Grey tightened his grip and stroked toward the side. Halfway across, as if on cue, Furtado rolled. Instead of fighting it, Grey threw all his energy in the same direction. They rolled twice, and the surprised instructor struggled for a breath. Grey muscled his way on top and took a few strokes with Furtado pinned beneath him. *Take that, bitch.* He could hear the laughter of students on the pool deck. *Time for a change.* Grey rolled again and again, all the while struggling toward the side of the pool. Thoroughly winded, he finally made it to safety. Furtado was too out of breath to speak.

"Pass," Osgood said, noting Furtado's condition. "Nice work, sir."

Grey felt an elation he seldom enjoyed. He had won. He had subdued an instructor, broken him like a horse. The trainees in line clapped him on the back as he joined the next group. The rest of the test was a breeze. Brimming with confidence, Grey took charge of each rescue and quickly defeated one instructor after another.

The afternoon wore on painfully: two hours of log PT, an hour of IBS, and a conditioning run. The instructors definitely weren't letting up for Hell Week. Grey limped back to the barracks beat but satisfied. Not only did he run his fastest four-mile timed run ever, but he also thoroughly embarrassed Furtado, a dangerous but fulfilling turn of events. Only one thing stood in his way: Redman was determined to see him fail. *He'll have to kill me. I'm not quitting.*

The week proceeded normally until Friday. The students spent two hours in medical receiving a whole slug of shots as protection against the numerous bacterial and viral infections that their battered bodies would be exposed to during Hell Week. *Hell Week.* It was on everyone's mind. It kept them up at night; it was the subject of countless rumors; and it even made twelve students quit. The thought of even starting the week was too much for some to handle, and Smurf was among the quitters. The class never saw him again. Because the Academy kids had been commissioned as officers several weeks before Grey and Rogers, they chose the next class leader. It was Pollock, the red-faced walking temper tantrum. Grey was a bundle of nerves as he received his Hell Week issue: two pairs of spandex underwear to limit chafing, and two pairs of COOLMAX socks with liners. Everything he had worked for, everything he wanted, everything he feared would be put on the line next week. Chief Baldwin released the class early and told them to report no later than ten o'clock on Sunday morning. The mood was somber as students contemplated the week that lay ahead.

"Remember, boss. It's written in blood now," Murray said, holding up his arm.

"I know. I won't let you down."

Grey stripped off his camouflage uniform and lay down on the grass outside his room. The ocean breeze whipped over his nearly nude body, caressing his damp skin. He closed his eyes and imagined lying in the surf night after night. It felt strange to voluntarily enlist in something that would take every last ounce of fortitude to survive. Grey resigned himself to the coming pain, the sleeplessness, the infections, the struggle.

"'All we are asked to bear we can bear. That is the law of the spiritual life. The only hindrance to the working of this law, as of all benign laws, is fear.'"

Grey tilted his head back and looked behind him. Rogers was standing in the doorway to their room.

"I'm not afraid," Grey lied.

"I am. But I know we can get through it."

"Give me another one—another quote."

"Okay," Rogers said. He scratched his chin, then proclaimed, "'Go forth to meet the shadowy future without fear and with a manly heart.'"

"I like that. Who was it?"

"Longfellow."

"'Shadowy future' is right. . . ." Grey slowly rose to his feet and walked past Rogers into the room. After a quick shower he threw on a pair of blue jeans and a clean shirt and grabbed his car keys.

"Where you headed?" Rogers asked.

"UCLA. I have a relationship to patch up before the hell begins. The last thing I need is to go through next week knowing the love of my life won't be waiting for me when I'm through."

"Ah, *l'amour.*" Rogers sighed. "A romantic journey to the City of Angels to profess your undying love to your exotic beauty. Good luck, Romeo. Don't forget flowers."

"Thanks. See you Sunday morning."

"Ciao."

Grey jumped in his jeep and sped off base and over the bridge to Interstate 5. Traffic would be horrible, but he didn't care. Nothing would keep him from Vanessa. His black eye had healed, his hair had grown in slightly, and he looked almost human. As he drove, he ran over the last few weeks in his mind. The fight, the black eye, Vanessa's disappointment in him. They hadn't talked much since. Things had continued to slide, and Grey was determined to salvage all that he could from their relationship. Sure, once he was in the Teams he could have his pick of the Frog Hogs, but he wasn't interested in some SEAL groupie. He wanted his intelligent, incredibly sexy Indian princess back.

He weaved through traffic, soliciting a few middle fingers and a number of angry horn blasts. Grey always responded the same way—with a friendly wave. It always threw people off guard. Traffic came to a snarled stop in Orange County, and he impatiently watched the minutes tick by. He took the toll road to the 405, and an hour later he was in Westwood, home of UCLA. Vanessa lived in a reasonably nice apartment in a complex dominated by law students. Grey parked his jeep on the street and started toward the stairway that led to the third floor. A man in his mid-thirties raced up in his BMW and jumped out brandishing a bouquet of flowers. He was obviously in a hurry. After brushing past Grey, he jogged up the steps to the third floor. Grey followed. The man stopped in front of Vanessa's door. *What the fuck?* Grey started forward, then stopped. The man shot him a confused look as the door opened. Grey immediately turned his back and ran down the stairs. He was horrified. *Who is he?*

Grey stopped at a gas station and picked up his cell phone. He dialed Vanessa's number twice but hung up before she answered. He ran over what he would say again and again in his head. He would yell . . . no . . . he would play innocent. On the third try he followed through, and Vanessa's silky voice answered the phone.

"Hello?"

"Vanessa?"

"Mark?" She sounded surprised. "How are you?"

"Not bad. And you?"

"Fine." There was a lengthy pause. Grey could hear her speaking to someone else in the room. "Sorry. I'm back."

"Is this a bad time?"

"Uh . . . no . . . well, yes, actually, it is."

"Hot date?"

"What are you talking about, Mark?"

"I saw the guy with the flowers. I'm sure he's a good catch. A lawyer, right?"

"Mark, what are you doing? Where are you?"

"It doesn't matter. I came to see you, but I guess I picked an inconvenient time. I'll let you get on with your night. I brought flowers, too, but I don't think they're quite as nice as your new friend's."

"Stop it. Just let me explain—"

"Is he your date or not?"

"Yes, but it's not that simple—"

"That's all I need to hear. Take care of yourself, Vanessa. Maybe we'll run into each other someday down the line."

"Mark—"

He hung up the phone. He grabbed the somewhat wilted bouquet he had picked up at the supermarket and walked into the gas station. A middle-aged Hispanic lady with tired eyes sat behind the counter.

"For you," Grey said, holding out the flowers.

"Me?" She looked incredulous. "Sir, I can't take those."

"Please do," Grey insisted. "I want you to have them."

She smiled, showing a mouthful of silver filings. "*Gracias*. They're very nice."

"You have a pleasant evening," Grey said. He jumped back in his jeep and fought his way south through the Friday-night traffic. The world flew past his jeep in a blur of artificial light, and Grey felt his eyes tearing up. *Must be the wind.*

NINE

GREY SPENT SATURDAY EATING and drinking as much as he could. In the evening he went out with Rogers and watched a bad movie about some bullshit mission to recover a U.S. space station hijacked by Russian terrorists. Knowing it would be his last night of sleep for a whole week, he naturally couldn't relax enough to make use of it. After several sleepless hours, Grey pulled on a pair of shorts and a T-shirt and stepped into the cool night air. He walked past several quiet rooms and entered the courtyard. The moon shone brightly through a break in the coastal clouds, casting a pale white light across the metal drying cages full of students' gear. He was hanging from one of the rusty pull-up bars, stretching his back, when a clatter of falling equipment rang out from a drying cage. Murray emerged seconds later with a bulky green seabag slung over his shoulder.

"Murray, what the hell are you doing out here?"

Murray visibly jumped. He lowered his seabag to the ground and shrugged. "I've got some personal crap I've been keeping in the cages. The instructors never search the cages the same way they search our rooms."

Grey dropped from the pull-up bar. "You should have just asked me to stow it in my car. That's the safest place of all. Strictly off limits to instructors."

"I wouldn't want to be an inconvenience."

"You'll always be an inconvenience."

"Thanks, boss." Murray smiled. "And why the hell are you out here, sir?"

"Can't sleep. I keep thinking about Hell Week."

"Me too."

Grey walked over to Murray's seabag. It was secured with a padlock. "What's the precious cargo?" He reached for it.

"Don't," Murray said quickly. He blocked Grey's access to the seabag with his body. "It's just some seriously hard-core porn, assorted sex toys for the ladies, and a few body parts."

"If you say so." Grey studied Murray's face. *What is he up to?*

"I should get going. My buddy's going to watch my crap for me. He's in the Indoc barracks, waiting to start First Phase."

"He's awake this time of night?"

"Of course." Murray hoisted the seabag over his shoulder with a noticeable effort. "He's on duty right now."

"And who's the watch supervisor?"

"I think it's Redman. I saw his car in the instructor lot."

"You're out of your mind. If he catches you snooping around, you can kiss your precious seabag good-bye. Not to mention the fact that he'll kick the shit out of you just before you start Hell Week."

Murray displayed the pink scar on his arm. "Blood brothers. I won't let you down."

"Get some sleep when you come back."

"I will."

Grey watched Murray walk past the drying cages and disappear down Trident Way. He walked back to his door and started to turn the knob, but the ghostly reflection of the sand berm in his window stopped him. He turned and trudged up the sandy embankment, taking a seat at the crest. The ocean was alive, throwing huge waves toward the shore in a thunder of spray and whitewash. Grey imagined landing his boat on a pile of rocks during night rock portage. The crack of each wave as it curled seemed a warning of broken bones and concussions. He studied the heaving sea for a few minutes, then turned and trudged to his room. He tossed and turned all night and woke up in the morning feeling like he hadn't slept at all.

Toting a seabag full of camouflage uniforms and extra socks, Grey walked toward the BUD/S compound. A red-faced Murray joined him minutes later.

"What's up, shipmate?" Grey asked.

Murray was out of breath. "Trouble, sir."

"What's wrong now?"

"Armstrong," Murray said. "He's gone. I can't get in touch with him."

"He's the retired SEAL you met in Imperial Beach, right?" Grey asked.

"Yeah."

"And he's not answering his phone?"

"I've called him a million times. He promised to be around this morning. I made him swear on it."

"Why is it so important to talk to him this morning?"

"Armstrong's an insider. He has dirt on Redman, knows something about this arms-smuggling ring in Imperial Beach. After that gun-store owner disappeared, it seems a bit of a coincidence that I can't reach him, doesn't it?"

"This whole thing is starting to smell like shit."

"You're telling me," Murray said. "I don't like it at all. But what the hell am I supposed to do now? We're going into Hell Week. We're disappearing from the face of the Earth for a week. This isn't something I can afford to worry about."

"It definitely isn't," Grey agreed. He walked on silently, turning the situation over in his mind. "I don't like this whole thing any more than you do, but I don't know what we're supposed to do about it. I guess you could contact the police."

"And tell them what?" Murray asked. "Forget it. Besides, there's one thing for damn sure: we can't afford any distractions during Hell Week. It's just you and me and the hardest five days of our lives."

"And we're gonna make it."

"Damn straight we are."

They walked into the compound and into the First Phase classroom, which was already filled with anxious students. Pollock, the new class OIC, stood at the whiteboard and kept track of the muster. He wiped the board clean with his sleeve and wrote 47 in big numbers.

"That's it?" Grey asked. "I thought we were still at fifty-four."

"We lost a few more over the weekend," Rogers said as he walked to Grey's side. "You ready for this?"

"I think so."

"What do you mean, 'I think so'?"

"Never mind. I just want to get the week over with." Grey took a seat at the back of the class and waited for their proctor. Several minutes later Chief Baldwin strolled in and made his way to the front of the classroom.

"Gentlemen," he said, stroking his mustache. The class immediately fell silent. "Gentlemen, you are being presented with the opportunity of a lifetime." He paused for effect, surveying the class with his cold blue eyes. "If you make it through this week, you will have accomplished something that every SEAL holds dear to his heart. Nobody forgets their Hell Week. No one. And more importantly, you will earn a modicum of respect from us, your instructor staff. We'll still treat you like shit, but you will have proved that you have the tenacity to make it through this program." He reached into his blue instructor jacket, pulled out a brown T-shirt, and held it up for everyone to see. "You'll be worthy of the fabled brown shirt. For those of you that make it, we'll have one waiting with your name stenciled on it. Better yet, I'll buy each of you a beer."

The class cheered.

"And you'll have taken one step closer to earning your trident—your passport to pussy!"

The class cheered even louder.

"So what's it gonna be, Class Two-eighty-three? How about a no-bell Hell Week?"

The class went crazy after Baldwin suggested a nearly impossible feat—a Hell Week with no quitters. Murray and Grey exchanged glances. Murray thumped his hand against his heart.

"The chaplain wants a word with you. Those of you who are nonreligious or non-Christian, feel free to take your leave. For those of you that stay—don't get too wrapped up in the whole 'God is my protector' bit. If you're religious, more power to you. Just remember that no one but Yours Truly is going to get you through the shit we have lined up. Just suck it up, guys. That's all you have to do. It's simple. Suck it up and shut up. Painful and simple." His eyes twinkled. "Meet back here in half an hour." A third of the class got up and filed out the door. Chief Baldwin followed them out, and several minutes later a gray-haired commander walked in. He held himself proudly erect, and his eyes cut quickly back and forth across the room.

"I'm Chaplain Patstone, to those of you who haven't met me. I've seen twenty-four classes get through Hell Week, so I'm not exactly new to this. What you are about to face, gentlemen, is a challenge that defies the understanding of the outside world. It's a sacrifice. You will give up all of your strength and all of your courage to see the week to its end. All of you that walk through this door on Friday afternoon will get one of these." Chaplain Patstone held up a camouflage Bible with a trident emblazoned on it. "Your own personal Bible. You can't go wrong with the Good Book."

"Hallelujah! Praise the righteous!" Jackson yelled, jumping to his feet.

The chaplain stared at him with thinly masked disdain. "I'm a Lutheran. We don't do that sort of thing, sailor."

A shadow crossed Jackson's face. "But we both accept Christ as our Savior and King. I don't think a little enthusiasm will anger the Lord."

"That may be true." He chuckled and smiled, showing off a row of perfect white teeth. "But if you would let me continue . . ."

Jackson looked hurt as he took his seat. Rogers leaned over toward Grey. "This guy's an asshole. I'm out of here." He stood up and stalked out of the room.

"I was just getting started," Patstone called after him. He snapped his fingers, and a frail old woman entered the classroom carrying a huge box. She set it on the ground and started passing out Bibles. "Please open your Bibles to Isaiah 40:29."

Grey didn't need to open his Bible. The chaplain had picked the one verse he knew by heart. Grey recited along with the class:

> He giveth power to the faint; and to them that have no might he increaseth strength. Even the youths shall faint and be weary, and the young men shall utterly fall: But they that wait upon the Lord shall renew their strength; they shall mount up with wings as eagles; they shall run, and not be weary; and they shall walk, and not faint.

"Beautiful words for a beautiful message," the chaplain said quietly. "This is your time of trial. Draw strength from the Lord. Trust in him. Let your faith carry you through the impossible moments. I hope you all make it through; I'll be expecting to congratulate all of you personally on Friday. Normally I would say more, but I have business to attend to.

But before I leave, how about the Nicene Creed?" He led the class through the recitation and then smiled graciously and slipped out of the classroom, followed by his waifish assistant.

Grey lowered his head onto his desk and closed his eyes. *Too much to think about.* Vanessa, Murray, Hell Week. *120 hours. That's not so long. Everything will come together. Just survive.* Maybe five days of torture would take his mind off his problems.

The rest of the class filed back into the room, followed by Baldwin.

"Movie time. You guys brought something to watch, didn't you?"

Murray's hand shot up.

"Murray?"

He jumped to his feet. "I brought *Carnal Desire* and *Big-Breasted Babes Who—*"

Baldwin cut him off impatiently. "We have ladies that work on this compound, you juvenile horndog. You can watch all the porno you want next weekend."

Murray sat down.

"Don't you have something violent and inspiring? *Road Warrior? Scarface?*"

"I brought *Braveheart,*" Warrior called out.

Baldwin mused, "A little bit of a downer, but definitely some good shit. What do you guys say?"

The room erupted into a shouting match. Half wanted to watch *Reservoir Dogs,* half *Braveheart.*

"*Braveheart* it is," Baldwin said, shutting off the lights. He popped the movie in, and the two televisions in each corner of the classroom lit up. Grey stretched out on the floor. This would be his last chance to relax, and he forced himself to take advantage of the opportunity to grab a little rest. He slept sporadically through the film, occasionally regaining consciousness long enough to watch a severed head fly through the air followed by a geyser of blood. The soundtrack ingrained itself in his head. The mournful tones of the bagpipes made him long to be far away— somewhere warm—naked, wrapped in a giant blanket with Vanessa in his arms, a fire burning in the hearth, children playing outside in the green hills. Anywhere but here . . .

"Freedom!" Mel Gibson yelled in his dying moment. Grey's eyes snapped open. The class watched mesmerized as the hero's life ended on the executioner's platform. The mood among the students was incredibly somber, but Grey could detect an underlying current of determination. Hell Week couldn't be *that* bad. Pollock roused the class from their trance and formed them up for a run to the chow hall.

"Fuck, I'm all fired up!" Murray exclaimed, falling into line next to Grey. The gleam in his eyes told Grey he wasn't lying. "Just let them try to stop me. Ain't no way, sir!"

"I'm already tired just thinking about it," Grey said. In truth, he was as determined as ever, but the realization that his boat crew would be targeted for "extra love" from the instructors was not pleasing.

The class ran to chow in silence. The students moved down the road like a giant organic life-form, each part moving efficiently in its assigned place. They were really starting to pull together as a class, and Grey knew that Hell Week would fuse the few trainees who survived into an inseparable unit. The somber mood persisted through chow. Occasionally a student, often Murray, would crack a joke in an attempt to lighten the mood, but most of the trainees kept on their war faces.

Chow ended and the class filtered out onto the street. The sun, obscured by a heavy layer of gray clouds, slowly slid below the horizon and cast a gloomy shadow over the base. The weather forecast for Hell Week held little promise: cloudy skies, air in the low sixties, water in the upper fifties. The class once again ran in silence, the slap of boots on pavement and the rustle of uniforms the only sound. Because it was Sunday evening, traffic was extremely light. *The real people with real lives are home with their families, watching television, cooking dinner, reading the paper.* As they ran past the Bachelor Officer Quarters, Grey felt the tug of the good life beckoning him. *Hot showers, a comfy bed, no instructors.*

"Maybe in my next life," Grey muttered under his breath.

The class turned onto the beach and ran toward three enormous cloth tents that had been erected on the beach. Chief Baldwin stood in the entrance to one of the rectangular green tents, arms crossed, jaw set firmly.

"There are exactly enough cots for everyone," he said. "I suggest you guys get as much rest as you can. Don't stay up chatting with each other. You're going to need every bit of sleep you can get. If you need to take a piss, use the beach. If you need to shit, get the attention of one of the roll backs and he'll escort you to the head." A roll back was a student from a previous class who had survived Hell Week, sustained an injury, and was waiting to start training again. Also known as brown shirts, there were always a few lingering around the base. "I'll see you gentlemen later tonight. Are there any questions?"

The class milled about silently.

"Anyone want to quit?"

A red-haired petty officer slipped through the crowd and whispered something to Baldwin.

"I was only kidding, but as long as we've got one, anyone else want out?"

The petty officer hung his head in shame, and Grey suddenly despised Baldwin for embarrassing the sailor in front of his peers. *As if quitting isn't hard enough . . .*

"Until we meet again," Baldwin said. He shot the class a stern look. "No more quitters!" With that he strode down the beach toward the compound.

Murray followed a brown-shirt escort to the head as students crowded into the tents and jockeyed for ideal cot position. The center of the tent went first. Grey found himself sitting on the edge of his raggedy military cot directly next to the tent's opening. When the instructors ambushed the class, he would be directly in the line of fire. *Great.* He saved a cot for Murray and tried to get some sleep. There was no way. The tent hummed with tension. Students started talking to one another, quietly at first, then gradually louder and louder until the air was filled with anxious voices.

"I heard we're doing night rock portage right after breakout."

"Bullshit. It's never the first night."

"I wonder who's on the midnight-to-eight shift. I hope it's not Osgood. . . ."

"Did you hear about the guy in the last class who got flesh-eating bacteria?"

"I heard it helps if you wear two pair of socks. Nylon underneath . . ."

Grey looked up at the roof of the tent. There was a large hole in the cloth directly above his head but no trace of the night sky. The air was thick with moisture, and the fog blocked out the moonlight. Grey brought his knees up to his chest and hugged his legs, conserving warmth. Murray slipped through the tent and looked around in confusion.

"Right here, Murray," Grey said, patting the empty cot.

Murray squinted and carefully sat down. "Grey?"

"Yeah?"

"This is it."

"I know. Get some sleep."

Murray sat rigidly on the edge of his cot. "I'll sleep Friday."

Half an hour passed by, and the students gradually wound down and curled up on their cots. The last thing Grey remembered before closing his eyes was the image of Murray sitting motionless in the darkness.

TEN

BURSTS OF LIGHT DANCED into the tent as the deafening roar of an M-60 machine gun shattered the night air. Suddenly a huge figure in full face paint and camouflage gear appeared in the entrance to the tent.

"Wake-up call!" A string of hot casings streamed from the machine gun and landed on Grey's chest. He wildly slapped the burning hot metal off his body and watched as the huge instructor made his way through the tent. "Wake up, shitbirds! Get a muster, now!"

Grey squeezed out of the tent and was soon joined by his frenzied classmates. They milled about aimlessly as instructors armed with M-60s pranced about, spreading mayhem. Back in the compound, simulated mortar rounds whistled shrilly before detonating with a bang. Mass confusion reigned. Murray grabbed Grey's arm.

"Where is your boat crew?" An instructor with a megaphone rushed up and held the device inches from Grey's head. "Where is your boat crew, sir? Get a muster!"

Ears ringing, Grey held six fingers in the air. Six was the number of his new boat crew, and he hoped that his men would see it. "Six," he yelled. "Six!"

Suddenly another hand latched on to his arm. It was Jones. Warrior emerged from the darkness next, followed by the Reverend Jackson. Several long seconds later a soft-looking kid with a big nose, named Kurtz, joined the group.

"All present," Grey yelled at the instructor.

The instructor's face almost burst with anger. "Get in the compound! Now, now, now!"

Ducking as if avoiding imaginary bullets, Grey and his boat crew stumbled through the beach gate and into the staff parking lot. Instructors emerged from the darkness, yelling, pointing, gesticulating wildly. The noise was deafening. Up ahead dozens of glow sticks were mounted on the perimeter of the grinder. With his crew trailing him like a string of ducklings, Grey moved toward the light.

"Get over here!" The shadow of an instructor holding a hose emerged from the gloom. "Drop down!"

Grey dropped into the push-up position and cranked out twenty. Meanwhile, the instructor with the hose doused the entire boat crew with frigid water.

"On your backs! Flutter kicks!"

Grey flipped over onto his back and started levering his legs up and down. The instructor leaned over and aimed the stream of water at Grey's face. Water splashed into his mouth, his nose, and his eyes, blurring his vision.

"What's your muster?" The voice yelled.

The world shimmered as Grey searched for his men. It was like trying to see in a dark swimming pool. He held a hand up next to his eyes, blocking the water, and managed to make out four figures doing flutter kicks nearby.

"Five!" Grey yelled. "Five accounted for!"

The instructor partially covered the end of the hose with his thumb, increasing the velocity of the water that pelted Grey's face. "Where's your sixth man?"

Grey shook his head as he struggled for air. *I don't know.*

"You better find him, sir! Never lose a man! Never!"

Grey started to climb to his feet.

"Get back down there. I didn't say you could recover. I want you to bear-crawl!" the instructor barked. "Now get out of here!"

Moving on his hands and feet, Grey started across the grinder, signaling for his men to follow. Another instructor with a hose emerged from the darkness and gave them a shower. They moved on, making their way back toward the beach. Grey turned and scanned the faces following him. Murray was still missing.

"Murray!" Grey yelled. "Murray!" He slowly navigated the parking lot, weaving between boat crews and their tormentors. Simulated mortar rounds whistled and exploded, and bursts of light flashed from an instructor's hot M-60. In the far corner of the parking lot, a huge instructor squatted next to a student who was lying with his straightened legs inches off the ground. Grey recognized the muscular form instantly. *Redman.*

Grey crawled over, followed by his boat crew. As he got closer, he saw that the student being tormented was indeed Murray. Redman looked up as they approached. "Drop down, assholes!"

Murray gave Grey a helpless look. It was obvious he was already in pain. His legs trembled violently.

"Keep those legs off the deck!" Redman yelled, nudging Murray in the stomach with his boot. "Drop them again and we'll stay here all night."

Grey completed his push-ups and waited, unsure of what to do.

"Push 'em out!" Redman yelled again.

Twenty push-ups. Twenty more push-ups. Twenty more push-ups. The routine continued for minutes. Grey's arms burned, and he felt beads of sweat pop up beneath his icy uniform. Murray's whole body shook as he held his outstretched legs and arms in the air. Redman flashed a rare smile.

"Just think, less than one hour down, and five long days to go." Redman glanced into the darkness beyond his captive trainees and grunted, "Recover."

Instructor Osgood emerged from the gloom and jerked his bald head toward the beach. "Join the rest of your class."

The bombs and blank rounds ceased as they ran through the parking lot toward the beach. With a crash and a thump, a trainee tripped on a curb and sprawled out across the asphalt. It was the new guy, Kurtz. Grey pulled him to his feet. His uniform sleeve was ripped, and blood oozed from the torn-up flesh on his arm.

"You okay?" Grey asked.

Kurtz nodded, and they continued on to the beach. The rest of the class had formed a push-up chain. Each student had his legs propped on the shoulders of the student behind him. They clumsily executed push-ups while Furtado yelled at the class leader.

"What the fuck is your muster?" He waited impatiently for an answer. "Hell Week sucks, but believe me, you'll make it a whole lot worse if you can't handle your musters. Now give me an answer, or I'll put you in the surf until the whole class quits."

"Up six," Grey yelled as they joined the group.

Pollock looked over his shoulder. "We have a full muster, Instructor Furtado!"

"It's about time! Now we're going to play a little game called whistle drills. One whistle means stand up. Two whistles means low crawl toward the sound. And three whistles means hit the deck—cross your legs, let your mouth hang open, and hold your hands over your ears." He placed a plastic whistle between his lips.

Two shrill whistles pierced the night air, but they didn't come from Furtado's mouth. They came from somewhere behind the group. Immediately the push-up chain collapsed as students turned toward the sound. The anonymous whistle blasted twice again, and the students crawled on their stomachs into the darkness. Since he had been part of the last group to join the push-ups chain, Grey was at the front of the pack as they crawled through the sand. Three blasts sounded, and Grey crossed his legs and clamped his hands over his ears. Two whistles. Grey continued crawling. He could barely make out a stumpy bald instructor perched on top of the berm ahead. Thinking there might be a prize for first place, Grey turned up the pace, using his elbows to pull himself through the sand as his legs kicked behind him. He was completely winded by the time he started up the berm. Just when he was within reach of Osgood's boots, two blasts of a whistle sounded, this time from the opposite direction. The class turned, and the drill continued. Now Grey was in last place. He felt his motivation slip.

"What? Now that you're in last place, you give up? We don't need quitters in the Teams. Why don't you just ring out right now?" Furtado kicked sand in Grey's face. "Quit, sir. Quit!"

Grey picked up the pace and found himself staring at the heels of the student in front of him.

"Crawl over him, sir. Don't stay in last place. I'll give you five seconds. . . ."

Apologizing between breaths, Grey pulled himself up over the back of a student ahead of him. He continued pulling himself up over other students until he was firmly wedged in the middle of the pack. One whistle blast. Grey stood up. Two blasts. He fell back onto his stomach.

"Too slow!" Osgood yelled. "You shitheads better look alive, or we'll just keep practicing until you get it right."

One whistle. Up. Two whistles. Down. *Up. Down. Up. Down.* Grey found he could cover extra territory by moving forward as he stood. One whistle. Up, step, step. Two whistles. Down—face full of sand. A slithering mass of sand-encrusted students crawled over the berm and down to the water's edge.

"I don't know about you guys, but I swear I hear a whistle out there somewhere," Jones said.

The class crawled into the ocean. Waves slapped against Grey's face, filling his mouth with briny water. The salt stung his abraded thighs, and his privates ached from the cold.

"Make yourself at home," Osgood said. "Get on your backs and link arms."

The class quickly turned over and lay down in the surf. Grey grabbed on to Murray and Jones and pulled them close for warmth. The night was pitch black, the moon hidden behind a thick bank of clouds. Grey could barely make out Osgood standing on the beach.

"Keep your heads down," he shouted. "I only want to see your eyes and your mouth."

Grey tilted his head back until he was looking straight up. The ocean closed over his ears, filling his head with the muted rush of crumbling waves. Deprived of hearing and with nothing but the darkness to stare at, Grey struggled to keep his mind off the cold. He sang songs in his head. He fantasized about Vanessa. He struggled to remember the name of every student in the class. Suddenly the human chain jerked. Grey tilted his head forward and watched as three students broke ranks and ran for shore. The quitting had begun in earnest. Soon the entire line was shaking. The tremors created by dozens of shivering bodies traveled up and down the line.

Grey clenched his jaw firmly and flexed his leg muscles in an attempt to stop them from spasming.

"Feet!" The command was barely audible, a faint whisper in Grey's clouded mind. He lifted his head clear of the water.

"Get on your feet, you slow motherfuckers!"

Grey tried to stand up and immediately toppled over backward, bringing Murray and Jones down with him. His second attempt brought more success. The three of them stumbled toward shore on numb, uncooperative legs.

"Line up!" Osgood yelled.

The class obediently formed a chain from north to south.

"Double arm interval!"

The students lifted their arms and spread out. Doc Anderson, one of the full-time navy physicians employed by the Special Warfare Center, moved from student to student, shining a flashlight in their faces, occasionally asking a simple question or two. He stopped in front of a blue-lipped kid named Dibble. After examining his eyes, Doc Anderson escorted him to the ambulance.

"Take off your tops," Osgood ordered. "You look too comfortable."

Grey clumsily unbuttoned his camouflage top and pulled it off. It took his numb fingers a few attempts to accomplish the task.

"Lose the shirts, too."

Grey pulled his white T-shirt over his head.

"With your shirt in one hand and your top in the other, hold your arms out to the sides."

Grey did as he was instructed. The cool ocean breeze on his wet back was nearly unbearable. Soon his whole body began jackhammering. His armpits were particularly sensitive, and the rush of cold air past the newly exposed skin was maddening. After a few minutes the simple act of holding his clothes at arms length became difficult, but at least the physical effort took his mind off the misery of being cold.

Dibble did not return to the lineup. The reason was simple—hypothermia. In one of the great injustices of BUD/S training, you could be dropped from training for becoming hypothermic. According to the doctors, one incidence of hypothermia made a student more susceptible to recurrences. Dibble had most likely produced a thermometer reading that suggested his core temperature had dropped dangerously.

"About-face!"

No way. Grey couldn't believe his ears.

"Drop your shirts!"

The students let their T-shirts and camouflage tops drop to the sand.

"Forward march!"

The shivering class marched out into the surf.

"About-face! Take your seats!"

Once again Grey found himself staring into the blackness, holding his breath as waves rushed overhead. For a brief moment the water provided a strange comfort. Being wet seemed preferable to an icy wind blowing on exposed skin. The sentiment didn't last. Grey prayed to God for salvation from the cold. Murray squeezed his arm in encouragement, sensing his struggle. *This is insane. Fucking insane. Five more days of this?*

Osgood called the class back to shore, and the drill repeated itself. Doc Anderson made his rounds, asked questions, examined faces, and occasionally dragged a protesting student to the ambulance for a core-temperature reading.

"About-face!" Osgood yelled.

Four students broke ranks. The thought of another round of surf torture was too much.

"About-face!"

The class turned around, greatly relieved. It was a bluff. They were done.

"About-face!"

Another student broke from the line. One of his buddies lunged for his arm, but the determined trainee managed to squirm free and run to the safety of the ambulance. Grey braced himself for another dip.

"Forward march!"

The class trudged onward into the ocean. Grey resigned himself to misery. *Don't fight it, and don't expect anything,* he told himself. He refused to fall victim to the classic Hell Week mind-fuck: *always anticipate the worst.*

Osgood only kept them in the ocean for a few minutes. He was weeding out the ranks, skillfully using mental games to pry all but the most determined trainees from the class.

"Get dressed and form it up. Make it quick."

The class milled about, dumbfounded. Their clothes had vanished. Grey spotted a camouflage sleeve protruding from a large lump in the sand farther down the beach. He jogged toward it, tripping over clumps of rotting kelp as he stumbled along. Dropping to his hands and knees, he started digging uniform articles out of the sand and passing them to the students who had followed him. He called out the names stenciled on the white strips of name-tape as he worked. "Gracy, Burke, Sharpe, D'Allessandro, Lopez, O'Henry . . ."

Pollok marched past the frenzy of dressing students, robotically chanting, "Hurry up, or you'll be late. Hurry up, or you'll be late." He smartly executed an about-face and marched the other direction, chanting the same mantra. From the smirk on his face, Grey could tell the instructors had put him up to it.

Grey extracted his shirt from the sandy mess and pulled it over his head. He found his top moments later, but his numb fingers wouldn't work the buttons. Rogers witnessed his plight and hurried over.

"Need a hand?" Rogers's blue eyes were clouded, and his usually pale face had an undertone of violet to it. He giggled quietly as he tried to button Grey up. "Don't work very well, do they?" He nodded at his trembling hands.

"Apparently they work better than mine," Grey said.

Rogers tamed the last button. "Got it. You look beautiful, darling."

Osgood yelled from down the beach. "Get your boats and line up on me! And hurry the fuck up, or I'll put you back in the drink!"

Grey ran over the berm and into the compound. Murray and Jones were already waiting next to the boat; Warrior, Kurtz, and Jackson arrived seconds later. Four green glow sticks decorated the boat so the instructors could keep tabs on them in the darkness. Six Pro-Tec helmets and six life jackets outfitted with glow sticks sat in the center of the craft. Grey's crew quickly threw on their jackets and helmets and hoisted the boat onto their heads.

"What's next?" Jackson asked.

"Rock portage," Grey said, "hence the helmets."

Night rock portage was the most dangerous evolution they would complete during Hell Week, requiring them to land their boats in heavy surf on a jagged array of boulders. Rock portage always occurred in the first half of the week. The class would become so sleep-deprived later that the task would be suicidal. Executing the maneuver properly took a clear head and sharp reflexes, and the pressure on the boat-crew leaders to call out the commands properly was intense.

Grey's crew lowered their boat at the edge of the surf. Osgood stood waiting for the coxswains, and Grey sprinted to take his place in the lineup.

"Ensign Grey reporting. Boat Crew Six standing by, manned, rigged, and ready for sea!"

"Shut up," Osgood grumbled. "Save your breath."

Grey stood silently at parade rest, his paddle extended in front of him like a rifle. Osgood waited for the other boat-crew leaders to assemble before dishing out instructions with his usual gusto.

"All right, knuckleheads, here's the deal. I want you to paddle through the surf, dump boat, and then assemble in a boat pool. Once you have a full muster you can paddle north. Big Blue"—he gestured at the diesel truck parked on the beach—"will parallel your course. It will shine its headlights directly out to sea when you're lined up on the rocks. You will then promptly get another muster and wait offshore for the signal to begin your approach. There will be four designated landing spots. Therefore, using your little pea brains, I'm sure you've deduced that only four boats can make an approach at any one time." Osgood spat in the sand and glared at the boat-crew leaders. "Make sense?"

"Hoo-yah, Instructor Osgood," came the collective answer.

"Hoo-fuckin'-yah is right," he drawled. "It's time for a little carnage. Surf's up tonight, gents. I timed the tides just for you. How about a little 'Thank you, Instructor Osgood'?"

"Thank you, Instructor Osgood."

"'Thank you' is right. This will be the most fun you have all week—for those of you that have balls, that is. Now hit it."

Grey dashed back to his boat crew and helped push the craft into the surf. As they paddled through the breakers, he quickly realized that the most challenging aspect of navigating the frothy inshore was spotting the waves before they were right on top of the boat. They got swamped several times before making it to safety.

"Muster!" Pollock yelled, holding a paddle in the air.

Grey steered his boat toward the class leader. Within a minute all the boat crews but one floated together.

"Where's Five?" Pollock asked. "Where's Rogers?"

Great. Rogers had most likely been dumped in the surf zone. They bobbed on the black ocean, large swells rolling beneath them as they waited. Several minutes later a boat reared into the sky as it crested an immense wave. It slapped the water with a crack as its bow dropped back to the surface, sending a sheet of water into the air.

"Sorry we're late!" Rogers yelled. "We had a little trouble getting out."

"No kidding," Pollock said. "We've got a full muster. Let's get moving."

Grey dipped his paddle into the water and swung the boat to the north. "Murray, give us a cadence."

"Aye, aye, skipper." Murray began chanting. "Stroke, stroke, stroke." After several minutes he became bored with his task and altered his cadence. "Stroke it, pet it, touch it, dip it." They moved along in the middle of the pack, paddling at a moderate rate. Grey was still freezing, but the act of paddling generated just enough warmth to keep him sane. Finally they arrived at their designated spot. Big Blue's headlights were shining straight out to sea, and the red roof of the Hotel del Coronado loomed imposingly over the white sand beach. Grey could barely make out half a dozen figures standing on a huge pile of rocks at the water's edge. Suddenly the light from four sets of batons pierced the darkness. Four of the instructors held the glowing rods above their heads.

"Boat Crews One through Four," Pollock yelled, "pick your approach!"

Four boats pulled clear from the pack and lined up parallel to shore.

"Give the signal when you're ready!"

The crew members simultaneously held their paddles in the air. The instructors lowered their arms, holding the batons out to the side. The students dipped their paddles into the water. The batons dropped, and the four boat crews started paddling frantically toward shore.

Oh no. Grey felt a series of huge swells pass beneath the boat. The instructors had timed the approaching waves so that they would be clobbered by a monster set. Suddenly the glow sticks that marked all four boat crews disappeared behind the backside of a large wave. Grey held his breath. Several seconds after the wave erupted into a sheet of spray, four empty boats slammed into the rocks. Green glow sticks bobbed eerily in the surf.

"Fuck me," Murray whispered reverently. "Not a single boat made it."

"We'll be the first. It's all about timing," Grey said, feigning confidence. "Piece of cake."

A minute later the set had passed by, and the boat crews managed to reassemble and paddle out to sea. A group of breathless, waterlogged trainees pulled up next to Grey.

"How was it?"

An Academy officer named Carlson simply shook his head. Blood streamed from his nose.

"That bad?"

"You'll see," Carlson said. "Try to time the sets, or you'll end up getting hammered like we did."

"Right." Grey studied the shore. The batons appeared once again. "All right Boat Crew Six. The moment of truth approaches."

They pulled away from the boat pool and took the southernmost approach. They held their paddles over their heads, then stroked hard when the instructor lowered his glowing batons. Grey felt the bottom of the raft ripple as a large swell moved beneath them.

"Hold on!" Grey yelled. "Slow it down!"

They slowed their pace, barely dipping their paddles into the water. To someone on the beach it might look like they were stroking hard, but they were hardly moving. A series of huge swells rippled past them.

"Slower!" Grey yelled.

They were dead in the water, paddling air. Two more huge swells rolled toward shore, and Grey looked over his shoulder apprehensively. It felt like a lull.

"Hit it! We need to move now! This is our chance."

They dug their paddles into the ocean with all their might, and the boat lurched forward. They picked up speed quickly, and the rock pile crept closer. Grey checked over his shoulder again. *Looks good.* He could still clearly make out the bobbing light sticks attached to the crews waiting in the boat pool. If they disappeared, it meant a large wall of water was on the way. Grey looked forward again and shook his head with disbelief. The instructor waved them off.

"What gives?" Jackson complained. "Man, we had a perfect approach all set up."

The instructor was a big man, and his wide smile was visible in the darkness. "It's Redman!" Grey yelled. "He's fucking with us. He just wants to see us get trashed."

"So let's land anyway," Murray suggested.

"Can't do it. He'd fail us for not following instructions. He might even give me a safety violation." Grey shook his head. "Fucking bastard." He dipped his paddle in the water and spun them around so that the bow pointed out to sea. "Paddle hard! We may not have a choice about landing," Grey warned. The bobbing glow sticks blinked out behind a mound of water.

They paddled furiously as a curling six-foot wave approached. Jones shrieked as the monster reared out of the darkness a few feet in front of them. Suddenly the bow jerked upward as they raced up the face. Jones and Murray fell back through the air from their positions at the bow. They collided with Kurtz and Jackson, who in turn crashed into Grey and Warrior. A paddle cracked Grey on the helmet as he fell backward into the ocean. The world exploded into a frenzy of whitewash, human bodies, and wooden paddles. Grey struggled toward the bottom, but the buoyancy of the vest kept him firmly in the grasp of the wave. He popped back to the surface just in time to brace himself for impact with a huge boulder. Remembering what the instructors had told them about minimizing the chances of injury, he swung his legs around in front of him just in time to absorb some of the blow. The weight of the water mashed him against the rock, and he desperately grabbed for a handhold before the receding wave stripped him away. He dug his fingers into a crack and hung on as the water surged back from the shore, and he winced as the rough stone tore the flesh on his fingers. Just as Grey turned to check for his teammates, another wave slammed into him, cracking his chest against the rocks.

"Where's your crew?" Redman yelled from atop the rocks. "Where's your goddamn boat?"

Why don't you tell me? Grey waited for the set to subside, then released his grip on the rock. Warrior and Jackson already had control of the boat, which had drifted a good distance south, and Murray, Kurtz, and Jones were lodged in the rocks several feet away.

"Let's go," Grey yelled, dropping back into the water. "We don't have much time until the next set moves through."

The four of them waded over to the boat and climbed in. Warrior and Jackson were already in position, paddles in hand. Grey experienced a moment of panic as he realized his paddle was long gone. A coxswain without a paddle was completely useless, and he didn't want to take one from someone else.

"Missing something?" Murray asked, holding out a paddle.

Grey managed a quick thanks before urging on the crew. "We need to beat the next set and avoid a replay. Let's go!"

They paddled harder than ever before, fiercely digging into the churning ocean. Grey kept his eye on the green lights just beyond the breaker zone. They made good progress, and so far the seas had been kind. Just as they were about to make it to safety, the bobbing light sticks disappeared.

"Incoming!" Grey yelled. "Paddle through it!"

They strained against the sea as their boat raced up the face of the wave. The crest started to curl over, but the collective force of the crew's frantic paddling punched them through the top of the wave, lifting the bow of the craft high into the air. It came down with a smack as they continued stroking toward safety. Exhausted, scraped up, and dripping salt water, they finally reached the boat pool. Grey slumped down in the back of the craft, resting his helmet against the hard rubber.

"I don't want to do it," Kurtz said, looking back at Grey. "I don't want to do it again." His eyes were wide, rimmed underneath with dark blue. "I can't."

Grey shook his head. "I don't know what to say. I guess you could swim in if you really want to. But why don't you hold off—give it one more try. Maybe you'll change your mind."

"I don't know," he kept repeating. "I don't know."

"C'mon," Murray said, joining in. "What's the worst that could happen? A slow and painful death? Where's your heart, man?"

"Murray, you're not helping. In all seriousness, though, if we fuck up the next approach you can just wade right up to an instructor and quit on the spot. But if we make it, you stay. How does that sound?"

"Okay. I guess," Kurtz said. He shook gently, and his knuckles shone white from clutching his paddle so hard.

"Hey, check it out," Jackson said, pointing at the water behind the boat. "We've got a visitor."

Grey turned and scanned the water. It took his eyes a moment to pick out the hooded head that slowly moved toward them. The approaching figure pushed a waterproof bag in front of him and made a concerted effort to move very quietly.

"It's SIN," Warrior said. "Don't look at him; you'll give his position away."

"What's sin?" Jones whispered in his hillbilly twang. "Ain't never heard of no sin. That his name?"

"No, Jones," Grey said. "SIN stands for Student Information Network. He's coming to bring us goodies." SIN was an underground group that operated at BUD/S. Classes who had already been through Hell Week always managed to get access to the current Hell Week schedule and made food drops at various points throughout the week.

"Howdy boys," the hooded figure whispered, grabbing on to the boat's safety line. "How about some junk food?"

"Yes, please," Jones said.

The mystery man opened his plastic bag, pulled out six Snickers bars, and scattered them in the bottom of the boat. "Anyone here dip?" he asked.

"Goddamn," Warrior murmured, "you are a godsend. I'll take a pinch." He reached into the tin that was offered up and pinched a huge glob of Copenhagen between his thumb and forefinger. With apparent relish, he deposited the dip between his lower lip and his gums and smiled. "Beautiful. You keep bringing me dip all week, and there's no way these fuckers will stop me."

"Good luck, guys," the hooded figure whispered before disappearing into the darkness. He moved so gracefully that he hardly left a ripple in the surface of the ocean.

Grey greedily tore off the wrapper to his Snickers bar and crammed most of it in his mouth. "We don't have much time," he sputtered, spraying little food particles everywhere. "We'll be up soon, so eat while you can. And Warrior, be careful you don't swallow your dip on the way in."

"No one's taking my dip away," Warrior said. "I'd die first."

"Good to know." Grey looked toward shore. At least one boat crew had made it safely to the rocks. *Four successful landings,* Osgood had said. *That's all I ask.* The task was a daunting one. They'd be here all night at the rate they were going.

"Let's try a different approach, boss," Murray suggested. "I think we should avoid Redman at all costs. You know he's never going to pass us."

"You're right. Let's head north."

They paddled into position at the northern end of the lineup. Minutes later they charged toward shore, racing the swells they knew were on the way. A three-foot wave reared up behind them, nudging the boat forward.

"Go with it!' Grey yelled. "Paddle." The wave seemed manageable, and catching it might save them from the bone crushers that would follow. They surged down the face while Grey strained to keep the bow pointed straight ahead. The rocks approached quickly, and Grey yelled for Warrior to ready the bowline.

"Bowline man out!" The boat slammed into a jagged boulder, throwing Grey forward and knocking his helmet against Jackson's back. Clenching the bowline in his right hand, Warrior jumped from the boat and scampered up onto the boulders. Just as he had nearly wedged himself into a secure position, an enormous wall of water picked up the boat and hurled it toward him. He tried to lunge to the side, but his leg disappeared in a hole between two rocks. Grey watched horror-stricken as his boat rose into the air and slammed down on Warrior's leg, pinning it against the rock. Warrior howled in pain, clawing at his leg as the ebb of the wave pulled the boat backward. The bowline slid from his hand, causing the boat to drift helplessly back into the surf. Grey desperately wanted to help Warrior, but he knew there was little he could do. He had to focus on landing his boat or someone else might get hurt.

"Murray, take the line!" Grey yelled. "Forward, paddle!"

The remaining crew members dug their paddles in, and the boat pushed up against the rocks again. Seizing his opportunity, Murray leaped onto a slippery boulder. He scampered high up into the rocks before wrapping the rope behind his waist and wedging himself in a crack.

"Paddles forward!" Grey yelled.

The remaining boat crew members passed their paddles to Jackson, who had moved to the bow of the boat.

"Paddle man out!"

Arms laden with slippery wooden paddles, Jackson climbed onto the rocks and made his way to safety.

"All out port side!"

Kurtz, Grey, and Jones climbed out of the boat and stood in waist-deep water. Another wave rumbled in, and Grey braced himself for impact, leaning heavily on the raft as he tightened his grip on a handle. The boat and its four parasites surged forward, crashing into the rocks, and then back again, pulling away from shore. The bowline went taut as Murray strained against the pull of the ocean, groaning with effort.

"Dump boat!" Grey yelled, anticipating a lull in the surf. "Dump it!"

The four of them strained against the weight of the water in the boat, shaking with effort as they slowly overturned the raft. A torrent of salt water spilled from the boat, reducing its weight tenfold. They immediately turned the raft on its side and lifted it onto the rocks.

"Ready! Up, heave!" Grey yelled as they inched the raft forward. The rocks were slick, and his footing was precarious. One wrong step could mean a twisted ankle, or worse, a broken leg. Two instructors quickly pulled Warrior off the rocks several feet away.

"Hurry it up, sir!" Instructor Heisler yelled. "Get your boat to safety!"

Foot by precious foot, they picked their way over the rocks, struggling to maintain their precarious grip on the boat.

"Incoming!" Murray yelled, his eyes wide as saucers.

Grey turned his head a second too late. An avalanche of white water crashed into his legs, throwing him forward and breaking his grip on the raft. He grasped wildly for a handhold on the rocks, but his hands slid helplessly over the slick stone. The water rushed back from the shore, sweeping him off his feet and pulling him into a hole between two rocks. As he slipped downward, the skin on his calf ripped painfully against a jagged edge, opening a six-inch gash. Warm blood pumped down his leg as he struggled to regain his bearing. On the rocks above, Jackson, Kurtz, and

Jones managed to keep the raft under control. Grey clawed his way up to the group and helped them move the boat the last few feet to safety. The scene that greeted his eyes on the other side of the rock unnerved him. Approximately thirty feet beyond the rocks, a band of yellow police line cordoned off the training area. A large group of tourists, undoubtedly from the Hotel del Coronado, watched the spectacle of the rock portage with thinly disguised excitement.

"Who needs a corpsman?" Senior Chief Lundin asked as they dropped their boat in the sand. "It looks like you could use a Band-Aid, sir," he said, nodding at Grey's bleeding wound.

"It's nothing." Grey looked toward the ambulance. "How's Warrior doing?"

"Who knows? Looks like a fairly serious break. Don't plan on seeing him again for a while." Grey's face fell, and Lundin immediately added, "He wouldn't have made it anyway, sir. Not with those stress fractures he was developing. I'm surprised the docs even let him start Hell Week in the first place."

First Ramirez, then Warrior. How many do I have to lose? Grey didn't have long to feel sorry for himself. Instructor Heisler slammed the door of the ambulance shut and ran back to the group. He looked nothing like his normal upbeat self. His spiky blond hair looked menacing rather than comical. His usually friendly eyes blazed beneath a furrowed brow.

"Drop the fuck down!" he yelled, spittle flying from his mouth. "Push 'em out!"

Grey dropped into the push-up position and started counting out repetitions.

Heisler looked up at the instructors still perched on the rocks. "Call them off! No more approaches until the ambulance gets back!"

Grey cursed his bad luck. While most of the class bobbed offshore munching candy, his boat crew would enjoy the collective attention of a dozen bored instructors. Sure enough, once the approaching boat crews turned and stationed themselves safely offshore, the instructors climbed down from the rocks and surrounded Boat Crew Six. A short distance to the north, the group that had landed before them was lying in a shallow puddle, trying not to attract any extra attention by shivering excessively.

"Well, well. What have we got here?" Redman asked.

Furtado ran his metal tongue stud across his moist lips. "Looks like a sorry shipwrecked crew to me. You sailors get lost in the storm? Scared by the big waves? Awww," he cooed. "We'll make you feel better." He glanced around at the group of instructors. "What do you say, guys?"

"Fuckin' put 'em in the surf," Osgood grunted. "Get 'em wet."

"They're already wet enough," Heisler said. "I think a little PT might be just what they need, but I'm willing to compensate. How about some four-count flutter kicks in that puddle over there." He pointed to the north and did a double take. His eyes narrowed to slits as he squinted in the darkness. "I almost didn't notice that other boat crew, they're so quiet. They can join in the fun, too. We love everyone equally here, boys and girls. No favorites."

"Fuck that," Osgood grumbled, "I *hate* you all equally, and I do have favorites."

"Well, what are you waiting for?" Heisler nodded toward the puddle. "Get busy."

Grey climbed to his feet and ran to the puddle. It was just deep enough so that when he lay down he had to extend his neck to keep his mouth above the water. The tourists, decked out in their fancy clothes, watched with interest from the other side of the yellow line as the students started flutter kicks. Their legs moved up and down methodically, churning the stagnant water like eggbeaters.

"Listen up," Senior Chief Lundin began from his perch on a rock. "I'm going to tell you why you don't want to be a SEAL. While you're doing flutter kicks, I want you to really concentrate on the words that are coming from my lips. I'm the closest thing to a friend that you guys will ever have here. I have a reputation as a pretty nice guy. Maybe a little too friendly, according to some of my colleagues." He looked to the other instructors for affirmation and received nods all around. "Like I said, maybe a little too nice. But I'm not going to sit here and feed you a bunch of bullshit about how glorious it is to be a SEAL. I won't tell you how great it is to free-fall from thirty thousand feet or how exciting it is to blow some poor bastard away with an M-60. That's all Hollywood, gentlemen. If you think you're going to spend your days doing that kind of stuff, you're sadly mistaken. Sure, you might get the occasional jump, and you definitely will spend a lot of time at the firing range, but the bulk of what you will do is not glorious at all. In fact, it just sucks."

He paused for effect. Grey suspected he had delivered this monologue more than a few times.

"Just to illustrate my point, I'm going to tell you about what I did for two years in South America. It might give you an indication of just how unglamorous and downright frustrating life as a SEAL can be. I was sent down to a country, whose name I can't reveal, to train a foreign military in counterinsurgency. Doesn't sound too bad, right? Teach a bunch of new recruits how to shoot guns and set ambushes? Well, the first day we got there I realized what our first obstacle was. The guys we were supposed to train were between fourteen and twenty years old. Sure, there was the occasional twenty-five-year-old, but for the most part we were dealing with kids. They didn't want to fight. They were drafted. Most of them had never seen a gun before in their lives. That was a big enough obstacle in itself, but on top of everything else, these guys were all sick. They had the shits, they were tired all the time, they were just generally in horrible shape. So what do we do? We give them antibiotics, of course. You should have seen the looks on some of their faces. It was like they were reborn. They had never felt so good in their lives. Unfortunately, they didn't seem to accept the idea that a certain dosage was optimal. A bunch of guys wolfed down all the pills we gave them at once, making them even sicker. Others discovered that they could sell the pills in the cities for more money than they received in their annual paycheck. Worst of all, we had to turn away hundreds of women and children who had heard about the miracle drugs and lined up outside the base every day to beg for help."

Grey's stomach was starting to cramp up from the flutter kicks, but he was so cold he hardly noticed. Occasionally he would lower his head into the water to rest his neck. Lundin's voice faded into the background as Grey's ears dipped below the surface.

"And clothes—these guys had, no uniforms. No shoes! We issued them all boots, but to our disgust nearly everyone came down with jungle rot within one week. We couldn't figure it out. We never had any problems with our own feet. Well, after walking through the barracks one night, I caught on real quick. These guys refused to take their boots off at night. They wouldn't air out their feet because they were afraid someone would steal their boots. It turns out that owning a pair of boots raised them at least one level on the societal ladder—they were no longer peasants—and they weren't about to risk losing their newfound wealth by saving their feet."

He's playing good cop, Grey thought to himself. *He gets all buddy-buddy with us, then he tries to sap our motivation with depressing stories. Nice try, old guy.*

"And the operations . . ." Lundin glanced over at the crowd of tourists, who probably couldn't hear a word he was saying. "I can't really tell you about the operations, but I will leave you with this thought: forty-five days to train a bunch of kids to kill like SEALs. On graduation day they could barely hold their M-16s, let alone use them effectively. The missions were, well . . . interesting." Lundin looked down at the students kicking away madly below him and shook his head. "Why you would work so hard for this kind of a life is beyond me. It doesn't get easier in the Teams, gents. It's different, but just as hard." With that he jumped down from the rock, spat into the puddle, and stalked away into the darkness.

"Well, that's fucking depressing," Murray mumbled. "That's not like Lundin at all, telling us all that shit."

Grey closed his eyes and tried to tune out the grunts and groans of the other students. The effort of keeping his face out of the water quickly surpassed the pain in his abs. His neck cramped up, but every time he relaxed he swallowed a mouthful of water. The instructors had devised a clever system to keep students from cheating.

"Man your boats!" Osgood yelled. The ambulance was back, minus Warrior.

Boat Crew Six ran to their raft and manned their positions. Grey stood awkwardly at the back of the raft. Because they were missing a crew member, only four men would paddle. Ideally, a boat crew would have six paddlers and one coxswain. They were seriously undermanned.

"I dunno. . . ." Kurtz moaned softly, hugging his arms across his chest. "I just dunno. . . ."

"Not again," Murray grumbled. "Stop your blubberin', Kurtz."

"Now we only have five. . . . We can't land with five. . . . I dunno. . . ."

Grey could tell he was going to quit. If he was having such doubts on the first night of Hell Week, he would never survive when things got really interesting. He didn't want to encourage the kid to quit, but he also didn't want to handicap his boat crew with someone who didn't want to be there.

"Look, Kurtz, you've got to pull yourself together. Yes, it's true you might get hurt, but that's part of the deal. If you want to stick it out, we'd love to have you. But I need you to make up your mind. Are you going to do this thing, or aren't you?"

Kurtz's eyes darted back and forth between Grey and Murray. His lower lip trembled. "I dunno—"

"Fuck this!" Murray said, shaking his head. "The guy's going to get us killed with his half-assed attitude. Let him go."

"Well?" Grey asked, "What's it gonna be?"

"If that's what you want . . . fine . . ."

"Fine, what?" Grey's patience was waning.

"I'm gone." Head bowed, Kurtz approached Instructor Osgood. Seconds later he was gone, ushered away into the darkness. Osgood walked over to the boat and sized up the crew.

"You shitbirds think you can get through the surf with four men?" He was looking at Grey.

No way. "Of course, Instructor Osgood."

"We'll see about that." His intense stare made Grey uneasy. "Here's what I want you to do. Make a few good landings with four men, and I'll give you two solid guys when you get back."

"Aye, aye, Instructor Osgood."

"What's this 'Aye, aye' shit? You sound like Popeye."

"Sorry," Grey said stupidly.

Osgood climbed onto the pile of rocks and peered out to sea. He turned back toward the beach. "Walk north past the rock pile and enter the surf there. Once you're clear of the breakers, paddle south and rejoin the boat pool."

"Up boat!" Grey ordered. The four of them hoisted the boat onto their heads and trotted north past the rock pile. The surf was still huge, judging by the explosive rumbles that shattered the stillness of the night. They waded into the ocean without uttering a word. Tension hummed in the air. With the surf so big, getting out safely would be a miracle.

"Murray, I want you to get an approximate interval on these waves. I'll try to figure out how frequently these sets are rolling in."

The other boat crew paddled out into the darkness, and a short while later their overturned craft rushed toward the beach without them. Osgood wouldn't be happy that Grey was trying to wait out the set, but he didn't have much of a choice. It was his only chance. Murray counted aloud as they stood their ground.

"I've got about ten seconds for wave interval—"

Grey held up a hand to silence him. "Wait." He strained his eyes as he searched the surface of the ocean for incoming swells. A six-foot crusher rushed toward shore, the whitewash dissipating as it rumbled along. "Now!" Grey yelled.

Grey and Jones jumped into the stern and paddled furiously while Murray and Jackson stroked from the bow. The blackness of the night made the journey terrifying. It was virtually impossible to spot a wave until it was right on top of the boat. Grey held his breath and offered up a prayer. *God, deliver us from broken backs and concussions, drowning and fractured skulls. Please save us.* They stroked mightily but moved forward at an agonizingly slow rate.

"Incoming!" Jackson yelled.

Grey saw it a split second later. A sheer eight-foot wall of water loomed over the boat. For a terror-stricken moment, Grey looked up in awe and stopped paddling. As they surged up the face Grey regained his wits. "Stroke through it!"

Their forward motion stopped at the crest of the wave, and Grey felt himself tipping backward.

"Sweet Jesus, deliver us!" Jackson yelled, digging in with his paddle.

Suddenly the boat flopped forward and the wave passed beneath them, dragging them backward several yards before releasing them from its grip.

"Ten seconds," Grey warned. "We're not safe yet."

They paddled and paddled, rolling over several swells before coming to a rest offshore. The crew breathed heavily and collapsed in various positions inside the boat.

"Dang. Forget surf torture. You want me to run home to momma, you keep throwin' these waves my way," Jones drawled. "I'm 'bout ready to retire."

Grey smiled and allowed himself a moment of happiness. What they had just accomplished was no small feat of seamanship, and Osgood would surely recognize their skill. Murray winked from the bow and put an arm around Jackson.

"We don't need six. We can kick everyone's ass with four!"

After taking a five-minute break, they made three successful landings in a row. Their fourth was a disaster. Jones dipped his paddle at the wrong moment, spinning the raft sideways as a big wave overturned them. Grey received a nice knock on the head, but he eventually managed to pull his crew together and get the raft over the rocks.

"What the fuck was that?" Redman yelled. "Am I dealing with a bunch of crackheads?"

"It was my fault," Grey said. "My timing was off."

"You could say that again, sir," Redman snarled. "You almost fucking killed your crew." He glanced at the shivering group of students and shook his head. "Not that it would be a big loss. That's a pathetic bunch you've got there."

Grey averted his gaze and held his tongue.

"Get out here. Join your class."

The four of them lifted the boat onto their heads and jogged back to the puddle. The boat crews had arranged themselves in a line facing south, with the bow of each boat in the chain touching the stern of the boat ahead. Grey maneuvered his crew to the back of the line.

"Short a few, sir?" Osgood asked, emerging from the darkness.

"Yes, Instructor Osgood."

"Who do you want?"

"Excuse me?"

"I asked you who you wanted, fuck nut."

Grey was taken aback. "I'm not sure."

"I'm not sure," Osgood repeated sourly. "I give you a chance to create the ideal boat crew, and you're not sure. Well, I guess I'll pick them for you." Osgood jumped up onto a rock. "Down boat!" he yelled.

The crews simultaneously lowered their boats into the shallow puddle.

"Give me a height line. Shortest man to the north. You have one minute."

The class erupted into a flurry of activity as students tried to arrange
themselves in order of height. They were in trouble. It was taking far too
long to accomplish such a simple task.

"Too slow. Time to pay." Osgood jerked a thumb toward the surf to
the north. "Link arms up north, past the rocks."

With somewhat diminished enthusiasm, the class splashed north
through the puddle, stopping on the beach a few yards from the water.
Grey linked arms with Jones and Jackson, and the three of them shivered together, anticipating the bone-numbing cold.

"Forward march!"

Grey stepped out toward the water. He quickly noticed that the closer
they got to the ocean, the smaller the students' steps became. Soon they
were hardly moving at all. *Give me a break.* Grey dreaded the cold as much
as anyone else, but they were only asking for trouble by chickening
out. Jackson snorted a quick laugh next to him.

"I see I'm not the only brother who hates the cold," Jackson murmured.

"Get in the water, now!" Osgood screamed, genuinely disgusted.
"Every second you delay is another ten minutes in the surf!"

The class quickly trotted into the ocean. Rivers of varying temperatures ran through the coastal water. They had just wandered into what felt
like a strong Alaskan current. Grey fought back a wave of panic. The first
minute was unreal. His body tensed up as his breath came in shallow
gasps. Jones moaned softly on one side, and Jackson gripped his other arm
with such force it felt like it would snap off. Grey wanted to tell Jackson to
take it easy, but the words blurred into a feeble moan.

"Hoo-yah!" The defiant, drawn-out cry came from somewhere down
the line.

One by one, the class picked up the chant, and Grey moaned along.
At the very least it took his mind off the cold. Maybe it would even inspire
the instructors to go easy on them and take them out of the surf.

"Shut up!" Osgood yelled. "Shut up!"

"Don't listen to him!" Petty Officer Larsen yelled. "C'mon! Louder!"

"Hoo-yah!" The class yelled continuously. Individually their voices
were hoarse and weak from the cold, but the collective cry was mildly

inspiring. Grey's numb lips formed a smile. He squeezed Jackson's arm, and Jackson squeezed back. After several minutes the class realized that they would receive no special treatment for their vocal efforts and faded into silence. Grey closed his eyes and was immediately transported to a world of blue-gray icebergs and frigid winter winds. He rose up into the air, gently moving skyward. As he turned his eyes back to Earth, he saw his own emaciated body bobbing in the surf. His lips were blue, his eyelids frost covered. Ice had formed in his hair, and the blue veins that snaked throughout his body pulsed weakly beneath translucent skin.

"Snap out of it," someone slurred, nudging Grey clumsily with an elbow.

Grey's eyes snapped open and he looked toward the voice. He found himself staring at a mouth full of broken, yellowed teeth. *Jones.* "Sorry."

"Don't apologize," Jones said. "Just snap out of it."

"I'm good," Grey mumbled. "I'm fine." He looked to his other side. Jackson's eyes were glazed over, he was staring straight ahead, and his body had stopped shaking. *Oh crap.* He jostled Jackson's arm. "I'm taking you in, buddy."

Jackson shook his head slowly. *No.* A tendril of spit hung from the corner of his mouth.

"Yes. We're going in right—"

"On your feet!" Osgood's voice boomed through a megaphone.

"Let's go," Grey said, grabbing Jackson beneath the arms. The preacher's body was almost entirely dead weight. With the help of Jones and Murray, Grey managed to prop him upright. They slowly marched forward, supporting Jackson from three sides. Occasionally Jackson's knees would buckle, and the three of them would strain to keep him from belly flopping in the shallow water.

"Corpsman!" Grey yelled. "We need a corpsman!"

Instructor Heisler emerged from the darkness and jogged over. He took one glance at Jackson and nodded toward the ambulance. "Bring him over."

They stumbled to the back of the ambulance. Instructor Heisler eased Jackson into a sitting position. "Get out of here," he said quietly. "Join the class."

"But—"

"Don't test me," Heisler said frostily. He looked genuinely upset.

Jones, Grey, and Murray joined the height line that had formed on the beach. They all fit slightly forward of the halfway point—above-average height.

"Break off at intervals of seven, starting at the back of the line!" Osgood yelled. "And if you want to cheat, that's your own damn problem. You'll only be screwing each other over." As an afterthought he added, "Ensign Grey, only take five men. Leave a spot for Jackson."

New boat crews quickly formed, and Grey made a hasty survey of his group: Murray, Jones, Larsen, Polkowski, and Rogers. *Rogers?* Grey sized up the class. A number of students had bolted during the latest round of surf torture. A few boat crews, including his own, would have more than one officer.

"Welcome aboard," Grey said, smiling at Larsen and Polkowski. "You, too, Renaissance Boy," Grey said, punching Rogers lightly on the shoulder.

"Thank you, sir," Rogers quipped, rendering a sarcastic salute. "My orders, sir?"

"At least we know who's in charge." Murray looked Rogers over. "You're the poetry guy, right? I bet you'll be spouting all kinds of crap in a few days."

"Not crap," Rogers corrected with a wag of his finger, "poetry. Prose . . ." He sighed and shook his head sadly. "The peasantry will never understand."

"Peasant? What the fuck?" Murray's eyes narrowed. "You better watch—"

"Form it up! Boat-crew order facing south! Now!" Osgood paced back and forth in front of the mob of students. "Get your sorry asses in gear or I'll eat you alive."

Boat Crew Six hoisted their boat onto their heads and fell in line. They stood toward the rear of the train, which worked to their disadvantage. The instructors called these treks "elephant runs." If a crew's boat lost contact with the stern of the boat in front of them, they first received a stern warning to keep up. If they still couldn't keep up, the students found themselves at the receiving end of one of Osgood's beat sessions. Being at the rear of the train was a disadvantage because of the accordion effect: as the boats at the front changed speed, the boat crews at the rear were forced to sprint and then slow to a jog repeatedly to maintain contact.

"Moving!" The shout came from the front of the line.

Grey lurched forward as the boat to the rear slammed into them.

"Pick it up! Let's go!"

"Sorry!" Grey yelled over his shoulder. They broke into a steady run, and the boat immediately began bouncing on their heads. Grey's skull was positioned under the stern of the craft, a fairly easy position to occupy. Because of the gentle curve of the boat and the weight of any residual water, the middle of the craft was the heaviest. Polkowski and Larsen groaned with discomfort as they bore the brunt of the burden. Polkowski normally had poor posture—his shoulders slumped—but now he looked like a hunchback underneath his burden.

"Straighten out!" Murray yelled from the front. "You're fucking killing me!"

"I am straight!" Polkowski yelled back.

At the head of the line, Osgood jogged through the soft sand, occasionally turning to yell at the lead boat crew. Grey stumbled along underneath his boat, cringing as the hard rubber of the stern slapped against his skull. Polkowski continued to slouch, and the port side of the boat listed dangerously. If Grey didn't do something quickly they would drop the boat.

"Polkowski, I'm switching you out!" Grey yelled. He slid forward to Polkowski's position and sent him back to the stern. As he positioned his head under one of the main tubes, he immediately doubted the wisdom of the switch. His head burned, and the sheer weight of the craft forced him to run by sliding his feet forward rather than lifting them. *Fuck me.* Grey's spine warped into an S shape as he struggled to find a better place for his head. He glanced to the right, his vision blurred with pain. Larsen's back was straight, his head was solidly under the boat, and his unfeeling icy-blue eyes were fixed on Jones's back. *How does he do that?* The agony came in waves that intensified as they sprinted to keep up with the boat in front of them. *Sprint, jog, sprint, jog.*

"Motherfucker!" Polkowski cursed from the rear. "Goddamn piece of shit. Fuckin' heavy-ass raft! Killing me! Killing me!"

"Knock it off," Rogers said. "Everyone's carrying as much weight as you. Besides, Grey just switched you out. You should be pleased."

"Pleased? Fuck that! This sucks! Are you happy, sir?"

"Me?" Rogers asked, his voice light and whimsical. "Oh definitely. I've been waiting my whole life for this. You know, back in the old days they used to do this with wooden boats." He paused and groaned softly as he shifted positions. "That's right. Wooden boats that weighed a thousand pounds dry. And on top of that, they had to wear steel boots and plate armor and carry battle-axes. You think this is hard?" Rogers clucked like a mother hen. "This is nothing, my son."

Grey found himself laughing despite the intense pain that radiated through every joint in his body. "It's true. This is a piece of cake. Not only were the boats wooden, but the instructors used to sit in them while you ran."

"True," Rogers noted. "How very right you are, Mr. Grey. So you see, Seaman Polkowski, there is no reason for your foul language."

"Fuck it! You guys are crazy."

Suddenly the weight on Grey's head increased tenfold. His knees buckled, and a strange electric sensation rippled up and down his spine.

"Get back under the boat!" Rogers screamed. Grey had never heard him yell so loud. "You're killing Grey!"

Delirious from the agonizing pressure on his head, Grey glanced over his shoulder and saw Polkowski jogging next to the raft. His hand was still on the handle, as if that somehow symbolized his attachment to the boat, but his head was underneath nothing but black sky. Grey suddenly saw nothing but red. He was so mad his heart trembled.

"What's this?" Instructor Heisler ran up next to the Polkowski. "What do you think you're doing, you worthless turd? You're a weak link, aren't you? You're holding back your boat crew, aren't you?"

Polkowski didn't answer. Instead he ducked back under the boat as if nothing had happened.

"Nice try, no-load. Get back out here. You're not helping anyway."

Polkowski obediently stepped out from underneath the boat.

"Who's in charge here?"

"I am," Grey hissed through gritted teeth.

"Are you in pain, sir?" Heisler asked. He studied Grey's face. "You don't look very comfortable." His voice rose several decibels. "Could it be because you have a weak link in this boat crew?"

"Could be."

"Is that a yes?"

"No."

"No?" Heisler's eyes flashed dangerously in the darkness. "Are you telling me you want to keep this piece of trash?"

"Yes."

"Fine. You keep Polkowski for now, but you won't be pleased when you get medically dropped for having compressed disks and a thoroughly trashed back. He's only holding you back." Heisler moved back to Polkowski's position. "I'll be watching you," he warned. "If that ugly knob of yours leaves that raft one more time, I'll drop you on the spot. Understand?"

"Hoo-yah, Instructor Heisler!"

"If you can yell that loud you aren't expending enough energy. Just look at Mr. Grey. The man can't even talk, he's hurting so bad. That's what we like to see."

I'm sure you do, Grey thought. His suffering decreased a notch as Polkowski assumed some of the burden. For a few minutes they ran in relative silence. The rumble of the surf drifted in and out with the wind, tempering the harsh groaning and grumbling of the students. Grey's crew started to lag behind. Two boat crews passed them up, and now they were positioned at the rear of the elephant train. Redman was waiting.

"A new batch of losers," Redman mused from the truck. "Welcome to hell, gentlemen. You want breakfast today?"

Food. Food is good. Grey's stomach rumbled.

"Too bad. Because every second that you lose contact with the boat crew ahead of you, I'll take a minute away from your chow time—a minute you'll spend with your boat at extended-arm carry."

"Let's go!" Grey urged. "We need this!"

They surged ahead, bumping into the boat in front of them. Maintaining steady contact between the last two boats in the train was nearly impossible. Grey's legs burned with lactic acid as he urged his crew to keep pushing.

"There's one minute," Redman noted. "Is that Murray I see up there?" The truck revved closer. "It is. Lucky Boat Crew Six. Since you have such a shitbird in your crew, I'm raising the stakes a little. Instead of one minute for every second, let's try two."

The bow of the boat slipped back several feet as the elephant train surged ahead.

"Four minutes. Six minutes. Eight minutes. Ten minutes."

"Let's pick it up!" Grey yelled. The thought of spending breakfast outside, boat held aloft on shaking arms, was none too pleasant.

"You need to fire up this crew, sir! Especially Murray. He's worthless."

The elephant train snaked back and forth across the sand berm, further spreading out the pack. Grey wanted to throw down the boat in disgust. He was giving it everything, and they still floundered in last place. *So much for breakfast.* They ran farther down the beach, then turned and passed through the gate and crossed on to the base. Big Blue, the lead truck, turned on its sirens and blocked the intersection on the Silver Strand Boulevard as the train bumped and stumbled across the street. They were truly in the public's eye now, and the instructors picked up the intensity even further, dishing out extra verbal incentive to keep up.

"Any boat crew that falls back gets boat squats all morning!"

"Get up there! Bow to stern! The whole class hits the surf if you can't keep up!"

"Make us look bad and you will pay!"

Grey focused on the shrinking distance to the chow hall. The possibility that the pain would continue through breakfast was overwhelming. He tried to convince himself that Redman was bluffing. *There's no way he won't let us eat. He has to. We'll die.* With the boat trampolining on his already tender skull, Grey pushed onward. A group of marines marched by on the sidewalk; a few even dared a sidelong glance at the strange spectacle that was being played out before their eyes. *Think you're tough? Think boot camp was challenging? Come on over, devil dogs. I'll show you pain.*

"Thank the Lord," Rogers mumbled as they approached the chow hall. Grey let himself relax slightly as the elephant train eased into the parking lot. Osgood stopped the train, then suddenly took off sprinting. The boat crews struggled to keep up as Osgood disappeared around the corner of a maintenance shed. The boats slammed into one another as the lead crew slowed for the turn. Another sprint, another turn, another sprint. They ran laps around the small shed. The boats bounced wildly, inflicting a serious beating on the heads of the students who vainly tried to keep pace with Osgood.

Big Blue was parked a short distance away from the never-ending loop of sprinting boat crews. Furtado sat behind the PA system, grinning wickedly. "Never gonna end. Never gonna end," he droned in a monotone voice. "Minimum wage. Minimum wage. Pain. Pain. Your kids will never know you. Kids will never know you. Your wife will leave you. Wife will leave you. Tired. Tired. Never gonna end. Never gonna end. Head hurts. Head hurts. Legs hurt. Hungry. Hungry. Wife in Tijuana, legs spread behind her ears. Wife in TJ, giving it up. Minimum wage. Minimum wage."

Grey suppressed a groan of anguish as the boat continued to slam against his skull. He couldn't hold out much longer. This was unreal, unbearable—the purest form of pain he had ever voluntarily endured. Sensing the trainees were reaching their threshold, Osgood steered them behind the chow hall.

"Down boat!" he yelled.

Rogers beamed at Grey as they lowered the boat to the ground. Grey smiled back.

"Not you, dipshits!" Redman yelled from the window of a parked truck. He climbed out and casually strolled over to Boat Crew Six. "Extended-arm carry. Now!"

They hoisted the boat to their heads, then extended their arms, holding the craft high in the air. *This isn't so bad,* Grey thought. *At least the damn thing's not bouncing on my head.* Redman stood by silently.

"You taking care of these guys?" Osgood asked.

Redman nodded and folded his arms over his massive chest. "I think you guys owe me the whole chow period. Isn't that right? I know you lost contact for at least thirty seconds. Thirty multiplied by two is sixty. Yes, gents, sixty minutes. That's too bad, because I really wanted some breakfast. Now I have to stand out here and watch you guys, because I know if I turn my back for a second, you'll cheat."

Within a few minutes Grey's arms trembled from the strain of keep the boat aloft. The novelty of this new position quickly wore off. Grey wanted the boat back on his head.

"I'll let you in on a little secret," Redman said. He lowered his voice conspiratorially. "I actually have to let you turds eat. Commander's rules. Can you believe that? Lucky for you, I brought some food along with me." Redman turned and strode back to the truck. He returned carrying seven MREs. The Meals Ready to Eat were suction-sealed in brown plastic wrapping, with the name of the main entrée printed in block letters across the front.

"I always enjoyed chicken with rice," Redman mused. "Tuna noodles isn't so bad either. Let me take a look at what we've got here, and you losers can fight over who gets what." Redman sorted through the MREs, pausing to read off the contents of each. "Reconstituted pork slice." He shrugged. "Beef franks. Not bad, not bad . . . spaghetti . . . another pork slice . . . sweet and sour chicken." Redman made a sour face. "Stay away from that one. Tastes like shit." He continued sorting. "Barbecued monkey entrails, and my favorite, scrambled eggs." He held up a brown packet. "Whoever gets the scrambled eggs should feel lucky. The factory stopped producing these a few years back. Apparently it wasn't a popular dish. Well, some lucky trainee is going to dine in style courtesy of Yours Truly." He dropped the scrambled eggs. "Now you guys need to figure out a way to eat breakfast while keeping the boat at extended-arm carry."

Grey's stomach turned. Not at the thought of eating an MRE, which was usually a decent meal, but at the thought of keeping the boat in the air for an hour with five people. His lower back shuddered in anticipation.

"We'll do this one at a time," Grey said, "starting at the front. Murray, you first. Grab an MRE and eat it as fast as you can."

Murray kneeled down and tore at the wrapper on his MRE. Each part of the meal was vacuum-packed in a separate bag, and Murray ripped into each one with gusto. He squeezed gummy spaghetti into his mouth, inhaled two giant crackers, slurped up some applesauce, and devoured a tiny candy bar, all in less than two minutes. Redman walked across the parking lot and leaned against a truck. He picked at his teeth and watched the groaning students with mild amusement.

"Can't hold out," Polkowski groaned. "Motherfucker. Piece of shit. Goddamn heavy piece of motherfuckin' shit."

"Shut the hell up!" Murray yelled. "If you don't shut your trap I'm going to kick your ass, Polkowski!"

"Fuck you! It's harder for me!"

"Like hell it is!" Murray threw down his empty MRE bag and pushed Polkowski out of his position. "Go eat, you pussy."

Polkowski needed no further encouragement. He ate ravenously. Just as he finished, the ambulance pulled up and Jackson climbed out. His brown skin still had an ominous undertone of blue, but he at least looked coherent. Without a word he rejoined the crew. Grey felt like Atlas, holding up the world on his weary arms. The pain wasn't as intense as having a boat slam against his head, but it was constant and it was wearing him down steadily. He would give anything to let the boat drop to the ground.

After Rogers quickly scarfed down an MRE, Jackson took his turn. Grey at last let his arms drop to his side. *Thank you, God.* The relief was incredible, almost orgasmic. Grey fell to his knees and ripped open the last MRE. *Scrambled eggs.* He should have guessed. The eggs were atrocious. Despite his hunger, he felt himself choking up. Not only did they taste like crap, but they looked like they could have been scraped from puke-covered Bourbon Street during Mardi Gras. Grey scarfed down the eggs, inhaled a package of gummy Spanish-style rice, and pushed a dry loaf of pound cake into his mouth. Still chewing the unappetizing mixture of foods, he rejoined his crew. Immediately the flush of lactic acid swept back into his arms. The minutes ticked by, slowly, slowly. The rest of the class filed out of the chow hall refreshed and ready for more.

ELEVEN

INSTRUCTOR REDMAN AND THE rest of the night crew disappeared, and a new gang of instructors took charge. Grey immediately focused on Instructor Logan, the sunflower-seed-spitting goon that had been the bane of his existence during Indoctrination. Logan scratched at his neck and returned Grey's gaze with an icy stare. The other instructors were a mixture of First Phase staff and a number of sadistic SEALs who took time away from their real jobs to volunteer for Hell Week duty. Logan barked an order, and the class took off at a run.

A fire raged on Grey's scalp. They were carrying their boats again, and the constant abrasion of it against his head was pulling his hair out. The class hurried across the Silver Strand Boulevard and onto the beach. Having Jackson back was a relief; he didn't shy from the weight of the boat. Polkowski continued to swear, and Murray kept telling him to shut the hell up. They stopped just outside the BUD/S compound and dropped their boats on the sand.

"What's this?" Polkowski asked, eyes wide. "Why the rest?"

"Hygiene check," Grey said. "I've heard we get a five-second shower and then an examination by the docs."

"Sounds good," Rogers added. "Maybe they'll rub my feet. I could use a nice foot rub. I swear, nothing's as good as a nice foot rub."

Larsen turned to look at him. "Homo."

Rogers glared back. "What? You in the closet? Come on out, the air's a lot nicer outside. I'll even let you rub my feet."

"You're fuckin' weird, sir," Larsen muttered. "Must be a Princeton thing."

"Speaking of fucking," Murray said. "How's your woman, Mr. Grey? She's one hell of a piece of ass, you lucky dog."

Grey shook his head. "Vanessa two-timed me. She's seeing some old guy up at school."

"Who's she boning, her professor?" Murray asked loudly. "I'm sorry to hear that, sir. What a waste! She must be fucking crazy to give you up!"

"Let's not talk about it," Grey suggested. But it was too late. The damage was done. He remembered how good it used to feel to wrap his arms around her smooth, warm body. Then he thought of her sleeping with some old-fart lawyer and felt his stomach churn. The eggs were coming up. He could feel it. Pushing his way past his crew, he knelt at the edge of the sand and vomited an acidic stream of eggs, rice, and pound cake.

"It's that bad, is it?" Rogers asked, placing a sympathetic hand on his shoulder. "You must really love the girl."

My girlfriend left me, my boat crew is the slowest in the class, and my body is already killing me. Grey cherished the moment of self-pity, then pried himself to his feet, wiped a sandy hand across his mouth, and joined his boat crew.

"Guess what I heard," Murray said as they fell into line.

"What's that?" Grey asked weakly.

"I heard that all the cold we're exposed to this week actually makes the hair on our balls grow faster. You know, extra warmth and all that. I think I might have to shave myself when the week's over. Can't get any play when you look like a Wookiee, if you know what I mean."

"What? What are you talking about?"

"Hairy balls, sir. Hairy balls."

Grey held up a hand. *Enough.* The shower line progressed quickly, and soon Grey found himself shuffling through the dripping-wet passageway of the old barracks. A giant fan was set up at the end of the corridor, blowing a torrent of cold air past the already chilled students. Grey stripped off his camouflage uniform and dropped it onto the pile that had formed. A roll back clad in a brown shirt and khaki shorts handed Grey a spongy scrub brush sealed in plastic wrap.

"One minute," the brown shirt said. "Any longer and you'll regret it. You won't be able to get out. Trust me."

"Thanks," Grey mumbled. He stepped into the communal shower and was immediately overwhelmed by the heat. He basked in the glory of the warm water, scrubbing absentmindedly as he relished the sensation of the heated water against his numb skin.

"Thirty seconds," the brown shirt reminded him.

Grey reluctantly stepped out of the shower and pulled a new pair of spandex underpants from a plastic bag hanging from the wall. After slipping them on, he ventured down another hallway and directly into the blast of a massive fan. Cold reclaimed his body as a brown shirt escorted him to medical. He shivered at the back door of the small clinic, patiently waiting his turn. Finally a doctor waved him in. Grey crossed the smooth floor in bare feet and stood at attention in front of the doc.

"At ease, sailor," Doc Anderson said with a smile. He was a huge man, almost comically muscular. He had served as a SEAL for ten years before attending medical school and becoming a navy physician. "Any complaints?"

Grey shook his head.

"Good." The doc peered in Grey's eyes, then examined his torn up hands. His eyes wandered downward and stopped on his legs. "Rock portage?" he asked.

Grey looked down at the huge scrape on his leg. "Tore it on a rock."

The doc scrubbed at the wound and poured disinfectant on it. "Watch it carefully. If your cut starts to smell bad or turn green, let a corpsman know."

"Don't worry. I will."

"Hang in there," Anderson said. "Only four and a half days to go."

Fuck you, too. "Thanks, doc."

Grey shuffled out the back door of the clinic. A young brown shirt grabbed him by the arm and sat him down on a picnic table.

"Don't get too excited," the kid warned as he slathered Grey's feet with a medicated salve. "Everyone gets the same treatment."

Grey didn't want to admit it, but the foot massage felt incredible.

"Okay. You're done. Go get dressed."

Grey searched through the purple milk crates lined up against the wall, finally locating one with his name scrawled on it. Just as he started to pull on his clean set of pants, Instructor Petrillo wandered over with a garden hose. With his blue eyes, black hair, and perfect dark skin, Instructor Petrillo was undoubtedly a lady-killer. He was also one of Grey's favorites. The man didn't have a mean bone in his body.

"Having fun yet?" Petrillo asked, holding the hose above Grey's head.

"Now that you're hosing me down, I am."

"Nothing personal, man," Petrillo said. "Just doing my job."

"I know." Grey managed a smile. As much as he hated the cold stream of water that soaked his recently dry change of clothes, he felt no bitterness toward the instructor. "You missed a spot," Grey said, pointing at his shoulder.

"Thanks," Petrillo said, watering down the dry patch of material. "Wouldn't want to be accused of being too easy on you guys."

"No. You wouldn't want that." Grey sat down on the concrete and pulled a pair of socks from the crate. The name McWharter was stenciled on them in big clumsy letters. *I don't even get my own socks?* Grey looked in a few other crates. Sure enough, the socks were universally mismatched.

"It don't matter," Petrillo said, noting Grey's frustration. "A little bit of athlete's foot is nothing to worry about, especially when you consider all the shit you guys are exposed to this week."

Grey pulled the socks on and then slipped into his boots. Petrillo moved on as more students searched for their milk crates. The coastal wind picked up, chilling Grey's skin beneath his drenched uniform. A few rays of light slanted through the holes in the cloud cover that loomed over the island, but they weren't enough to generate any kind of heat. Grey climbed to his feet and moved along the ranks of changing students, looking for someone who needed help.

"Mr. Grey," Murray crowed, "could you hold my cock while I put on my boots?"

Grey moved on. Sometimes it was better not to encourage him. Jones was standing in front of his crate with a dumbfounded look on his face.

"What's the matter, Jones?"

"Socks. Ain't got no socks, sir."

"Finish getting dressed. I'll find some for you." Grey wandered to the end of the row. A huge pile of socks sat moldering next to the last crate.

Grey grabbed the cleanest-looking pair and brought them back to Jones.

"This is the best I could do," Grey said, offering up the damp socks.

"Ain't no matter. I spent half my life in bare feet, digging chiggers from my skin. A little dampness won't hurt me. 'Sides, look at you. You're soakin' wet."

"Petrillo will find you. Don't get too excited about your dry uniform."

Instructor Logan rounded the corner of the building, and immediately the atmosphere changed. Students dressed more urgently, and Petrillo no longer smiled as he hosed them down.

"Get the fuck out of here!" Logan yelled. "You think you can just take your time, don't you? You're all dead! You're all fucking dead! The second you finish pulling on your nasty uniforms, hit the surf and line up on the beach!"

Grey joined most of the class as they sprinted around the barracks, through the gate, over the sand berm, and into the ocean. A few trainees whooped with forced enthusiasm, but most of the class immersed themselves in the frothy surf in silence. Logan was waiting when they returned.

"Get in your boat crews, now! I don't care how many people you have; I want those boats on your head!" Half-chewed sunflower seeds spewed from his mouth like casings from a machine gun.

Grey took a quick muster of his crew. Jones and Murray sprinted onto the beach, arms windmilling wildly with effort. Jackson, Polkowski, Rogers, and Larsen were nowhere to be seen.

"Prepare to up boat!" Grey yelled. Jones and Murray took positions on either side of the boat. "Up boat!" They heaved mightily against their handles, torquing their backs as they lifted the craft from the ground. It didn't help that it was full of sand. The instructors must have decided that an inflatable boat wasn't heavy enough by itself.

"Fuck," Murray complained. "There's no way we can handle this piece of shit with three people. Not with all this sand."

"What the hell did you say?" Logan asked, jogging over. "Can't handle it? If you think this is bad, you haven't experienced pain. Squatting position, move!"

The three of them bent their knees at ninety-degree angles. The boat immediately started wobbling as they strained to keep their legs from giving out. Grey knew they wouldn't last more than thirty seconds.

"You drop that thing, and you turds will be my bitches for the rest of the day."

"Let's keep it up," Grey groaned. "We can do this."

Jackson, Polkowski, and Rogers appeared and joined the effort. Larsen stuffed his lanky frame beneath the boat seconds later. The pain in Grey's legs diminished, but he knew he wouldn't last. He felt tears squeeze themselves out of the corners of his eyes, and he felt ashamed as they trickled down his cheek. He wasn't feeling sorry for himself; his body was just reacting to the stress.

"Recover," Logan muttered. "Not fuckin' bad for a bunch of no-loads." He turned his attention to the class. "Now, gents, the moment you've been waiting for! Log PT!"

"Please, no," Polkowski whispered.

"Lord, deliver us," Jackson murmured.

"Motherfucker!" Murray yelled.

"What?" Logan snapped his gaze in Murray's direction. "Who said that?"

"I did," Murray said. "I said 'motherfucker,' Instructor Logan."

"I know you did." Logan looked confused, as if he had forgotten what upset him. He spat out a stream of seeds and returned his attention to the class. "You have two minutes to be in the ready position with your logs. Move!"

Boat Crew Six ran to the log pile. They hoisted a splintery telephone pole onto their shoulders and jogged back to Instructor Logan. *Lift, squat, press, sprint.* The next two hours consisted of a series of excruciating exercises. They sprinted back and forth to the surf, dunking their logs each time for that extra bit of weight. They held the cursed poles over their heads for minutes on end and even survived a lengthy stint with Old Misery. The session ended with a dose of surf torture. Murray and Grey clamped themselves around Jackson in an attempt to trap warmth in his trembling body. They carried him from the surf half an hour later. He was babbling and foaming slightly at the mouth, but he managed to pass the corpsman's inspection. Grey and Murray leaned against him, keeping him upright as he answered the standard questions.

"What's your name? Where are you from? What's your rank?" Heisler looked at Grey leaning up against his freezing teammate and shot him a look as if to say *I know what you're up to*. He shook his head and moved on.

"The cold, sir," Jackson stammered. "It's gonna kill me. It's worse for the black man. Wish I was Scandinavian. Ain't no Arctic water in Africa."

"You'll make it, Jackson," Grey said. "Just stick close to me. I'll keep you warm."

"Thanks, sir."

Logan directed them back to their milk crates by the barracks. He gave them five minutes to suit up for a one-and-a-half-mile ocean swim. Grey knew this would be the easiest evolution during Hell Week: no harassment, a wet suit top, and a chance to work the kinks out of their already-destroyed muscles. He pulled on his UDT life jacket, strapped on his web belt, secured his dive knife and flare, pulled on his hood and booties, and spit in his mask to keep it from fogging up. As always, fish-eyed Murray would be his swim buddy.

The class waded into the ocean and kicked beneath the large breakers rolling toward shore. Grey kept one hand locked onto Murray's web belt. He didn't want a wave to separate them. A safety violation was the last thing he needed. Once they reached the calm offshore waters and Pollock reported a full muster, the class was off and swimming. Murray kept looking over at Grey with his ridiculously large eyes. Fish eyes in a round face with a round fish mouth. Grey laughed, inhaling a stream of salt water. He slowed the pace as he struggled to recover. The instructors wouldn't be recording times during Hell Week, so Grey was in no hurry to make it back to the start. In fact, he crossed the finish line with a pang of regret. It would only get worse from here.

Grey and Murray swam in to shore and stripped off their swim gear. They were one of the last pairs in, so they had to hurry to get back into uniform. Less than a minute later Boat Crew Six was formed up on the beach. They hoisted the boat onto their heads and waited for Logan. They didn't wait long. The instructor stepped onto the beach and immediately began running north. The class struggled to keep up, their legs shuffling clumsily in soft sand as the boats bounced crazily on their bobbing heads.

The goofy-looking blond instructor named Dullard ran next to the class, screaming at boat crews, warning them to stay bow to stern. The class shuffled along next to the towering sand berm. Suddenly Dullard sprinted to the top of the berm and continued shadowing the class. *What the hell is he doing?* Time seemed to slow as Grey watched him pick up speed then hurl himself through the air with a violent leap. He arced skyward, then came down with a crash on top of Pollock's boat crew. A scream of pain pierced the damp morning air as a student fell to the sand. Grey had to stop his boat crew to avoid running the injured man over. Dullard jumped down from the boat as the class froze, unbelieving.

"Instructor Dullard!" Rogers yelled. "What's wrong with you? You probably broke that guy's back!"

A murmur of surprise rippled through the class. Accusing an instructor of anything was generally a bad idea, but Dullard was clearly in the wrong. He had the look of a schoolboy caught with his hand in the cookie jar. Grey was outraged and embarrassed for the other instructors. *How could he be so stupid?*

The ambulance raced over, and the corpsman jumped out. He trembled with anger as he rolled the crippled student onto a backboard. Dullard watched guiltily as the student was lifted into the ambulance and the doors slammed shut behind him. Ensign Ryder, an old former chief who had earned his officer commission late in life, grabbed Dullard by the arm and marched him back toward the BUD/S compound.

"His career's over," Rogers said. "And he deserves it, too."

"You're right about that one," Jackson added. "Anybody know the guy who went down?"

"His name's Smith," Polkowski said. "Lives next door to me. Quiet guy. Nice."

"What a waste." Grey shook his head in disbelief. "What an amazing waste."

"Shit happens," Larsen said. "Big fucking deal."

Rogers lunged at Larsen and clamped a hand around his throat. "Listen up, you pathetic headbanging piece of white trash. You ever say anything like that again, and I'll snap your neck. I mean it." Rogers's eyes were wild.

"Good Lord," Jackson said, prying Rogers's hands away. "I didn't know you had it in you, sir."

"Neither did I. But I won't tolerate that kind of disrespect. I'm absolutely certain about one thing: I never want to operate with someone who could care less about his teammates—someone like you, Larsen."

Larsen looked at the rest of the boat crew to see if anyone was outraged by Rogers's behavior. No one was. He turned away in shame. Red warning lights went off in Grey's head. A factious boat crew would be the end of the road. It was crucial that they all at least tolerate one another if they wanted to survive the week.

Grey put a hand on Larsen's shoulder. "Maybe if you apologize we can forget this whole thing. I don't want hard feelings between anyone in my crew."

"I'll apologize if Mr. Rogers apologizes for choking me out," Larsen sulked.

Grey looked at Rogers. "Well?"

Rogers nodded his agreement, and Larsen apologized. Rogers returned the apology, and the two shook hands.

"Look," Grey said, "our mood swings are only going to get worse as the week progresses. Let's try to keep our feelings in check. Just survive this week, then you guys can duke it out behind the berm all you want. Deal?"

Boat Crew Six murmured their agreement. Grey quickly took in his surroundings, watching the instructors with interest. They seemed even more disturbed than the class. Instructor Logan's face betrayed his amazement and disgust at the events of the last few minutes, but it wasn't long before he pulled himself together and had the class holding their boats at extended-arm carry. The ambulance rumbled back onto the beach, and Instructor Logan took off running. The class crossed the Silver Strand Boulevard, navigated the streets of the amphibious base, and then completed twelve laps around the maintenance shed before crashing to a halt behind the chow hall.

Still sopping wet, Grey filed into the building after his class. Felicia grabbed his arm as he passed the cash register. She pressed a candy bar into his hand. Without turning, Grey stuffed it into his pocket, murmured his thanks, and continued down the line. Despite their huge meals, a caloric snack like a candy bar was a welcome treat during the long nights.

"Why you so skinny?" an old Filipino food server asked. "You need to eat more." She wagged a gnarled finger at Grey. "Eat. Eat."

"I'll eat as much as you want to give me, ma'am."

"Good." Moving with excruciating slowness, she piled three slices of meatloaf, two hot dogs, a mound of mashed potatoes, and a pile of rice on his plate. She passed it back with a shy smile. "Now you eat."

"I will." Grey returned her smile and continued down the line. Three glasses of milk, two glasses of Gatorade, and two cheesecakes later, his tray was completely covered. Grey carried his load into the dining room and took a seat with his boat crew.

Jackson sat with his head bowed and mumbled grace. Jones ate with the ferocity of a starving rat, cramming huge spoonfuls of mashed potato into his mouth. Rogers picked small gray lumps out of his meatloaf, placing them on a dish reserved for the task of holding the unwanted mystery particles. Polkowski's head rested limply on the tabletop, Larsen examined the torn-up flesh on his hands, and Murray watched the instructors.

"What a lively crew," Grey exclaimed. "It looks like Jones is the only one who knows how to get things done. The rest of you should eat up."

"Sir," Jones drawled, "I must confess I have an advantage over these other folks. I grew up fightin' four brothers and two sisters for food at every meal. You learn to eat fast or not at all." As Jones spoke, he continued shoveling food between his smacking lips.

"Chew with your mouth shut, sailor," Rogers urged. "You keep this up, and we'll have to send you to finishing school."

"Now, pardon my saying so, but not all us boys have the means or the brains to attend your pretty-boy college, sir. Dang, I should take you home with me sometime. We'll take away your silver spoon and replace it with a nice wooden one. Show you some real livin'." Jones smiled. "You know I'm just teasing, sir, but I have to ask you one question: You ever killed anything you ate?"

"No," Rogers answered, without the slightest trace of animosity. "I've never killed anything. But I would love to see where you grew up sometime. I don't want you to think that just because I'm a Princeton man that I'm stuck up."

"Naw," Jones said. "Naw. Not stuck up. Just lucky."

Stoop-shouldered Polkowski finally lifted his head from the table. He glanced around with tired eyes, then pushed his chair back and stood up. "See you guys later. I'm done."

"Sit down," Rogers said. "Don't be ridiculous."

"I'm not kidding. I've had enough."

"So that's it?" Jones asked. "After all that we've been through, you're just going to walk away?"

"Sorry. I just don't want it bad enough anymore. Good luck to all of you." Polkowski slinked away and headed for the instructor table. He approached Instructor Logan and was ushered out the door an instant later.

"Well, what's next on the agenda today?" Grey asked, changing the subject. "Any guesses?"

"Surf torture," Jones muttered.

"More elephant runs." Jackson gingerly touched the top of his battered skull. "I think I'm growing a ridge on my head. I'd give anything to run a step without that boat jackhammering on my noggin."

"Whatever it is, it shouldn't be that bad," Larsen said. "They save the real bad stuff for the night shift."

Grey shifted his attention to Murray, who hadn't said a word during chow. His face was pale, and every few minutes he would let out a series of hacking coughs.

"You alright, shipmate?" Grey asked. "You sound like crap."

"I'm fine," Murray said, forcing a smile. "I love this shit."

Instructor Logan wandered over to the student tables, and the room grew quiet. He picked a muffin off a student's tray and bit into it. As he chewed, he said, "I know none of you are tired yet. But just keep in mind, as the week progresses, you will be very tempted to fall asleep in my chow hall." He shook his head. "Don't do it. The punishment for sleeping during meals involves eating or drinking a concoction of my choice. I guarantee it will not be gentle on the palate. I have a penchant for Tabasco sauce, gents, and I will use it freely. By the way, chow time is over. On your feet." He stuffed the remainder of the muffin into his mouth and wandered back to the instructor table.

The class filed outside and clustered around the boats. Logan followed them out, and soon they were off and running again, this time to the east end of the base. They jogged along the main road before turning onto a poorly maintained athletic field. After dropping their boats on the muddy grass, the class climbed down a cement retaining wall at the edge of the field and lined up along the bay. The small sliver of beach was covered with molding weed and gave off an unpleasant odor. The brownish green bay water looked equally uninviting.

"Listen up, ladies," Instructor Logan yelled from atop the wall. "The next event of the day is called Logan's Lope. I would love to take credit for the name, but I'm afraid this uncomfortable exercise predates my reign as an instructor." Logan tilted his head back and spewed a stream of sunflower seeds into the wind. "Like everything else, this is a race. And it involves boat crews, not individuals. Basically, you'll be lying on your back with your legs wrapped around the waist of the next guy in line. The whole boat crew will form a chain in this manner. Only the last guy in line will have free legs. The rest of you will have to use your arms for propulsion. Pretty simple, right? You're just moving along like a caterpillar or a giant water bug. Why don't we have someone demonstrate? Any volunteers?"

Ensign Pollock's hand shot up immediately.

"Okay, class leader. Take your boat crew and show us how it's done."

Pollock's boat crew waded out into the bay. They wrapped their legs around each other's waist, lay on their backs, and started stroking. Their arm movements were uncoordinated, and one of the students was clearly having trouble keeping his head above the water. To make matters worse, Pollock was at the head of the chain, flailing away wildly and doing nothing to maintain a steady course.

"Enough!" Logan yelled. "What a pathetic display! If the rest of you look as bad as they did, we'll be here until midnight." Logan pointed to a dock that extended fifty yards out into the bay. "You'll start there." He moved his finger to the north. "And you'll paddle over to those rocks— about a quarter mile. Then you'll climb the rocks, run south along the street, do a lap around the field, run north, climb back in the water, and paddle back here. Any questions?" He waited a fraction of a second. "Good. Go line up."

Grey stepped into the bay and waded toward the dock. The mud sucked at his boots with every step, nearly prying them from his feet. Suddenly the bottom disappeared and Grey found himself swimming toward the dock. He was grateful for the life preserver he was wearing. Treading water in full uniform without any kind of buoyancy compensation got old very quickly.

"Line up on me," Grey said. "I'll lead."

Boat Crew Six linked up and lay back in the water and waited.

Logan yelled from the shore, "Remember, it pays to be a winner! Now get moving!"

Grey stroked backward and quickly realized that they would have to synchronize their efforts if they wanted to get anywhere. "Murray, give us a cadence!"

"Stroke! Stroke! Stroke!"

They slowly picked up speed, gliding north through the murky water of the bay. Grey was already starting to shiver from the cold, and he knew this operation would last most of the afternoon.

"Fuckin' A!" Larsen yelled. "You're crushing my nuts, Murray. Move just a little bit that way." The chain rippled as Murray shifted uneasily. "Okay, better."

Grey had his legs wrapped around Rogers's waist, and he could tell his friend was having trouble keeping his head above the surface. Grey tried to lean back farther, easing the pressure on Rogers's torso.

"Better," Rogers gasped. "Thanks."

Most of the boat crews floundered by the pier, but one had pulled its act together and managed to establish a large lead. Grey continued flailing in time to Murray's cadence, trying to keep his mind on anything but the cold or Vanessa with another man, anything but the image of Ramirez alone in the hospital, anything but vengeful arms brokers. The instructors followed their progress from the shore as they inched through the water.

The clouds thickened overhead as they continued paddling. The water started to dance with tiny ripples as raindrops splattered against Grey's face.

"Who the hell was Logan anyway?" Larsen asked. "What kind of sick fuck makes up something like this? Logan can take his goddamn Logan's Lope and shove it up his ass—"

"Hey," Grey cut in. "Enough complaining. Let's win this race and get it over with."

"Yeah, Larsen, shut up or I'll crush your nuts again," Murray warned. His threat was followed by a chorus of throaty coughs.

They stroked and stroked, fighting the tide that pulled water into the bay. Grey's thoughts had scattered into an incoherent jumble by the time they stopped at the rock pile. His entire crew shivered violently in the rain as they climbed up the rocks and out of the bay. They began running clumsily, working heat back into their numb limbs.

Instructor Petrillo called out to them as they ran by, "You need to win this one, guys. Trust me, it will be worth it. There's only one boat crew ahead of you. Catch them. You won't regret it."

Grey surged ahead, urging his crew on. He could see the lead pack turning a corner on the field in the distance. "Petrillo wouldn't lie to us. We need to catch them. Maybe we'll get a rest."

"Bullshit," Larsen said. "It's all bullshit. They tell you that winning has its reward, but it doesn't. The only reward I've ever gotten is surf torture like everyone else."

"Look at it this way; the faster we run, the warmer we'll get. Now let's go."

They picked up the pace and slowly closed the distance to the lead group. The two competing boat crews scrambled down the rocks together and entered the water at the same time. Grey waded out into the bay and took his place at the head of the chain. For several minutes they stroked neck and neck with their competition. Suddenly the other crew turned toward shallower water. *What the hell are they doing?* Grey continued his determined paddling and was surprised when the other crew suddenly shot forward.

"They're using their legs on the bottom!" Murray yelled.

Grey saw that he was right. The last man in the chain was nearly standing upright, pushing against the bottom with his feet.

"Hey, knock it off," Grey yelled. "That's not cool."

"If you ain't cheatin', you ain't tryin'," came the reply from the boat-crew leader.

"Academy puke!" Larsen yelled. "Why don't you take your ring and shove it up your ass!"

Grey smiled as his boat crew exchanged insults with the cheaters. At least a little animosity would keep his men fired up. They stroked harder and harder, but they couldn't keep pace with the other crew.

"Fine," Grey said, "we'll play their game. I'm taking us shallow." He steered the human chain into shallow water. "Murray, give us some power."

They surged forward quickly as Murray kicked against the bottom. They thrashed and thrashed, but it was clear they wouldn't be able to erase the other crew's lead. They waded into the beach just behind the cheaters.

"And we have a winner," Instructor Logan exclaimed. He addressed the winning crew. "Go ahead and get comfortable. Sit butts to nuts over there on the beach. Keep each other warm, but don't sleep." He turned to Grey's team. "You know what second place means, don't you?"

"What's that?" Grey asked with little enthusiasm.

"You're the first losers. Take off your vests."

They stripped off their life jackets and dropped them on the beach.

"Now get out there!" Logan pointed to the bay.

Grey waded back into the murky water. He turned around and linked arms with his boat crew.

"Take your seats!"

They sat back in the water as two more boat crews waded to shore.

"Hide the trainee!" Logan yelled.

Fuck. Grey held his breath and disappeared beneath the surface. Cold water closed around his head and pushed against his lips. After what seemed like five seconds, Grey poked his head out of the bay.

"Hide the trainee!"

They repeated the drill. *Hide the trainee. Hide the trainee.* Grey tried to calm himself. His frustration mounted. Logan briefly lost interest in them as the remainder of the crews struggled toward shore.

"I'll hide my dick in your ass," Murray grumbled, spitting bay water in Logan's direction. "How'd you like that, big man?"

For two hours, the class alternated push-ups on the beach with hide-the-trainee drills in the bay. The rain faded into a gentle drizzle as the afternoon progressed. Shaking violently became second nature to Grey. The masseter muscles in his cheeks cramped up from the constant chattering of his teeth, and he had to work his jaw repeatedly to keep it from locking up completely.

"Entertain me!" Logan yelled. "This shit is getting boring. One good story or joke, and I'll let you turds crawl out of the bay."

The students looked at each other expectantly. Everyone was afraid to volunteer. Finally Rogers raised his hand. The class groaned.

"Ah, Shakespeare," Logan said. "What have you got for us this time? A love poem?"

"No. I was thinking about something a little more sobering. Something to put suffering in perspective."

"And what might that be?"

"Well, the Vikings are always a good bet when you're looking for something dark. How about a nice bit of prose from a rune? How about some true masochism?"

"Whatever you say, sir. Get on with it before I lose my patience."

"Right." Rogers stood tall in the water. "I think you'll appreciate this one. The Vikings actually believed that chaos and evil would prevail in the final battle between the gods." He adopted his deep theatrical voice.

> Brothers will battle
> And kill each other,
> Sister's kin
> Commit foul acts.
> There's woe in the world,
> Lechery rampant;
> An axe-age, a sword-age,
> Shields are sundered;
> A storm-age, a wolf-age,
> Before the world crumbles.
> No mercy or quarter
> Will man give to man.

"Shut the fuck up!" Logan barked. "Sounds like heaven to me! You are one goofy little turd, sir. You are the shining example of the adverse effects of too much education. Amusing, but not good enough. Hide the trainee!"

The snickering stopped as the students held their breath and disappeared beneath the surface. The drills continued until dinnertime, at which point the students lifted their boats back onto their heads and raced to the chow hall. The next instructor shift waited in the parking lot. Grey looked for familiar faces. He immediately picked Chief Baldwin and Senior Chief Lundin from the menacing crowd. At least he could count on Lundin to temper the sadistic impulses of the others.

The trainees hosed off their hands and boots at a spigot before filing into the building. Grey smiled at Felicia as he moved past the register and into the chow line. The food servers wrinkled their noses as the students held out their plates.

"You smell like sewer!"

Grey hadn't noticed. He was so cold and so tired his brain wouldn't allow him the luxury of fretting over bad smells. As always, he sat with his boat crew and wolfed down a generous helping of navy slop. Grey found himself shivering despite being indoors. It was awfully drafty in the chow hall. He looked up. The ceiling fans were turning at full speed. Murray followed his gaze.

"Bet you anything the instructors are behind those damn fans."

"I definitely wouldn't put it past them." Grey stood up. "I'm getting hot chocolate. Anyone else want some?"

The whole table raised their hands.

"Okay, but I might need some help." Grey looked at Murray.

"Aye, aye, sir." Murray gingerly rose from his seat and followed Grey back to the food line. The packets of cocoa powder were gone, but the hot-water container was full. Grey filled six cups with steaming water and handed three to Murray. They shuffled back to the table and passed the cups out.

"I thought you were getting hot chocolate," Larsen complained.

"Hey, at least it's hot," Grey said. He held his cup to his cheek. The warmth was heavenly. He desperately wanted to wrap his whole body around the steaming cup. He shifted the cup from one cheek to the other, then pressed it to his chest. There just wasn't enough of it to go around. The rest of the table looked equally frustrated. They were enthralled by the warmth of the water, but they didn't know what to do with it. Finally Grey put the cup back on the table and wrapped his arms tightly around his chest.

Murray coughed violently and held a napkin to his mouth. Once his hacking subsided, he glanced at his napkin, quickly crumpled it into a ball, and jammed it in his pocket.

"What's that all about?" Grey asked.

"What are you talking about?" Murray couldn't meet his gaze.

"I'm talking about that cough. You sound like crap. And why were you in such a hurry to hide that napkin?"

"It's covered in snot, sir," Murray explained. "I wouldn't want to offend Rogers."

"Knock off the bullshit," Grey said. "Let me see the napkin."

Murray leaned in close to Grey and whispered, "Blood brothers, right?"

"Of course," Grey whispered back.

Murray suppressed a cough. "I think I'm in deep shit, sir."

"Do I need to turn you in to medical?"

"You wouldn't dare," Murray hissed. "A promise is a promise. The only way they're getting me out of this class is by carrying me out in a coffin."

"Give me the napkin," Grey insisted. "Let me see it."

Murray pressed a crumpled napkin into Grey's hand under the table. Grey opened it up and recoiled in disgust. It was coated with slimy pinkish froth.

"This is serious, Murray," Grey whispered. "I can't let you continue."

"It's not your choice."

Not my choice? Grey suppressed his anger. "I can't let you."

"Sir, we have a pact." Murray shot him a plaintive look. "Blood brothers."

Grey handed the napkin back to Murray. "I won't tell if you promise not to hide your condition if it gets much worse."

Murray smiled. "Deal."

"I don't feel good about this."

"Don't worry so much. Plenty of students have made it to the end of Hell Week with pulmonary edema."

"What are you two whispering about?" Rogers asked.

"Nothing exciting." Grey rolled his neck and looked away. "We were just speculating about the beat-down we'll get tonight."

"Time to go, gents," Chief Baldwin called out. "Say good-bye to the sun, because you won't be seeing it for quite some time."

The class stepped outside into the fading light. The air was still heavy with moisture, ensuring that the class would never enjoy a dry moment. Grey and his crew hauled the boat onto their heads and waited for instructions.

The lean instructor named Barefoot stepped in front of the class. With his big eyes, big ears, and small face, he bore a striking resemblance to a mouse. Unfortunately, he was a notoriously fast runner. "I'm going to haul ass back to the compound, so don't get left behind. Stragglers will pay dearly." Barefoot took off at a dead sprint.

The boat pounded Grey's tender skull as he tried to keep up. Big Blue pulled up next to his crew, and Chief Baldwin leaned out the window.

"Motivate me, gents. How about a little ditty?"

Murray didn't hesitate. He coughed loudly, then launched into one of his favorite chants:

> I had a dog whose name was Blue.
> Blue wanted to be a SEAL, too.
> Bought him a mask and four tiny fins,
> Went to the ocean and—

"Shut up!" Barefoot yelled over his shoulder. "I hate that lame-ass jody. Keep it up and I'll run you dipshits into the ground."

"So much for that one," Murray muttered.

Chief Baldwin winked from his truck. "Better luck next time."

The class sprinted across the highway and onto the beach. Barefoot stopped at the surf line and ordered the class to extended-arm carry. "You guys ready for a long paddle?"

"Hoo-yah!" the class responded. Paddling was infinitely less painful than running with a boat crashing up and down on their skulls.

"Too bad, lazy turds. We're running." Barefoot's mouse eyes fixed themselves on Boat Crew Six. "And you know why? I'll tell you why. Because of that stupid jody you dumb shits started on the run over here. Hell Week is not a time for celebration. This is a somber fuckin' experience, and I expect you to act accordingly."

"Bullshit," Murray coughed.

"Did I hear something?"

"Negative," Murray said innocently.

"Listen, shithead, I know you're a bad egg. You don't want to play along? Then you're fucked. You won't make it through this week. You *will* not survive Hell Week. Am I making myself clear?"

"Crystal clear." Murray looked at his feet.

Without another word, Barefoot turned and broke into a run. Cursing freely, the class followed him south along the water's edge. Every step was a jolt of pain, and there was no end in sight. The mess of lights across the border grew brighter as the class limped toward Imperial Beach.

"Where are we going?" Larsen asked. "Tijuana? Five-dollar blow jobs?"

"Damn, that sounds good." Murray grunted like an animal. "I could use a little girly action. Too bad we're headed for the mud pits."

"What?" Larsen asked.

"The mud pits. South end of the bay. Down by the marina."

"You serious?"

"I'm willing to bet money on it. Prepare yourself for the bacterial invasion."

"What you guys talkin' about, bacterial invasion?" Jones asked. "I'm lookin' forward to a nice mud bath. Good for the complexion and all."

Barefoot picked up the pace, and the elephant train lurched forward, propelled by the threats of instructors riding in diesel trucks alongside them.

"Switch me out, man! Switch me out! I can't take it anymore!" Larsen's neck folded over so that the boat bounced wildly on the side of his head.

"I got it!" Grey yelled. He moved from his position at the stern and edged Larsen out of the way. Grey had never taken the bow position. It was an extremely unpleasant change. Not only had a load of sand slid toward the front of the boat, but instead of being pulled along by the momentum of the crew, Grey felt like he was being pushed over from behind. *Please let us stop soon. Please.*

Barefoot kept right on running. Several minutes later he veered to the east and sprinted across the soft sand. The class followed. Soon they were limping through a large tunnel that crossed beneath the Silver Strand Boulevard. The headlights from the truck behind them played eerily against the dirty walls, and the slap of dozens of boots on concrete echoed in the confines of the tunnel. Barefoot sprinted through the tunnel and disappeared on the other side. As Boat Crew Six lurched back onto the sand, Grey immediately picked Barefoot out at the bottom of a gentle slope. Strangely, the water that stretched for fifty yards behind him didn't shimmer. It stood still. Perfectly still. As his boat crew got closer, Grey realized his error. It wasn't water. It was mud.

"Way to call it, Murray," Jackson said. "Time to play in the mud."

Barefoot ordered them to drop their boats at the edge of the sludge and line up in boat crews. "Time for a relay race. We'll start with the basics. Each member of your crew will run to the far end of the mud flats and back. Those boat crews that have six members, pick one person to run twice." Barefoot glared at the class. "Any questions?"

A student raised his hand. "How do we know when we're at the end of the flats?"

"You'll know because you'll be swimming, you stupid piece of shit. The mud changes to bay water in matter of a few feet. Keep right on going if you want. I don't give a shit."

"Mighty Mouse sure says 'shit' a lot," Murray mumbled quietly.

"Who wants to run twice?" Grey asked. No hands went up. "Fine. I will."

"Ready . . ." Barefoot raised an arm. "Go." His arm cut downward, and the first competitors sprinted off in a flurry of arms and legs.

Grey flew forward for several steps before the ground gave away. His forward momentum flung him facedown in the mud as his legs stuck knee-deep in the ooze. Grey struggled to get himself upright. He futilely pushed against the mud with his arms. It squished past his elbows, moving all the way up to his shoulders. Now his head was the only part of his body clear of the mess. He spent several seconds frantically trying to reach something solid with his hands. His fingertips grazed against a rock, but he couldn't leverage enough power from the hard surface to pull his upper body free. Working slowly against the weight of the mud, Grey pulled his legs underneath him so that he was kneeling. Then he gingerly squatted until he was standing knee deep in the filth. The stench of the putrid muck overpowered him. Grey tried to take another step, but stopped when he felt his boot sucking off of his foot. A quick glance around gave him a small degree of comfort. No one was making much progress.

"Hurry it up, turds!" Barefoot yelled. "If you don't want to play this game, I'm sure we can find something else to do. Something a little more challenging."

Grey slowly pulled one foot free from the mud. He threw the loose leg forward and lost his balance again as the muck swallowed it back up. *Fuck.* Grey tried another approach. He was already on his stomach, so he simply kicked against the semisolid bottom of the mud flat. His progress was slow, but it was progress.

"That's the way, sir!" Jones yelled. "Just like a bird dog in a pond!"

A bird dog . . . Grey kicked and kicked. The mud oozed through the neck of his shirt and down the front of his body. It slicked over his groin and slipped down his legs. The other students watched his progress and imitated his technique. Grey's arms finally plunged into a substance that might pass as water. He turned around and started the journey back.

"This is ridiculous," Grey moaned as he pulled himself from the muck.

"Good job." Rogers slapped Grey's mud-slicked back. "We're in first place."

"Now watch this here," Jones said. "I'll show you city boys how it's done." He took a few steps backward, then took off at a dead sprint. At the edge of the mud flat he launched himself into the air. Grey smiled as he watched Jones fly gracefully through the darkness. He sailed a good ten feet before his body slapped into the muck with a crack and a slurp. Jones immediately rose to his feet and moved forward. His technique looked absurd, but he made progress. Jones jerked his legs up and down rapidly, keeping the mud from establishing a firm hold on his legs. By the time he reached the far side of the flats, Grey could see that his sides were heaving with effort.

"I'm finished," Jones croaked, collapsing at the starting line. Jackson leaped into the mud and thrashed toward the far side. Then came Larsen, then Murray, and then Grey was up again. He did slightly better this time, although he was once again forced to pull himself along on his stomach. He lurched across the finish line in first place.

"Sit butts to nuts in the mud," Barefoot ordered. "Pays to be a winner."

Grey gathered his crew and they waded into the mud and sat down, sandwiching their bodies tightly together to conserve warmth. Despite the nauseating smell, the mud was strangely soothing. Grey watched, satisfied, as the rest of the class repeated the race. *I'll close my eyes, just for a second.* He awoke with a snap as Murray's palm connected with his head.

"Next race, boss."

"Already?"

"Already." Murray helped Grey to his feet, and they slurped back over to the starting line.

"Time for something a little more fun," Barefoot said. His big eyes shone in the darkness. "You all know how to do somersaults, right? Of course you do. The relay race is the same, only you will somersault to the end and back." Without missing a beat he added, "Ready, go."

Grey stepped to the edge of the mud flats and reluctantly lowered his head into the filth. It seeped around his ears, his eyes, his nose, blocking all his senses. He felt himself suffocating in darkness. He kicked with his legs and couldn't seem to bring them over his head. As his head slipped farther into the mud, two slimy tendrils of ooze snaked up his nose and into his ears. He tried his legs again. No luck. *Shit. Shit. Shit.* Grey desperately tried to yank his head free. It wouldn't budge. He was getting hypoxic. *To die like this. To die with my head in the mud . . .* A raw sense of rage gripped his body as he strained against the mud with all his might. His head slid upward, then popped back into the night air. Grey wheezed a desperately needed breath. He gingerly opened his eyes; everything was brown. He couldn't hear a word. He tried to pick the mud from his ears, but only managed to push it in farther. Suddenly a figure appeared at his side. Grey turned in surprise. Judging by the brown vein that stood out on Barefoot's brown face, the instructor was yelling.

"Get back down there," came the muffled order. "What is this? Some kind of rest break? Bullshit. You haven't gone anywhere yet."

Stomach churning with fear, Grey plunged his head back into the mud. *Slurp.* The world went completely silent. Grey kicked and kicked. Ever so slowly, he managed to direct his momentum forward. He rolled onto his back, then pulled himself to his knees. The mud swallowed his head again, and the process repeated itself. Every few turns his head would get stuck, leading to a panic-induced rage. By the time Grey made it back to the start he was cursing and sputtering with anger.

Jackson mouthed a few words in Grey's direction. Something went pop in Grey's ear, and he caught the end of Jackson's sentence. ". . . over this."

"Over?"

"I don't get your meaning," Jackson said with a perplexed look.

"I couldn't hear you."

"I was just saying you shouldn't get all worked up over this ridiculous parade. I've never seen you so worked up. You were cursing like a sailor."

"Just wait until it's your turn to drown in the mud," Grey said as he glanced at Murray. Grey did a double take. Murray lay face down in the mud, and Instructor Barefoot had a boot planted against the back of his neck.

"What's going on?" Grey yelled.

"This doesn't concern you, sir."

"Yes it does. That's a member of my boat crew that you're drowning."

"I'm not drowning him, fuck nut." Barefoot lifted his boot, and Murray flung his head upward, gasping for air. "Since you're so concerned, maybe you should take his place."

Grey pulled Murray from the mud and then dropped to his knees. He heard Murray protesting as Grey lowered his head into the filth. He rolled and rolled, propelled forward by raw hatred, the strongest hatred he had felt toward anyone in years. *Fuck you, fuck you, fuck you,* he chanted in his head. *Someday I'll be your OIC, and I'll ruin you. I'll absolutely destroy you. I don't care if this is supposed to make me stronger. I will find a way.* Grey rolled right onto Larsen's boots. He stood up and staggered to the end of the line. The drills continued well into the night. Somersaults, backward running, wheelbarrow races. Nearly deaf and blind from the mud, Grey strained to decipher Chief Baldwin's instructions.

". . . mud men . . . time . . . paddle . . . chow . . ."

Grey looked at Murray in confusion. Murray nodded, signaling that he understood the orders. Grey followed his crew back to the boat. Together they picked it up, perched it on their heads, and carried it across the mud flats. Grey pushed the boat from the stern as they dropped it into the murky water. Soon he was in above his head. After swimming behind the boat for a few strokes, Grey pulled himself in.

"Wow. You sure clean up nice," Murray exclaimed, noting Grey's wet uniform. "I think I'll take a dunk myself." He slipped over the side of the boat and into the bay, and the rest of the crew followed suit.

"I'm just happy I can hear again," Grey muttered to himself.

A mess of wet bodies flopped back into the boat. Grey looked at Murray expectantly. "What's the word?"

"We're supposed to paddle north and guide off Big Blue's headlights at the edge of the amphibious base. Shouldn't take more than a few hours. Of course, Barefoot did call it a race."

"Let's get moving. Murray, you can start with the cadence. We'll rotate positions at the halfway point."

They stroked in time with Murray's voice, gliding north through the bay. The lights of the downtown glowed in the distance beneath the arc of the Coronado Bay Bridge. To the east Grey could barely make out the ghostly outlines of old ships in the maritime graveyard. The battered hulls had long since been abandoned, left to rot in the southern reaches of the bay. They continued on, quietly dipping their wooden paddles beneath the smooth surface of the water.

"Stop splashing me," Larsen complained.

"Sorry," Jones drawled. "Didn't mean to."

Two bright dots appeared in the distance. *Headlights.* They looked deceptively close. Grey continued to paddle patiently, but the lights remained stubbornly out of reach.

"I said stop splashing me!" Larsen screamed.

"Quiet down!" Rogers scolded. "Jones doesn't mean to do it. Give him a break."

"You try getting splashed with cold water every other stroke."

Jones turned and looked at Larsen. "Hey, no need to make a big fuss. I'll change places with you right now. Then you can splash me all you want, okay?"

"Fine." Larsen climbed into the bow, and Jones scooted backward.

They stroked onward. Two boat crews had a commanding lead on them, and three were trailing behind. Grey knew they didn't have to win. Winning was nice, but the key to survival was not losing. Getting beat during Hell Week was more than just a discomfort. Everyone had a breaking point, and each additional beating brought their abused bodies one step closer to failure.

"Sir, why'd you join up?" Murray asked, looking back at Grey.

"What?" Grey was caught off guard. "Why'd I join up?" His mind blanked. "Why'd you join?"

"Nice try. I asked you first."

Grey watched the swirling wake behind his paddle. "Because this is hard."

"Because it's hard?" Murray asked. "Jesus. I'll give you a two-hundred-pound pack and put you on a six-month forced march. There has to be something more than that."

Grey thought about it. "Camaraderie. The chance to prove to myself that I could hack it." He smiled. "And of course, to blow shit up and kick down doors."

"That's more like it. You were scaring me for a second."

"What about you, Murray? Why the SEALs?"

"To kick ass, plain and simple. To kick fucking ass and take names. To be the best. And of course, to go back to my high school reunion and have all those chicks who ignored me line up for a piece of my Johnson."

The whole boat crew erupted into laughter.

"I didn't even think of that one," Larsen said. "Damn, that's good. There's no way I'm ringing out now. I can already see all those skanks lined up on their knees."

Jackson shook his head. "A little graphic, brothers. I'm no angel myself, but could you spare me the details of your white-bread honky fantasies?"

"Don't even try to tell me you don't think about that," Murray scoffed. "You're full of shit, Reverend."

"I'm just saying I don't need to hear it. I'm trying to live a good life."

Silence overtook the boat crew as they focused their attention on paddling. They were almost there; Big Blue sat in plain sight at the edge of the amphibious base. After reaching the shallows, they jumped out of the boat and pushed it to shore. Instructor Barefoot accosted them the moment they stepped on dry ground.

"Extended-arm carry!"

They hoisted the boat above their heads.

"Don't move." Barefoot walked away and climbed back into the truck.

"I knew we should have dumped boat," Murray grumbled. "This thing is heavier than shit."

"Shit's not heavy," Rogers corrected.

They held the boat up for several minutes before breaking down and taking periodic rests. They repeatedly lowered the boat onto their heads, stored up energy, then pushed it up again. Barefoot was bound to notice eventually, but Grey knew they simply couldn't keep the waterlogged craft in the air for any length of time.

"You guys are letting me down," droned a sarcastic voice. "This is not acceptable."

What? Grey was sure he was hearing things. He searched the darkness for several seconds before he noticed a figure squatting next to a pile of rocks, perfectly motionless, watching.

"You don't want to play Barefoot's reindeer games?" The figure stood up, and a familiar face emerged from the shadows. Chief Baldwin pointed toward the bay. "Get out there. I don't want to see any part of your body but your eyes and your mouths."

"Cold." That was all Jackson could say after half an hour of immersion in sub-sixty-degree water. A deep blue tint had crept into his full lips. He clumsily formed them around the word again. "Cold."

"Bring it in, gents." Chief Baldwin waved them back to shore.

Grey helped Jackson out of the water. The Reverend leaned heavily against him, knees buckling and arms twitching sporadically. Chief Baldwin took one look at him and summoned the corpsman. A moment later the ambulance whisked Jackson away.

Why? Heavy-hearted, Grey watched the red taillights fade into darkness.

"Drop down."

Grey stared ahead blankly.

"I said 'Drop down,' sir!"

Grey snapped out of his trance and assumed the push-up position. He only managed sixty before his arms gave out. The rest of the crew didn't fare any better. They lay sprawled out on the crumbling pavement, shivering, hoping Baldwin would ignore them. For once, he did.

"Get up." Barefoot climbed out of Big Blue. "Go get wet."

They ran to the bay, dunked themselves, and ran back.

"Get wet."

The drill continued until the last boat crew emerged from the darkness of the bay. Barefoot glanced at his watch and ordered the class to line up for an elephant run. Grey's tenderized scalp screamed in protest as the boat settled on his head. Barefoot trotted away, and the class followed. They wound through the amphibious base, finally lurching to a halt in front of the chow hall. It was time for midnight rations, the much-anticipated fourth meal of the day. The director of the chow hall allowed the SEALs use of the facilities late at night during Hell Week. The mess specialists simply scraped all their leftovers from dinner into containers and stored them for later use by the instructors.

Grey was working on his third cup of hot chocolate when Jackson hobbled in the door accompanied by the corpsman. He made a beeline for the leftover chow. Several minutes later he appeared at the table with a plate full of steaming food.

"Good to see you back," Grey said.

"Thanks." Jackson's voice was weary. "The docs wanted to roll me back to the next class, but I convinced them not to. They said if I got hypothermia again, I'd be a goner for sure."

"They'd roll you just for getting cold?" Rogers asked incredulously. "It's not like getting cold is an accident. The instructors have complete control over how long we're in the water." He shook his head. "That's ridiculous."

"My core temp was ninety degrees," Jackson explained. "Anything below ninety-four is a one-way ticket to a world of trouble. I was on a downward spiral."

"Still . . ."

"Don't worry, brother," Jackson said. "I just thank the Lord for giving me another chance. Let's just hope I can keep my body temp up. The doc said I needed to eat a lot and drink a lot to keep the fire inside raging." He patted his stomach with one hand as he forked meatloaf into his mouth. "God willing, this will all be a bad memory someday."

"Bad memory?" Murray raised an eyebrow. "Hell, this will be a fucking great memory. What other excuse do I have in life to sandwich myself between sexy men like you guys to keep warm?"

"Fag," Larsen grumbled. "Keep your homo tendencies to yourself."

"You're just jealous that I'm not giving you any love." Murray's smile faded as he hacked violently and spat into his napkin.

"Just stay away from me." Larsen scooted his tray over and shifted seats.

Grey sat quietly, cupping his mug of hot chocolate in both hands. His body trembled gently. The damn ceiling fans whirred away, pushing cold air all over the room. Grey had only been up for about thirty-six hours, yet he was already finding his eyelids impossibly heavy.

TWELVE

THE MIDNIGHT CREW STORMED in, jolting Grey out of his daze.

"Get the hell outside!" Osgood screamed. "Move, move!"

Grey jogged through the door, his crew at his heels.

"Get your boat at extended-arm carry! Keep it up there!" Redman, Heisler, and Osgood moved through the ranks like wolves through a herd of sheep. In the background, Furtado's cynical voice echoed through the truck loudspeaker. *Tired. Tired. Want to go home. Sick of it. Sick of it. Leave me alone. I'm gonna quit. I'm gonna quit. The recruiter lied. This sucks. This sucks. I could be somewhere safe and warm. I could be on USS* Neverdock, *whacking in my rack. I could be spanking, but I'm cold. Never gonna end. Never gonna end.* The harassment came to an abrupt halt as Osgood strode to the front of the class.

"Time for a little more land portage, 'cause I know you shitbirds love running. The next evolution is called the base tour. I'm feeling gracious tonight, so I've decided to be your tour guide. I'm going to point out certain landmarks on this fine base, and I expect you to remember them. There will be a test later in the week."

Osgood darted away on his stumpy legs. Boats bounced against one another as the class fell into line. The tour led them all over the amphibious base. Osgood stopped at various buildings and shouted out the location. Personnel Services Division. Post office. Base library. Helicopter pad. SWCC building—Special Warfare Combat Crewman—the SEAL junior-varsity team. Base theater. They flew along the deserted streets, boats bouncing, heads and necks aching. Finally Osgood steered them back to the empty sports field next to the bay. The moment they lowered their boats, Osgood ordered them into the water.

"No, brother," Jackson pleaded, grabbing Grey's arm. "Please."

"Don't look at me," Grey said helplessly. "I hate this crap, too."

"Please." His deep brown eyes were wide. "Please."

Grey waded into the mucky water, dragging Jackson alongside him. They settled in among the slimy tendrils of sea grass that peppered the mucky bottom. Grey pulled Jackson close. They were both shivering in a matter of seconds, as much out of reflex as the actual cold. Murray moved in close on Jackson's other side.

"Wow." Jackson managed a weak smile. "I think the water got warmer."

"Naw," Murray laughed. "I'm pissing on you."

"Well, just keep right on pissin', brother."

"I got you covered next," Grey said. He waited a few minutes, then positioned himself even closer to Jackson and emptied the contents of his bladder.

"Yeah," Jackson moaned. "Oh, yeah."

"I can't hardly believe this," Jones drawled. "My brothers would take me out back and beat the livin' daylights out of me if they knew about this—if they knew I'm buddies with a bunch of guys who piss on each other to stay warm."

"Desperate measures for desperate times," Rogers chattered. "I think it's beautiful, really. Just think about it."

"I'm thinkin', and I don't see no beauty in it. I don't know about you Princeton types, though. If you get excited over this kind of thing, I guess that's okay by me."

The mood lightened considerably. Grey could tell Jackson was distracted; he didn't have the lost look in his eyes that signaled trouble. If a little piss was all it took, Grey would save it all for his hypothermia-prone buddy. They shivered together long into the night. Osgood periodically brought them out for a few minutes of calisthenics, then ordered them back into the bay. Delirium set in. The cold and the sleep deprivation started to take their toll on the students of Class 283. Four trainees bolted for the safety of the instructor truck, leaving the class total at thirty-four.

Grey shivered as dark thoughts wormed back into his head. A familiar scene unfolded. He floated above the Arctic, looking back down on his blue-skinned body immersed in the dark ocean. What little hair he had was frozen solid; his eyes were red, unfeeling, cracked. His chest moved up and down gently, his body past the point of shivering. *Boats.* A fleet of inflatable boats drifted toward him. *Boats. Thank God.*

"Get under your boats!" Osgood yelled.

"Sir!" Murray yelled impatiently. "Let's go!"

Grey stumbled to his feet and slogged out of the bay. Jackson and Murray stuck close to his side. Osgood approached the trio and studied them. He looked Grey in the eye. Grey did his best to stare back confidently.

"Fucking cold, isn't it?" Osgood asked.

Grey nodded.

"I asked you a question, dipshit."

"Yes, it's cold, Instructor Osgood."

"How'd you like to go back in?"

"I would like that very much, Instructor Osgood."

Osgood grinned. "Sir, you're full of shit." He stared Grey down for a few intense seconds before turning and stalking away.

The class lifted their boats onto their heads and followed Osgood to chow. All Grey could think of was a nice steaming cup of hot chocolate. He could already feel it warming his numb fingers, could feel the cup against his cheek, could feel the warm liquid sloshing in his stomach.

"Morning Felicia," Grey croaked.

Felicia's mouth dropped open. "Sir! Mr. Grey! What they do to you?"

"What do you mean?"

"You look bad. You look very tired."

"Felicia, it's Hell Week," Grey explained patiently, "and it's only Tuesday. Wait until you see me on Friday."

Felicia shook her head sadly. "Why a nice man like you do this?"

"Why does a good-looking girl like you do that?" He nodded toward the cash register. "Aren't you headed for Hollywood?"

"As soon as I learn to speak English good." She glanced over at the instructor table. "You better go."

"I'll see you at lunch."

"Eat lots."

"I will." Grey moved down the line, paying little attention to the food that the cafeteria workers slopped on his plate. He could only think of the hot chocolate. Glorious hot chocolate. Grey filled a cup with steaming water, grabbed two pouches of powdered cocoa, and marched over to a table. He sat next to Murray and immediately pressed the cup against his cheek. *Yes.*

"Eat, sir," Murray mumbled between mouthfuls of egg. "It's more important than that shit. Calories, sir. Calories."

Grey reluctantly put down his cup and forked hash browns into his mouth. The crew ate in silence, intently focused on the act of shoveling food down the hatch. Osgood wandered between tables, searching for sleeping students. Fear kept them awake. It was clear no one wanted to experience the Osgood Tabasco Treatment. Chow ended and the class waddled outside. After sitting soaking wet in his plastic chair, Grey was incredibly stiff. The skin between his legs was raw despite the Hell Week–issue spandex. Osgood took a few minutes to reorganize boat crews. Grey's crew remained unchanged with six members. The other five boat crews merged into four, and the instructors strapped the extra boat to the top of Big Blue. Grey was now the lead officer of Boat Crew Five.

"Saddle up, dipshits. Time for a run." Osgood took off down the road.

Grey chanted an old mantra in his head with every step. *Pain. Pain. In my head. Pain. Pain. In my feet. Pain. Pain. In my legs. Pain. Pain. In my knees.* Despite the dark message, Grey found the chant soothing. Anything to keep his mind occupied. The class stumbled to a halt on the beach behind the BUD/S compound.

"Shower time!" Murray exclaimed. He hacked violently then danced a little jig. "Shower time, baby!"

"Where do you get the energy?" Rogers asked. "It baffles me."

Larsen scoffed, "It'll be gone tonight. Just wait. Steel Pier will get him."

Grey stripped off his soggy uniform and walked into the barracks. A windstorm generated by a giant fan greeted him as he navigated the passageway and stepped into the bathroom. The shower felt too good. Grey couldn't bring himself to leave. He tried to hide in the corner, but a brown shirt caught on and called him out. The warm water evaporated under the blast of another fan, and Grey resumed shivering as he trudged toward the medical clinic.

"Any problems?" Doc Anderson asked, giving Grey the once over. Grey simply shook his head.

"Let me see those cuts." He pulled on a latex glove and poked around Grey's oozing leg wound. The red skin around the gash exuded heat. "Not good. I'm going to put you on antibiotics." He scrawled something on a tab of paper, ripped off the top sheet, and handed it to Grey. "Bring this over to the corpsman. He'll take care of you."

"Thanks."

"Hang in there, ensign."

Grey walked across the smooth clinic floor and stopped at the corpsman's table. He handed over his prescription. The corpsman, a weasely little man with thick glasses, snatched the slip from Grey's hands without an upward glance. Seconds later his hand reappeared cupping two large pills. He jerked his head toward the water fountain.

Instructor Petrillo had already positioned himself next to the crates of dry uniforms and was hosing them down. He whistled merrily as he watered his new garden. Grey leaned over his crate and felt a cold stream of water run down his back.

"How's it going, sir?"

"I'm alive."

"Nasty cuts you got on your legs there."

Grey shrugged. "Rock portage. I'm on antibiotics."

"Got a girlfriend?"

The change of subject caught Grey off guard. "Yes. Well, no, I guess not."

"Sir, that doesn't sound too promising. She screwing around behind your back?"

"I don't know."

"Let her go," Petrillo advised. "You don't want a girlfriend in the Teams. Trust me. It's nothing but a heartache. Nothing but a shitty sex life because you're traveling so much. Nothing but a waste of your precious energy, sir."

"Thanks. I'll keep that in mind."

"Just looking out for you," Petrillo said. "Besides, Team guys get more pussy than rock stars. It's hard to be exposed to that and not get a piece for yourself." Petrillo continued whistling as he sauntered down the line, casually hosing students as they frantically pulled on their camouflage uniforms.

Murray appeared at Grey's side. "They don't have a clue."

"Who?"

"Medical. They have no idea I'm on the verge of coughing up a lung."

"And this is a great accomplishment?"

Murray smiled. "It will be a great accomplishment when they secure Hell Week and I've survived five days of this shit with bleeding lungs."

"Is it getting worse?"

"No." Murray slapped Grey on the back. "A little blood never hurt anyone, did it? This isn't preschool, sir, this is a SEAL breeding ground."

"If you say so." Grey finished tying his boots and helped dazed trainees find their gear. When Logan rounded the corner, all the students who had finished dressing sprinted toward the beach. They didn't need any verbal encouragement. Grey arrived at his boat to find a skinny instructor known as Batman sitting on the main tube, paddle in hand. Instructor Batman was a Second Phase instructor, meaning he had volunteered for Hell Week duty. Rumor had it that Instructor Batman thought his chosen name made him more intimidating. Grey thought it was comical. To make matters worse, Batman always sported a pair of trendy sunglasses that hugged his narrow face. Batman stood up, stretched, flexed his tiny muscles, and regarded Grey coolly. Without a word he dug the paddle into the sand and started filling up the boat. Grey grabbed another paddle and scooped the sand out as fast as he could. The two of them worked quickly, but Batman had an advantage. Every third stroke he would aim a paddle full of sand at Grey's face, blinding him for several seconds. Grey would stop, blink rapidly, then resume his digging.

"Sandbox warfare," Logan said, observing the two of the them. He spit a wad of sunflower seeds at Grey's head. "Looks like you're losing, sir."

Jackson and Murray joined him, and together they quickly turned the tide against Batman.

"All three of you, hit the surf," Logan ordered.

They sprinted over the sand berm and into the ocean, and by the time they got back, their boat was completely filled. Batman had already moved on to another boat crew.

"Gather round, children," Logan called out. "Time to get on with the day's plan. The next evolution is a relay race. Each boat crew will run down the beach, together, hanging on to a paddle. Every little turd in the boat crew must have a hand on the paddle at all times. Big Blue will be the halfway point. You will go clockwise around Big Blue and then run back here. If you have any questions you're a fucking retard. The race starts now."

"Let's go," Grey yelled. He was ecstatic. Running without a boat bouncing on his head seemed like a nice break. He picked up a paddle and held it out for the other crew members. Once six hands were grasping the wood, Grey led the way over the berm and down to the hard-packed sand. They passed two boat crews and took the lead. Jackson was the only member of the crew without great running credentials, but he didn't seem to have any problem keeping up.

Big Blue slowed down so that it cruised alongside the lead mass of runners. Instructor Logan leaned out the window. "Well, boys, isn't it nice to be in first place? You've already built a commanding lead, and everyone knows winning has its privileges." Logan shook his head. "Sadly, I saw Mr. Grey's hand leave the paddle. That means all you homos need to jog down to the surf zone, get completely wet, and get on with the race."

"That's bullshit," Grey complained as they turned toward the surf. They had to lay down carefully to avoid accidentally breaking contact with the paddle. Jackson groaned as the frigid water washed over him. The cold didn't bother Grey so much; after all, they would be running in a matter of seconds. But the sand that filtered down his pants legs and stuck between his thighs infuriated him. The flesh between his legs was already raw. Running with sandy thighs would only aggravate the situation.

"Your lead is shrinking," Logan noted. "I bet if you guys hit the surf one more time you'll fall into second place. Who wants to test my theory?"

They ran on. Logan continued to watch them like a hawk. "Oops, it looks like Seaman Murray is testing me. Hit the surf."

Logan continued to heckle them long after they had lost their lead. "Just give me a fair race, and I'll destroy you. I'll eat you for breakfast and leave you crying for Mommy." Grey's anger only fueled his desire to win.

They managed to move ahead despite hitting the surf every few minutes. Finally Big Blue pulled away and raced ahead to mark the turnaround point.

"Let's do this," Grey urged. "Let's show that pussy what we're about."

"I'm dying," Jackson grunted. "I don't have those runner's legs like you."

"Do your best."

They slowly closed on the leaders. By the time they ran around Big Blue they were right on the heels of the lead boat crew. They pulled up alongside their competition. It was Pollock's gang. The two crews ran side by side, feeding off each other, pushing the pace continually. The finish line was less than a quarter mile away when Big Blue roared up alongside them.

"Who's it gonna be?" Logan asked. "Who's gonna sit and relax during the next evolution? This is not a race you want to lose. . . ."

Grey watched Logan from the corner of his eye. The instructor wasn't even looking at Pollock's crew.

"Oh, no!" Logan called out dramatically. "Boat Crew Five, hit the surf. Seaman Murray just screwed you guys over."

Grey led his crew into the ocean. They didn't bother getting out immediately. The race was lost, and the cold water actually felt nice for a change. They lay in the shallows, piled on top of one another, chests heaving. Finally Grey climbed to his feet and helped everyone else up.

"That was our race. It was ours," he said quietly.

"Ah, the elusive laurel wreath," Rogers sighed. "There is something beautifully tragic about our boat crew. It's almost poetic."

"You and your beauty," Jones drawled. "I sure don't see it, sir. But I'll keep my eyes open just in case I'm blessed with one of them revelations."

They walked across the finish line in protest and were immediately sent to the surf by Logan. They huddled together in silence, staring at the gray clouds gliding overhead. The three remaining boat crews limped across the line and joined them in the shallows. The mass of bodies rolled back and forth on the tide, limp, exhausted. Logan paced up and down the beach, checking his watch every few minutes.

"Bring it in!" he yelled. "New game!"

The class waded out of the water and gathered round.

Logan spit a flurry of sunflower seeds into the wind. "How about an old-fashioned puke-fest? You guys would like that, wouldn't you?" He offered a rare smile, flashing teeth speckled with the black and gray remnants of his chewing habit. "Of course you would. Here's how it works. This will be yet another relay race. Each boat crew member will position his head against the paddle like so." Logan stood a paddle upright on the sand and bent over so that his forehead touched the tip. "Then you will spin, like so." Logan spun around the paddle, maintaining contact between the paddle and his head. "You will spin twenty times clockwise as fast as you can. Then you will run to Instructor Batman." Logan choked as he mentioned the name. Even he had a hard time keeping a straight face. "Instructor Batman"—he coughed loudly—"will watch you as you spin twenty times counterclockwise. Then you will run back here. *Capiche?*"

The class nodded. Grey turned to his crew. "Who wants to lead?"

"I will," Murray said. "But I think you should anchor. You're the fastest runner."

"Ready . . ." Logan chanted. "Get set . . . go!"

Murray spun wildly around the paddle. After ten cycles he fell on his butt. He jumped back to his feet and continued spinning. Dropping the paddle, Murray sprinted away, his body positioned at an unnatural slant. He was headed for the sand berm. As he corrected his bearing he tripped. He got up and fell again. Finally he stumbled over to Instructor Batman. Spin, spin, spin. Murray sprinted, fell, sprinted, fell. A sickening shade of green flooded into his face. Reaching the finish, Murray fell to his knees. A stream of puke gushed from his open mouth as Jones started spinning.

"We have a winner!" Logan exclaimed ecstatically. "Feels good, doesn't it? You didn't want that chow anyway."

Grey watched the rest of his boat crew spin, turn green, sprint, and collapse. Jackson and Jones puked. Larsen and Rogers didn't. Now it was his turn. He placed his forehead against the paddle and spun wildly. His head was reeling after ten revolutions. By twenty his stomach churned uneasily. *Time to kick some ass,* Grey thought. *I can outrun anyone here.* His vision blurred, he bolted across the sand. The class erupted into laughter. Grey felt his boot splash against water. He realized with horror that he was at the edge of the ocean. He corrected himself and stumbled over to Batman.

"Having a little trouble, sir?" Batman asked, grinning stupidly.

Grey picked up the paddle and spun counterclockwise. As he ran back across the stretch of beach, he flexed his stomach muscles in a vain attempt to keep breakfast down. An acidic mess surged up his throat, and he puked on his uniform as he continued running.

"Nice!" Instructor Logan cheered. "Very nice!"

Grey stumbled across the finish line in second place.

"Go clean yourself off in the surf zone, you filthy pig."

Grey flopped into the ocean and wiped the puke from his shirt with his hand. His mouth still burned from the contents of his stomach. *Water.* Grey stumbled back to Instructor Logan.

"Go hydrate," Logan ordered. "And hurry it up."

Grey poured the contents of his canteen all over his face, gulping and gagging down as much as he could. He rejoined the class, which was already forming up for the next relay race. The instructions required them to roll like a log to Instructor Batman, perform a perfect handstand, and then roll back. More puking, more nausea, more headaches, more thirst. Grey struggled to do a handstand. It took him several minutes to regain enough balance to keep himself inverted.

The sun reached its zenith behind the thick layer of clouds, a faint white spot in a sea of gray. The class formed up for the run to chow. Grey switched positions with Larsen, who had been holding the hardest spot in the middle of the boat all day.

"I don't think I'm going to last," Larsen stated matter-of-factly. "My fucking shins are crapping out. Stress fractures."

"Can you run through it?" Murray asked. "Hold on until Thursday night?"

"Doubt it. I've been sucking it up the last two days. I'm destroying my legs."

"Did you tell the doc?" Grey asked.

"No."

"Why not?"

"Didn't want to get rolled. Starting back at day one doesn't excite me."

"That's understandable, but if you destroy your legs like you say, there's no way you'll ever get through five more months of this."

Larsen shrugged and continued running. His face was distorted with pain by the time they stopped at the chow hall. He reported in to the corpsman, and Grey knew that was the last he'd see of Larsen all week.

"I'm sick of losing guys," Grey said as he moved down the chow line. "No more. I'm putting a cap on injuries and DORs, effective immediately."

"Cool, because I was thinking about quitting," Murray said, voice dripping with sarcasm. "Now I have a reason to stay."

"Seriously, though, doesn't it get to you?"

"Of course it does, sir, but that's the nature of the beast. The statistics speak for themselves."

Grey picked up his traditional cup of hot chocolate and took a seat. The mood at the table was grim. Now that Larsen was gone, they were down to five people. Logan walked over to the group, followed by a square-jawed thirty-four-year-old petty officer named Simpson. Simpson was a former Recon Marine who had managed to get an age waiver so that he could attend training. The usual cutoff age was twenty-nine.

"Here's your new man," Logan said, nodding toward Simpson.

"Welcome," Jones said sleepily. "Take a seat."

"Thanks."

Grey could tell square-jawed Simpson was all business. The guy sat like a marine, looked like a marine, talked like marine. No wonder the instructors didn't like him. He had a good reputation with the students, though. Grey felt strange about the prospect of leading a seasoned soldier who was ten years his senior.

After chow Logan ran the class back to the beach. He claimed the surf was up and it was a perfect time for a little surf passage. The boat crews lined up at the edge of the ocean, and the coxswains reported.

"Ensign Grey reporting, Boat Crew Five standing by, manned, rigged, and ready for sea." He saluted with his paddle.

"Very well," Logan said. He looked the coxswains over. "As you can see, we've got some nice sets rolling through this afternoon. I want some quality entertainment. Quality, gents. None of this pansy-ass *timing the sets* crap. I want carnage. I want bodies flying through the air. You are here to entertain us this afternoon. Failure to do so will result in surf torture." He spat a gob of chewed-up sunflower seeds onto Grey's boot. "First race is to paddle out to the buoy, dump boat, then paddle back in with the boat upside down. Any questions?"

"Do we have to paddle with the bow facing forward?" Pollock asked. "I don't fucking care," Logan growled. "What kind of stupid-ass question is that? All I demand is that you paddle in upside down. Now get out of my face." He dismissed the boat crew leaders with a flick of his hand.

Grey turned and ran toward his crew. "Hit the surf!" He caught up with them as they carried the boat into the shallows. A huge set had just rumbled in. The timing was right, and Grey knew they needed to act quickly. Murray called cadence as Grey urged them on. They bumped over a few lines of whitewash before crashing through the curling lip of a wave. A few more powerful strokes and they were safely offshore.

"What's the race?" Rogers asked.

"Around the buoy, dump boat, and paddle in upside down."

"What? Upside down?"

"That's the order," Grey said. "Should be interesting."

"Interesting?" Jones drawled. "I think they pay you officer types just to be optimistic. Beauty in everything, everything interesting . . ." He shook his head.

After they paddled around the buoy, Grey collected all the paddles and abandoned ship along with the two students on the port side of the craft. The three remaining crew members pulled the boat upside down. Grey handed the paddles up to Simpson, who was now positioned atop the slippery craft. The three of them left in the water scampered aboard and grabbed their paddles. Soon they were all kneeling and stroking toward shore. With nothing to hold on to and no exposed tubing to brace themselves against, their balance was precarious at best. As they slowly inched toward shore, a series of large swells rose up behind them, forcing them to lie back to avoid slipping off the bow of the boat. *Logan wants entertainment,* Grey thought, *and that's what he's going to get.* They approached the break zone, and the crew members looked at one another and shook their heads. They didn't have a chance. Six-foot surf was hard enough to manage right side up.

"Good Lord, guide us and protect us," Jackson mumbled. "Deliver us from angry seas and broken backs."

"Sir, I recommend we hold off until the next set rolls through," Simpson offered.

"Can't do it, Simpson," Grey said. "Logan's orders. No chickenshit. We are here to entertain. Full speed ahead, shipmates."

They continued stroking as the large swells became increasingly steep. *This is it.* Grey eyed a mammoth wall of water bearing down on them. Murray smirked, Jackson cringed, Simpson sat steely eyed. There was no way to brace for impact, so they simply waited for disaster. The wave picked up the stern and dropped the bow, catapulting Grey over the heads of his crewmen. He slapped into the water and immediately struggled for the bottom. He relaxed as the world spun in a whirlwind of churning water, a stray foot, a paddle. Once his lungs started to burn with oxygen deprivation, Grey pushed off for the surface. The boat was nowhere to be seen. Although the roar of the surf muffled their voices, Grey could hear the instructors cheering from shore.

Grey stroked awkwardly, holding his paddle with one arm as he pulled with the other. The rest of his crew struggled over, and they waded to shore together.

"Nice show!" Logan yelled, genuinely pleased. "Jones, that was a nice backflip. You do that on purpose?"

"Of course," Jones said, grinning from ear to ear.

"Well, you turds win this round. Take a seat. Get comfy."

They sat butts to nuts in the sand, pressing their shivering bodies together. They watched the next round of surf passage and cheered as boats shot into the air, scattering bodies to the wind. The instructors commented on the performances as crews struggled toward shore.

"Fucking Pollock," Batman said. "What a pussy. Did you see him hesitate?"

"I saw it," Logan grumbled. "Surf torture for those pansies."

The crews jogged up the beach, dragging their boats along with them. They stopped in front of Logan and looked at him expectantly.

"Ensign Pollock, Boat Crew Three, standing by, manned, rigged, and—"

"Shut up!" Logan yelled. "You don't deserve to be a boat crew leader. You disobeyed my orders. I said no hesitation."

"But—"

"But what? You fail. You fail. You fail." Logan worked himself into a rage. "You like the sound of that, don't you? Failure! Failure! Failure!" He kicked sand at the shivering crew. "Pollock, take your worthless Academy ass and your worthless crew and take a seat in the surf."

The boat drills continued throughout the afternoon. They paddled facing backward, they swam their boats in, they purposely let the waves catch them sideways. Mass carnage reigned supreme. Finally the night crew took over and ran the class to chow.

"Wow," Rogers groaned. "I've got a bit of a headache."

"No shit," Murray added. "I think we all left a few brain cells behind."

Felicia pressed another candy bar into Grey's hand as they filed past the cash register. He mouthed his thanks and continued on. Instructor Barefoot watched Grey with big mouse eyes.

"Tuesday night," Murray said as they sat down together. "The big test. This is it. I heard once you make it past Tuesday night, you're almost there."

"That's because Tuesday night is the worst," Jones said. "Steel Pier ain't no joke."

Grey greedily inhaled his spaghetti and meatballs. The afternoon's adventures had given him a ravenous appetite. Six pieces of cake later he was still hungry. Grey filed back through the chow line and got seconds.

"Hungry?" Jackson asked, raising an eyebrow at Grey's gluttony.

"Yup," Grey said. "You should eat more. It's going to be a cold night. You'll need all the energy you can get.

"I'm working on it, sir," Jackson said, holding a forkful of mashed potatoes before his lips. "Don't know about you, whitey, but I was raised with manners."

Grey smiled. "There's a place for everything, Jackson. And let me tell you, there is absolutely no place for manners this week. Survival is the name of the game." He pointed his fork at Jackson's plate. "And that's why you should eat."

Chief Baldwin ushered the class out into the humid evening air. "Feels like rain, gents. Looks like you guys will get the full benefit tonight."

Instructor Barefoot appeared at the front of the class and smiled wickedly. "Ready to freeze your asses off? If I was you, I'd quit right now. Tonight will be no fun, I promise you that. Just think about it. Think about the coldest you've ever been, then think ten times colder. We're going to bring you to the edge and leave you there."

A shy young seaman named Gracy stepped out from under his boat. His crew leader lunged for his arm, but Gracy sidestepped him.

"No harm in quitting," Barefoot said as Baldwin ushered Gracy away. "This is not for everyone. Hell, I wouldn't do it again."

Let's get on with it. Cut the propaganda. Grey's scalp was raw, his back was torqued, his legs were horribly infected, his skin was chaffed, his lips were chapped, his privates tenderized from sand. Despite his ills, he was more determined than ever to see the week through. Barefoot's speech only added fuel to the fire.

The class spent the next hour following Barefoot around the base. The skinny instructor ran impossibly fast, and a virtual symphony of groans, grunts, and the occasional whimper rose into the air as they followed his lead. Finally Barefoot came to a halt next to a long pier that jutted north into the bay. Five metal sheets, six feet long and three feet wide, sat at the base of the pier. Ice cubes completely covered the sheets.

"No," Jackson whispered. "Please God, no."

"Can't be that bad," Murray said, placing a comforting hand on Jackson's shoulder. "What's the worst that will happen?" He shrugged. "You'll die, that's all. But you're a religious man, so you have nothing to worry about."

"Welcome to the Arctic research station," Barefoot said. He pointed to the metal sheets. "We've got ice." He pointed to three large fans. "We've got freezing winds." He pointed to the bay. "And we've got cold water. What else could you ask for?"

Chief Baldwin cut in. "Before I let Instructor Barefoot have his fun with you, we're going to practice some survival skills. Everyone pick a partner."

Grey turned his eyes toward Murray, who nodded in affirmation.

"You and your partner will enter the water next to the pier. One at a time, you will take off your boots, tie them around your neck, and then make a flotation device out of your pants like we taught you. Once you're done, stand by for further instructions."

Grey and Murray filed down the pier and jumped into the bay. The briny water was only slightly warmer than the ocean. Grey treaded water while his partner struggled with his boots between violent coughs. Murray's head disappeared below the surface, then reappeared seconds later as he gasped for air. After several minutes he lifted a pair of boots from the water and tied the laces together. He slung the boots around his neck, pulled his pants off, and tied the legs together. Grasping his pants by the waist, he flung them over his head and into the water, trapping a massive pocket of air in the legs. Holding the waist shut, Murray slipped his head through his new life preserver.

"Your turn," Murray said.

"Right." Grey took a deep breath, then disappeared below the surface. The absence of light and the murkiness of the water made it extremely difficult to see his boots. He groped blindly, trying to undo his knots with numb fingers. When his breath ran out he jerked for the surface. After several minutes of frustration, Grey finally managed to strip his boots off and tie them around his neck. His pants came off with less trouble. He tied the legs, whipped the pants over his head, and clasped the waist closed.

Murray and Grey bobbed together in the bay, shivering, eyes turned expectantly toward the pier. Baldwin paced back and forth with a grim expression on his face, watching the students struggle. The class waited and waited. The shivering grew more intense, more desperate. Baldwin continued pacing.

"This blows," Murray chattered.

"I know." Grey forced a weak smile. "I don't see how it can get much worse."

"Everyone out!" Baldwin yelled. "And make it quick!"

The class made a mad dash for the single ladder that led back to the pier. One by one, they climbed out of the bay and filed down to the metal sheets. Instructor Barefoot eyed them hungrily.

"First of all, get rid of your uniforms and boots. I want you in your underpants. Then I want Boat Crews One through Three to stay here. Boat Crews Four and Five, report to Senior Chief Lundin at the windstorm station."

Grey unbuttoned his camouflage top, stripped off his white T-shirt, pulled off his socks, and dropped them all in a pile along with his pants and boots. Herding his boat crew ahead of him, Grey shivered over to

Senior Chief Lundin. Three metal fans with enormous blades sat behind the somber instructor.

"I'd like to tell you this isn't going to suck," Lundin said. "But I'm not a liar. Just remember, this can't last forever." He arranged the frigid students in a line, then placed his hand on a switch. "Keep your arms out. I want exposed pits." With a flourish he flicked the switch, and a torrent of cold night air whipped over the students. He turned the other two fans on, then stepped aside and watched the trainees squirm.

Grey closed his eyes as the wind caressed his dripping body. His body lurched and jerked involuntarily as it reacted to the new chill. The fans hummed, the students cursed, and the raindrops started to fall. Lundin looked up and shook his head in disbelief.

"You unlucky bastards. You poor souls."

They shivered, jerked, and drooled, moaned, groaned, and whimpered.

"Let's try to lighten the mood a little, shall we?" Lundin asked. "Who's got a story or a poem, or something to share with the class."

Murray raised his hand.

"Yes, Murray . . ."

"I have something for show-and-tell," Murray chattered.

"Well, what could that be?" Lundin asked patronizingly.

Murray pulled down his white spandex underwear. "The world's smallest cock and balls, courtesy of BUD/S training."

Lundin didn't bat an eye. "Very nice, Murray. Anyone else?"

Rogers raised his hand.

"Yes, Princeton . . ."

"I have a few lines of verse."

"Of course you do, sir."

"They're from *The Tempest* by Shakespeare."

Lundin nodded. "Fitting."

Rogers started reciting, but he was chattering so hard he could barely form the words. Finally he pulled himself together enough to whip through a few lines. Grey tried to listen, but the verse went right through him. Something about "ebbing Neptune," "mutinous winds," and "heavenly music."

"Nicely done, sir," Lundin said. "Now kindly remove the silver spoon from your mouth and keep suffering."

Jones snorted a laugh. Grey dreamed of hot chocolate.

"Time for a rotation," Lundin said. "Go report to Instructor Barefoot."

Grey stumbled away from the whirring fans and padded through the rain toward the dreaded metal sheets. Boat Crews One, Two, and Three passed by, looking like the living dead with their blue skin and sunken, wild eyes.

"Welcome," Instructor Barefoot said. He gestured toward the ice-laden metal sheets. "Please, lay down. Make yourselves comfortable."

"Do we have to?" Murray asked.

"Shut the fuck up." The smile was gone. "Get down there. Now."

Grey chose a spot next to Murray and Jackson. He stepped onto the sheet, and his feet immediately burned. He sat down, and his ass was on fire. Finally he lay back and cringed as a million little campfires erupted across his body.

"Put your heads down," Barefoot ordered. "Don't try to cheat the system."

Grey lowered his head onto the cubes of ice and shuddered. It felt like someone was cracking a ball-peen hammer against his skull.

"I want you to lay there and think about what you're doing. I mean, why the fuck are you putting up with this? This is ridiculous. You should be home in bed, and you're lying on a metal sheet covered with ice."

Soon a drumlike rattle filled the air. It gradually grew in intensity, and Grey realized it was the sound of frozen bodies shivering and bouncing on top of the metal sheets. *Ratta-tat-tat.* Grey clenched his jaw shut to stop the chattering of his teeth. Jackson mumbled next him. "Oh, God. Oh, Lord."

"On your stomachs," Barefoot ordered.

Grey rolled over and had to bite his hand to keep from screaming. His testicles sang with pain. He looked over at Murray, hoping to gain some comfort from his friend. Instead, he was met with a blank stare, a look totally devoid of feeling.

"Murray?" Grey hissed. "You okay?"

Murray's eyes flickered. "What?"

"You okay?"

"A little cold, but that's part of the game."

"Okay. Just checking."

"On your backs," Barefoot ordered.

Grey rolled back over. *Ratta-tat-tat.* The drum roll of clattering bodies started again. Grey tried to bring himself to another place, tried to imagine himself in bed with Vanessa, but then he remembered the old man and his flowers. He tried to picture himself in Palm Springs, lounging by a pool in the desert heat. No good. *Too fucking cold.*

"Up, up, up," Barefoot ordered. "Go take a dunk in the bay and report back to Senior Chief Lundin."

Grey tried to stand up but slipped on a piece of ice. He crashed down on his ass, scattering cubes everywhere. Moving more cautiously, Grey slowly rose to his feet. He tested his balance, taking a few delicate steps. Satisfied with his coordination, he shivered over to the side of the pier and jumped into the bay.

The water was warm. So warm . . . like a Jacuzzi. Nothing like a little ice to put things in perspective. Grey worked the feeling back into his limbs.

"Hot damn!" Jones exulted. "I never thought the bay would feel so good."

"Lundin's waiting," Grey said. "Sorry to disappoint, but we better get moving."

They climbed up the ladder and back into the windstorm. They did four rotations through the circuit: windstorm, ice, bay. By the time the drill ended, Grey's mind slipped and misfired constantly. Jackson was another story altogether. He refused to answer any of Grey's questions. He simply shook his head when asked if he was okay. Grey and Murray sandwiched him, trying to force some warmth back into his body. They huddled at the back of the group as Barefoot addressed the class.

"All right, girls, enough of this cold bullshit. I prefer running. Get dressed and get under your boats. Make it quick."

Grey quickly pulled on his pants, his shirt, and his top. He yanked on his socks and slipped into his boots, only to look up and see that Jackson hadn't moved. He was still standing in his underwear in the midst of a group of dressing students. *Shit.*

"Jackson, buddy, time to get dressed," Grey said, gently shaking

Jackson's arm. He picked up a pair of pants and held them out. No response. He could see this would be a challenge. "Murray, get over here."

Murray appeared at his side. "Jackson, bro, pull it together."

Grey grasped Jackson by the shoulders. "Lay down," he ordered.

Jackson slowly lowered himself to the concrete. Grey started yanking the pants on his legs while Murray worked on his T-shirt.

"What the fuck is going on here?" Barefoot asked.

"Nothing," Grey lied. "Jackson's fingers are numb. He's having trouble with his buttons." *Wake up, Jackson. Snap out of it.*

Murray subtly inched his hand toward Jackson's pants. Moving with lighting speed, he grabbed Jackson's balls and gave them a hard squeeze. The dazed trainee sat bolt upright, eyes wide.

"See, he's fine," Grey said.

"You guys are pathetic," Barefoot sneered. "Just hurry it up. Don't make the class wait for you. I can always put you back on the ice."

Jackson slowly regained his alertness as Grey and Murray pulled on his boots. They sprinted to their boat just as Barefoot led the elephant train away from the pier.

"Up boat!" Grey yelled. They lifted the boat onto their heads and took off at a full run. Barefoot led the class across the amphibious base, across the highway, and onto the beach. He turned north and ran past the rock pile, past the Hotel del Coronado, past the gate to the North Island Naval Air Station. The bouncing boat was as uncomfortable as ever, but Grey had grown partially numb to the constant pounding on his skull. They had covered at least three miles by the time Barefoot stopped the elephant train.

THIRTEEN

THE MIDNIGHT CREW WAS already positioned on the beach, waiting to take over. Instructor Osgood emerged from the shadows. "It's my show now, turds. We're playing a new game. It's called Escape and Evasion. First, why don't you refresh yourselves and hit the surf."

The class ran into the shallows, flopped down, and ran back.

"Now that you're suitably cold again, I want each boat crew to dig a shelter. It should be a pit big enough to fit seven people inside. You can use your boat as a roof. Just make sure you conceal the damn thing. You have thirty minutes."

Grey chose a patch of sand at the edge of the beach bordering a large stand of dense bushes. Each member of his boat crew grabbed a paddle and dug quickly. Once they had excavated a good-size pit, they flopped their boat on top of it and covered the whole thing with sand. As a final touch, Murray ripped a plant from the sandy soil behind them and placed it on top of their shelter. *Not bad.* Grey crawled inside. *A bit cozy, but workable.*

"Time's up, dipshits!" Osgood yelled.

Grey scrambled out of the shelter. He joined the class in a school circle around Instructor Osgood.

"Like I said, this is Escape and Evasion. Your goal is to not get caught." He scanned the fatigued faces in front of him. "Trust me, you don't want to get caught. Your goal is to get from the drop-off point to your shelter without getting intercepted by one of the hostiles. You'll have a few hours, so don't try that bullshit where you think you can sprint the whole way. None of that. You should be on your bellies most of the time. Use any cover available and keep a low profile. By the way, you're operating in swim pairs, not boat crews. I recommend staying away from big groups. Now form it up for a run. Instructor Redman is going to take you to the start."

The class formed into three ranks, and Instructor Redman stationed his hulking form at the front of the formation. The run was relaxing. Grey knew he could outpace Redman in a heartbeat, and now that he didn't have a boat on his head, he felt surprisingly good. They ran for several minutes before coming to a stop next to Big Blue. Furtado and Heisler regarded the class coolly from the warmth of the truck.

"Stay off the airfield," Redman ordered. "Stay off the roads. Use common sense. Prisoners will be tortured. Now get lost."

Grey scanned his surroundings. A straight shot along the beach would be suicide. No cover. A shallow gully ran to the east, ending at a playing field ringed by trees. Beyond that was the airfield and the Navy Lodge. They would have to try their luck with the gully. Grey and Murray ran over a small sand berm and dropped into the gully.

"The farther we get in our first few minutes, the better," Grey said.

"Good call," Murray agreed. "Let's at least get to the field."

They ran at a crouch, shuffling through the soft sand at the bottom of the gully. Once they reached the perimeter of the field, Grey dropped to a prone position. He crawled along the edge of trees, moving toward the airfield with Murray at his side.

Murray put a hand on Grey's shoulder. Grey froze. Someone with a flashlight moved slowly along the opposite side of the field. They slowly backed behind a tree. The figure prowled around for a few minutes before turning to the south. They continued crawling until they reached the end of the field. Across a narrow road lay a large dirt field, approximately fifty yards on a side. A small shack sat in the center of the clearing. Grey pointed across the sparsely vegetated terrain and shrugged. He knew the instructors wouldn't expect them to cross over to the Navy Lodge at the far end of the clearing. Murray nodded his assent.

They scrambled across the road and dropped onto their stomachs. The field provided little cover, just a few knee-high brambles. Grey crawled quickly, dragging his torso across the dirt. He stopped behind the sheet-metal shack to catch his breath. Murray appeared at his side seconds later.

"I'm never going to forget this," Murray whispered.

"Forget what?"

"This week. Everything. All the shit we've been through."

Grey nodded. It wasn't like Murray to get all nostalgic.

"Thanks for always looking out for me." He coughed loudly into his hand and wiped the reddish goo on his pants.

"You should turn yourself in," Grey said quietly. "This is getting ridiculous."

"I'll be fine." Murray smiled weakly.

Grey squeezed Murray's shoulder before continuing across the field. A two-foot-high cement wall surrounded the clearing to the east. Grey gave a quick glance over his shoulder then rolled over the wall and flattened himself against the pavement on the other side. Murray flopped down next to him, and they surveyed the parking lot. The area was cluttered with cars—good cover. It was past midnight, and most of the hotel-room windows were dark. Moving from car to car, Grey crawled on his hands and knees toward the building.

Suddenly a beam of light cut toward them. Murray and Grey hit the deck and held their breath. Footsteps sounded in the parking lot, and the light bounced from car to car. Murray started to lift his head, but Grey yanked him back down. Whoever was roaming the parking lot was looking for something—probably them.

Grey lay a short distance from an open corridor that cut through the center of the hotel. The north side of the hotel bordered a sizable plot of land covered with thick, head-high bushes. The vegetation would provide optimal cover, but Grey knew they couldn't risk moving that far. They would have to try their luck with the corridor. The light suddenly vanished. Grey ventured a peek over the hood of the Mustang he was using as cover. A lone figure slowly worked the parking lot in the opposite direction, sweeping a beam of light back and forth to the south.

"We're taking the corridor," Grey whispered. "I'll lead. I'm going straight through. I'll look for cover at the opposite end. Give me a few minutes before you follow."

"Good luck." Murray winked.

Moving as quietly as he could, Grey darted from the Mustang, scurried down a short walkway, and flattened himself against the wall of the corridor. He advanced thirty feet and stopped at the intersection of another hallway that cut to the north. He peeked around the corner. *Nothing.* He continued on. Just as he reached the far end of the hotel, a door squeaked open behind him. Grey froze. He couldn't make himself turn around.

"Are you an army soldier?" It was the voice of a young child.

Crap. Grey slowly turned. A boy, probably four years old, clutched a stuffed bear to his chest and regarded him with wide eyes.

"No," Grey whispered. He corrected himself. "Yes. Yes I am." Grey reached into his pocket and pulled out the soggy Snickers bar, which Felicia had given him that afternoon. He held it out. "Here. I'll give you this candy bar if you don't tell your parents I'm here."

The kid took one look at the mostly crushed, sand-coated Snickers bar and burst into tears. He disappeared into his room and pulled the door shut behind him. *Fuck me. I'm fucked. Shit. Shit.* Grey exited the corridor to the east and frantically looked for cover. No bushes. No cars. A row of lush trees bordered a road that ran from north to south. Without thinking twice, Grey scrambled up the nearest tree. He climbed into the high branches and froze. A dense layer of leaves obscured his vision.

"Where did you see him? Can you show daddy?"

"Over there."

"Did he really offer you a candy bar?"

"Yeah, but it was smashed. Yucky."

"Go back inside. I'll wait here and see if he comes back."

Grey hit his head gently against the trunk of the tree as he considered his situation. Murray was stranded at the other end of the building. Hopefully he would spot the man standing in the hallway and abandon Grey's route. If he did, Murray had three choices: stay hidden behind the Mustang, navigate the dense bushes on the north side of the hotel, or work his way south through the parking lot. *He'll go north.* It made the most sense. Staying in the parking lot was too risky.

Grey couldn't move with the man loitering in the hallway. He'd have to wait until the man retreated to his room. Grey clung to the tree and listened, yearning for the sound of a closing door. He was far from his shelter on the beach, and he knew that failing to make it back within the time limit would result in severe punishment. Another hour in the surf was not a pleasant thought.

The man coughed. Grey waited. The man wandered out onto the street. Grey hugged his tree and held his breath. The man sat down on the curb below the tree. He held his head in his hands. *Great. This guy obviously has something else on his mind.* After several long minutes, he rose to his feet and disappeared into the corridor. A door slammed shut.

Grey hung from one of the tree's lower limbs and dropped to the ground. He tiptoed down the corridor, gingerly making his way to the western side of the building. He peeked around the corner. No sign of an instructor.

"Murray," he hissed. "Murray, let's get out of here."

No reply.

Grey dodged from car to car to the north. He stopped at the thick stand of bushes that bordered the hotel.

"Murray, let's go. It's all clear."

Silence.

Grey turned and darted from car to car to the south. *Must have taken the southern route.* It made sense. Once the figure with the flashlight moved on, there was no reason not to take that approach. Grey crouched in the shadow of a tree at the far end of the hotel.

"Murray," he pleaded. "Let's go."

The wind whispered from the beach.

Crap. Murray could have moved on without him. Grey tried to imagine his friend leaving him behind. *No way.* It was strictly forbidden to leave your swim buddy behind, and Murray was loyal beyond question. *Maybe an instructor nabbed him.* That would spell the end for both of them. *Fuck.* Grey sprinted across the parking lot, vaulted off the retaining wall, and churned through the soft sand of the gully toward the beach. His breath came in heaving gasps as he passed the metal shack. *Murray, where are you?*

Grey suddenly dropped onto his stomach behind a small sand berm.

Not far ahead, Grey could make out two instructors escorting a student toward the surf. He strained his eyes to positively identify his swim buddy. It had to be him. *He's caught.*

"Stupid fuck. If you're going to screw your swim buddy, you might as well not come back for him and get nailed."

Grey's heart pounded as he looked over his shoulder. It was Heisler.

"You never leave your swim buddy behind, sir." He shook his head sadly. "Never."

Heisler didn't need to say anything more. Grey knew a serious beating was in store.

"Get off your ass and follow me."

"Can I rejoin Murray?" Grey asked.

"Don't worry about him." Heisler smiled. "He's in good hands."

Heisler marched Grey toward the beach, veering to the south of the path taken by Murray and his two escorts. Grey scanned the surf for his friend. A human form lay prone in the shallows, shivering violently beneath the watchful eye of two familiar instructors. *Redman and Furtado. Fuck.*

Grey marched south in the darkness with Heisler's palm planted firmly on his back. They halted in front of Instructor Osgood, who sat on a small sand berm overlooking the ocean.

"This officer lost his swim buddy," Heisler said quietly. "And he lost him in territory that was off-limits. I think he needs a little remediation."

"Welcome to my world of pain," Osgood growled. "Drop on down, fuck stick."

Grey dropped into the push-up position.

"Bear crawl," Osgood ordered. The stocky instructor stood and walked backward, leading Grey toward the surf. "So you lost your swim buddy in territory that was off-limits?" he asked. "I can't think of a more serious fuck-up. I just can't. You will pay dearly for your stupidity. Start praying to whatever gods you believe in, sir. You're gonna need their help to survive the next hour."

Grey crawled into the ocean and lay down facing the beach. His mouth cleared the surface, but every ten seconds a large breaker would roll toward shore and surge over his face. Osgood stood silently on the beach, arms crossed, legs spread. Grey lost feeling in his hands first, then his lower legs.

A patch of clear sky opened up overhead. When Grey's face wasn't submerged, he focused on the stars that twinkled in the coal-black sky. He felt himself slipping away. Hoping to find another warm body to latch on to, he reached to the side. Nothing. No Murray to crack a joke. No Jackson to put suffering into perspective with his jackhammering body. No Jones with his hillbilly twang. Just as Grey's jaw muscles froze up, Osgood ordered him out of the water. He stood and fell repeatedly and finally gave up and crawled to Osgood's feet.

"On your feet," Osgood ordered impatiently.

Grey carefully rose to a standing position.

"On your back."

Grey flopped over backward, slamming into the sand.

"On your belly."

Grey rolled onto his belly.

"On your feet."

The cycle continued endlessly: Osgood spitting out commands like a robot, Grey rising and dropping and rolling.

"Instructor Osgood," Grey croaked. "I want you to know it wasn't Murray's idea to split up. It was my idea."

"Shut up! Don't try to play the martyr!" Osgood pointed back toward the surf. "Get out there and think about how you failed as a leader and as a teammate."

Just as Grey started toward the surf, the wail of the ambulance siren pierced the night.

Grey turned and watched the huge SUV, lights flashing, race to the north. *Oh shit.*

Big Blue's loudspeaker crackled to life from darkness to the south. "Fall in on Big Blue immediately. This is not a drill."

"Stand fast, shitbag," Osgood barked, clamping his hand on Grey's arm. He listened intently to the cackle of his radio. *Man down. Man down.*

Grey's heart dropped. "Who is it?" he asked urgently.

"Shut the fuck up," Osgood ordered.

Grey broke free from Osgood's grip and sprinted to the north, moving as fast as his numb legs would carry him. Osgood followed behind, cursing loudly. Grey fixed his gaze on the red flashing lights of the ambulance and increased his pace. He watched in horror as Redman and Furtado rolled a limp body onto a hard plastic backboard and loaded it into the back of the SUV.

"No!" Grey yelled.

Osgood tackled Grey from behind, dropping him to the sand.

"Sir, you better fuckin' control yourself, or I'll make sure you never end up in the Teams."

Grey lay sprawled face-first on the beach with a mouth full of sand as the ambulance sped past, siren blaring. He tried to stifle his tears, but they ran freely into the sand. *No. No fucking way.*

"Get a grip," Osgood growled. "We need to get back to Big Blue and muster. I'll deal with you later."

Grey wiped his sleeve against his eyes. He tried to control his breathing. "Is he dead?"

"Could be," Osgood said. "Now get off your ass."

Grey rose to his hands and knees.

"Get up, sir."

Grey stood.

"Now pretend for one minute that you're a man. Pretend that you have a sack." Osgood kicked at the sand in frustration. "We're training you to be a warrior, not a chaplain. You can cry all you want after Hell Week, but you need to stow that shit."

Grey dragged a sandy sleeve across his eyes. He couldn't stop thinking about Murray. Not only had Grey agreed to help hide Murray's condition from the doctors, but he'd also abandoned his swim buddy, breaking a cardinal rule of the BUD/S trainee. *It's over for me. It's over.*

Osgood planted a hand on Grey's back and began pushing him, stumbling, toward the gathering crowd of trainees down the beach. "Run, you dumb shit. Run."

Grey tried to force his legs in the steady rhythm of a quick run, but he couldn't do it. His body felt like a wet noodle, and his knees kept buckling. By the time Grey reached his fellow students, Ensign Ryder, the crusty old SEAL in charge of the night shift, had already gathered the class into a school circle. Osgood roughly pushed Grey to his knees behind Rogers.

"Listen up, tadpoles," Ensign Ryder said. "We lost a man tonight. All I'm going to say is this: it's a goddamn shame, and if any of you mother-fuckers want to hide a medical condition from us, do so at your own risk. Murray had pulmonary edema." Ensign Ryder glared at Grey. "His condition should have been apparent to the other members of his boat crew. His death was absolutely fucking unnecessary. We're on lockdown, gents. This is serious shit, and if I had my way, you'd all be paying for the man for what happened. We're on standby until we hear from the CO."

Grey turned the situation over in his mind. He knew Murray had pulmonary edema, and he had been suffering. But dying from a little surf torture? *No way.*

"Cupcake," a voice whispered. "You don't think you're going to sit here on dry ground until the commanding officer checks in, do you?"

Shit.

"Not a chance." Osgood grabbed the collar of Grey's camouflage top and yanked him to his feet. "Give me a hundred squats."

Grey's rubbery legs barely held him up as he began squats. Osgood looked on with disgust, barking encouragement whenever Grey's legs failed and he collapsed to the sand. The rest of the class looked on with empty eyes. Hell Week had long ago beat the compassion out of them. When Grey couldn't perform another squat, Osgood switched to push-ups.

"Between every repetition, you will repeat the following: 'I am a worthless turd, and I will never be a leader.'"

Grey started his push-ups with pulverized arms, grunting the declaration every time his arms locked. At fifty reps, his body failed.

"Slither to the surf like a dirty snake," Osgood ordered.

Grey wormed his way down to the water's edge.

"I only want to see your eyeballs."

I can't take this. Grey crawled into the shallows, his head already spinning deliriously. He rolled onto his back. *I'm going to quit. I'm going to count to ten, and I'm going to quit, then I'm going to walk away forever and never look back. One. Two. Thr—* A surge of salt water rushed over his face and into his mouth. He choked and spat. *Three. Four.* Images flashed through Grey's mind in rapid succession: Murray tackling Instructor Redman. Murray drunk, coming to Grey's defense. Murray laughing, swearing, winking. *Five. Six. Seven.* Grey steeled himself for his encounter with Osgood. He would just walk right up to him and say it. *Eight. Nine. Murray wouldn't quit.* The realization hit Grey like a ton of bricks. Another wave of cold water rushed over his face. *Blood brothers. Promise you won't quit. Promise.*

"What the hell am I supposed to do?" Grey asked the sky. "What?"

The stars spun above his head. Murray's voice flitted through his consciousness. *Finish it, boss. Don't let the fuckers beat you down. Win. Win.*

"Win what?"

Grey vaguely felt a hand close around his arm. He was being dragged from the water. The feel of dry sand scraping against his sopping uniform jolted him back to reality. Osgood kneeled next to him.

"Sir," he said quietly but firmly, "don't make me send you to the ambulance. I don't want you to wash out of this program. I want you to learn. I'm creating you. I'm making you a man. Give me a reason to keep you here. Snap out of it."

"I'm fine," Grey said weakly. "The cold . . ."

Osgood snorted in disgust and stood up. "Push-ups," he barked.

Grey completed push-up after push-up. He slipped into a level of consciousness beyond pain. His arms were so utterly destroyed they ceased to feel much of anything. He was on autopilot, moving mechanically. The push-ups turned to sit-ups, which turned to leg levers, which turned to squats, which turned to more push-ups. Osgood finally ordered Grey to join his class.

"Grey, get your ass over here!" Ensign Ryder barked.

Grey obediently broke through the school circle of trainees and stopped in front of the silver-haired instructor. "Reporting as ordered, Ensign Ryder."

"Shut up with that crap." Ensign Ryder scowled. "Just give me a straight answer. Did you know about Murray's condition?"

"I knew he was struggling, sir."

"Bullshit. You knew he was dying."

The insult hit Grey like a slug to the chest.

"Anything to say for yourself?"

Grey struggled to form the right words. His mind still sputtered at the edge of coherent thought. "I cared about Murray. I protected him from the instructors, from his own class. . . ." He wiped his sleeve against his cheek. "We were brothers."

"Well, isn't that sweet," Ensign Ryder said. "An officer and an enlisted man, best buddies."

"I couldn't stop him."

"So you're telling me you can't control your men?" Ensign Ryder asked.

"Not Murray."

"Why not?"

Grey searched for the right words. *Because I promised him I wouldn't?* Grey instinctively glanced at the pink scar on his arm, the only evidence of his pact with Murray.

"I'm waiting," Ryder said.

"Murray was different."

"Shit." Ensign Ryder cracked his knuckles noisily. "A man's dead, and all you can say is that he was different."

Grey clumsily wiped away a trickle of salt water leaking from his nose. "I'm ready to be judged."

"What the fuck?" Ensign Ryder beckoned for Instructor Osgood.

Osgood jogged over on his stubby legs. He spat a glop of chewing tobacco onto the sand. "What's up?"

"Jim, what did you do to this guy?"

"I beat him up pretty bad," Osgood confessed. "Fucker deserved it."

"You were one of our top guys," Ensign Ryder said, kicking sand onto Grey's boots. "You lost contact with your swim buddy, and now he's dead. If it were anyone but Murray, I'd recommend that we process you out of this class." His eyes narrowed. "He was a shitbag anyway, right?"

"No, sir, he was not."

"You're defending a dead man?"

Grey swallowed hard. "Yes."

"So it's your fault that he died?"

"No."

"So you're halfway acknowledging culpability, but unwilling to accept full responsibility for your actions as an officer."

"No, sir."

"What exactly do you mean, then?"

He's fucking with me. Grey knew that Ensign Ryder was toying with his sleep-deprived, half-frozen mind, and it made him furious. A wave of heat flooded into his cheeks. He opened his mouth to speak.

"What?" Ryder said.

A torrent of insults coursed through Grey's mind, but each time he tried to pull one from the soupy morass churning in his skull, he came up empty.

"He's speechless, sir," Osgood noted. "I'm afraid he's impaired."

"You need the silver bullet?" Ensign Ryder asked.

Grey shook his head. *Motherfucker.*

"Well, I think you're a borderline case. We need to do something to warm you up." Ensign Ryder nodded at Osgood. "Take Grey up the beach and have him dig a hole in the soft sand. Have him make a nice bed and get cozy."

"Aye, aye, sir," Osgood growled.

"And you," Ensign Ryder said quietly, grabbing Grey by the arm. "We'll talk later."

Grey broke free of Ensign Ryder's grip and marched north along the beach. After the nervous chatter of BUD/S Class 283 faded into the background, Osgood ordered him to stop. Without waiting for his next command, Grey dropped to his knees and began clawing away at the sand. *Why? Why? Why?* A small hole appeared and quickly expanded as Grey channeled his anger into the gritty particles beneath his fingertips. *Fucker. Murray. Motherfucker.*

"Why didn't you show such goddamn enthusiasm when I asked you to run back to your class?" Osgood asked. "It's like digging this hole is gonna bring him back. It won't."

Grey didn't respond. He was busy tunneling into the earth, flinging sand with as much energy as he could muster. *Why? Why? Why?* Grey felt tears welling up in his eyes again. *Sand. Goddamn sand. Vanessa. Green hills. Vanessa. Hot chocolate.* Grey groaned, a deep roiling noise rising from his chest. *Pulmonary edema. Bloody hands. Bloody lungs. Redman. Furtado. Fucker.*

Osgood stood silently next to Grey, his beefy arms crossed over his chest. Periodically he spat a stream of chew onto Grey's head or kicked sand back into the hole. Grey didn't notice. He clawed and clawed, his eyes fixed on the beach beneath him.

"That's enough."

Grey continued his frantic excavation.

"Stop!" Osgood yelled, grabbing Grey by the shoulders.

Grey twisted around and looked up at Osgood. The instructor's face showed little emotion. Where Grey expected to find hatred, he found only emptiness. Osgood calmly flipped Grey onto his back in the hole and began pushing sand over Grey's body with his foot. Grey didn't resist. He couldn't. He turned his gaze to the night sky and surrendered.

"Sleep."

Grey awoke to a slight tickling sensation in his ear. Osgood dropped the strand of kelp he had been using to wake Grey and grunted an inaudible command at the officer.

"What?" Grey croaked. His arms broke free from the sand.

"CO called in, says it's time to resume training. You in?"

You in? Grey repeated the question in his head. Osgood muttered the words so casually, as if he were asking Grey to join him for a night of drinking.

"Is Murray dead?" Grey asked.

"Yes, he's dead."

"Who killed him?" Grey pushed his upper body free of the sand and sat up in the pit. "Was it Redman?"

"You don't know what you're talking about."

"He's dead."

"I know."

"How long have I been asleep?"

Osgood looked at him quizzically. "Long enough. Maybe an hour, maybe less."

"And I'm supposed to just continue on like nothing happened?"

Osgood's eyes narrowed. "If we were engaged in a war, do you think that God would just come down and say, 'Stop! One of Ensign Grey's enlisted buddies died?' This isn't prep school, sir. Your friends will die in this business. Your job as a leader is to continue on."

"Where's my boat crew?"

"Down the beach. Waiting."

Grey eased himself to his feet and dusted the sand from his uniform.

The short span of sleep Osgood had granted him left him feeling surprisingly alert. He jogged behind Osgood through the darkness, his eyes trained on the instructor's back. Soon the sounds of his suffering class filled his ears. Ensign Ryder was making up for lost time. While waiting for the CO's go-ahead, the class had grown complacent. The instructors darted among the trainees, shocking them back to life with a mixture of pain and cold. Grey joined his crew. He struggled through a series of push-ups, then bear-crawled to the surf. He squashed himself between Rogers and Jackson in the shallows.

"I'm sorry about Murray," Rogers said gently. "He was a good friend."

"Amen," Jackson said. "I know you would have saved him if you could."

Grey desperately wanted to tell them that Murray's death couldn't have been caused by pulmonary edema, that Redman and Furtado had drowned him, but he couldn't. Hell Week would take a large enough toll on his crew's psyche. Survival would take every ounce of strength they had. Grey's crew shivered and chattered and writhed with discomfort. Osgood called them back from the surf, ordered them to roll in the sand, then directed them to prepare to move out. He took his position at the front of the elephant chain, and the class followed him south along the beach, racing the falling moon and the rising sun. The sand gave way to concrete as they turned through the beach gate. Cars honked encouragement as they sprinted across the highway and navigated the streets of the amphibious base. Osgood raced them around the parking lot behind the chow hall before finally letting them drop their boats. Grey's head was battered beyond the point of discomfort. The top of his skull was so bruised, simply touching it sent jolts of pain up and down his spine.

"You look bad," Felicia observed as Grey moved past the register. "You need sleep. Get some rest."

"I would love to," Grey said, "but that's not about to happen. Three more days, Felicia. Three more days."

Felicia shook her head sadly at Grey's deplorable condition as he moved on. The old Filipino food servers clucked their disapproval and piled extra food on his plate. *Oh, sir, you too skinny. You need eat more. Have more bacon, sir. More eggs. More French toast.* Grey wasn't in the mood for conversation. He forced a smile and moved on.

The table felt empty without Murray. The five remaining members of Boat Crew Five ate in silence, sloppily shoveling mountains of food into their mouths. Grey scraped his plate clean and stared into his cup of hot chocolate. His head dropped repeatedly as he lapsed in and out of consciousness.

"We have a winner," Osgood announced from behind Grey's chair.

Grey's eyes snapped open. A bottle of Tabasco sauce slammed down on the table in front of him. Instructor Osgood snatched a donut from Jackson's tray and coated it with salt from a salt shaker. Then he dripped soy sauce over it, and finally, as the crowning touch, he saturated the donut with Tabasco.

"Eat up."

Grey's stomach turned as he looked at the red-and-brown donut.

"Eat up, sir. You're racking up penalty points."

Grey popped the donut in his mouth and chewed. A fire raged in his mouth. He had to fight the instinct to spit the mess all over his tray.

"Swallow, sir."

Grey swallowed and felt the spongy bits of flame sear a path into his stomach.

"Now are you going to stay awake?"

Fuck you. Grey reached for a glass of water and gulped it down. Osgood wandered off, chuckling happily, looking for another victim.

"Harsh," Jackson muttered as Grey choked.

"Have some milk, sir," Jones offered, pushing a full glass toward Grey.

Grey tilted his head back and chugged, spilling milk from the corners of his mouth. He didn't bother wiping. The day shift wandered into the chow hall and took charge.

"Outside," Logan said, jerking a thumb over his shoulder. "Saddle up."

The class filed out of the chow hall and hefted the boats onto their heads. Logan ran them to the athletic field at the east end of the amphibious base. After a few fast laps around the field, Logan stopped the class and ordered them to drop their boats.

"Relays," Logan said. He stuffed a handful of sunflower seeds into his mouth. "You guys love relays, right?"

The class managed a weak "Hoo-yah."

"Goddamn right you do. Here's the deal: your entire boat crew will low-crawl across the field and back. Then one swim pair will wheelbarrow across the field and back. After that, some lucky bastard will play rolling pin and roll across the field." Logan smirked. "Extra points for not puking. Lastly, the remaining swim pair will run the perimeter of the field—in a fireman's carry."

"Shoot," Jones said. "None of them options sounds too appealing to me. I'll volunteer for the wheelbarrow."

"And I'll join you on that one," Jackson added quickly.

"I'll do the fireman's carry," Simpson volunteered.

Rogers looked over at Grey. "Well?"

"Fuck it," Grey said. "You join him. I'll puke it out. I need to get the Tabasco out of my system anyway."

Logan started the race, and all five members of Grey's crew low-crawled across the grass. It was tough going and very hard on the elbows. They finished the hundred-yard crawl, and Jones and Jackson wheelbarrowed each other across the field. Jackson's arms failed constantly, resulting in a series of face-plants as a light-headed Jones plowed him into the earth. They switched places at the halfway point, and Jones emulated Jackson's performance nicely.

Grey was next. He dropped onto his stomach and started rolling. The world spun wildly as his breakfast slowly crept up his esophagus. He wasn't even at the halfway point when he started forcefully throwing up. After a short stop, he rolled on. And on. And on. Grey's head felt like it was swelling. The pressure became nearly unbearable. He finally rolled onto Jackson's feet and dry-heaved twice.

Logan laughed and spit sunflower seeds on Grey's head as he lay immobile. By the time he managed to rise to his knees, Simpson had already crossed the finish line with Jones over his shoulder. Simpson hardly looked winded at all. His posture was perfect, almost too strong. *Looks like someone took a ramrod to his asshole,* Grey thought.

The races continued. The next event required that each crew run twenty laps around the road surrounding the athletic field. They were well into their fourth lap and had built up a sizable lead when Jones inexplicably stopped in the middle of the road and unbuttoned his fly. He smiled stupidly as he urinated all over the pavement.

"Jones," Simpson barked, "cut that out. We have the lead."

"I gotta take a piss," Jones said. "Sorry, it just can't be helped. Nature calls sometimes, and you just gotta answer. Know what I mean, Devil Dog?"

Simpson's face turned red and his cheek twitched. "Don't push me."

"Hold your horses, Leatherneck."

"Jones!" Rogers exclaimed.

"Sorry, I was just trying to tell this jarhead that pissing is a natural thing, like eating and sleeping. You just can't avoid it."

Simpson turned his back to Jones as another boat crew ran by. Grey knew Jones was simply a little punch-drunk from all the PT and the lack of sleep. He was the last guy on Earth to be belligerent. Jones buttoned his fly back up and they continued on. They crossed the finish line in second place and spent the next two hours immersing themselves in the bay and warming up with calisthenics. Another run around the base, and it was chow time.

Instructor Petrillo pulled Grey aside as the class funneled into the mess hall.

"I'm sorry about Murray. I know you two were tight."

"I'm sorry, too."

Instructor Petrillo thrust his hands into the pockets of his blue windbreaker. "It's not your fault."

Grey stared at Petrillo. "Who said anything about it being my fault?"

"Word on the street is that you knew he was dying."

"Who said that?"

"The night shift." Petrillo's eyes dropped to the concrete. "Redman and Furtado, among others. They're claiming you killed him, that you should have pulled him out twenty-four hours ago. I know you, sir, and I think it's bullshit. If you were keeping Murray's secret, I know he put you up to it."

Grey opened his mouth to reply, but Petrillo had already moved on. *Redman and Furtado. They're the fucking murderers.* Grey moved through the chow line mechanically. His mind clumsily sorted the events of the last few weeks: *gun store owner murdered; Master at Arms reports poor ammo inventories at BUD/S; Murray investigates; Murray disappears.* Grey sat down and tried to make a compelling case out of the facts clanging in his head. He couldn't do it. He needed more.

"You okay, sir?" Jackson asked. "Besides being absolutely miserable?"

"Don't worry about it. Let's just get through this week." Grey didn't even look up. He methodically forked food into his mouth. His stomach churned as he remembered his last glimpse of Murray stumbling toward the surf with Redman and Furtado behind him.

Logan herded the class out of the building and led the elephant train across the highway and back onto the BUD/S compound. Now that the week was well underway, Logan had subdued his manner somewhat. His temper evened out as inflicting suffering took less and less energy. Every step the class took was pain, every waking minute a tribute to discomfort.

Grey stripped out of his clothes, filed down the windswept hallway, and stepped into the steamy shower. The warm water stung at first, and by the time Grey started to relax, it was time to step out. Doc Anderson probed and prodded Grey's oozing leg wound.

"Good thing I put you on antibiotics," Anderson said. He pointed at several red streaks extending upward from Grey's cut. "You were developing a nice case of cellulitis. Keep taking those pills, and you should pull through. You're borderline for a medical drop, though."

"Don't even think about it," Grey said, staring the hulking doctor in the eye. "I'm not going away. If you have to amputate, so be it."

Anderson smiled and slapped Grey on the back. "Like I said, keep taking the pills."

Grey turned to walk out of the clinic, but stopped short. "Doc?"

"Yes?"

"How did Murray die?"

Anderson froze. "Why?"

"I need to know. He was a member of my boat crew. He was my responsibility."

"Well . . ." Anderson's cheeks flushed, as if what he was about to say embarrassed him. "Pulmonary edema. Blood in the lungs. He drowned."

"Drowned in his own blood," Grey repeated softly.

"I should have caught it earlier. I—"

"It's not your fault, Doc. Murray was keeping a secret."

"That's a damn hard secret to keep. Usually we know when someone is that far gone."

Grey scanned Anderson's face. He could sense the doctor held himself accountable. "Maybe it wasn't an accident."

Anderson shook his head. "You're tired. Your head will clear once this week is over. Now get out of here."

Grey shuffled over to the corpsman, swallowed his pills, and stepped outside. As always, Petrillo hosed him down as he dressed himself in his clean uniform. Petrillo was silent for once, brooding over something. He sprayed Grey absentmindedly and then moved on. The class assembled back on the beach.

"Line up and link arms," Logan ordered casually. "You know the drill. Out you go. Out into the warm ocean. Out where you belong."

After a half hour of shivering in the shallows, Osgood recalled the class and directed them over the berm. A half dozen instructors wielding paddles stood by silently.

"I want you to bury yourselves," Logan said. "Get comfortable. Dig into that nice warm sand and cover yourselves with it."

The students obediently dropped onto their backs and started pushing sand onto their chests. The instructors helped out with their paddles, generously heaping sand on their heads.

"Lights out," Logan ordered.

FOURTEEN

GREY WOKE UP WITH a start. A hideous cackle squawked from Logan's megaphone. *What's going on?* Grey knew he couldn't have slept more than five minutes.

"Rise and shine, ladies!" Logan yelled. "Hit the surf."

For the first time in nearly three days, Grey felt warm and dry. The sun poked through the clouds, and the sand on his chest radiated like a furnace. He didn't want to move.

"I said hit the surf, dipshits!"

Grey struggled to his feet. His quadriceps stretched painfully as he hobbled over the sand berm and down to the ocean. The class linked arms at the water's edge.

"I thought I'd died and went to heaven," Jackson said as they marched into the frigid shallows. "Damn, that was good."

"And I tell you what," Jones added. "I ain't never complaining about where I sleep again. Ever."

The warmth ebbed from Grey's body as he lay back in the water. The notion that the week would never end flooded back in its place. Grey tried to relax, to become one with the cold, to accept the discomfort. He closed his eyes and visualized a better life. A cottage in the countryside with a fireplace that burned year-round, even in the summer. A beautiful dark-skinned woman that looked remarkably like Vanessa to keep him warm. A gigantic bowl of steaming hot chocolate, and a never-ending supply of Big Macs and French fries. A huge hot tub that overlooked miles and miles of empty rolling hills. *I will never take these things for granted. Never.*

Logan called them in from the surf, and they spent the rest of the afternoon executing boat drills. The waves had died down, so paddling to the offshore area and back presented little challenge. Logan quickly grew bored.

"Out and back upside down," he barked. "And I want a good show."

Too exhausted to provide any entertainment, they obediently paddled in and out of the surf with their boats flipped upside down. The carnage was minimal. Logan expressed his displeasure by ordering another round of surf torture. More blue skin, more violent shivering, and more urination to stay warm. Logan finally stalked off the beach when the evening shift arrived.

"Get under your boats," Barefoot ordered.

Grey immediately felt uneasy. The instructor glared at him with his big mouse eyes as Grey hoisted his boat onto his head. Grey met the instructor's stare: there was more than disgust in it. Genuine hatred brewed somewhere in Barefoot's big-eared head.

"I want your crew in the lead position," Barefoot said, "and if you don't keep up, we'll spend some quality time together over dinner."

Great. Grey urged his crew on as Barefoot ran north through the sand. They stayed on his heels for a short distance, but the pace was just too fast. They fell back, and another boat crew passed them up.

"C'mon now," Jones said. "I want dinner. Let's get a move on."

Grey knew it was futile. They were the only crew with five people, and Jackson could barely walk, let alone run. Jackson's legs were so chafed that he had to waddle, and the rest of the crew ended up virtually dragging him along with them. The elephant train weaved through the amphibious base, finally stopping at the chow hall. Grey's crew ended up solidly in last place. Barefoot was delighted.

"Well, well, not only did you not keep up," he crooned, "you slow motherfuckers ended up in last place. Extended-arm carry."

They held the boat above their heads. Barefoot returned with an armful of MREs.

"Not again," Jones moaned.

"What? You've done this before?" Barefoot asked. He sounded disappointed.

"Sure have," Jones answered. "Once is enough, don't you think?"

"Nice try, hillbilly." He dropped the MREs on the ground. "You know the drill. Eat up, but don't let that boat touch your heads."

Barefoot sat in Big Blue and watched them struggle. *Evil man. Evil, evil man.* Jones ate first, and by the time he had scarfed down his vacuum-packed chicken and rice, the boat was wobbling out of control. They struggled, groaned, and shifted the weight of the craft from one hand to the other. The boat slipped from Grey's grasp and flipped over onto the concrete with a crash.

"What the fuck?" Barefoot yelled. "That's bullshit! Bullshit! You never drop your boat! Never!" His large eyes bulged from his narrow face. "You don't want to play my games? Fine. We'll do something else. Get down in the push-up position."

Grey and the rest of his crew dropped onto their hands.

"Now eat up, but don't let me catch your knees touching the ground."

Holding himself up with one hand, Grey picked up an MRE with the other and tore the thick brown wrapper open with his teeth. He worked on opening part of his meal until his supporting arm couldn't bear the weight any longer, then he switched arms and started again. Ten minutes later he had eaten most of his tuna noodles, but he was thoroughly exhausted and needed the support of both arms. He would have to forgo the rest of his meal.

They spent the entire dinner period in the push-up position. Grey almost felt thankful when they lifted the boats onto their tenderized heads and followed Barefoot back to the beach. His relief was short-lived. They ran south on the beach toward the compound, but instead of stopping, Barefoot kept right on running.

"Lord, have mercy," Jackson moaned. "My legs are as raw as a bleedin' side of pork."

"It can't last forever," Simpson stated.

Grey looked over in surprise. Simpson almost never spoke.

"You're right, Simpson," Rogers chimed in. "Absolutely right. The only eternal pain is the Inferno, and even Dante wielded a sarcastic pen when he wrote his book."

"You talking about hell, brother?" Jackson asked.

Rogers laughed. "Dante's version of it."

"Can't be much worse than this," Jackson said.

"Oh, yes it can," Grey said. "Trust me, it can and it is."

Rogers groaned. "Will you stop being so cryptic and just say what's on your mind?"

"Later. You'll have to wait. Trust me, it's not something you need to be stressing about right now."

The last traces of sunlight faded away as Barefoot stopped the elephant train half a mile south of the obstacle course.

"Here's what I want," Barefoot began. "It's a simple task. If you execute it according to plan, you will be rewarded. You fuck up, you'll be punished. Makes sense, right?" Barefoot snatched a paddle from one of the boats. "You will use paddles to dig a pit—a rectangular pit three feet deep, ten feet in width, and twenty feet in length. You have less than an hour. Get started."

Ensign Pollock, the red-faced class OIC, immediately took charge and started directing the digging. The class had cleared away about a foot of sand when Instructor Barefoot strolled back over to the group.

"You guys look like you're heating up."

"We're doing just fine, Instructor Barefoot," Jackson said. "Nobody here is cold."

"No," Barefoot corrected. "I think you're getting overheated. Hit the surf, all of you. Wet and sandy. Make it quick."

Grey ran with his class through the damp evening air and dunked himself in the ocean. Moving as quickly as possible to generate heat, Grey ran back to his paddle and started digging frantically. He managed to stay fairly warm by flailing away at the sand with all his strength.

Once the pit was dug, Instructor Barefoot had the class sit down while individual students climbed onto the lip of the pit and told jokes. Grey didn't pay attention. He knew the routine. If the jokes sucked, the class hit the surf. If they were good, they stayed put. *Murray would have saved us. Only he could come up with a joke raunchy enough to make instructors laugh.*

The jokes sucked and the class got wet. Repeatedly. The class would laugh extra hard at stupid jokes in the hopes that the laughter would somehow be contagious and the instructors would play along. No such luck.

"You guys are the worst group of joke tellers I've ever encountered," Barefoot said. "I've been here a year, and you are hands down the worst. Poor performance results in poor treatment, ladies. Now for our next game." He grinned from ear to ear. "This one's my favorite. Let's start by hitting the surf."

The class turned and trotted toward the ocean. They were in no hurry. Whatever was in store would not be pleasant. Suddenly the beach lit up with a dazzling display of flickering yellow light. It took Grey a moment to realize what he was seeing as he rose from the water. The instructors had ignited a huge bonfire farther to the south. *Warmth.* Grey could imagine how good it would feel to stand next to the blaze and dry out his uniform. Barefoot met them as they slogged out of the ocean.

"Nice little fire, isn't it? Why don't we take a little walk down the beach and get a closer look?"

Barefoot led the class down the beach, stopping twenty feet from the fire.

"You can almost feel it, can't you? Almost feel the beautiful warmth enveloping you? It's good, isn't it? You want to get closer, don't you?"

The class nodded vigorously. *Yes. Take us closer.*

"Too fucking bad for you guys. If you had managed to tell one good joke—just one—you would be warm and toasty right now. Instead you're going to suffer. Line up in a semicircle around the fire, but keep twenty feet away."

The class spread out around the fire. Grey fought the impulse to charge forward and flop down in front of the blaze. Rivulets of water streamed from his uniform, and if he could just get a little closer . . .

"Now take off your tops and your shirts and drop them on the ground."

The class obeyed, and soon twenty-nine bare-backed students shivered in the ocean breeze.

"Now drop your pants around your ankles."

Grey unbuttoned his pants and shoved them down around his ankles.

He stood transfixed by the fire, shivering, hugging his chest with his arms.

"Now hold your arms out to the side."

No. God no. Grey slowly lifted his arms and immediately cringed as the cold breeze whipped over his damp skin, burning past his exposed armpits.

"Now, gentlemen, we're going to watch the fire die. What a shame. What a God-awful shame. All that heat, and you'll never get a taste of it."

This is really perverse. This is beyond sadistic. This is nothing short of evil. Grey looked over at Jackson. The Reverend's jaw clattered noisily, and a moist sheen coated his brown eyes. Grey shivered so hard that his back muscles cramped up. He thought of Murray, and his throat constricted painfully. The fire grew smaller and smaller as the flames consumed the pile of wood. Eventually a faint orange glow from a mound of ash was all that remained.

"Bye-bye, fire," Barefoot squeaked in a girlish voice. "Bye-bye, warmth. Time for more cold." He pointed toward the surf. Two students broke away from the crowd and headed for Big Blue, which was parked off in the darkness. Grey recognized one as Simpson.

"Hey!" Grey yelled. "Hey, Simpson! Get back over here!"

The proud marine kept walking and didn't look back. *Another one. Beautiful.* Grey joined his class in the surf zone. Barefoot ordered them out of the ocean half an hour later, frigid, stumbling, delirious. After a round of poorly executed push-ups and sit-ups, the class reorganized boat crews. After a new wave of DORs, the class was now down to twenty-four students. The students voted on which boat crew should be dissolved. Pollock's crew was the unanimous choice, and he was clearly devastated. In truth, taking away the class leader's boat crew demonstrated a disturbing lack of confidence in his leadership. Grey's crew, renamed Boat Crew Three, took on two new crew members: a beefy-looking kid with deep-set green eyes named Smurr, and a redhead named O'Patry. Grey welcomed them to his crew unenthusiastically as they hefted their boat and followed Barefoot to the chow hall.

Despite the running, Grey remained chilled to the bone as they stopped in the parking lot next to the cafeteria. He could hardly wait to get his hands on a nice steaming cup of hot cocoa. Jackson, Jones, and Rogers were equally addicted to the cocoa, the only comfort they could count on.

Grey piled his tray with leftovers from dinner and moved on to the container of hot water. He filled a cup with the steaming liquid and thrust his hand into the bin containing the cocoa packets. It was empty. Grey looked around in panic. Jones was moving away toward a table, head down, muttering.

"Any hot cocoa?" Grey yelled, directing his question toward the brown shirts who served food.

"All out," they replied in unison.

Grey's heart sank. His eyes watered. He needed that cocoa. Needed it like oxygen. He stood motionless for a minute, then dragged himself to the table where his boat crew had assembled.

"Here," Jackson said, pushing his cup toward Grey. "Take a sip. I know you want it. It's written all over your face."

Grey looked down. The cup was filled with chocolaty warmth. It swirled beautifully, little whirlpools of taste and comfort. Grey smiled sheepishly and took a long sip. He closed his eyes and savored the moment before passing the cup back.

"Thanks," Grey said. "You saved me."

"Not a problem, sir," Jackson answered. "It's my Christian duty to share."

Grey ate in silence, brooding over the remaining forty hours of training. He knew the worst of it had passed, but the sleep deprivation was getting ridiculous. After every third or fourth bite of food his head dropped. Each time he'd look around in alarm, expecting a bottle of Tabasco sauce to appear on the table.

A familiar figure strolled into the chow hall. *Redman.* Grey could barely contain his hatred. *You will go down, you cowardly bastard. And I will be there to watch it all.* Furtado followed, sliding his glinting tongue stud along his moist lips. *You too, fucker.*

The class filed outside and immediately resumed shivering.

"Time for the treasure hunt," Furtado said. "I'm going to give you a clue, and you dumb assholes are going to try to figure out where you're supposed to go. If you guess wrong, it's a thirty-second penalty. You will keep guessing until you get it right. Then you will go to the location and check in with the instructor who is there. He'll give you the next clue, and the race will continue. Any questions?"

Jones raised his hand.

"What do you want, Uncle Jeb?"

"What's the prize for winnin'?"

"I won't beat the shit out of you. How's that sound?"

"Sounds great," Jones drawled. "Sounds like a party."

"Here's your first clue: cake eaters sleep here with full checkbooks and full bellies."

"Easy," Grey whispered. "The Bachelor Officer Quarters."

His crew nodded in agreement, and Grey ran over to Instructor Furtado.

"The BOQ," he blurted.

"Wow," Furtado exclaimed in mock surprise, "amazing powers of perception. I knew you went to college for a reason. Now get moving."

Grey's crew limped down the road toward the BOQ. The rest of the class followed close on their heels. Another crew overtook them, and they reached the high-rise building in second place. Instructor Heisler waited in Big Blue.

"Second place equals the first losers," Heisler reminded them. "Extended-arm carry."

As his crew held the boat above their heads on shaky arms, Grey reported in for his next clue.

"Since I was such a fucking nerd in high school, this is where I spent all my time."

Easy. Grey didn't need his crew's help for the this one. "Base library," he answered.

"You are absolutely correct," Heisler crooned in his game-show voice. "You win a fabulous trip to the base library, departing now."

Grey turned and rejoined his crew. They spent the next two hours crisscrossing the base, limping from one location to another and solving simple riddles. Instructor Redman finally guided the class through the fence that bordered the outdoor swimming pool.

Instructor Furtado addressed the class from his perch on the three-meter platform.

"I don't want you to get the impression that the midnight shift is no fun. You don't have that impression, do you?"

"No, Instructor Furtado," the class answered in unison.

"Good, because we've decided to spend some time in the pool playing games—fun games like water polo and king of the mountain."

You've got to be kidding me. Grey warily eyed an inflatable boat positioned at the edge of the pool. He didn't need a closer look; he could see the ice cubes from where he stood.

"We'll start with water polo. Winners will get a warm shower. Losers will get the ice boat. Boat Crews One and Two are shirts, Three and Four are skins. I'm the referee, and any decision I make stands firm. Any questions?"

Grey and his crew stripped off their clothes. Clad in nothing but spandex underwear, they jumped in the sixty-two-degree pool and treaded water. The two new guys, Smurr and O'Patry, were accomplished water polo players. Grey's team quickly took control of the first game. O'Patry hurled the ball past the opposing team's defense with frightening speed. He was a fish in the water, confident, quick, and ruthless. Grey was delighted. A warm shower awaited.

Furtado blew his whistle. "Team Two wins, four to nothing. Team Two, you have five minutes to enjoy a victory shower. Team One, line up by the ice boat."

Grey pulled himself out of the pool and padded into the bathroom. Twelve shower nozzles spouted warm water, filling the room with steam.

"Praise be to God," Jackson cried, positioning himself underneath a stream of warm water. "I've never played water polo before, but I love the sport already."

Grey thawed out underneath the heavenly spray, relishing the strange sensation of hot water against his skin. A chorus of ecstatic moans echoed in the tiled room. The minutes flew by, and Furtado strode into the bathroom far too quickly.

"Back in the pool," he ordered. "Time for round two. Only this time, O'Patry and Smurr are going to the other team. Maybe that will give Team One a fighting chance."

Grey's heart sank. He knew the game was lost already. The pool felt exceptionally cold after the hot shower, and he had a hard time rousing any enthusiasm from his exhausted body. As he expected, they were crushed three to zero. Smurr and O'Patry moved like lightning and instantly took control of the game.

"Into the boat," Redman ordered, pointing at the mixture of ice and water. "Everyone should spend at least five seconds in there. If you try to cheat me, I'll remediate you with extra time."

Grey uneasily watched his teammates flop down in the boat and emerge seconds later with faces contorted with pain. Grey waited his turn, then lowered himself into the icy mix. A tiny hammer cracked against his skull, sending a wave of pain up and down his spine. His whole body throbbed as a thousand explosions spread fire across his skin. Grey patiently counted to five and then crawled out of the boat. *Must get back in the pool.* He eyed the mass of chlorinated water hungrily. The wind raked against his ice-coated skin like a set of claws.

Several minutes later a satisfied-looking Team One strolled out of the bathroom. Furtado switched up the teams again, and the games continued. Grey's group won two more matches and lost two more. The juxtaposition of ice and hot water was dizzying, but it sure beat surf torture. Finally Furtado grew tired of water polo and gathered the class around him.

"New game," he said. "It's called King of the Mountain. The rules are simple. Two boats will be positioned upside down in the pool. Whichever team takes over the boats and manages to keep all opposing players off wins. It's simple."

A crew of brown shirts carried two inflatable boats to the edge of the pool and threw them in. Then they jumped into the water and secured the boats in the middle of the pool using lines that attached to the bottom.

"Team One is shirts, Team Two skins. Line up on either side of the pool."

Grey led his shirtless team to the far end of the pool. They lined up along the edge of the water and coiled their muscles, ready to explode into action.

"Go!"

Grey jumped headfirst into the water and took a few strokes beneath the surface. In an instant he was next to one of the boats. He pulled himself up onto the slippery surface of the craft and immediately engaged in combat. A skinny kid in an oversized white shirt grappled with him, vying for supremacy. Grey easily tossed him into the pool. He glanced around and surveyed the situation. Three skins and one stubborn shirt battled on the boat. Grey pushed against the huge body of an opposing player, heaving with all his might. Just as the massive body teetered over the edge, a meaty arm reached back and grabbed Grey's ankle. Grey struggled to stay on the raft, but the weight of the huge student pulled him over the side.

Bruises and scratches, inhaled water and torn shirts—the pool raged in absolute chaos. Finally one of the students yelled victory. The shirtless team sat proudly on the boats. *Shower time.*

Grey enjoyed another round of warm water. He could definitely get used to this. Furtado kicked them out of the bathroom after a five-minute break.

"Round two," Furtado announced. "Only this time, I want some narration." He looked toward Rogers. "Sir, why don't you entertain us with some moving shit like one of your pansy poems? Go ahead, climb up on the high platform. When you start reciting, the rest of the class will start fighting."

Grey lined up on the edge of the pool with the rest of his team while Rogers climbed the stairs to the three-meter platform. The poet took a deep breath, and the class leaned forward in anticipation. Puffing out his chest, Rogers held out one hand and recited in his manliest voice.

> *"Thou guardian power of Cilla the divine,*
> *Thou source of light! whom Tenedos adores,*

Twenty-three students simultaneously launched themselves into the water, battle-ready and eager for bloodshed.

> *"And whose bright presence gilds thy Chrysa's shores:*
> *If e'er with wreaths I hung thy sacred fane,*

Grey pulled himself onto a boat and immediately threw himself against a struggling white shirt. Their bodies collided, and they both rolled back into the pool, a tangle of arms and legs and fists. Grey looked toward the sky. Rogers stood proudly above them, oblivious to the chill wind blowing across his drenched body. His recitation rang out above the grunts and battle cries of the frenzied warriors below.

> *"Or fed the flames with fat of oxen slain;*
> *God of the silver bow! thy shafts employ,*
> *Avenge thy servant, and the Greeks destroy.*

The instructors roared with laughter. Jones stood buck naked on top of one of the rafts, flexing his lean muscles and howling with rage. A student surfaced in the pool and sheepishly tossed a pair of underpants toward him. Jones pulled them on as his teammates defended his position.

> *"Thus Chryses pray'd:—the favouring power attends,*
> *And from Olympus' lofty tops descends.*
> *Bent was his bow, the Grecian hearts to wound;*
> *Fierce as he moved, his silver shafts resound."*

Rogers cut his recitation short and executed a perfect swan dive into the pool. The surface barely rippled as he disappeared from sight. Seconds later he joined the fray, climbing over everyone in his way.

"Yeah, white shirts, yeah," Jackson yelled, jumping up and down on a raft. "Who's yo daddy now? That's right!"

Furtado blew his whistle, and the chaos died as quickly as it had begun. Grey's crew made another trip to the shower while Team One lined up on the ice boats. The battles continued until the first rays of muted sunlight filtered through the morning clouds.

The class saddled up and followed Furtado to chow.

"Thursday morning," Jones drawled somberly. "Ain't but a day to go."

One day. It sounded impossibly long. Grey smiled weakly at Felicia as he moved down the chow line. The line snagged up as students waited for a new batch of scrambled eggs, and Grey immediately fell into a series of microsleeps. His head would drop, he'd lean forward dangerously, then he'd snap back into reality just before doing a face-plant on the deck. He progressed zombielike through the crowd. The old Filipino women didn't even make an attempt at conversation. Grey simply held out his plate and watched them pile on the food. Calculations started running through his head. Simple math was difficult, but he figured that he'd been up for eighty-four hours without any real sleep since Hell Week began. That equaled almost ninety-six hours without sleep if he factored in being up all day Sunday. *Goddamn*, Grey thought. *I'm going to make it.*

Furtado rounded up the students after breakfast and ran them back to the compound for their hygiene check. The brown shirts who ushered them in and out of the shower winked and offered encouragement. *You're almost there. The last day is easy. Hang in there. Look for us tonight, during Around the World.*

Grey scrubbed his cuts and winced as he touched the messy tear in his leg. He limped out of the shower and slowly made his way over to the medical center.

"Doesn't look good," Doc Anderson muttered, poking at Grey's cut. "I really should medically roll you—"

"But you won't," Grey added quickly.

"I won't, but I'll need to take a culture." He produced a long Q-tip and poked at the pussy mess around Grey's wound. He placed a protective plastic sheathing over the swab and looked Grey in the eye. "How you feeling?"

"Fine," Grey said.

"No complaints other than your cut?"

"No."

"And your mind?"

"What?"

"You're not still obsessing over Murray, are you?"

Grey's mood immediately darkened. He resisted the urge to punch the doctor. "I'm managing."

"Okay, I'll see you tomorrow. Make sure the corpsmen remembers your antibiotics."

Grey swallowed his pills and padded out the back of the clinic in his bare feet. He searched the crates for his name.

"One more day, sir," Petrillo said as he hosed him down. "One more day. Easy stuff. The worst is over."

"Thanks," Grey mumbled. He tried to imagine the relief of finishing Hell Week. Murray's death muted everything. On a primal level, he would be happy when the pain ended, but he wouldn't be exuberant. He couldn't be: he had some serious investigation to do once he became lucid again.

"No deep thoughts, sir," Petrillo said. "Minute to minute. Just live minute to minute. Survive."

Grey knew he was right. He had to keep his mind focused on surviving the week. After pulling on his already soaked uniform, he helped Jackson find an unclaimed pair of socks. Once Jackson was on his feet and fully clothed, Grey jogged out to the beach.

Logan sat on the edge of Grey's boat, thoughtfully chewing a mouthful of sunflower seeds. His bald head gleamed in the early morning sunlight.

"You know what I think, sir?"

"What's that, Instructor Logan?"

"I think it's a good thing your little friend dropped out."

"He didn't drop out," Grey hissed, "for Christ's sake!"

"Just making sure you're still alive," Logan said calmly. He turned his back and walked away.

Grey glared after him. He desperately wanted to hurl a paddle at the stocky instructor's bare head. It would be so simple—so satisfying. *And so stupid.*

Logan ordered the class into running formation. The elephant train loped south, winding back and forth over the sand berms. Grey's legs burned as they hauled their boat up and over the small mountains of sand. His boat crew had fallen into last place by the time Logan stopped the procession. Instructor Batman, the skinny petty officer perpetually hidden behind sleek sunglasses, corrected their lack of motivation with ten minutes of boat squats. White blotches blurred Grey's vision by the time they dropped their boat onto the sand.

"Time for a break," Logan called out.

The class cheered.

"We're going to play a little hide-and-seek. You hide, we seek. We find, you pay. You pay, you hurt, we laugh. Got it?"

The class nodded. Grey scanned his surroundings. They were just south of the obstacle course. An old burned-out, twin-rotored helicopter lay wedged in the sand, and a multitude of large corrugated metal pipes littered the area.

"We'll go to the other side of the berm and wait five minutes. Be ready."

Logan and his entourage of instructors climbed the berm and disappeared down the far side. Grey loped across the sand and searched the pipes. A pipe open on two ends provided too much background light; he would be easy to spot lying inside it. Finally Grey settled on a pipe half buried in the sand. He crawled inside and peeked through a tiny hole in the corrugated metal. A continuous stream of gray clouds passed overhead, lulling him into a trance. *I'll just close my eyes for a minute.*

He awoke with a start. A stream of putrid liquid jetted through the hole and onto his face. Someone whistled happily outside. Grey scooted farther into the pipe until he was out of the way of the shower. The stream slowed to a drizzle, then stopped. Grey wiped his hand across his face. *Piss.*

Seconds later Logan's head appeared at the end of the pipe. "Hi there, sir."

"You pissed on me."

"I didn't know you were there. Come on out and join the losers."

Grey inched himself out of the pipe. The thought of piss spattering across his face made him sick to his stomach.

"Go clean yourself off in the surf and report to Instructor Batman."

Grey sprinted across the wide field of sand, up the berm, and down to the water's edge. He did a belly flop in the shallows and rubbed his hands over his face. *Fucking prick. Disgusting.* A crowd of losers crawled across the beach on their bellies, following the ever-elusive Instructor Batman and his whistle. Grey joined the group and slithered across the beach for the next half hour.

"I think I'll be a snake in my next life," a sand-encrusted student muttered. "I hate whistle drills."

Grey barely recognized the face. "Rogers?"

"Yeah, it's me."

"Where'd you hide?"

"I buried myself in the sand. It almost worked, too. Logan spotted my eyes."

Just then Instructor Logan charged over the berm. A few dazed students limped after him, vainly attempting to keep up.

"Time for a little PT," Logan growled, "and since we have four winners, I'll let them pick the exercises." He slapped Jones on the back. "Hill-billy Bob, you go first."

The class spread into PT formation and watched Jones expectantly.

"The first exercise is a personal favorite of mine. It's called the groin stretch." He dropped onto the sand and assumed the correct position. "Ready, stretch."

Surprisingly, the instructors didn't object. Jones stretched the class for a few minutes before the other three students had their turn. More stretching ensued.

"Enough of this stretching bullshit," Logan muttered. "Time for some good shit."

The class groaned. Grey steeled himself for another round of pain.

"The next exercise is the eyelid stretch. When I say 'one,' you close your eyes. When I say 'two,' you open them. Think you can handle that?"

"Hoo-yah!" A few students even cracked smiles.

"One," Logan shouted.

Grey closed his eyes.

"Two."

He opened them

"One."

Grey closed his eyes. The beach grew quiet. He felt himself slip away, lulled to sleep by the warm sand and the rush of the surf.

"One."

Grey's eyes shot open. His mind raced as he struggled to figure out how long he had been asleep.

"You stupid fucks," Logan yelled. "I said 'one,' which means close your beady little eyes. Half of you are sitting there with your eyes open. All of you, hit the surf!"

The eyelid drills continued well into the day. Grey wanted to sleep so badly he felt like screaming. Every time he truly relaxed, he inevitably misinterpreted Logan's commands and ended up getting wet. When lunchtime rolled around, Grey was grateful to get moving again. He didn't miss the sleep as much when he was active. The class followed Logan across the base and into the chow hall.

"Beefsteak, chicken steak, gravy steak, turtle steak," Jones drawled as he shuffled along.

"What are you talking about?" asked O'Patry.

"Steak, steak, steak, give me some fries." Jones smiled, a brief flash of mangled teeth. "Ain't no real man's food here."

"He gets weird when he's tired," Grey explained. "The boy needs his sleep."

"Sleep, sleep. We don't sleep in the hills."

Grey ignored the muttering of his shipmate and proceeded through the line. Felicia wasn't behind the register, and Grey found that he missed her smile. Lunch disappeared in a flash of semiconsciousness. The meal flickered in his mind, a hazy memory completely void of detail. Grey assembled his boat crew outside.

They spent the afternoon sitting in the bay and paddling out to the edge of the shipping lanes and back. Occasionally Logan would throw in a few sets of leg levers or sit-ups, and less often, push-ups. The class was physically ruined. Every movement Grey made took effort, but the various pains in his body had faded into a distant throbbing sensation. *Never gonna end.*

FIFTEEN

THE NIGHT SHIFT TOOK over as the class sat down for their evening meal. Barefoot stalked between the students, warning them not to fall asleep. Heads nodded, and one trainee even managed to fall out of his chair. Barefoot punished the unfortunate student with a concoction of Tabasco sauce, tuna casserole, and chocolate milk.

After dinner the class followed Barefoot across the base and onto the beach. He turned south as the sun set, leading them along the hard-packed sand at the water's edge. The class managed to stay bow to stern as they limped toward Mexico. Grey's mind wandered ceaselessly, bouncing from one subject to another in an endless succession. *Head hurts. Must have lost some hair. Vanessa has to take me back. She doesn't want an old man. Murray should be here. I bet we're going back to the mud flats.*

The elephant train snaked beneath the highway and stopped just short of the bay. They were at the mud flats.

"Ready for a long paddle?"

"Hoo-yah," the class yelled.

"Good. Because this time you're going to get it." Barefoot gestured to the north, toward the lights of downtown. "This is called Around the World, gentlemen, and it will take all night. You will paddle, you will hallucinate, you will fight, and you will be watched. Don't get lost, and for Christ's sake, don't come in last place. This is the Big Race, shitbirds. Pays to be a winner. Starting here, you will paddle north through the bay, under the bridge, past an aircraft carrier, and then bend around to the west, following the contours of the island. An instructor will be stationed at the northwest end of the island. You will check in with him before continuing. He will give you additional directions. Understand?"

"Hoo-yah!"

Grey couldn't wait to paddle. It was infinitely more relaxing than running with a boat flopping on his head.

"Then get moving," Barefoot yelled.

Grey and his crew slogged through the mud, nearly dropping their boat several times as they lost their balance in the viscous muck. Once they reached water, they dropped their boat and climbed in. Grey pointed the boat to the north as his crew stroked quietly.

"Let's not lose this one," Grey urged. "We can't lose."

They glided through the inky black water, their paddles creating swirling white whirlpools with each stroke. The city lights shimmered and sparkled, teasing Grey with thoughts of couples sitting happily on sofas in cozy apartments, watching television with steaming cups of hot cocoa clasped in warm hands. His boat settled into the middle position, with two crews ahead and two behind.

"Hold up," Jones drawled, raising a hand. "Stop just a minute."

"Jones, we can't stop. We'll lose our position," Rogers explained.

"Trust me. Just stop."

The crew stopped paddling. Grey squinted into the distance. Suddenly it came into focus. A giant brick wall extended across the bay, stretching underneath the entire span of the Coronado Bay Bridge. His mouth dropped open as he tried to make the apparition disappear. *Can't be real.* He closed his eyes, then opened them again. It was still there.

"Lord almighty," Jackson breathed. "That's one mother of a wall."

"There's no wall," O'Patry said impatiently. "Get it together."

"Hey, carrottop, there's a gosh darn wall, okay?" Jones said loudly.

"Hey, hey, hey," Rogers exclaimed. "Let's pull it together. First of all, I see what appears to be a wall. In truth, it is just our minds playing tricks with the light. Second of all, even if there was really a wall, what should stop us from paddling closer for a better look?"

Jones grumbled as they continued paddling. *Just a vision,* Grey thought. They stroked onward to the north. The wall loomed closer and closer, a brick slab of monstrous proportions. Suddenly they were through it, stroking beneath the graceful arc of the bridge. Grey steered the boat through a cluster of yachts moored near the shore. The boats rocked gently, and a dim yellow light filtered through the round portholes in several cabins.

"Rich bastards," O'Patry mumbled. "Comfortable, rich bastards."

"No reason you can't be rich," Rogers said. "Start saving today. If you set aside twenty percent of your income in an account that generates thirty-percent interest, you will have half a million dollars by the time you retire." He sighed. "Of course, thirty percent is a great return by any stockbroker's standard."

"Money talk," Jackson grumbled. "You white boys need to start thinking about the real investment. I'm talking about the Good Lord Jesus Christ."

Grey found the comment amusing, but he couldn't find the energy to laugh. He was having trouble steering. They paddled onward in the darkness, cruising along the coast of the island.

Grey pointed. "Look." A figure swam toward the raft.

"What?" Jones asked. "I don't see nothin'."

The figure moved closer, and Grey recognized the impish face. "Murray!" he yelled. "What the fuck are you doing here?" The smiling eyes winked, then the face melted into the ocean as Grey's crewmates prodded him with their paddles.

"Wake up, sir. Snap out of it. It's not Murray."

"Sorry," Grey groaned. He felt completely empty. Drained of energy, sapped of inner strength, and miles distant, as if he were viewing his life from above. His fatigue was contagious. Another boat crew caught them, then slipped past as Grey and his crew struggled to stay awake. Jones nodded off constantly, and Jackson resorted to splashing him with cold bay water to keep him alert. Two strokes, a violent head jerk, then a splash. The cycle repeated itself until Jackson himself started to nod off. Suddenly Jones disappeared over the side of the boat.

"Man overboard," Grey muttered. He turned the boat around and they paddled to where Jones bobbed in the bay. "Get in, shipwreck."

"Sorry about that," Jones murmured. "I reckon I must have dozed off."

Grey reached down and pulled Jones back into the boat.

Another figure clad in a wetsuit glided toward them from shore.

Grey was too nervous to say anything. *What if it's another apparition?* He didn't want his boat crew to think he had lost it.

"Hey," the figure whispered. "Hold up."

The boat slowly slid to a stop as the figure grabbed the safety line on the craft. Grey's crew watched with slack jaws as the hooded man opened a waterproof bag and threw a handful of candy and energy bars into the boat.

"You're going to love this," he said, flashing a toothy grin. He reached into his bag and pulled out six plastic pouches the size of his palm. "Just break the seal on the packets by twisting them, and voilà, you have heat."

Grey urinated in his pants. The thought of heat was so attractive he just couldn't help himself. He passed out the packs and then turned to thank the swimmer, but the mysterious figure was gone.

"Hallelujah," Jackson said, and he breathed. "Check this out." He cracked the pack and dropped it down his pants. "Oh baby! Warm balls!"

"Good idea," Jones said as he did the same. He smiled broadly. "You should try this, boss."

Grey cracked his pack and thrust it down his spandex underwear. The heat was delicious, almost overwhelming. The whole crew stopped paddling and basked in the luscious warmth.

"God bless SIN," Jackson murmured.

"Do you realize what you just said?" Rogers asked. "The irony is beautiful. An organization named SIN just brought us comfort, and you gave it God's blessing. God bless sin. The intersection of the divine and the earthly. Ingenious. Remarkable."

Jackson shook his head. "Whatever you say, sir. I just like the heat."

They tore the wrappers from the candy bars and gobbled them down. When the last bit of food was gone, they reluctantly paddled onward. The heat in Grey's groin slowly faded. The immense bulk of an aircraft carrier loomed overhead for several minutes as they paddled past. Grey turned the boat to the west, guiding them past the North Island Air Station.

"Look," Jones drawled, pointing at the shore. "See the light?"

"I see it." Grey barely made out the shape of two instructors standing on the rocks. One of them held a flashlight. They bobbed closer, and Grey recognized Redman's massive body. The instructor glared at him as they pulled their boat up on the rocks.

"I'm saving you shitheads a little effort," Redman growled. "Instead of paddling all the way around the jetty, you turds get to rock portage about fifty yards and save yourselves an hour of effort."

They dragged their boat up and over the jagged boulders that lined the shore. The instructors had stationed themselves on the northwestern corner of the air base at the intersection of two poorly paved roads. Grey's crew lifted the boat and trudged to the south.

"You turds are in third place," Redman said as he walked next to Grey. "You're already in deep shit. Just don't lose. I'll personally kill all of you."

And he means it, murdering bastard, Grey thought. Suddenly his foot struck something hard, and he fell to the pavement. His crew members lost control of the craft, and it crashed down on Grey's head.

"Clumsiness is no joke," Redman said. "You're just like your friend Murray. Too clumsy to be an operator."

Yeah, and that's why I'm the fastest guy on the obstacle course. Grey pushed the boat off his back and stood up.

The other instructor stepped out of the darkness next to Big Blue. It was Furtado. "You're a fucking klutz, sir. Why don't you do yourself a favor and ring out? They'll eat you alive in Third Phase." His tongue stud flashed in the darkness. Grey desperately wanted to yank it from his mouth.

Grey and his crew hoisted the boat back onto their heads and walked down to the west, facing shore. They lowered their craft into the water and climbed in.

"Look for headlights about a mile down the beach," Redman ordered. "That's where you may or may not get midnight rations. Judging by the way you're performing, my guess is that you'll go hungry."

Grey pushed off from the shore and they paddled to the south.

"He tripped you," Jones muttered angrily.

"Who did? Redman?"

"Yes, sir, none other. I saw it with my own eyes."

"I saw it, too," Rogers said quietly.

Motherfucker's going down. Grey wanted to say it aloud. He wanted to share his dreams of revenge with his crew. Someone had to answer for Murray's death, and Grey was sure it would be Redman. At this point, though, he knew it would be foolish to involve the rest of his crew and arouse any extra attention.

They continued their ritual of paddling and sleeping until Grey spotted a pair of headlights blazing from the beach. They stroked for shore, timing their approach carefully to avoid being caught in front of a large wave. A whitecap rose up in the darkness behind the boat.

"Keep it steady," Grey ordered as he leaned back against his paddle. The wave caught them, and they slipped down the face. They started to veer heavily to the starboard side, but Grey leaned even harder against his paddle and managed to straighten their course. Heisler waited on the beach, arms crossed, a scowl upon his face.

"Drag your boat clear of the water," he ordered. "Then get your sorry asses back in the surf. I heard rumors that you were sleeping. Time to pay the man."

Grey and his crew dragged their boat several yards up the hard-packed sand, then turned, linked arms, and marched back into the surf. Grey shuddered. Even after four and a half days of constant immersion in freezing water, the bite of the ocean took his breath away. Heisler kept them in surf for a few minutes, then ordered them to join their class.

A large white diesel pickup filled with boxes of MREs sat on the beach. Heisler climbed into the bed and hurled unopened packets at them. *How generous.* They would eat after all.

"Anyone want to trade for beef franks?" Jackson asked.

"Nice try," Jones said. "I ain't trading my ravioli for nothin'."

They sat cross-legged on the beach and devoured their meals. Grey managed to get sand all over his food, but he ate it anyway. Along with several packets of food and basic condiments, every MRE contained a packet of coffee grounds. Grey stuffed the cheap stuff in his mouth in hopes of regaining even a fraction of his former alertness. His mind skipped like a damaged record, flashing to other places, other times. Strangely, he kept thinking about sex. He knew he didn't have enough energy to complete the task, but the thought of making love to Vanessa was more appealing than ever. *Maybe it's the warmth.* Not that it would happen anyway; not at the moment.

Redman and Furtado roared into the makeshift camp in Big Blue.

Eyes flashing, Redman jumped from the cab and kicked sand all over their unfinished meals.

"Snack time is over, girls. Your voyage isn't done. You have two minutes to get through the surf zone. And if you aren't back at the compound in two hours, I'll rip your head off and piss down your throat." He belched loudly. "That's a promise."

Grey jumped to his feet and rushed to the boat. He was joined by Jackson, O'Patry, Rogers, and Smurr. *Jones. Where's Jones?*

"Get started," Grey ordered. "I'll catch up. I have to find Jones."

His crew ran down the beach with the boat while Grey frantically scanned the camp. MRE wrappers littered the beach. A few brown shirts moved slowly across the sand, picking up trash. Redman and Furtado glared at him from their truck. *Where the hell are you?* He squinted into the darkness. *There.* Jones lay nestled at the base of a sand dune, deep in sleep. Grey sprinted over and walloped him in the ass with his boot.

"Ow," Jones complained. "Didja have to kick me, sir?"

"We're late. Get up."

Jones scrambled to his feet and took in his surroundings. His eyes widened in panic as the rest of the class paddled through the surf zone. Sprinting at full speed, Grey and Jones flew across the beach and into the ocean. The other four crew members sat in the boat and held it steady in waist-deep water. Grey pulled himself in and took his position at the stern. After a flurry of energetic strokes, they glided past the breakers and turned south.

"Sorry," Jones muttered, addressing the whole crew. "I'm real sorry."

"Forget about it," Rogers said. "We can hardly blame you for feeling sleepy."

"Yeah, no sweat, Hillbilly Bob," Jackson added. "Ain't no thang."

"Thanks," Jones murmured. He looked genuinely relieved.

They paddled south, guiding off the lights of the Hotel del Coronado. No one spoke. They rhythmically dipped their paddles into the black ocean, creating a steady splash and swish that was only interrupted when someone fell into a microsleep and let his paddle drag. The minutes turned into an hour, and the Hotel del Coronado slowly slid past. The moon had nearly completed its journey across the sky by the time they turned toward shore to make their approach to the compound.

They landed without incident and pulled their boat from the water in last place. To their astonishment, the instructors didn't harass them. Heisler simply instructed Grey to position his boat at the back of the elephant train. Still wet from the waist down, they began what Grey knew might be the last chow run of Hell Week. He wouldn't miss the journey. He particularly hated the traditional sprint across the highway, which always managed to strip another clump of hair from his pulverized scalp.

"You gonna make it, Mr. Grey," Felicia cooed. "You need sleep."

"I know, Felicia. I think you've mentioned that before. I'll be sound asleep in less than twelve hours." *Less than twelve hours.* A quick rush of elation coursed through his veins as he contemplated finishing Hell Week, but his enthusiasm died as he thought of Murray.

"I proud of you, Mr. Grey," Felicia said. She flashed her award-winning smile. "I know you can make it. I never understand why, but I know if anyone can do it, you can."

"Thanks." He was genuinely grateful for Felicia's support, but he found responding to her compliment difficult. He pressed his hand against hers. "You're the best."

Grey filled two mugs with steaming water and grabbed two packets of cocoa powder. For the first ten minutes of chow he ignored his plate of bacon, eggs, and hash browns. He cupped his mugs, one in each hand, and savored the warmth that spread from his palms. It was unlike any comfort he had experienced before, a comfort only someone who had been on the edge of hypothermia for five days could fathom.

"Like the little match girl," Rogers said quietly.

"What?" Jackson said. "You okay, sir?"

"It's like the little match girl, the way Grey holds those two mugs, feeling the heat run out of them. You know the story. The girl has to sell books of matches or she can't come home. One night when she can't sell a single book, she is forced to stay outside and light the matches for warmth. Just look at him." Rogers smiled and nodded at Grey. "It's tragic. Beautiful and tragic."

"You and your dang beauty," Jones muttered. "I swear, you'd think this place was some kind of artsy-fartsy academy."

"Beauty is everywhere," Rogers said. "And it's definitely here, in the suffering, in that cup of hot cocoa. This place is sinister and beautiful. I'm definitely writing a poem about this week. It's epic, really"—he smiled sheepishly—"when you think about it."

"Okay. Let's not push it," Grey interjected. "Epic or not, I want it over with."

"Amen to that," Jackson said.

"Yeah, no joke," Jones drawled.

"And what about Murray?" Grey asked. "What in the hell is the beauty about him dying on us?"

Rogers's smile faded. "I said beauty is everywhere, not in everything. Murray was a free spirit, a true man's man, and a good friend to you. That's beautiful. His death isn't."

The table fell into silence. Grey knew everyone was thinking about Murray. The situation reeked of foul play, but unlike him, they didn't have anything to base their gut instincts on.

The morning crew filtered through the door to the chow hall. Logan ushered them outside and led the class down to the edge of the bay by the playing field.

"Get wet," he ordered.

The students dropped their boats and waded into the bay without complaint.

"Out of the water," Logan ordered seconds later. "I like a quiet class. Instead of freezing, you'll do a little paddling. You tired fuckers would like that, wouldn't you?"

Grey considered the proposition. His hands were bright red and spotted with painful blisters. He could hardly hold a paddle without wincing. Still, it was better than the cold.

"I want you to paddle south along the bay, but instead of going all the way to the mud flats, I want you to stop at the marina just to the north. Everyone know the place I'm referring to?"

The class nodded absentmindedly. Grey had no idea. He counted on following the other boat crews. He knew it was poor leadership, but at this point he didn't give a shit.

"Then get going. Remember, the week's not over, gents. If you don't keep the energy level up, I just might volunteer to stay here until Saturday. I really don't care. I'll do it. You know I'm that crazy."

Yeah, we know, Grey thought. He pushed their boat out into the smelly bay water and climbed in behind his crew. They paddled slowly down the bay, squinting against the glare of the morning sun on the still water. *Stroke, stroke, stroke.* Grey could hear Murray calling cadence. *Stroke it, pet it, touch it, feel it.* He burst out laughing. His crewmates shook their heads sadly and continued paddling.

They trailed the other boat crews, unconcerned about the punishment a late arrival might bring. The week was almost over. Although it wouldn't be enjoyable, Grey knew they could all bear another round of surf torture.

Logan yelled at them from the bed of Big Blue as they rounded the corner of a cove and paddled into a marina full of sailboats.

"Everyone out of the boat!"

Grey's crew obediently rolled over the side of the craft and into the bay.

"Dump boat!"

Fucking idiot. In order to dump his boat, Grey needed at least two people to stay inside, a detail Logan had missed. Grey nodded at Jones, and they both climbed onto the main tube. They reached across to the far side of the boat, grabbed the nylon handles anchored to the main tube, and pulled backward. The boat rose up onto its side, then crashed over backward.

"Now, Mr. Princeton, you bathrobe-wearing, poetry-spouting, intellectual pig-fucker, climb up there and assume the George Washington position."

Rogers pulled himself onto the flat bottom of the raft and crawled to the bow. He stood and raised a hand to his brow.

"The rest of you shitheads—give me a storm. Start shaking that boat. I want monster seas."

The rest of Grey's crew latched onto the side of the boat and pushed and pulled, jerking the craft up and down in the water.

"Now give the thing a little forward propulsion. We don't have all day."

They kicked hard and slowly moved through the water.

Rogers smiled as he tried to maintain his historic pose.

"Dump him!" Logan ordered.

"I will not surrender," Rogers yelled back. "I will not let you and your Hessian dogs snuff out of the seeds of true freedom. You can not suppress the rights of men any longer, you imperial bastards!"

"Dump him!" Logan's voice was joined by other instructors and students in the class. "Dump him!"

"Sorry, Rogers," Grey said. "This is a democracy, and the overwhelming vote is against you."

Jackson and Grey heaved on one side of the boat, while Smurr, Jones, and O'Patry worked the other side. The boat rolled mightily, and Rogers tumbled headfirst into the bay. The beach party cheered.

Rogers rose to the surface sputtering. "You just killed the American dream."

"Yeah, sorry 'bout that," Jones drawled. "I guess you just don't have the makin's of a president." He flashed a smile, then added, "No offense intended."

"None taken."

They pushed their boat to shore, and Heisler immediately ordered them to the rear of the elephant train. Logan ran them across the highway, then turned north along the soft sand. They bounced along at a quick pace, finally stopping next to the demolition pits. A barbed-wire fence surrounded the pits. They dropped their boat next to the fence and followed Logan through the gate.

"You remember whistle drills?" Logan asked.

"Hoo-yah," the class responded.

No sooner had the cry left their lips than a deafening explosion rocked the enclosed area. Grey dropped onto his stomach and covered his ears. Chief Baldwin stood twenty yards away, just beyond a dozen strands of barbed wire strung less than a foot above the rocky ground. The corners of his brown mustache twitched as he placed a whistle between his teeth. Two shrill blasts rang out in the morning air. Grey crawled toward Baldwin on his stomach, grinding his legs and arms into the gravel as he snaked forward. A strand of barbed wire caught his shirt and tore his uniform. The rest of the class followed on his heels, urging him on. Periodically a high-pitched whine grew in intensity for several seconds, followed by an ear-busting explosion. The students tried to anticipate the explosions, crossing their legs and covering their ears moments before detonation. Baldwin continued moving backward, leading the class under more barbed wire and across an endless stretch of thorns and gravel. Grey's elbows and the inside of his knees became tenderized within minutes. Three flares dropped onto the sand upwind of the students, and a nauseating sweet green smoke rolled over them.

Mass chaos, Grey thought. *Nicely done.* He couldn't see a thing, his ears rang, and instructors with bullhorns barked unintelligible commands. He continued to follow Baldwin, who finally stopped next to a three-foot-diameter cement tube that protruded from a gentle hillside. Baldwin pointed into the tube. Grey crawled in, and the explosions became even more deafening. The tube slanted downward at a fairly steep angle. Grey slid forward on his stomach. Several seconds later the tunnel came to an abrupt end, and he found himself lying in the most putrid puddle of water he had ever encountered. It was chocolaty brown, and little bits of plant life and dead insects floated on the surface. Two thirty-foot lines ran across the pit. The top line was positioned about four feet above the lower one. Logan stood at the upper lip of the pit, firing blanks from his massive M-60.

"Get down!" Instructor Batman yelled through his megaphone. "I should only see your eyes!"

Grey slunk down into the nauseating pool of gunk as he waited for the rest of the class to filter in. The students slid out of the pipe one by one until all twenty-four formed a large circle around the perimeter of the pit. The M-60 fell silent, and the simulated mortar rounds stopped thundering in.

"Time for a little rodeo fun!" Logan yelled. "Officers first. How about you?" Logan pointed at the class leader. "Your leadership skills during the week have been less than ideal. Here's a chance to vindicate yourself. If you can make it all the way across those lines, I'll secure your whole class right here and now. That's a promise."

Pollock adjusted his mud-caked camouflage hat, then rose out of the stinking pool and climbed up to the two lines. Grey realized where the challenge lay. He hadn't noticed a series of thin lines tied to the two larger ones. Four brown shirts stood at the side of the pit, ready to jerk Pollock from his perch.

"If the roll backs can't get you off the line in less than a minute, they all take a dunk in the pond of pain. How's that sound?"

The four brown shirts belted out a loud "Hoo-yah."

Pollock stepped onto the lower line and grabbed the upper one. Moving deliberately, he inched outward over the pool. The brown shirts pulled at the line, gently at first, then more violently as Pollock advanced farther. Once he was safely above water, they jumped up and down, yanking on their lines with all their might. Pollock's feet slipped off the bottom line, but he managed to keep his grip on the upper one. The thirty-foot rope jerked four feet to each side at a dizzying speed. After a brief fight, Pollock lost his grip and flew headlong through the air. He landed flat on his back, sending a sheet of mud into the air. The students and instructors cheered loudly.

"Not bad," Logan said, "but not good enough. I want a real cattle rustler."

"I ain't a cattle rustler," Jones piped up, "but I've tamed my fair share of mustangs."

"Since we have no Texas trash in this class, I guess we'll settle for a Tennessee hillbilly."

Jones climbed up onto the lines. He moved with lighting speed, catching the brown shirts by surprise. By the time they reacted and started jerking the lines, he had already managed to scamper a considerable distance. After a few yards of hard-earned progress, his feet slipped from the line. Instead of dangling free like Pollock did, Jones wrapped his legs around the upper line and clung to it like a koala bear. The brown shirts heaved and strained, but Jones wouldn't be deterred. He slowly inched onward. By the time he hit the halfway point, the brown shirts were sweating from effort. The line whipped eight feet to each side, and Jones looked like a human bumblebee, zooming back and forth across the pit at lightning speed.

"Yee-hah!" Jones whooped, inching even farther across.

"They're going to kill him," Grey muttered. "This is ridiculous."

"No joke," Rogers said. "At that velocity he might—"

The audience whooped with excitement as Jones shot free from the line and catapulted into the air. He flipped end over end and splashed into the pond several feet from Grey's head.

"That's a record!" Logan yelled. "Not bad, Uncle Jeb!"

Jones rubbed his head and grinned from ear to ear. "Don't ask me to do it again."

The mood in the pit shifted dramatically. The instructors laughed and offered words of encouragement from above while the students tested their strength on the line. It almost felt as if Hell Week were already over. Grey's turn came, and he performed dismally. His mud-slicked hands slipped free from the line almost immediately. The instructors shook their heads in disgust as he belly flopped into the muck.

Chief Baldwin stood at the edge of the pit with a megaphone in hand and waited for the laughter to subside.

"Gentlemen," he said, "you have been through the hardest week of training anywhere in the world. You have done things that would make ordinary men run home and cry to momma. You have surmounted obstacles that most people will never be able to comprehend. And now, gentlemen, I have just four words for you."

"Four words?" Rogers whispered. "That can't be right."

"Four simple words that will change your life forever," Baldwin continued.

Hell Week secure? Grey mulled it over in his sleep-deprived mind. *Hell Week secure.* That was only three words. His heart sank.

"Get under your boats!" Baldwin yelled.

A collective groan echoed throughout the pit.

"That's right. It's not over yet, motherfuckers!" Logan shouted. "Get moving!"

Grey scaled the steep sides of the pit and ran through the gate surrounding the compound. Once his crew had assembled, he gave the order to prepare for an elephant run. Logan appeared moments later, chuckling softly to himself.

"This is going to suck," he said, "real bad."

The class struggled to keep up as Logan took off at a sprint. They ran along a loose sand road at the edge of the highway. Just when Grey managed to close the gap between his bow and the stern of the boat ahead, Logan turned up the pace a notch. The rumble of a diesel truck grew louder as the instructors closely tailed the struggling class.

"What the heck is that?" Jones asked.

A nursery rhyme reverberated through the morning air.

This old man, he played three,
He played knick-knack on my knee.
With a knick-knack, paddy whack,
Give a dog a bone,
This old man came rolling home.

It took Grey a moment to process what he was hearing. It wasn't his fatigue-warped mind playing tricks on him. The familiar song blared from the PA system on Big Blue. Despite the painful slap of the boat as it bounced on his inflamed scalp, Grey managed a smile. *Sick bastards.*

Logan turned up the pace even more as they neared the BUD/S compound. Instead of running directly to the gate, he zigzagged up and down the sand berm, occasionally looking over his shoulder to shout insults at the lagging boat crews. After several minutes of agonizing berm sprints, the stocky instructor headed for the gate in the chain-link fence. *Please, please, please.*

Logan turned at the last second and doubled back toward the berm. Jackson's breath came in ragged gasps, and Smurr limped badly. Grey didn't know how much longer his crew would last. Logan took them back and forth over the berm six more times before finally leading the class into the compound. After ordering the crews to drop their boats in the parking lot, Logan led them onto the grinder. They stood at attention as Chief Baldwin strolled through an office door.

Several minutes later a gray-haired admiral decked out in dress blues strode purposefully to the front of the formation. The gold trident that marked him as a SEAL gleamed above a chest full of ribbons. He cleared his throat, then spoke in a low, resonant voice. "I don't need to lecture you guys on the hardships you endured. Any one of you could describe the pain, the discomfort, the freezing temperatures, the sleeplessness. I've been there, the instructors have been there, and so has every SEAL. By completing this week you have taken a huge step in the realization of a dream. Not many will understand what you have gone through. It is an experience unlike any other. Every SEAL remembers his Hell Week, and every SEAL draws upon the misery he endured during those long nights when the going gets tough. You are changed forever, men. You will never look at a hot shower the same way again."

A few students laughed quietly. A few choked back tears. Grey floated in a stage of foggy disbelief. It couldn't be over. It was another trick.

"I'm proud of each and every one of you. I've heard good things about this class, and I'm honored to have the opportunity to say the words you've looked forward to hearing for one sleepless week." The admiral paused for effect, then said solemnly, "Hell Week secure."

The instructors smiled, and Grey suddenly felt more tired than he ever had in his life. The admiral moved down the line, shaking hands and offering his congratulations. After he departed, Chief Baldwin ushered the class back to the showers. Grey examined his wounds as a stream of warm water splashed over his filthy body. The inside of his thighs oozed yellow fluid from tender pink patches of flesh. The gash on his leg was a veritable rainbow of colors: rings of red, white, yellow, green, and black circled the deep wound. Grey reached up and felt the top of his head. His scalp was a patchwork of tender coin-size bare spots.

As he stepped out of the shower, he received a clean pair of shorts, sandals, and a brown T-shirt with his name already stenciled on the front and back. He pulled the shirt over his chest and checked himself in the mirror. A zombie stared back at him. His eyes were deeply sunk and rimmed with red, and his face sported five days worth of stubble. Suddenly the tile floor looked extremely inviting. Grey wanted to curl up and fall into a prolonged coma.

"Chief Baldwin wants you back in the classroom," a brown shirt said. "The sooner you get out there, the sooner you can sleep."

Grey slipped into his sandals and shuffled across the grinder and into the First Phase classroom. He sank into a hard plastic seat and flipped open the lid of the pizza box sitting on his desk. He ate quickly, but the food gave him no satisfaction. The other students scarfed down slices of greasy pizza with blank faces. No celebration, no cheering, just dumbfounded silence.

"Well, shitbirds, you're done," Baldwin said, striding into the room. He rubbed his mustache thoughtfully. "I think the admiral pretty well summed it up. Good job on surviving Hell Week. You started the week with forty-seven, and the twenty-four of you made it. I'm going to pull a bus into the compound in about ten minutes. I'll give you guys a ride back to the barracks. Before I can cut you loose, though, there are a couple of things you need to know. First of all, you need to elevate the end of your bed. If you don't keep your legs raised, they'll swell up like sausages. Use a drawer from your desk—just jam it under your mattress. Second, a crew of roll backs will be roaming the barracks, checking on you guys as you sleep. The X of masking tape on your door is to indicate that you're a Hell Week survivor. Don't take it off. We don't want any of you turds passing away in the night." Baldwin belched loudly. "Someone will wake you up tomorrow morning at eleven A.M. Be back at the clinic by twelve so the docs can check you out." He looked around the class-room, appraising the faces of the survivors. "Get some sleep."

Baldwin strode out of the room. After prying themselves from their chairs, the students limped out of the classroom and onto the grinder.

"Good job, men!" the chaplain shouted from across the pavement.

The class was too fatigued to respond. They helped one another across the grinder, the stronger students supporting those whose legs had locked up in the classroom. Jackson leaned heavily against Grey, apologizing under his breath for his weakness. They climbed aboard a white bus pi-loted by Chief Baldwin and rumbled back to the barracks.

Rogers opened the door to their room and stepped inside. Grey fol-lowed him in and immediately flopped down on his bed.

"Don't forget to elevate," Rogers said groggily.

"Right." Grey pulled a drawer from his dresser and slid it under his mattress.

Rogers examined their door. "I'll be damned."

"What?"

Rogers fingered the cross formed by white masking tape. "If this was made from lambs blood, we'd have a nice biblical parody on our hands. We are the chosen few."

"Right," Grey mumbled, "whatever you say."

"I'm hitting the sack. I recommend you do the same."

"I will."

Rogers flopped onto his bed and immediately fell into a deep sleep.

Grey peeled the strips of tape from the door. He didn't want anyone prowl-
ing his room. He pushed the door shut and locked it. As a final touch, he
took an empty glass bottle from his tiny fridge and propped it on top of the
doorknob. After easing himself onto his bed, Grey reached over and set his
alarm clock for 11:00. That done, he shut his eyes and immediately exited
the conscious world.

SIXTEEN

BULLETS OF SWEAT OOZED from Grey's forehead and back, saturating his brown shirt and soaking his sheets. Grey looked at the clock: 3:00 A.M. He stood up slowly, flinching in pain as his rigid muscles stretched. Taking baby six-inch steps, Grey tottered over to the bathroom and pulled a towel from the rack. After stripping off his shirt and wrapping his body in the towel, he inched back to his bed and closed his eyes.

Grey bolted upright in his bed. Groping blindly, he fumbled for his small alarm clock. Once his fingers closed over it, he hurled the clock across the room. It continued to buzz in the corner of his closet. Grey rubbed his eyes and scanned his room. Rogers snored like a chainsaw, sound asleep and dead to the world. Grey gingerly eased himself out of his bed and shook his roommate awake. Without a word, they both slipped into their shower sandals and limped toward the BUD/S clinic. The class was strung out along the road like a trail of refugees leaving a prison camp.

"What's up, sir?" Jackson asked as he caught up to the pair. "How you feeling?'"

"I'd be lying if I said I felt human," Grey said. "Truth is, I feel like I slept about ten minutes. Those damn cold sweats . . ."

"I know what you're saying, sir. It's like the thermostats in our bodies blew out."

"I slept like a baby," Rogers chirped. He smiled sheepishly. "Sorry. Inappropriate comment."

"Sir, it's simple, really. You're just some kind of freak," Jackson said. "We've come to expect that kind of nonsense from you."

Jones ambled up alongside them. "You wouldn't believe what I did last night."

"What'd you do?" Grey humored him.

"I knocked one of them brown shirts square in the jaw when he came to wake me up. Popped him a good one, just like this." Jones punched at the sky. "Poor guy didn't even hit me back. If he had been one of my brothers, I would've expected a good beatin'. But no, not this fella. He just shook his head and walked out of the room. Almost made me feel bad. 'Course, he should know better than to wake a man who hasn't slept in five days."

The four students walked on, arms slung around one anothers' shoulders.

"We made it," Jones said with finality. "I'll be damned."

"Amen, brother," Jackson added.

Grey touched his arm. *Blood brothers.* Celebrating didn't feel right without Murray around. After all, the scrappy seaman was the architect behind nearly every class celebration. Grey missed him deeply.

The class formed up behind the clinic and checked in for their last hygiene exam. Doc Anderson looked Grey over quickly.

"Nasty cut," he said, eyeing the green, black, and yellow tear on Grey's leg. "Our tests came back negative for any flesh-eating bacteria. It might look and smell foul, but you'll live. Just keep it clean, air it out, and keep taking antibiotics."

"Anything else I should know?"

"No, you're good to go," Anderson said. He slapped Grey on the shoulder. "Go get some more sleep. You still look like shit."

"Thanks."

Grey met up with Jones, Jackson, and Rogers and hobbled back toward the barracks.

"Sir, there is definitely somethin' you ain't tellin' us here," Jones drawled. "I know you too well by now. It's about Murray, ain't it?"

Rogers looked over with interest. "Tell us, Mark. You promised you would."

"I guess now's as good a time as any," Grey conceded. "But if I let you into my fucked-up world, you'll be sacrificing a lot of sleep, and I know you need it."

"Forget the sleep," Jackson said, his puffy, blistered lips turning up into a smile. "Sleep is for the weak. There's time for that later."

"And it will be dangerous," Grey added.

"We're training to be SEALs, not Girl Scouts, sir," Jones said. "Give me a break."

"Point well taken," Grey said. "So, who wants in?"

"As Murray would say, 'Fuckin' A,' sir!" Jones clapped Grey on the shoulder.

"I'm in," Rogers stated solemnly.

"Me too," Jackson said, "although I'd like to know what I'm getting into."

"Meet in my room in fifteen minutes," Grey said. "I'll fill you in then."

Jackson and Jones split up as Rogers and Grey walked to their room. Grey's head ached intensely. A vicelike pressure crushed his temples, only furthering his desire to crawl back into bed. *I should be done with this bullshit. I should be passed out, drooling happily on my pillow.* Grey knew his current condition made him extremely vulnerable. In addition to fighting the mental effects of countless hours of sleep debt, his body had been battered beyond recognition.

"I'll be back in a minute," Grey said. "There's a call I need to make."

Rogers nodded, and Grey stepped outside of their room, cell phone in hand. His heart still ached from the last attempt he had made to visit Vanessa, but he needed to hear her voice. She knew him better than anyone, and he wanted to straighten things out. He dialed her number, and seconds later the phone picked up.

"Hello?"

"Vanessa, it's me," Grey said softly. "I just finished Hell Week."

"I knew you'd make it," she said. "I never doubted you."

"I know," Grey said. He closed his eyes. "About last week—"

"Forget it," Vanessa cut in. "It wasn't what you think. He was a friend who got carried away." An uneasy silence followed. "I miss you. Can I come see you?"

"No, and that's part of the reason I called."

"What's going on?"

"I need you to stay in L.A. this weekend."

"Why?" Vanessa asked. "Why can't I come see you?"

"Because Murray died, and I know it wasn't an accident. My boys and I have some investigating to do, and just to be safe, I'd appreciate it if you'd lay low for this weekend."

"You'd 'appreciate it if I'd lay low,' " Vanessa repeated. "What in God's name is going on? Murray died? How did that happen?"

Grey leaned his head against the wall. "It was during Hell Week. He was sick, but he shouldn't have died. He drowned in his own blood, and the only people around were two instructors. I don't know much at this point, but I won't let them sweep this whole thing under the rug. Just please stay somewhere else this weekend. I don't know what I'm dealing with here, and I don't want to take any chances."

"Mark, this is ridiculous."

"Trust me. Please." Grey's tone shifted from impatience to anger. "Just do it." He usually loved Vanessa's headstrong ways, but today he was in no mood to argue.

"Fine." Her voice was uneasy. "Call me when you're done with this crap."

"I will," Grey said. "I'll call as soon as I can." He limped back to his room. His crew had already assembled.

Jones lay sprawled out on Grey's bed. He lifted his head. "Give it to us straight, boss."

Grey sat on the edge of the bed and relayed the events of the last few weeks, starting with Murray's decision to blackmail Redman. He covered the murder of the gun-store owner, the inventory problems at BUD/S, the disappearance of the retired SEAL, and finally, the details of his last moments with Murray.

"I don't like this at all," Jackson said, shaking his head. "This is nothing but trouble, plain and simple. But if someone thinks he can get away with taking down one of my shipmates, he's mistaken. I don't care what we're up against. We'll get to the bottom of this."

"Grey," Rogers said gently. "You mentioned that Murray had pulmonary edema. That's a very serious condition. Isn't it possible he essentially died of exposure?"

No. No way. Grey was on the defensive. He shook his head.

"That lung stuff is serious business," Jones chimed in, "but Murray shouldn't have died from it. He didn't look that weak."

"It's not that I doubt you," Rogers added, placing a hand on Grey's shoulder. "I've never doubted your judgment for a second. I just think that we're all fatigued and famished and generally lacking lucidity."

"Lacking what?" Jones asked. "Dang it, sir, we're too tired for your Princeton-speak."

"We're just tired," Rogers said. "I question our collective judgment."

"I'm behind Mr. Grey all the way," Jackson said. "He may be wrong about Murray's death, but we need to find out for sure. If that means we lose some more sleep, well then, that's just God's plan."

Rogers searched Grey's face. "You know I'll support you." He shrugged. "What's another few days of suffering?"

"So you're in?" Grey asked.

"I'm in."

"Good. I think our first order of business should be to get out of here," Grey said. "We're not safe in the barracks. We need to relocate."

"Hold on," Rogers said. "From what you've said, I'm still not sure that staying in the barracks puts us in danger. If Redman was after anyone, it was Murray, right?"

"But he knows we were buddies," Grey countered. "If Murray was going to confide in anyone, Redman knows it would have been me. And who knows what kind of attention he drew when he was poking his nose into that arms-dealing crap in Imperial Beach."

Rogers shrugged. "Either way, I could use a night away from this place. My sheets are drenched with sweat."

"Then let's get out of here." Grey opened a dresser drawer and pulled out a worn running shoe. He shook it, and a wad of cash fell to the floor. "I'll pay for the room. There's a place down the road, across the street from the Hotel del Coronado," Grey said. "It's close enough to be convenient, and the parking is underground. No one would think to look for us there."

"We need to make sure everyone has a cell phone," Rogers said. "That way we can split up."

"I'll take care of the phones," Jones said. He rolled off the bed and moved toward the door. "I'll be back in a few minutes."

"I'll search Murray's room," Grey offered. "We might need some of his phone numbers." He walked outside and followed the hallway to Murray's room. The door was locked. Grey knocked loudly before remembering that Murray's roommate had dropped out before Hell Week. Since then, Murray had been living alone. He tried the sliding-glass window, and it slid open with a satisfying *thunk*. Grey glanced around quickly then pulled himself through the window and dropped onto Murray's bed. The sheets had been stripped off the ratty mattress and thrown in a heap in the corner. The lock on Murray's closet was gone, and his desk drawers had been hastily pulled open. Grey sat down at the desk and filtered through the jumbled contents of each drawer. Nothing but old receipts, magazines, and a well-worn copy of J. R. R. Tolkien's *The Hobbit*. Grey turned his attention to the closet. The pockets of Murray's jeans had been turned inside out. Grey halfheartedly searched through the pile of clothes in the corner before moving on to the bathroom. *Nothing.* No phone numbers, no links to the outside world. He glanced through the window then stepped outside and pulled the locked door shut behind him.

The elderly woman behind the reservations counter at the hotel regarded Grey suspiciously. She was clearly revolted by his appearance. Like everyone else in his crew, he wore a T-shirt and shorts, which did little to hide his oozing leg wound. Grey smiled, picked up the key card she pushed across the counter, and walked back to the elevator. He descended into the basement, where the rest of his crew waited in Rogers's battered Toyota. In the ten minutes he'd been gone, they'd already fallen into a deep sleep, their faces mashed against the car's windows. Grey woke them up and herded them back into the elevator. Ten minutes later, they were all seated on the floor of the hotel room, formulating a plan.

"Murray apparently made contact with a retired SEAL. We need to find out where he lives," Rogers stated matter-of-factly. "It would be a step in the right direction."

"And how do you suggest we find his address?" Grey asked.

"Where would you go if you wanted to gather info about a salty old SEAL?"

"McP's," Jones drawled. "Every SEAL passes through that bar at one time or another."

"Exactly. Someone there will know how to get in touch with our contact," Rogers said. "What was his name again? Armstrong?"

"That's it," Grey said. "Retired chief, served with Redman."

"Why don't you and I go check it out?" Rogers asked.

"I'm game," Grey said. "But what if the instructors are there?"

"At three o'clock on a Saturday afternoon? They're not that pathetic. If we leave now we should beat the crowd."

"You gents have fun," Jones drawled. "The Good Reverend and I will guard the fort." He crawled on top of a bed and closed his eyes. "Wake us up when you get back."

"We will," Grey said. "Get some rest."

Even though the bar was only a few blocks away, Rogers pulled his car out of the underground garage and drove the distance. Grey didn't want an instructor to recognize them walking out the front door, and in reality, any kind of physical movement still presented an extremely painful challenge. Every step sent a firestorm of raw pain rushing up his legs.

With its pleasant white walls and green awning, McP's looked the part of a respectable Irish pub. A gated outdoor seating area flanked a well-appointed walnut bar, and a number of tourists happily sipped beers in the soft sunlight. Grey followed Rogers through the main door and scanned his surroundings. A middle-aged man with bushy brown hair and the massive shoulders and soft belly of a linebacker whose glory days had expired sat at the bar, chatting with a silver-haired bartender. They both looked up in annoyance and frowned at Grey and Rogers.

"Don't come back until you graduate," the brown-haired man said. "We don't need any tadpoles stinking up our joint."

Grey looked at Rogers in surprise. *How do they know?*

"Oh, come on, it's written all over your face, the way you walk. . . . I know a case of 'grinder reminder' when I see it," the man explained, shifting his hulking body so that he faced the intruders. "What are you guys? Class Two-eighty-three? You've got *Hell Week Survivor* written all over your face."

"You guessed correctly," Rogers answered politely. "But don't worry, we're not trying to claim a spot in your bar. I know we still have a long way to go before we earn our tridents. We just need to get in touch with an old SEAL, and we thought you gentlemen might know where to find him."

"We're not gentlemen," Mr. Linebacker shot back. "I hate that god-damn word. We're fighters. We work for a living."

The bartender reached across the counter and placed a hand on the large man's arm. "Bill, no need to be so hard on these guys. They just finished Hell Week. Remember how shitty that was? All they want is some info."

"Exactly," Grey said. "We're not trying to intrude prematurely into your world; we just need to talk to someone who knows their stuff. You two served in Vietnam, didn't you?"

"Fuckin' A, we did," Bill said. "Mekong Delta." He rolled his neck. "None of this pansy-ass shit they do these days."

The bartender stepped out from behind the bar and extended his hand. "Jake Davidson's the name." He nodded toward his friend. "Bill can barely walk because of all the shrapnel in his thigh. He's a little bitter."

"Am not."

"And he hates Hollywood SEALs. I don't feel quite as strongly as he does about it, but I have to admit the number of pretty-boy Team guys has grown exponentially in the last few years. I think they're more concerned with appearing in documentaries than they are about operating. You two aren't Hollywood types, are you?"

"Far from it," Rogers piped up, "although we know a few."

"Fucking pretty boys," Bill scoffed. "What an embarrassment. Can't even wipe their ass without a TV camera in their face."

"Bill, you're generalizing now," Jake said. He smiled, and the skin around his eyes erupted into a web of deep wrinkles. A small scar ran up from the edge of his eyebrow, lending him a ruggedly handsome appearance. "I'm sure you guys will do fine. What rank are you, anyway?"

"We're officers," Grey stated reluctantly.

"Goddamn!" Bill yelled, a little too loudly. "Cake eaters! Résumé builders!"

Jake angrily stormed back behind the bar, poured a double shot of tequila, and slammed it down in front of Bill. "Drink it and shut up, Bill. I'm trying to run a bar here."

Bill threw back his head, and the yellow liquid disappeared down his throat. He wiped his sleeve across his mouth. "Sorry. I'll quiet down."

"Thank you," Jake said. "I don't have any problem with officers. Just remember, always take care of your men. Take care of your men, and they'll do anything for you. Sell them out, and you're finished. I had a damn good OIC in Vietnam." His green eyes moved away from Grey's face. He shook his head, his mind clearly occupied with old memories. "Damn good."

"And listen to your chief," Bill muttered. "Listen to your chief or you're dead in the water. Chiefs run the navy, and it's the same in the Teams. If they take you under their wing, you're set."

"And don't get carried away in your search for glory," Jake added. "Don't be afraid to turn down a mission if you think the lives of your men are in jeopardy. Stay cool, think clearly. Your chance to prove yourself will come along. Pick your battles wisely."

Bill belched loudly. "Confucius say, 'He who kill opponent first always get last laugh.'"

"I told you to be quiet," Jake scolded. "Stop with your Confucius crap." He turned his attention back to Grey. "Now remind me, why are you here again? Not to soak up our wisdom, I'm sure."

"Actually, we lost contact with a friend of ours recently. He's a retired chief. Armstrong's his name."

"Goddamn Armstrong!" Bill yelled. "I know that pig fucker. Team Three, right?"

Jake reached over and boxed Bill on the ear. "For Christ's sake, quiet down, Bill."

Bill rubbed his ear and frowned at his empty shot glass. "Well, what about it? Am I right or am I right?"

"The Armstrong we're thinking of was an East Coast guy. Team Four, I think," Grey said. "But he retired out here. Lives somewhere in Imperial Beach."

"Armstrong, Armstrong." Jake repeated the name quietly to himself. "Don't know of anyone East Coast by that name."

"And trust us, if this Armstrong character really lived here in Imperial Beach, we'd know about him," Bill said. "Especially a retired chief." He shook his head. "I know of one Armstrong who served here on the West Coast his entire career before retiring in Montana, but I have to say, I think you guys must be confused. There's no East Coast Armstrong."

The door to the bar swung open, and the color drained from Rogers's face. Grey slowly turned around.

"What the fuck do we have here?" Osgood yelled. "What in the hell is this? You think you're SEALs now?" He chuckled merrily. "Oh boy. Oh boy."

Instructor Furtado and Instructor Redman pushed through the door and stopped short in surprise. They eyed the two battered students hungrily.

"You believe this crap?" Osgood asked. "Look who came to hang out with the big boys."

"Well, if it isn't my two favorite homos," Furtado said pleasantly. "Have a seat." He politely gestured toward two of the empty bar stools.

"We actually have to get going," Rogers said. "We're pretty exhausted—no condition to imbibe."

"Pretty exhausted?" Redman snarled. "Not exhausted enough, apparently. I'll fix that later."

Jake smiled at the instructors' antics. "These young lads actually came to ask me about a friend of theirs."

Grey's heartbeat increased dramatically. He looked at Jake pleadingly. *Please be quiet. Please.*

"Armstrong's his name. He's a retired chief, right?"

Grey nodded. He was too mortified to speak.

"You ever heard of a guy named Armstrong?" Jake asked, looking at the group of instructors. "Seal Team Four? Retired in Imperial Beach."

"Never heard of him," Furtado said quietly.

"No fucking clue," Osgood said.

"No such guy," Redman grunted. "If he was retired Team Four, I would know him."

"No matter." Osgood put an arm around Grey's shoulder. "Why

don't you have a seat, sir? You can spare a few minutes with your future teammates, can't you?" His eyes sparkled merrily.

Grey nervously sat down at the bar and shot Rogers a terrified look.

"Jake, fix my friend a drink," Osgood said. "I think you know what he wants."

"I can't, really," Grey said. "I'm driving."

"Pussy," Osgood snarled. His eyes flashed dangerously for a brief instant. He smiled, and his tone became pleasant again. "Well then, Mr. Rogers, I guess it's just you and us."

Jake filled the bottom of a double shot glass with Tabasco sauce, then filled it to the rim with tequila.

"One for each day of Hell Week," Osgood said.

Jake shot him an annoyed look.

"I'm paying," Osgood said. "Don't worry so much, shipmate." He pulled a twenty from his pocket and handed it to Jake. "Like I said, five shots."

Four more shots appeared on the table. The two other instructors gathered around and looked on with interest.

"This will put some hair on your homo chest, Plato," Osgood said. "Rapid succession. No puking, no complaining. Take it like a man."

Rogers sat down, rolled his shoulders, and breathed deeply.

"Cut the melodrama, fag boy," Furtado said.

Rogers threw back the first double shot, then the second, then the third. His eyes watered, but he managed to keep from gagging. He held the fourth shot in his hand and looked at it hesitantly.

"Get on with it," Osgood said. "You're only to Wednesday."

Rogers gulped down the fourth shot, and then with trembling hands, the fifth. His Adam's apple continued to work reflexively, and for a moment Grey was sure he would puke. He tottered unsteadily and cringed.

"Good stuff," Rogers croaked. "Nectar of the gods."

Osgood clapped him on the back. Even Redman smiled. Furtado clicked his tongue stud against his teeth and regarded Rogers coolly with his icy blue eyes.

"Not bad, sir," Osgood said, genuinely pleased. "Taken like a man. We might make something out of you after all."

"He's still a pussy in my book," Redman growled, "and I'm getting tired of looking at these two cake eaters. Don't you think it's about time they crawled home?"

"Feel free to leave, esteemed sirs," Osgood said. "Mr. Grey, I'm gonna kick the crap out of you on Monday for being a pussy. And I still haven't forgiven you for your Hell Week bullshit. Mr. Rogers, you just earned a one-day vacation. Good job."

"Thanks for the drinks," Rogers groaned as he lurched for the door.

"Hold up," Jake called out. He scrawled a name and phone number on a napkin and handed it to Grey. "Call this number and say that Jake referred you. The guy is an old buddy of mine. He knows everyone around here. If there really is an Armstrong from Team Four around here, he'll know how to find him."

"Thanks, Jake." Grey turned to leave and felt Furtado's icy stare burning through him. He stopped and returned the instructor's look. The hint of a smirk pulled at the corners of Furtado's mouth.

"Sleep well, pussy."

Grey turned and followed Rogers onto the street. Rogers made it halfway to the car before he fell to his knees and emptied his stomach into a tidy planter next to an upscale shop. The nicely dressed patrons looked on in shock, clearly horrified by the spectacle. Grey scooped Rogers up and laid him across the backseat of the old Toyota.

"I'm a good friend," Rogers stated matter-of-factly.

"I know you are," Grey answered.

"Those drinks were meant for you, buddy. Talk about taking one for the team." Rogers's body went limp, and he immediately began sawing deep, snuffling breaths. Grey climbed behind the wheel and wound his way through an upper-class neighborhood before turning back toward the hotel. He pulled the car into the underground lot and looked back at Rogers. Drool stains covered his shirt, and his eyes darted back and forth in the rapid eye movements usually reserved for deep sleep. His body was so deprived of rest that it skipped the initial stages of the sleep cycle, carrying him straight into dreamland. Grey opened the back door and cradled Rogers in his arms. Carting him to the elevator took all of his energy.

Grey knocked loudly on the door to his room with his elbow. After waiting several seconds, he knocked again. *No response.* He gently set Rogers on the ground and dug his key card out of his pocket. The lights were off and the shades drawn, but Grey could clearly make out two human forms on top of the two beds. Jackson lay wrapped in a thick comforter, shaking gently in his sleep. Jones slept swaddled in a white towel, beads of perspiration running down his face in tiny rivulets. Grey glanced back and forth between the two students, deciding whom to wake. Rogers clearly needed his own bed. Grey finally decided on Jones. Still cradling Rogers in his pulverized arms, Grey nudged Jones with his knee. The Tennessee Wonder instantly sprang into a sitting position and swung at Grey's head, nearly missing his nose.

"Easy, Tennessee," Grey said gently. "I need your help, buddy."

"What? What?" Jones glanced around in confusion. The anger in his face gradually subsided. "Sorry, boss. I thought you were gonna send me to the surf."

"I wouldn't do that to you, Jones," Grey said. "But I need you to give up your bed for a while. Rogers is hurting bad."

"What's going on?"

"We ran into a bunch of instructors at McP's."

"You're kidding," Jones drawled, shaking his head in disbelief. "You're full of it, sir. Ain't no way."

"I'm quite serious. They made Rogers take five double shots of tequila in about twenty seconds. It wasn't pretty. He needs sleep bad."

Jones stiffly crawled out of bed. "Here. Set him down nice and easy." He limped to the bathroom and came back holding two glasses of water.

After dumping Rogers onto the bed, Grey forced the water down his throat, ensuring that he was well hydrated before he passed out again. Rogers instantly curled into a fetal position and pulled the comforter up around his neck.

"Who was at the bar?" Jones asked.

"Redman, Furtado, and Osgood."

"This gets weirder by the minute, sir," Jones said. "Redman and Furtado were there? Ain't they the ones we think messed with Murray?"

Grey nodded. "Give me second. I need to make a call." He picked up the phone, pulled the napkin from his pocket, and dialed the number scrawled across the soiled paper. After six rings a woman answered the phone.

"Yeah."

"Is Mr. O'Dell there?"

"Who's asking?"

"My name's Mark Grey. I got referred to him by Jake, the bartender at McP's. I need to talk to him about a friend of mine."

"Hold on." Grey could hear her yelling in the background. Nearly a minute later, a man with a gravelly voice picked up.

"What?"

Grey waited a second. *Is that it?* When he realized that was the only greeting he would receive, he said, "Your buddy Jake told me to give you a call. I'm looking for a friend of mine by the name of Armstrong—retired SEAL chief, lives in Imperial Beach, served on Team Four."

"Don't know him," O'Dell growled. "In fact, I don't recall anyone by that name from Team Four. Are you sure you have his name right?"

"Pretty sure."

"If he was your friend, I imagine you'd know his name."

"I'm just tired. My class finished Hell Week yesterday."

"So you're a fucking tadpole?"

"Yes."

"Well, I'm sorry I can't help you." O'Dell paused, then said, "In the unlikely event that you make it through training, remember to listen to your chief. Ignore your chief and you're fucked. I'm sure my boys at McP's told you the same thing, but it's the damn truth. Your officers won't know shit. Your chief should be your role model. If you can't tolerate one of your junior officers, or he just gets too uptight, duct-tape him to a table and leave him behind."

Grey snorted a quick laugh. O'Dell clearly had no idea he was talking to an officer. "Thanks for the advice."

The phone line went dead.

"Figure it out?" Jones asked, opening one eye. His sat slumped in a plush blue chair, his skin still shiny with sweat.

"No. But I'm not discouraged yet." Grey faked enthusiasm, but he felt horrible. The "grinder reminder" on his ass cracked open as he rose from his chair. Sticky blood oozed from the newly opened wound, soaking through his underwear. To make matters worse, Murray's SEAL contact was starting to seem like an illusion. "I think we should get some food, but I need to clean up first."

"Whatever you say, boss. I'm ready whenever you are." Jones forced a smile and immediately closed his eyes and let his head roll back. Within seconds he was out cold.

Grey gingerly stepped into the bathroom and stripped off his clothes. He hesitated twice before summoning the courage to turn on the water. The first splatters of chilly water on his hand took his breath away. After climbing into the bathtub, he wrapped his arms around his chest and shook gently. Gradually warmth flooded into his stiff limbs, and he laid back and closed his eyes. *Grab some food, come back and sleep. Wake up and find out more about Armstrong.* It seemed straightforward. *Then what?* Grey's world melted away, replaced by the familiar salty coastal breeze and frigid ocean of the Silver Strand. Redman and Furtado stood on the berm above him, their bodies silhouetted against an endless bank of gray clouds. A wave washed over his face, then another, and another.

Grey gagged violently. His eyes shot open as he spat liquid from his mouth. Water cascaded over the side of the tub and rolled across the tile floor, saturating his clothes as it moved toward the door. Grey lunged for the water and shut it off. After opening the drain, he stripped a towel off the rack and threw it on the vast puddle that had formed. Grey stepped out of the tub and pushed the towel around with his foot. *Fuck it.* He stumbled out the door and found everything as he had left it. Jones snored noisily in the big blue chair as beads of sweat trickled down his face. Rogers slept under the comforter of one bed, while Jackson lay curled in the comforter on another.

"Jones," Grey said, shaking him gently. "Tennessee, wake up."

Jones swung, but Grey was ready this time. He stepped aside, and the punch sailed past his head.

"Is it morning already?"

"No, but we need to get some food for our shipmates. And I don't think we should go anywhere on the island. We're way too noticeable."

"I agree," Jones said. "I have to admit, some chow sounds damn good right now, sir."

"You've got to get up first," Grey said. "Let's go."

Jones eased himself to his feet and hobbled toward the door. Grey followed him into the elevator. They walked across the underground parking lot and climbed into Rogers's old Toyota. Grey's jeep was far too conspicuous; a Toyota would blend into traffic nicely. Minutes later they were cruising down the Silver Strand Boulevard past the BUD/S compound. Jones looked over at the obstacle course and shook his head.

"Hate that damn thing."

They raced toward Mexico, paralleling the beach they had run up and down countless times over the week.

"Hate that damn beach."

Grey smiled. "I sense a theme here. Why don't you take a nap? I'll wake you up when we get there."

"Don't need no damn sleep." Jones flashed his snaggletoothed smile and closed his eyes.

As they reached the sound end of the bay, the density of tired one-story houses increased. Grey shifted uncomfortably in his seat as they pulled into the McDonald's parking lot. His ass was bleeding again, and it kept sticking to his shorts. They cruised through the drive-in and ordered a dozen Big Macs and six large fries. Grey forked out the money, and they continued north toward Coronado, hungrily stuffing French fries into their mouths. Between swallows, Jones looked over at Grey and opened his mouth as if to speak.

"What?" Grey asked.

"It's silly, boss."

"Nothing's silly at this point. Life couldn't get stranger. Go ahead and say what you have to say."

Jones swallowed his next mouthful of French fry. "I was just gonna ask you a question." He looked out the window and studied the churning ocean. "Where would you be if you could be anywhere in the world right now?"

"Easy," Grey answered quickly. "I can think of the exact spot. I used to run up to a field in the hills above Stanford. There's a lookout near a small lake nestled below a ridge. It's always quiet, and the whole Bay Area is spread out below. The hills are amazing. They roll down toward the university like a green carpet." Grey smiled to himself. "In the distance Hoover Tower rises up from campus. And at the northern edge of the bay, San Francisco sparkles against the flawless sky." Grey paused. "I think the day I discovered that place was one of the happiest in my life. I found the lake in the middle of a perfect three-hour run; it was also the day Vanessa finally agreed to go out with me. I honestly can't remember being happier."

"It's not fair, is it?"

"What?"

"Finishing Hell Week is supposed to be one of the best darn days of our lives. Instead, it's just more of the same. Only instead of getting beat, we're playing with our lives."

"True," Grey agreed, "but even if everything worked out like it was supposed to and we were sleeping happily in our beds, it still wouldn't compare to the day Vanessa agreed to go out with me. I can still picture her face at that exact moment. God, I miss her."

"You really like that gal, don't you?" Jones asked.

"I do," Grey agreed. "More than I ever wanted to like anyone." He looked over at Jones and slapped his leg. "What about you, Tennessee? Where would you be, if you could be anywhere at this exact moment?"

Jones closed his eyes. "My favorite fishin' spot. I used to spend hours there. Sometimes when my mom would get mad at my dad and start yellin', my brothers and I would run there. Rain or shine, we always ended up at the same place. It's just a perfect pool below a waterfall. Each of my brothers had his own sittin' rock, and I swear them rocks got smooth from us sittin' around so much. Of course, we pretty much fished that little stream out, so it became more of a tradition than anything else. No one ever bothered us there, which is probably why it's still so special to me."

"Sounds nice," Grey said. "I would love to go there someday."

"And I'd like to take you," Jones said. "You've earned the right."

"I've earned the right?"

"Yeah, I don't go tellin' everybody that comes around about my secret fishin' spot. This is a big deal where I come from."

"Well, I'm honored then," Grey said. He looked over at Jones, who was searching Grey's face for a hint of sarcasm. "I'm serious, Jones. I mean it."

"Then I'm glad I told you," Jones said.

They drove on in silence. Minutes later Grey pulled the old Toyota into the hotel's underground parking lot. Grey picked up the bag of hamburgers and fries and rode the elevator up to their room. He pushed into the room and nudged Jackson and Rogers with his foot. Jackson woke up slowly, reluctantly prying himself from a deep sleep. Rogers bolted into a sitting position, his eyes darting back and forth wildly, sweat streaming down his face in tiny rivulets.

"This is outrageous," Rogers quipped. "My hypothalamus is really angering me." He touched the damp skin on his arm. "Am I hot? No. I am not hot, but my body seems to think it needs to purge every ounce of liquid directly through my skin." Looking forty years older than his actual age, he clumsily rose to his feet and tottered into the bathroom. "Good God, what happened in here? Who tried to flood us out?"

"Sorry," Grey said. "I fell asleep in the tub."

"Quite all right," Rogers said. "It happens to the best of—" A gagging sound cut off his sentence midstream. Grey heard a gush of liquid stream into the toilet.

"You okay?"

"Just purging out the last of that Mexican poison," Rogers said. "I'll be fine."

"Don't forget to hydrate."

"I won't."

Jackson gradually pried his eyes open and leaned up on his elbows. "What you got there, sir?" he asked, eyeing the bag in Grey's hand.

"Three Big Macs with your name on them. How does that sound?"

"Hallelujah," Jackson murmured. "I could use some food. I'm starved half to death."

While Rogers showered, the three of them sat on the beds and wolfed down their hamburgers and fries. Grey found himself barely satiated after 2,000 fat-filled calories.

"So what's next?" Jackson asked, wiping his hand across his mouth. "What's the plan, sir?"

"We're done for the day. I'm in no condition to stay up much longer, and I'd just assume we all get some more sleep. Tomorrow morning I'll take someone to check out the gun store with me. Hopefully we'll pick up some more info."

Rogers emerged from the bathroom wrapped in a towel. "Let's hear it. Give me the scoop."

"What scoop?" Grey asked. "You've already heard everything. We just got some food."

"Oh," Rogers said, his brow furrowing in concentration. "My God, I think I'm losing my mind."

"And that's why I think we're useless tonight," Grey said. "Playing Sherlock Holmes on no sleep is idiotic. Everyone should hit the rack."

"I get to share a bed with the Good Reverend," Jones drawled, nudging Jackson in the ribs. "He don't sweat as much as you, Mr. Rogers."

"I wouldn't want an officer and a sailor sharing a bed anyway," Rogers sniffed, feigning snobbishness. "You might dirty my linens."

Jones snorted a laugh and flopped back on the bed. Grey found a dry spot on his own bed and instantly fell into a restless sleep.

SEVENTEEN

MARK, WAKE UP. IT'S three o'clock." Rogers gently shook Grey's arm.

"Three?"

"That's fifteen hundred, military time, sailor."

"Shit." Grey sat up and surveyed the dimly lit room. Jackson and Jones sat side by side on the edge of their bed, dressed and ready for action.

"Shit ain't an order I understand, sir," Jones drawled. "You're gonna have to do a little better than that."

Grey frantically sorted through the contents of his foggy head. Assorted bits of information flashed into his mind and then disappeared before he could assemble them into any semblance of order. He pulled the thin comforter up around his shoulders.

"I'll help you out," Rogers offered. "First of all, we have almost no leads. We know Redman might have killed Murray because he hated him, and on top of that, Murray supposedly knew Redman demonstrated a propensity for pilfering explosives, gun parts, and ammunition at his last command. I'm just not sure the pieces fit together."

"So where does that leave us?" Jones asked. "We don't got a dang thing."

"Circumstantial evidence," Rogers said. "That's all we've got. But I think Mark was right when he suggested that a visit to the gun shop might bring up a few interesting leads. However, I think we need to do a little preparation before we go there."

"Like what?" Grey asked.

"If we want to have someone at the gun shop positively ID an instructor who's been making visits, we need pictures."

"And where will we find pictures?" Grey asked.

"Back behind the Second Phase area at BUD/S there's a filing room that has a picture of every SEAL," Rogers explained. "I think we can manage to pilfer a picture or two without getting caught."

"Sounds good. We'll hit the compound first and then the gun shop." Grey picked up the TV remote and handed it to Jackson. He wasn't comfortable having his enlisted men risk their careers by sneaking around on base. "You and Jones will stay here. Take advantage of the rest."

"Aw c'mon," Jones protested. "I feel like the dang little brother again. Feels like I'm being left behind while you big boys go on a huntin' trip."

"Sorry Jones," Grey said. "You can come next time."

Jones shook his head sadly. "And I get the same old line. Next time," he muttered.

"Get some rest," Grey placed his hands on Jones's shoulders and gently pushed him down into a sitting position on the bed. "Relax, but watch your phone."

Grey grabbed a complimentary notepad and pen from the dresser and headed for the door. After a short drive, Rogers and Grey limped the quarter mile from the student parking lot to the BUD/S compound. A seamless wall of gray obscured the sun, casting a dull light over the sandy pavement. The side gate to the compound was locked shut, so Grey walked around to the quarterdeck.

"What's up?" It was Rupert, an enlisted trainee who had been medically dropped from Grey's class during Indoctrination. He leaned over the counter and smiled. "What are you two doing here anyway? Shouldn't you be passed out somewhere?"

"Should be," Grey replied, "but I've got other things on my mind. I need to ask a big favor."

Rupert raised an eyebrow. "A favor? What's on your mind?"

"I need to get into the storage room back behind Second Phase."

"Why?"

"I can't say. But trust me, you'd be breaking the rules for a very good reason."

"I'm just supposed to take that on faith?" Rupert asked skeptically.

Grey pulled three twenty-dollar bills from his pocket. He laid them on the table. Rupert glanced around, then placed his hand over the money and slid it off the counter.

"I can't leave the quarterdeck until Mason gets back," Rupert explained. "He went to get us some McD's for lunch. I'll just tell him I need to take you to the copier."

Grey and Rogers waited impatiently for several minutes until Mason showed up.

"Congratulations, gentlemen," Mason said, extending a hand. "I'm glad you made it."

"Thanks." Grey was restless. He didn't want to waste any time.

Rupert addressed Mason. "I'm taking Grey and Rogers to the copier. I'll be back in ten minutes. Don't even think about eating my fries."

"Who me?" Mason looked offended.

Rupert led Grey and Rogers back behind the grinder. He stopped in front of a small building positioned next to the dive tower. After pulling a set of keys from his pocket, he tried them one by one in the old lock. *Click.* They were in. Rupert stepped into a dark hallway and walked several feet to a nondescript door. He pushed it open and flipped on a light switch. Grey peered into the room. Six large filing cabinets lined the walls, three on either side. Another door sat squarely at the back of the room.

Rogers slumped against the wall. "I'll watch the door."

"And I'm getting the fuck out of here," Rupert said. "Anything happens, I didn't let you in." He glared at Grey. "Right, sir?"

"Of course not. This shouldn't take long." Grey pulled open a filing drawer. The student data was arranged by class number. *Redman's a petty officer. Probably went through training ten years ago.* Grey found the file for Class 195. Redman's name didn't appear on the roster. Grey worked his way down year by year. He stopped when he saw Heisler's name. Curiosity made Grey pull out the instructor's file and flip through it. "Born in Ventura, California. Entered BUD/S training at age 17. Outstanding PT scores. High marks for aptitude. Graduated Honor Man." Grey replaced the folder. A teenage honor man was unheard of.

Grey continued flipping. He stopped at Class 190. "Joseph Redman. Born in Sweenee, North Dakota. Entered BUD/S at age 21." Grey scoffed.

"Slow run times. Mediocre PT scores. Below-average aptitude." He read further. "Finished training despite an Administrative Review Board for a DUI. Issued a warning for starting a fight with a fellow student." Grey shook his head in disbelief. *Not only did they graduate this guy, but they made him an instructor!* He studied the picture of a more youthful and less muscle-bound Redman. Over the years his icy stare hadn't changed. The same coal-black eyes glared from the photograph. Grey plucked the picture from the file and slipped it between two pages of the notepad. He quickly jotted down a few sentences about Redman's record and then continued his search. After almost ten minutes of searching, he managed to locate Furtado's file. *Mediocre* was the only word that came to mind as Grey reviewed his stats.

Suddenly Rogers slipped into the room and gently shut the door behind him. "The closet. Go!" he whispered urgently. Grey bolted for the door at the back of the room. He opened it quietly and stepped inside. Rogers turned off the lights and followed him in. Grey felt around in the blackness. The closet was full of janitorial supplies. He stumbled toward the back, and after moving about six feet, he hit a wall. Rogers put a hand on his shoulder.

"Sit down," he whispered. "Get under the tarp." He pulled up the corner of a smelly sheet and handed Grey an edge.

Grey sat cross-legged against the wall and pulled the tarp over his head. Rogers sat next to him and propped some mops against the lump formed by their bodies. The outer door opened with a crash. Light flooded under the doorway to the closet, and a series of footsteps clicked on the tile floor. Grey held his breath. The footsteps grew closer. *Fuck me. We're done.* The closet door crashed open, and the room flooded with light. *Kill me and get it over with.* Silence. In the next heartbeat the door slammed shut and the light blinked out. The footsteps crossed the floor, and the outer door crashed shut.

Grey and Rogers sat perfectly still for several minutes. Finally Rogers pulled down the tarp and they stood up. Moving quietly but with a sense of urgency, they stepped out of the closet and skittered across the storage room. Seconds later they eased out of the building and into the sunlight.

"Well, well. What the fuck do we have here?"

Grey spun to his right. *Oh, God.*

Instructor Redman stood with one arm draped lazily over the edge of a water trough used for cleaning dive gear. "What do you think, Lance?"

Instructor Furtado emerged from of the doorway of a Second Phase equipment room. "Looks like these two homos are playing Sherlock Holmes."

"Nah. More like the Hardy Boys. Those fuckers had a certain gayness that these two faggots share."

"True," Furtado said.

Grey felt Rogers tense up. *We should run.*

"Don't even think about it, dumb fuck," Furtado said, walking toward Grey. "You might have been a fast runner before Hell Week, but you're a worthless piece of shit now."

Grey knew he was right. Running would get him nowhere. "We were just checking out the—"

"Shut up," Redman growled. He walked over to Grey and snatched the notebook from his hands. "What's this?"

"It's just some information about our favorite staff members, Instructor Redman," Rogers said quickly. "We heard that at the end of First Phase, we get to roast the staff. What could be better preparation than checking out their service records?"

"You're so full of shit," Furtado hissed. "You've always been full of shit. You're a walking cum-and-shit receptacle, you fuckin' faggot."

"Is he right?" Redman asked. "Are you of the homosexual persuasion?"

"I'm not interested, if that's what you're getting at," Rogers replied coolly.

"You just added a few hours to your torture session." Redman flipped open Grey's notebook. "I thought you were gathering information on the entire First Phase staff. Where are the rest of the instructors? And why the fuck is my picture in here?"

Grey stood silently, his heart throbbing in his chest.

"I know what they're doing," Furtado said. He glanced at Redman.

"Stupid fucks," Redman grunted. "Goddamn stupid fucks."

Furtado strolled over to one of the dip tanks behind the Second Phase classrooms. Large metal half-cylinders, the tanks were reportedly a favorite torture device of the Second Phase instructors. "Grey, get over here," he ordered.

Grey hobbled to Furtado's side.

Furtado glanced at the bulge in the pocket of Grey's shorts. "Give me your cell phone."

Grey handed it over.

"Now get in."

Grey rolled over the top edge of the dip tank and splashed into the frigid water. When he tried to sit up and take a breath, Furtado pushed his head backward violently. Grey's skull cracked against the back of the tank. He didn't fight the pressure of Furtado's palm against his forehead. As he lay at the bottom of the tank, he looked up at Furtado's face. The instructor's image rippled grotesquely above him, a devilish smile on his face.

The silence of the tank was oddly soothing. A pink cloud fanned out in front of Grey's eyes. He could feel the blood seeping from the torn scab on his head. As he lay there passively, the fire in his lungs growing more urgent every second, he thought back to the lifesaving drills. *I beat you before, you weak pig fucker. I'll beat you again.*

Rogers splashed down at the opposite end of the tank, but Grey paid little attention. He knew he was close to blacking out. *I beat you before. I'll beat you—*

Suddenly Furtado's grip shifted, and Grey felt himself rushing for the sunlight. His face broke the surface, and he sawed in a ragged breath.

"This is only the beginning, sir," Furtado said. "If you don't quit tonight, I'll kill you. I swear it."

"Like you killed Murray?" Grey choked.

Furtado drove Grey's head beneath the surface, smashing it against the bottom of the tank. This time it hurt. Grey felt the remainder of his scab rip free. Furtado's grip shifted again, and he clutched Grey's T-shirt with both hands. With surprising strength, the instructor heaved Grey up and out of the tank. Grey dropped to the asphalt and lay sprawled out on his back.

"I ought to fucking kill you right now," Furtado said quietly. "But I'm going to use my better judgment and draw it out over the course of the night. How's that sound?"

"Fuck you."

Furtado placed a foot on Grey's chest. "I'm afraid that might make Mr. Rogers jealous."

Redman, who had been repeatedly dunking Rogers in the tank, suddenly grunted with effort and heaved Rogers onto the pavement next to Grey.

"I was looking forward to a relaxing evening with some of San Diego's finest Frog Hogs, but now I'm stuck with you two turds," Redman mused. "You're going to pay for ruining my night."

Rogers turned his head to the side and looked at Grey. His eyes said everything. *We're finished.*

"I think you both should know, I voted for kicking the shit out of you when you showed up at McP's," Furtado said. "But Osgood would have none of it. Bet you didn't know he was such a softy, did you?"

"I'll be sure to thank him later," Rogers murmured.

"I don't think you understand. There is no later." Furtado pressed his foot harder against Grey's chest. "Both of you are finished tonight. Of course, you could make things easier for yourself and tell me who is in on your little team of investigators. Did Mason open the file room for you?"

"No," Rogers stated firmly.

"Then it must have been Rupert. I always knew he was a dirty bird."

"It wasn't him, either," Grey wheezed. He couldn't barely speak with Furtado's foot crushing his chest.

"So you just magically found your way into our files?" Redman asked.

"Something like that," Rogers said.

"And what about other members of your boat crew?" Furtado asked. "I know two officers would never work alone. You cake eaters need at least one enlisted man to carry your notebook for you." He pushed hard against Grey's chest. "Well, who else is working with you?"

"No one," Rogers said. "I'm very jealous of my relationship with Mark. I won't let any other sexy bitch interfere with our love."

"I told you they're fucking gay!" Furtado exclaimed triumphantly.

Despite the crushing pain in his chest and the hopelessness of his situation, Grey managed a snort of laughter at Rogers's fearlessness.

"Which one of you is the man in the relationship?" Redman asked. "Which one takes it in the brown star?"

When neither Grey nor Rogers responded, Furtado mused, "At least they know the joy of ass fucking." He ran his tongue stud along his lips. "There's nothing like riding a bitch in the ass and stealing her soul."

Stealing her soul? Grey shuddered at the thought of Furtado mounting some skank in the back of a dark club.

"Enough pillow talk," Redman growled. "It's time to pay the man, gents. Mr. Grey, I'll let you pick your first form of punishment. You have a choice of PT or surf torture."

Grey looked at Rogers. "What do you think?"

"PT."

"Mr. Grey, does Mr. Rogers speak for you?"

"PT is fine by me."

"Is that your final answer?"

"Yes."

"PT it is!" Redman announced. He strolled into a Second Phase building and disappeared from sight.

"While we're waiting, I just want you two to know something," Furtado said. He eased the pressure on Grey's chest. "I hate you two fuckers, but I'm not going to kill you."

Grey and Rogers remained silent.

"No, I'm not going to kill you," Furtado repeated. "You're going to kill yourselves."

That shouldn't be hard, Grey thought. His muscles were practically liquefied from Hell Week. Combined with the horribly infected gash on his leg, the still-bleeding cut on his head, and his weakened immune system, Grey knew he wouldn't withstand much punishment before breaking.

"What's going on here?"

Grey turned his head toward the familiar voice. *Chief Baldwin. Thank God.* The lanky instructor stood with his arms crossed over his chest at the edge of the Second Phase grinder.

"These worthless cake eaters were snooping around in our records," Furtado explained. "Instead of sleeping like good brown shirts, they decided to try to dig up some dirt on their hardworking instructor staff."

"Are you gentlemen out of your mind?" Baldwin asked. He stroked his mustache. "Wasn't Hell Week hard enough for you two?"

"It was plenty hard," Grey said. "We were just hoping to find some dirt on you guys so that we could roast you properly at the end of First Phase."

"And you got caught," Baldwin mused. "If you were operating in

Afghanistan and some half-starved extremists caught you, do you think you'd be alive?"

"Negative, Chief Baldwin," Grey said.

"Damn right. You'd be tortured first and then left for dead. Consider yourself lucky that you're only getting a serious beating tonight." Baldwin shook his head in disgust and turned to leave.

"Chief Baldwin, wait—"

"There's nothing more to say. The situation is out of my hands," Baldwin said over his shoulder. "To the victors go the spoils of war."

The spoils of war? Grey felt a surge of nausea rise up in his stomach. If Baldwin wouldn't help them out, no one would.

"You see, my little faggot friends, it's just you and two mean instructors. No one wants to hear your lame-ass story." Furtado paused and hocked a wad of spit onto Rogers's stomach. "I know your whole train of thought. You think that because I didn't go to college, you're smarter than I am?"

"Negative, Instructor Furtado," Rogers said quietly. Grey could tell that Baldwin's arrival and departure had taken a toll on Rogers's psyche.

"You're fucking stupid—that's what you are. I know exactly what you're thinking. . . ." His voice trailed off as he placed a shoe against Rogers's forehead. "It's going to be a long night."

Instructor Redman emerged from the Second Phase spaces heavily laden with diving gear. He wore one set of twin-80s on his back, and he carried the other set in both arms. Grey had heard about the primitive diving rigs the students learned to dive with. A twin-80 was an antiquated Jacque Cousteau–style rig with two giant tanks and twin hoses leading to an old-fashioned regulator that reportedly never worked properly.

"Mr. Grey, stand up," Redman ordered.

Grey stood up, and Redman handed him a set of tanks.

"Jock up."

Grey worked his way into the primitive web harnessing and tightened the straps. He nearly fell over backward from the weight of the cumbersome tanks.

"Rogers, get up." Redman took the other set of twin-80s from his back and held them out for Rogers. "Put this shit on."

Once they were both outfitted properly with their diving gear, Redman strode into one of the Second Phase garages and wheeled out a contraption that looked like a giant roulette wheel.

"Since you pansies will never know what Second Phase is like, I thought I'd give you a taste of what you'll be missing." Redman affectionately patted the roulette wheel. "Gentlemen, meet the Wheel of Misfortune."

Fuck. Grey had heard of the wheel and the damage it inflicted upon its victims. Painted on its surface was a nauseating array of punishments: 100 leg levers, 50 push-ups, 100 squats, 100 lunges. . . . With tanks on their backs, Grey knew they didn't stand a chance.

"Since I know you can't do leg levers with tanks on, we'll replace leg levers with tower sprints," Redman announced.

Grey glanced up at the dive tower. The twisting staircase that wrapped around the giant metal structure looked menacing. A misstep would mean broken bones.

Furtado stood on the opposite side of the wheel from Redman. "I think I should get to spin first." He gave the wheel a strong pull. "C'mon now! Big money!"

The sadistic click of the wheel as it moved from one punishment to the next sounded to Grey like nails against a blackboard. The pointer finally settled on 50 push-ups. Grey eased himself to the asphalt next to Rogers.

"Let's see it, turds!" Redman boomed. "I want perfect form. If you do it right the first time, I might let you two knuckleheads go home a few minutes early."

Grey's already battered hands burned with pain as he struggled with his push-ups.

"One, two, three," Redman counted. "Oh my! At this rate, I don't think you're gonna make it."

After ten push-ups, Rogers collapsed next to Grey.

"Get the fuck up!" Furtado yelled. "Get your faggot ass in the air where it belongs!"

Rogers groaned as he struggled to lift his chest off the ground. His arms spasmed violently.

Grey counted to himself. *Thirteen, fourteen, fifteen.* Hell Week had taken every ounce of strength from his body. He had nothing left. With a thud, his body slammed onto the asphalt.

"Get up! Get up! Get up!" Redman bellowed. "We can make things a lot worse than this, shitheads! Get the fuck up!"

Grey pushed with all his might, but his body wouldn't budge.

"On your feet, lazy turds!" Redman yelled. He gave the wheel another pull. *Click, click, click, click*—100 flutter kicks.

"You know what that means," Furtado said pleasantly. "It's time for some stairs."

Grey shuffled toward the dive tower, the twin tanks banging awkwardly against his lower back. As he reached the bottom of the stairs, he steeled himself for the climb.

"Let's go, buddy," Rogers said quietly. "We'll talk at the top."

Grey nodded and began his ascent. After a few steps lactic acid shot through his thighs, spreading fire up and down his spinal column. *My God.* He labored upward, carefully placing each foot to avoid a disastrous fall. Soon desperate breaths ripped in and out of his lungs.

"Hurry up!"

Redman's voice spurred Grey onward. He climbed and climbed, finally stumbling up to the diving platform. Rogers appeared seconds later.

"Why don't they just get it over with and finish us?" Rogers asked between ragged breaths.

"They're not going to kill us," Grey said. "They want us to ring out. They won't try anything too crazy with Chief Baldwin on duty."

"I don't think Baldwin is concerned about us." Rogers bent over and rested his hands on his knees. "My body is destroyed. I don't know if I can do this."

Grey looked down at the Second Phase grinder. Furtado and Redman were waiting with their arms crossed by the Wheel of Misfortune. "We have to try. We have to do it. We've come too far to give in to this bullshit."

"We're finished." Rogers turned and began limping down the dive-tower steps. Grey followed close behind, and soon they were standing in front of the wheel.

"Grey, give it a whirl," Furtado said. "Try your luck."

Grey stepped up to the wheel and yanked one edge downward. *Click, click, click, click.* The pointer settled on 50 squats.

"Aw shit," Redman said. "This one is gonna hurt."

Rogers and Grey began performing squats. The first few weren't bad. By number thirty Grey's field of vision began shimmering.

"Get up, you pansy-ass bitch!"

Grey's vision cleared, and he found himself looking up at Furtado's angry face. The instructor's tongue stud caught his eye, and he stared at it, mesmerized.

"What the fuck are you looking at?"

Grey didn't answer. He couldn't. He tried to drag himself back to reality, but his mind rebelled. The glimmering tongue stud held him captive.

"Looks like we've created a vegetable," Redman mused. "That's a first."

"Grey, are you okay?" Rogers bent over and shook Grey by the shoulders.

"I didn't say you could touch him, dumb shit!" Furtado yelled. "Finish your squats."

Rogers continued his squats as Grey struggled to sit up.

"The vegetable moves, but does it talk?" Redman asked.

"I'm fine," Grey slurred. He finally broke his gaze from Furtado's tongue stud.

"The vegetable does talk." Redman flashed a wicked smile. "And I think the vegetable is all steamed up. I like mine cold and crisp. What do you think I should do, Instructor Furtado?"

"Maybe a chilly dip would firm him up. But personally, I also like my vegetables salty. Maybe a trip to the surf is in order," Furtado offered.

No. No. No. Grey rolled over and startled crawling away on his hands and knees, his tanks awkwardly slumping to one side of his back. *Please. Please. No.*

"What the fuck is wrong with this guy?" Furtado asked with a laugh. "I think he's regressed to an infantile state."

"We better get the tanks off him," Redman said. He turned his attention from Rogers, who had collapsed after forty-two squats, and stepped to Grey's side. He reached beneath Grey and nimbly undid the straps holding on the twin-80s. After pulling the tanks from Grey's back, he strode into the Second Phase building.

"Don't think you're getting off easy just because your Stanford-educated brain is malfunctioning," Furtado said, nudging Grey in the ribs with his foot. "If you can't handle PT, you leave us with only one choice."

Grey looked over at Rogers, who was lying on his stomach several feet away. As much as the PT hurt, his mind refused to accept the possibility that he and Rogers would be surf-tortured. After Hell Week, surf torture was supposed to be a thing of the past, a punishment only inflicted under the direst of circumstances.

"Can you form a sentence yet?" Furtado asked.

"I can speak," Grey said quietly, still straining to collect his thoughts.

Furtado turned his attention to Rogers. "Give me your tanks."

Rogers slowly rose to his knees, pulled off his tanks, and handed them to Furtado.

"Don't go anywhere," Furtado ordered. He turned and walked into the Second Phase building, leaving the two trainees alone.

"Grey." Rogers crawled toward him. "Are you okay?"

"Fine," Grey muttered. "I'm fine. I just lost it for a second." He touched the sticky mess on top of his head where his scab used to be and then looked at the red stains on his hands. "This is insane."

"Should we run?" Rogers asked, glancing at the Second Phase building.

"And then what?" Grey shook his head. "Chief Baldwin knows about us, and he's a senior instructor. If he endorses this beat-down, there's not much we can do."

"What if we ring out?"

"Are you kidding?" Grey slowly eased himself to his feet. "No fucking way." He stood unsteadily, looking down at Rogers. "I'd rather die."

Grey extended a hand and pulled Rogers to his feet. The two trainees clung to each other for support.

"Mark, I don't know about this anymore," Rogers said. "I think we've outsmarted ourselves. I think Redman and Furtado had very little to do with Murray's death."

Grey's chest tightened. *He doesn't trust me.*

"It just doesn't make any sense. Nothing adds up. There is no Armstrong." Rogers stepped away from Grey and then collapsed backward onto his ass. He looked up at Grey and shook his head sadly. "We're insane." He slapped the asphalt in frustration with the palm of one hand.

"We are clinically insane, Mark. We haven't slept, our bodies are shutting down. We can't trust our own minds."

Maybe you're insane. I'm not.

"You can't even follow me," Rogers said in exasperation. "Do you understand what I'm saying?"

Grey nodded. *You think I'm insane.*

"Say something."

Grey extended his hand to Rogers. He spoke slowly. "We can't quit. That's all that matters now. We can't quit. Murray would never forgive us."

Rogers took Grey's hand, and Grey tried to pull him to his feet. Rogers was halfway off the ground when Grey pitched forward and crumpled on top of him.

"Fucking homos!" Furtado yelled. "You two just keep asking for trouble. You can't keep your hands off each other."

Redman grunted in disgust and walked past the two trainees, a folding beach chair clamped under one arm. He didn't look back as he walked toward the ocean.

"Follow him!" Furtado ordered. "Move!"

Grey and Murray rose to their feet and shuffled toward the beach. Furtado walked behind, whistling merrily. They trudged across the parking lot, over the sand berm, and across the beach. Redman, who had unfolded his chair and taken a seat at the edge of the surf, extended an arm toward the ocean.

Here it comes. Grey's body twitched uncontrollably as he stepped into the shallows.

"Down," Redman barked.

As Grey turned to face shore, he noted the tears streaming down Rogers's cheek. He squeezed Rogers's arm hard and took a deep breath. They flopped backward into the ocean, letting the icy coastal current surround them. Grey's body thrashed against the horror of the cold, and a fire raged on his scalp as the salt water saturated his wound. He tried in vain to bring his limbs under control. Rogers shivered next to him, and the hollow sounds of the ocean echoed in his ears. *Murray, keep a warm spot for me.* Grey's entire back seized up, and he gritted his teeth in pain. *Keep a spot for me, you dumb motherfucker.*

After a few minutes of immersion, Grey felt Rogers struggle to sit up. He grabbed the back of Rogers's shirt and pulled him back. *You're not quitting.* Grey closed his eyes and thought of Vanessa. He wanted to disappear between her perfect breasts, snuggle into a warm spot and hide forever. Her smooth skin, flawless and brown, radiated heat against his body. Her laughter rang in his ears. *God, I love you.*

On your feet. On your feet. On your feet. The phrase turned in Grey's head like the refrain from a musical. Grey felt Rogers struggle to sit up, and again Grey pulled him back. Rogers responded by grabbing Grey's testicles and squeezing hard. Grey's mouth opened in shock, and a stream of salt water rushed in. He lifted his head clear of the surf and coughed violently.

"Redman's calling for us," Rogers chattered. "Stop your games."

Grey gazed at the beach. Sure enough, Redman beckoned from the comfort of his folding chair. Coughing salt water and crippled by the searing pain in his groin, Grey rose to his feet and staggered toward shore.

Furtado intercepted the two chilled trainees as they trudged up the beach. "Halt."

They stopped. Grey knew what was next.

"Shirts off."

Rogers moaned softly as he stripped his drenched T-shirt from his body and dropped it on the sand.

"Arms out."

The coastal breeze scorched Grey's armpits with icy flames. Furtado watched him closely.

"What's your name?"

"Ensign Grey," Grey chattered.

"And you?" He nodded at Rogers.

"Ensign Buttercup."

Grey felt a flutter of joy in his stomach. Despite the pain, the never-ending progression of abuse, Rogers still had some life in him.

Furtado reached out and gently tweaked Rogers's nose. He spoke softly. "I thought you might make it through tonight, you fucking faggot. I thought you might have a little common sense in that Ivy League brain of yours. Now you're finished. You're finished."

Grey stood silently, mulling over Rogers's insolence. *Fearless, just like*

Murray. The thought didn't sit well. *Like Murray.* He remembered his swim buddy's devilish smile, his crazy blue eyes, the way he always had a joke ready. *Murray.*

After minutes of standing in silence, Furtado turned Grey and Rogers over to Redman, who ran them through a series of push-ups and berm sprints from his beach chair. The beefy instructor watched them impassively, barking out his orders mechanically. Unlike Furtado, who seemed to enjoy himself immensely, Redman was all business.

When their legs failed, Redman ordered Grey and Rogers to crawl to the surf. The sun slipped below the horizon, casting a purple glow over the beach. *Should be beautiful.* The water rose up to his thighs, then savagely slapped his crotch.

"And halt!"

Grey stopped.

"About-face."

Grey turned around just in time to watch Chief Baldwin lead Jones and Jackson over the sand berm.

"I found these two snooping around, looking for your prisoners," Baldwin announced. "Instructor Redman, they're all yours."

Redman nodded in reply. He motioned for Jones and Jackson to approach. Grey couldn't hear the conversation that ensued, but his friends' faces said it all. They knew they would be lucky to survive the night. Jones and Jackson listened intently to Redman, then turned and jogged toward the surf.

"Welcome to the party, shipmates," Grey said. "The water's nice and warm for you."

"Dang it, sir. This ain't good," Jones said, his eyes wide with terror. "I can't take any more of this cold. I just can't."

"Amen to that," Jackson said, dropping to his hands and knees next to Grey. "Cold and I don't agree with each other. We're well acquainted, but we just don't get along."

"It will be a long night," Grey said, "but we'll get through—"

"About-face!" Furtado yelled.

The four trainees turned and faced the oncoming waves.

"Forward crawl!"

They crawled deeper into the ocean, cringing as the whitewash slammed into their faces. Once they could no longer keep their heads above water, they planted their feet beneath them and continued walking. Furtado stopped them in chest-deep water. They linked arms and pulled each other close.

"What happened?" Jones asked. "We got worried when you didn't answer your cell phone."

"We were caught," Rogers chattered, "like a bunch of amateur sleuths. Like the Keystone Cops, except with less skill."

Grey's jaw ached violently from shivering so hard. It took a considerable effort to string together a few words. "We told you to say put," he chastised. "You should have listened to us."

"Well, excuse me for caring," Jones said. "Where I'm from, friends don't let friends suffer alone."

Grey gave his arm a feeble squeeze in reply. The four trainees endured the rest of the surf torture in silence. The minutes passed slowly, and Grey marked time by counting the waves that crashed into the back of his head. By the time Furtado called them back and they reached the shore, Jackson's eyes had glazed over. The minister's lips were blue, his body limp as a noodle. Grey and Rogers each took an arm and propped him up.

"This one's done," Furtado observed casually.

"He's done," Redman agreed.

Furtado inched closer to Jackson so that his nose nearly touched Jackson's forehead. "So what's it going to be, brother? Another round of surf torture, or is it quitting time?"

Jackson looked over at Grey pleadingly. Long strings of spittle dripped from the corners of his mouth.

"Don't even think it," Grey said.

Jackson released a deep, guttural sob. He turned his eyes back to Furtado. "I'm done."

"No!" Jones yelled. "C'mon now! No way!"

"He said it," Furtado observed. "The rest of you would be wise to follow his example, because we're not going to stop this game until you all quit."

Redman slowly rose from his beach chair. "You sure you want to do this?" he asked Jackson. "I've got no beef with you. It's these two cake eaters I want to get rid of."

"The cold . . . I can't do it anymore."

"Well, that's a fucking shame," Redman grumbled. He planted a palm on Jackson's back and pushed him toward the grinder.

Grey's heart sank as he watched the preacher stumble over the sand berm. *Follow him.* The thought flitted through his mind. A few steps was all it would take. *Grasp the lanyard, ring the bell, end the pain.* Grey glanced at his two remaining boat crew members, and his self-pity was quickly replaced by angry resolve. Rogers and Jones needed him to be strong.

"He wouldn't have made it anyway," Furtado observed. "He was a freak in the water. He would've drowned in Second Phase."

"Like hell he would have," Jones said. "Ain't no way."

Furtado sized him up. "You're not looking so good yourself, Hillbilly Bob. Are you next?"

"Not a chance."

Furtado turned to Rogers. His tongue stud clicked against his teeth. "How about you, Socrates?"

Rogers shook his head.

Furtado glanced at Grey. "I know it won't be you. You're too fucking stupid to quit." He rubbed his hands together. "Well, there's no sense in waiting for Instructor Redman to return. Go ahead and drop down."

Grey fell forward onto the sand and struggled through twenty push-ups. His arms spasmed wildly as he held himself in the upright position.

"You stupid fucks are failing," Furtado said. "If you can't do push-ups, we can always play in the ocean."

Three sharp peals of a bell rang out in the evening air.

"Hear that, gentlemen?" Furtado asked, kicking sand into the faces of the trainees. "That's the sound of freedom."

Rogers collapsed and lay motionless, his face buried in the sand.

Furtado nudged Rogers with his boot. "If that's the way you're going to be . . ." He bent over, grabbed Rogers under the arms, and dragged him into the shallows. "If you're gonna play dead, you're gonna play dead cold."

Grey turned around so that he was facing the ocean. "Request permission to join my shipmate."

"Me too," Jones added.

"You fucking homos want to join Socrates in the surf?" Furtado laughed. "Go ahead, and since you're a bunch of gay fucks, why don't you get really cozy."

Grey bear-crawled across the sand and settled down next to Rogers.

"I said get cozy!" Furtado yelled. "Get on top of him! Both of you!"

This fucker has a serious problem. Grey crawled up on Rogers's back, then Jones crawled on top of Grey.

"I don't think Ensign Rogers is getting any air," Grey said. He watched with concern as Rogers struggled to keep his face clear of the surging tide.

"A homo pyramid! Beautiful!" Furtado stepped into the ocean and squatted in front of the trainees. He lifted Rogers's head. "See. He can breathe just fine." A rush of icy water surged up the beach, and Rogers's face temporarily disappeared beneath the surface.

"This isn't safe," Grey said. *Motherfucker. I am two seconds away from killing you.*

Furtado scoffed. "Danger is the name of the—"

"Knock it off!"

Furtado spun around. "Chief Baldwin—"

"Jones, Grey, get off him!" Chief Baldwin strode to the waterline and watched as Grey and Jones climbed off Rogers's back. Redman followed close behind.

"They were getting carried away," Furtado explained casually.

Rogers shakily rose to his knees and coughed up a stream of salt water. Chief Baldwin stroked his mustache and eyed Furtado. For several tense seconds, all was quiet but the rush of the tide and the rumble of crumbling waves. Rogers stood up and swayed from side to side.

"This is unsat," Baldwin grumbled. "Mr. Rogers, get over here."

Rogers took one step, then flopped facedown in several inches of water. Baldwin strode to his side and lifted his head.

"What's your problem, sir?"

Rogers gurgled something comprehensible only to Baldwin.

"You what?"

Rogers struggled to rise to his knees, but his rubbery arms wouldn't lift his torso.

"You're finished, sir." A look of concern crossed Baldwin's face. "You should DOR." He grasped Rogers under the arms and yanked him to his feet with a violent heave. The officer's body was dead weight in his arms. "Sir, do you quit?" he asked slowly.

Rogers dangled helplessly, his chin resting on his chest.

"I heard him," Furtado said. "DOR."

Baldwin glared at him. "You should have pulled him earlier."

"He looked fine to me," Furtado said defensively.

Baldwin bent over, then effortlessly slung Rogers's body over his shoulder. "I don't want to see anything like this again," Baldwin grumbled. "If we lose a trainee tonight, we can all kiss our careers good-bye."

"Aye, aye, chief," Furtado said. "Understood."

"Redman, you're in charge," Baldwin said. "You're responsible for these two."

Redman nodded, his beady black eyes devoid of emotion. Baldwin turned and carried Rogers over the berm.

Once Baldwin had disappeared from sight, Furtado shattered the silence. "Ding-ding, ding-ding. Socrates, departing," he chimed.

Grey clenched and unclenched his fists. He wanted to knock Furtado out, but he knew he lacked the coordination for a well-placed punch.

"Jones, I suggest you ring out," Redman said gruffly. "This shit's about to get ugly, and you might as well spare yourself the discomfort."

"Heck no," Jones drawled. "I ain't leavin'."

"Suit yourself." Redman nodded toward the surf. "Get comfy."

Grey and Jones waded into the ocean and sat down. They linked arms and held each other close. Jones's quivering voice broke into a quiet rendition of John Denver's "Country Roads". After a few verses, Jones's jackhammering jaw forced him to stop.

"Hang in there, buddy," Grey slurred. "Do it for Murray. Stay strong."

Jones didn't reply. The two trainees suffered in silence, rolling forward and back with the surge of the tide, periodically spitting out a mouthful of salt water. Redman watched from his beach chair, and Furtado paced back and forth at the edge of the ocean.

Grey worked his mouth carefully, struggling to form words. "We were good friends."

"What?" Jones chattered.

"Murray. We were good friends."

"You liked him." Jones drew himself closer to Grey, greedily feeding off of his warmth.

Several minutes later Redman waved them in from the beach. Once they reached shore, he nodded at the sand berm. "Fireman's carry, up and down the berm. Go."

You've got to be kidding. Grey could barely stand, let alone carry Jones on his shoulders while scaling the sand berm.

"Move!" Furtado yelled. "You heard the man."

"I'll carry first." Grey clumsily bent over, and Jones sprawled sideways across his back. He straightened out and took a few faltering steps toward the berm.

"You fall, and you're going straight back into the surf," Redman warned.

Focusing all of his attention on each footfall, Grey carefully ascended the berm. His back and knees shimmered with pain, but he held his course. He descended successfully, and Redman looked away as Grey completed his journey. Jones dropped from Grey's shoulders and bent over to accept his cargo. They switched positions, and Jones lurched forward unsteadily.

"Same goes for you, Hillbilly Bob," Redman said. "You drop, you freeze."

Jones groaned beneath Grey's weight. He wisely cut a diagonal course up the berm, his brow furrowed in concentration. A bony shoulder jutted into Grey's stomach, making it an uncomfortable ride. *C'mon buddy. Don't drop me.*

"This is the moment of truth, gents," Furtado said. "Don't fall on the way down. I'd hate to see you get surf-tortured again."

Jones began his descent, and Grey felt him pitch forward dangerously. Grey leaned back to compensate, but he acted too late. The pair plunged headfirst down the sandy slope. Grey rolled over Jones's head and came to rest at Furtado's feet.

"Oh, no, it looks like someone got a boo-boo!" Furtado cried with mock concern.

Injured? Grey checked himself over quickly. *Nothing.* He turned his head and looked at Jones. A stream of blood trickled from his friend's nose and ran into his mouth. Jones didn't bother spitting it out.

"Hillbilly Bob, you okay?" Redman asked.

Jones nodded.

"The best thing for an injury like that is cold," Redman noted. "Grey, help him out. Join your buddy in the surf zone. Go all the way out this time. And don't come back until one of you wants to quit."

Grey obediently waded into the frigid sea with Jones at his side. They ducked beneath the whitewash crashing toward shore, only to march onward. They stopped once the water had risen to their chins.

"Should we swim for it?" Jones asked. "They won't follow us."

"We're too cold. We'll die."

"I'd rather die trying to escape than spend more time standin' here."

"That's not the point, Jones. We can leave anytime we want."

Jones mulled over Grey's answer. "Depressing, ain't it?"

"How's your nose?"

"Hurts like a bitch."

Grey turned and faced shore. "We just have to make it until morning. It can't last forever."

Twenty minutes later Grey watched with concern as Jones repeatedly let his head drop. After fishing his friend's head from the water a half dozen times, Grey crossed his arms over Jones's nearly lifeless body and pulled him toward shore. *This is ridiculous.*

"So who is it?" Redman asked as Grey pulled Jones onto the sand. "Who wants to quit?"

Grey's body trembled so severely, he couldn't respond.

"Well?"

Grey dropped to his knees and took Jones's pulse. *Still alive.*

Redman reluctantly climbed out of his chair and strode to Jones's side. He bent over and slapped the prone trainee across the face. "Hillbilly Bob, you okay?"

Jones's eyes moved to Redman's face, but he didn't respond.

"Seaman Jones, are you okay?" Redman repeated. He waited in vain for a response, then turned to Furtado. "He's done. Carry him to medical.

Fire up the hot tub. Make sure he doesn't die on us. I take his silence as a drop on request."

You fucker! Grey grabbed Redman's beefy arm and shook his head.

"Ensign Grey, get your hand off me," Redman ordered calmly. "You don't want another one of your crew members to die, do you?"

Grey willed his mouth to work. "No." He held his head in his hands.

Furtado grunted as he slung Jones over his back. "Life's not fair, cupcake. Get over it."

Redman returned to his chair as Furtado trudged back to the compound. Grey lifted his eyes to the full moon overhead. *This is not my life. This can't be my life. This is not how it ends. Vanessa . . . God.*

"Sir, it's just me and you," Redman observed. "We've got all night. I've got a bone to pick with you, and I'm in no hurry."

Grey touched the top of his head. A gooey mixture of sand and blood had adhered to his wound. He pulled his hand away and stared at the red smear on his fingers.

"Sure you don't want to quit?" Redman asked.

Grey looked away and extended the middle finger of his right hand.

"Fuck." Redman stood up and folded his beach chair. "Get up," he ordered.

Grey rose to his feet.

"Run south."

Grey contemplated the order. Redman was luring him farther away from the compound. The few rational cells left in his brain told him to sprint over the berm and find Chief Baldwin.

"I'll give you a thirty-second head start." Redman checked his watch. "One, two . . ."

Grey willed his frozen legs back to life. On any given day, he could crush Redman in a footrace. Tonight, however, was a different story. *This is it.* Grey took a deep breath and ran away from the compound along the water's edge. With every passing second, his legs loosened and his stride lengthened. *Let's go, you fucking murderer.* The reflection of the white moon rippled off the surging tide. *Beautiful fucking night.* He dodged clumps of kelp, dug deep, and increased his pace.

"I'm coming for you!"

The yell didn't inspire fear in Grey's heart. *I'm already gone.* He tilted his head back and didn't fight the tears flowing down his cheeks. *Murray, buddy. Murray, why?* The obstacle course sped past, then the helicopter wreckage, then nothing but open beach extended for miles. He was alone on the Silver Strand, an instructor hunting him down, breaking him. The lights of Imperial Beach twinkled in the distance. Grey could hear Redman's ragged breathing behind him. The instructor was closing the distance, wearing him down. Grey felt his mind detach from his body as his legs struggled to maintain their pace. *Not done yet.* The crunch of Redman's boots in the soft sand drew nearer. A hand touched Grey's bare shoulder, and he twisted away. *No pain.* He accelerated.

Why did you burden me, Murray? Why the secret? Why the blackmail? We could have made it. We could have made it. You and me. You and me.

Redman was panting behind him, just out of reach. Grey pleaded with his body, asking for another burst of speed. His legs burned, his pace slackened. *No.* With a grunt, Redman hurled himself at Grey, knocking him to the sand. The air rushed out of Grey's lungs, leaving him helpless. Redman kneeled on his back.

"Stupid shit," he gasped, struggling to regain his breath. "Where did that come from? Who the fuck are you? No one runs that fast. Not after what I put you through."

Grey closed his eyes.

Redman clamped a huge hand around Grey's neck. "You . . ." he breathed. "I've hated you right from the start."

And I, you.

"From the first day you showed up, with your fucking perfect PT scores and easy smile. You think this is some sort of grand adventure?"

Finish me. Finish me.

"Just another feather in your cap. Isn't that right? Isn't that what you want?"

Do it.

"Another bullet on your résumé." Redman squeezed Grey's neck.

Do it. Now.

The pressure on Grey's neck let up. Redman climbed to his feet and kicked a cloud of sand into the air. "Fuck!" he screamed.

Grey slowly opened his eyes.

"Fuck!" Redman stared down at him, his eyes black as the night sky.

"You are the toughest and the fucking stupidest . . ." He reached down, grabbed Grey by the ankles, and began dragging him toward the ocean.

Oh God.

"I don't think I could kill you if I tried." Redman released Grey's ankles, leaving him slumped in several inches of surging water. "Are you ready to listen?"

What?

"Are you ready to listen, you stubborn motherfucker?"

Just talk.

"Want to know who killed Murray?"

"You did," Grey said quietly.

"Wrong answer." Redman grabbed Grey's ankles and dragged him a few feet farther from shore. "One of us killed him, and it wasn't me."

No way.

"Murray was a stupid son of a bitch. He couldn't just let things be. I hated him, he hated me. That's the way things work at BUD/S. I had no reason to kill him."

A large breaker rolled into shore, surging over Grey's face. Redman was still talking when the water rushed away from the beach.

"—stupid fucker. He tried to set me up, tried to frame me."

What? Grey rose up on his elbows.

"The morning of Hell Week the bastard planted two MP-5s, ten frag grenades, and a few hundred rounds in the trunk of my car. I found the shit that evening, asked around, found out that Team Three was missing two MP-5s. So what did I do?"

Grey shook his head. He couldn't believe his ears.

"I returned the gear. Funny thing, I met up with a few Feds that night. They wanted to search my car. Said they had an anonymous tip. Something about a group of arms dealers in Imperial Beach."

Oh God.

"I consented to the search. They had nothing on me—said it sounded like blackmail. Took me awhile to figure out who did it. Pretty ballsy for a little trainee. I've got plenty of enemies, and it wasn't until I searched the little shit's room that I figured out it was him. He was stupid enough to keep an article about a murdered gun-store owner in one of his drawers."

Grey remembered the article, and how Murray's room had been ransacked during Hell Week. *Murray, you stupid, stupid bastard.* Grey remembered how Murray had guarded his seabag the night before Hell Week began. *You had it all planned out, thought you could beat the system. Goddamn it, Murray.*

Redman dropped to his knees in the icy water. He grasped Grey's head in his hands and squeezed hard. "You were in on it, weren't you?"

"No."

"Don't lie to me."

"I'm not lying."

"You obviously knew something. You should have been sleeping, you stupid fuck. You were digging through our files—"

"Wait." Grey's temples throbbed under Redman's vicelike grip. "Murray claimed he had dirt on you. I didn't want any part of it. I told him he was being stupid."

Redman released Grey's head and stood up. "I had no idea he had pulmonary edema. I knew he looked like shit, but a few minutes of surf torture shouldn't kill anyone. His death was an accident, sir. Plain and simple. In fact, if anyone was responsible for his death . . ."

"I was," Grey said quietly. His heart constricted painfully in his chest. *I was. I was. I was.* The phrase repeated itself in Grey's head. He looked up at Redman and thought he detected a trace of pity in the instructor's eyes. *Murray, how could you do this to me? Murray . . .*

"Goddamn right, you were responsible." Redman crossed his arms over his chest. "Say it again."

"I was responsible."

"Again."

"I was responsible." Grey felt his eyes well up.

"Again."

"I was responsible."

"Stupid fuck," Redman grunted. "I've hated you from the start. *Hated you.* But you're one tough son of a bitch. I'll never like you, sir, but I won't stop you, either." Redman gazed out at the ocean as a large set of breakers rolled toward shore.

Grey's sleep-deprived mind raced. *Full blackmail. God help him.* A wall of whitewash pushed Grey flat against the sandy bottom, and his field of vision went black. His insides twisted. *I did it. I kept the secret.* The water receded, and Grey stared up at Redman's extended hand.

"It's over."

Grey reached up and grasped the instructor's powerful hand. Redman jerked him to his feet.

"Now run," he growled.

"Which way?"

"I said it's over, you asshole. Which way do you think?"

Grey gazed at the dark compound several miles down the beach. "I'm only going back under one condition."

"Now you think *you* can give *me* conditions?" Redman asked.

"I'm not going back unless you reinstate my crew. What happened to them wasn't right. This was between you and me and Murray. They had no part in it."

"They quit."

"Can you honestly tell me you would have survived this bullshit?"

"Maybe," Redman grunted. "Maybe not. I didn't get caught."

Grey turned and looked toward Imperial Beach. "The choice is yours. I know the CO will be confused when I call him from a pay phone. It will make a great story. Two days after Hell Week is secured, a dead trainee's boat crew dissolves, and his crew leader is picked up at the Mexican border."

"You're a melodramatic little shit." Redman mulled over Grey's proposition, then shrugged. "Every class needs a fuckin' hillbilly, and a preacher, and a poetry-spouting egghead. Only Furtado and Chief Baldwin saw them quit. . . ."

"Fine. One more thing: don't expect any of us until Tuesday. We need a day of sleep. You can explain our absence to Chief Baldwin. He can smooth things over."

Redman nodded, and Grey ran north along the water's edge, coaxing life from his rubbery legs. He embraced the pain coursing through his body, used it as a scourge to drive the guilt away. *Murray dug his own grave.* His friend's big blue eyes and impish smile flitted through his mind. *I didn't stop him.* Grey turned inward, oblivious to Redman's heavy breathing behind him. He flew across the sand, punishing himself with every step.

Grey woke up wrapped tightly in his sweat-soaked military-issue blanket. Rogers sat at the edge of the bed.

"You're awake," he noted.

"Something like that."

Deep blue circles framed Rogers's sunken eyes. His voice was hoarse. "We need to talk."

"I know."

"I'll get Jackson and Jones."

A fearsome cramp seized Grey's legs, and he groaned in pain as he struggled to sit up. *My God.* A lonely beam of sunlight streamed past tattered curtains, illuminating the sand-strewn floor. The pungent smell of sweat and decay filled Grey's nostrils as he peeled off his sticky blanket. His head ached with a vicious, repetitive throbbing that ran from his temples to the base of his neck.

Vanessa. Murray. He ached for either one of them. Vanessa for comfort, Murray for a smile, a joke, anything . . .

"Sir, reporting for duty." It was Jones. Rogers and Jackson followed him into the room.

"Sit down," Grey said, gesturing at the rumpled bed.

"Smells like someone died in here," Jackson noted.

Grey got straight to the point. "You boys all think you're done, don't you?"

"It's lookin' like that might be the case," Jones answered. "None of us made it through the night, and 'sides, ain't no way Redman or Furtado would let us continue on."

"I think I saw God," Rogers said. "He had frost on his eyelashes."

"Amen, brother," Jackson added. "Darn near killed me too."

Grey examined the back of his hands. "I owe you all an apology."

"For what?" Jones asked indignantly. "You don't owe us nothin'. None of this is your fault."

Grey started to speak, then caught his breath. "I . . ."

His crew waited patiently for him to continue.

"It wasn't what I thought. I shouldn't have dragged any of you into this. Redman didn't kill Murray."

"Furtado, then?" Jones asked.

Grey shook his head. "Murray was worse off than I thought. I should have sent him to medical."

The room was silent. Rogers face flushed red.

"That's such a load of horseshit!" he blurted. "Goddamn it, Mark, that's absolute crap, and you know it!"

Grey reeled in the face of Rogers's uncharacteristic outburst.

"Yeah, that's a bunch of bull," Jones added.

Jackson shook his head slowly. "Ain't no way, sir."

Grey held up his hand to stop the stream of objections. "He was my responsibility. I knew he was sick. I kept it a secret. End of discussion."

Rogers pushed Grey with surprising strength, knocking his head against the windowsill. "Fuck you, Mark! You're not going to be a martyr! Not while I'm around! You protected Murray at every turn! If Redman and Furtado didn't kill him, then he effectively killed himself!"

Grey pushed himself back into a sitting position and rubbed his head. Jackson and Jones were speechless. They watched Rogers with thinly disguised fascination.

"Fuck this place. Fuck it." Rogers stood up. "They took Murray, and they broke all of us, including you. You might have survived the night, but they planted some evil seed in your head. They broke your insides."

Grey winced as he rose to his feet. He grasped Rogers's shoulders firmly. "Murray's death is for me to deal with. I called you in here to tell you that you're not done." He shook Rogers. "Do you hear me? You're not broken. You're back in training, starting tomorrow."

Rogers broke free from Grey's grasp and leaned heavily against the wall. His voice caught in his throat. "What did you say?"

"You're in. All of you."

"All of us?" Jones asked.

"That's what I said."

"But why?" Rogers asked softly.

"Redman acknowledged that last night was bullshit. We had a talk, and we came to an understanding. He has always hated my guts. Always will. But he realizes the shit he put us through last night was unreal. He agreed to let all of you back in."

"But why?" Rogers repeated. "Because he couldn't break you?"

Grey remembered his threat to call the CO from a pay phone at the Mexican border, and Redman's incredulous reaction. "He did it because he knew he was wrong. That's all."

"He didn't say anything else? He didn't talk about Murray?" Rogers asked.

"Murray made a bad call," Grey said quietly. "A very bad call."

The room was silent as his crew waited expectantly. "Well?" Jackson asked. "How about it, sir?"

Grey sat on his bed and cradled his head in his arms.

"What did he do?" Jackson asked.

"Leave him be," Jones said. "He'll answer when he's good and ready."

Grey closed his eyes and conjured up an image of Murray with a seabag slung over his shoulder in the middle of the night, eyes wide with surprise. *Stupid fuck. Stupid fuck. I should have known.*

"He tried to frame Redman," Grey mumbled. "He stashed weapons and ammo in his trunk and then tipped off the NCIS."

"What?" Rogers's eyes were wide with disbelief. "Why would he do that? Why would Murray do an asinine thing like that?"

"He thought Redman was going to force him out. He wanted him out of the picture."

"Well, I'll be." Jones whistled. "Damn crazy fool."

"You didn't know that while we were getting tortured, did you?" Rogers asked.

Grey shook his head. "No way."

Rogers sat down next to Grey and put an arm around his shoulder. "That only furthers my point, Mark. This wasn't your fault. None of it was."

Grey changed the subject. "We need to do something for Murray. I'll need your help tonight."

"With what?" Rogers studied Grey's face.

"It's time to say good-bye in our own way. I thought a burial at sea would be appropriate."

"Without the body?" Rogers asked.

"Without the body."

After a long silence, Rogers nodded in affirmation. "Brilliant. You see, Mark, I'm not the only one with a sense of the beautiful. I'm sure Murray will be delighted."

"I'll bet he laughs," Jones said. "Murray was like that, always laughin' and carryin' on."

Clad in freshly pressed camouflage uniforms, Grey, Rogers, Jones, and Jackson trudged through the sand toward the back gate of the BUD/S compound. Their movements were unhurried, and with the exception of Jackson, who had a canvas seabag slung over his shoulder, they walked unencumbered. A faint squeak interrupted the still night as an opening appeared in the twelve-foot chain-link fence. They walked past the sentry wordlessly. Working in unison, they pulled a black inflatable boat from a metal rack and laid it on the concrete. Jones pulled four wooden paddles from the rack and placed them in the boat. At a signal from Grey, they hoisted the rubber craft onto their heads and slipped back through the gate.

The coastal breeze picked up as they climbed over a steep sand berm and marched toward the sea. They continued past the ocean's edge, their pace never slowing as they waded into waist-deep water. With a nod from Grey, they lowered the craft into the frothy surf and climbed aboard. Their synchronized strokes eased them over the mounds of whitewash rolling toward shore. The gusty wind whipped trails of spray into their faces as they coaxed the craft out to sea, and the outline of the base grew distant, finally blending into the horizon.

"Here."

Jackson opened the seabag and pulled out a life jacket, a dive mask, and a sheathed knife. Working quickly with nimble fingers, he secured the mask and knife to the orange jacket with a length of line. After a moment of silence, he spoke:

"Never have I known a man with more determination and a greater love for life. I know he rests with the Lord, and his spirit will live with us forever. The Good Book says there is life beyond death for the righteous." He lowered the jacket into the rolling sea and gave it a gentle push. "We'll miss you, brother. See you on the other side."

"You were a good friend," Grey added, "even if you were a pain in the ass."

Jones spoke softy in his backwoods drawl. "Keep smilin', you silly bastard. Don't have too much fun without me."

Precariously balancing himself at the bow of the boat, Rogers rose to his feet and addressed the dark sky.

> *Did my eyes once seek solace in the night sky,*
> *stars falling with every breath?*
> *Have I not shivered in offshore winds,*
> *salt and iron bitter on my tongue?*
> *Without a backward glance, I faced the tide.*
> *It was a chance I had to take, and took.*

Grey sat on the berm behind the barracks, his eyes trained on the rolling surf. He compulsively scooped up handfuls of sand and let the grains sift through his fingers. The fog crept in, blanketing the beach in damp silence. He clenched his jaw and tightened the muscles in his throat—anything to fight the tears welling up in his eyes. *BUD/S. Goddamn beautiful place.*

Grey shuddered as the evening breeze whipped past his exposed torso. He had stripped off his shirt, hoping the discomfort would keep his emotions in check. A car door slammed in the parking lot next to the barracks, shattering his solitude. He was too tired to turn his head. *Tomorrow it starts again. Just you and me, buddy. Just you and me.*

Grey ignored the hushed footsteps in the sand behind him. He tracked the progress of a well-lit freighter as it silently steamed out of the bay. He didn't flinch when he felt two soft hands close over his shoulders.

"Mark?"

The voice was warm, familiar. The dam of tears threatened to break. He couldn't answer.

"You poor baby. You look terrible."

Grey's insides warmed as a pair of lips grazed his neck.

"And you smell like crap."

He wiped a bare arm across his eyes. *Hear that? I smell like crap.* He reached behind his head and stroked a smooth cheek. The freighter sounded its horn twice as it steamed into the open ocean. He closed his eyes. Class 283 was already moving on. His crew was a day late. *You said it best, buddy. This shit is paradise.*